War Woman

Also by Robert J. Conley

THE REAL PEOPLE

The Way of the Priests
The Dark Way
The White Path
The Way South
The Long Way Home
Dark Island
War Trail North
War Woman

The Rattlesnake Band and Other Poems
Back to Malachi
The Actor
The Witch of Goingsnake and Other Stories
Wilder and Wilder
Killing Time
Colfax
Quitting Time
The Saga of Henry Starr
Go-Ahead Rider
Ned Christie's War
Strange Company
Border Line
The Long Trail North
Nickajack
Mountain Windsong

War Woman

A Novel of the Real People

Robert J. Conley

ST. MARTIN'S PRESS
NEW YORK

Design by Ellen R. Sasahara

Library of Congress Cataloging-in-Publication Data

Conley, Robert J.
War woman: a novel of the real people / Robert Conley.
    p.   cm.
ISBN 0-312-17058-0
1. Indians of North America—Virginia—First contact with Europeans—Fiction.   2. Indians of North America—Florida—First contact with Europeans—Fiction.   3. Virginia—History—Colonial period, ca. 1600–1775—Fiction.   4. Florida—History—Spanish colony, 1565–1763—Fiction.   5. Cherokee Indians—Fiction.
            I. Title.
PS3553.O494W29   1997   97-18593
        813'.54—dc21   CIP

First Edition: November 1997

10   9   8   7   6   5   4   3   2   1

Author's Note

By 1673, according to Grace Steele Woodward in *The Cherokees* (University of Oklahoma Press, Norman, 1963), the Cherokees already had guns "presumably acquired when raiding Spanish settlements in Florida." We could as easily presume trade. History records neither. The raids or the trade could have taken place much earlier.

Archaeologists have discovered the ruins of an old Spanish gold mine in the Cherokee country, and again, there is little or no historical record of such activity.

Finally, some historians record that about seven hundred Cherokees moved to Virginia, near Jamestown, in 1654, to settle on an abandoned town site. The Virginia settlers had driven off the Powhatans by the 1640s. According to these historians, the Cherokees fought with the Virginians and won. Other historians dispute that the events ever actually took place.

This novel, *War Woman,* is a story about how all of these things might have happened.

I

1580

H E watched as Tobacco Flower said good-bye to her husband, Swift Deer. A handsome young man, Swift Deer was outfitted for hunting, and he would be gone for a few days at least, perhaps longer. The farewell was prolonged and loving, and somehow watching it made her angry. It disgusted her. She was a virgin, and she knew that everyone in New Town knew that she was a virgin. She didn't mind being a virgin. In fact, at sixteen, she still found the thought of men, at least in that way, to be more than a bit disgusting.

But she knew what the people of New Town thought about her. They either pitied her or laughed at her or thought that something was wrong with her—because she had never had a man. And she was sixteen years old—more than old enough in the minds of Ani-yunwi-ya, the Real People. She was old enough to be married even. She was almost as old as Tobacco Flower.

She hated the thought that people were talking about her behind her back, sniggering at her, feeling sorry for her and, when she watched Tobacco Flower and Swift Deer taking their loving leave, all of that hate surfaced. It focused on the young lovers who appeared to be so happy.

She watched as Swift Deer walked away from his wife's house headed for the passageway that would lead him out of New Town and on to the beginning of his journey. She hoped it would be a long one. She watched as Tobacco Flower gazed after her husband with big, soft doe eyes. She watched and it made her sick with disgust.

She waited until Tobacco Flower was just about to turn around and walk back into her house, and then, with long, quick strides, she walked straight toward Tobacco Flower. She called out in order to stop Tobacco Flower in her tracks, to catch her outside, before she disappeared into her house.

" '*Siyo*, Tobacco Flower!" she called out.

Tobacco Flower stopped and looked and saw her and did what any of the other residents of New Town would have done. Tobacco Flower stood there waiting, almost obedient, and she smiled a reluctant smile, and she returned the greeting.

" 'Siyo," Tobacco Flower said. *"Tohiju?"*

"I'm all right," the other replied. "So your man is going hunting?"

"Yes," said Tobacco Flower.

"I'm sure that he'll be successful."

Tobacco Flower blushed slightly and ducked her head. "Yes," she said. "He usually is. He's a good hunter. He provides well for me."

"He's good at other things, too," said the uninvited guest. "Isn't he?"

"At other things?" Tobacco Flower repeated. "Yes. Of course. He's a good ballplayer, and he's pretty good at the *gatayusti* game. He's young, and he hasn't yet had a chance to go to war, but when he does I'm sure that he'll do well."

Tobacco Flower was nervous, and it showed. She was quietly, secretly wishing that this disturbing young woman would go away and leave her alone. But the other did not. Instead, she pressed on deliberately with the unwelcome conversation.

"He's pretty good at night, too," she said, "under the bear rug that you have in your house."

Now Tobacco Flower was really embarrassed at this latest comment from the annoying young woman. It was not a thing she liked to talk about with anyone, but especially not with this unpleasant one. True, Tobacco Flower's sisters and her aunts occasionally teased her about it, but this one did not seem to be teasing. She seemed to be up to something more sinister somehow. Tobacco Flower wondered what it could be.

"Do you agree?" the other asked.

"Well, yes," said Tobacco Flower. "Of course. He's my husband." She wanted to add, "How do you know about the bear rug?" Instead she kept that thought to herself. This one, it was said, could be dangerous. She would have to be careful of her words.

"I found him to be very pleasant," the other said, "that time I lay with him in your place."

A sudden and uncontrolled expression of combined anger, rage, and shame came over the face of Tobacco Flower. She looked as if she wanted to fly at the other one with both of her tiny fists clenched and flailing. Instead she stood there trembling, her face turned bright red, almost purple. In her tight fists, held down at her sides, her nails dug into her palms. Her eyes glared rudely at the other one. She tried to talk, but she couldn't seem to finish a sentence.

"You—," she said. "You did . . . that time you—"

"It's all right," said Tobacco Flower's tormentor. "Calm yourself down. He's absolutely loyal to you. You don't have to worry about him. I know that to be true. You see, he doesn't even know that it was I. He thought I was you. Besides, I did it the other way around, too."

"What other way?" asked Tobacco Flower, her voice now trembling with barely controlled rage and, now, grotesque curiosity. "What do you mean?"

"I came to you once in the night," said the other. "Another time. I came in his shape. You didn't know that, did you? I wanted to find out what it felt like for a man, you know? I was curious, too, about how you would be. You're so tiny and delicate. You were all right, though. It was fun."

Then, a bright smile on her face, she turned abruptly and walked away, leaving poor Tobacco Flower to deal with this incredible revelation the best way she could. Swift Deer was not even where Tobacco Flower could reach him to talk to him about this claim. He would be on the road already and, even if she could talk to him, neither one of them would ever know if the astonishing story was true. The uncertainty would torment them both from this day on, for the rest of their lives together. It might even shorten their lives together, and that would be all right, too, the other one thought. It would serve them right.

Having so casually sown those terrible seeds of discontent, she suddenly felt much better. She felt smug and satisfied and lighthearted. She felt as if she had gotten even, for the time being at least, with all of those who were talking about her behind her back, laughing about her, even just silently thinking things about her.

Now at least these two would wonder whether or not she was actually a virgin. They would wonder how many men she had slept with in the guise of their wives and how many women she had slept with disguised as their husbands. They might even pass the tale on to others, and the others would begin to wonder, too. No woman in New Town would feel secure any longer in the arms of her own husband. No man would be sure what woman was lying beside him at night. No man would know if he was really the father of his own children. *But then, of course,* she asked herself, *does any man ever know that?* She laughed out loud in her delight.

SHE almost always got her own way. She knew it, and everyone else knew it. And she insisted upon it. It had been like that from the very beginning. As an infant, she screamed louder than her twin brother, and because she screamed the loudest, her mother always figured out what she wanted and gave it to her while her brother waited patiently for his turn.

As she grew older and played with other children, she always insisted that they play the games she wanted to play. If anyone else dared to suggest something, she almost always had another suggestion, and almost always hers was the suggestion that they followed.

Then when she became old enough to think about young men, even though she wasn't really interested in them yet, if another girl became interested in a particular young man, she would intervene and steal away his affections. Then she would wind up snubbing the young man and rejecting his attentions because, of course, she had never really wanted him in the first place.

Her twin brother, on the other hand, was well liked by all. Because of the dominance of his sister, he had really had no choice but to develop a patient and pleasant personality. He had grown up quiet, modest, almost self-effacing. Some of the people thought it remarkable that he seemed to harbor no resentments against his sister. On the contrary, he seemed to love her as much as any brother loves a sister, perhaps more. As far as anyone could tell, he was absolutely and sincerely devoted to her.

But she was devoted to no one but herself, to nothing but her own whims and always having her way. Because of that, she had few friends. Actually, she had no friends. She had companions. There was never a shortage of companions for her. She always wanted people her own age around her, and so they were always there. They were there because she wanted them there, and she always got her way. The people, young and old, disliked her, yet gave in to her, and those her own age were her constant companions because of one thing. They were afraid of her, all of them. There was a strongly held belief that out of every set of twins, one would be a witch. For that reason, often when twins were born one would be killed at infancy. But the twins of Osa, the Catawba woman, she who had been rescued by Asquani from the Spaniards, had both been allowed to live and, sure enough, the little girl had become a witch. Or so the people believed. For there was more. Not only was she a twin, she had also been started off in life by Uyona, the Horn, the old woman whom everyone had feared throughout her unnaturally long life.

Pregnant and alone, since her husband had been killed accidentally by his best friend, Osa had gone to Uyona for help. In exchange for her help, Uyona had demanded the girl child for herself. Osa had not wanted to give up her child, but she had promised and she, like the others, feared the old woman. They believed Uyona to be a Raven Mocker, one who lived to extreme old age by stealing time from the lives of others to add to her own life.

Osa had kept her word and given the girl child to Uyona, and the child had been raised by the old woman until she at long last died. Then Osa had taken her infant back, but already the child was spoiled and headstrong. There were some who would gladly have killed her even then, but Osa protected her from them. By that time, the people were already convinced that the infant girl was a witch. They were all almost certain that Uyona had kept the child from seeing anyone but herself for the specified number of days and, for that same number of days, had fed her a special diet in order to purposefully raise her to be a witch. No one had any evidence of this, of course. No one had seen anything to back up these beliefs. Yet they knew that the child was a witch. Did she not always have her own way?

"And she can change her shape at will," they said. "Be careful what you say about her. You might think that you're talking to your own brother, and it might really be her."

"And she can dive into the earth and swim through it as if it were water."

These things and more were said about her.

Her name was Gano luh' sguh, Whirlwind. Uyona had given her that name. And, out of a sense of loyalty, responsibility, or fear, Osa had kept the name. Her girl child was Whirlwind and she belonged to the Bird Clan, Ani-tsisquah, the clan that had adopted her mother. This had become another sore point for the people of New Town. "She is not even a Real Person," they would say. "Her mother is a Catawba woman with a Spanish name. She was adopted because she had no home."

"And she was only adopted because of her husband. They wanted Asquani's wife to have a home here among us."

"But he, too, was adopted. He was adopted by Ani-wahya, the Wolf

People. His mother was Timucua, the one called Potmaker. She was rescued from the Spaniards by Carrier, the trader, when he went south to the land the Spaniards are now calling La Florida."

"Yes. And, though Asquani was raised here among us by Carrier and Potmaker, Carrier was not really his father. Some unknown Spaniard was his father."

"Asquani, the Spaniard, was well named. He was not a Real Person. His father was Spanish and his mother Timucua."

"And his wife is a Catawba. Therefore, his children are not Real People at all. They're Spanish, Timucua, and Catawba."

Usually these kinds of things did not matter to the Real People. What mattered was only whether one belonged to a clan, whether born to it or adopted into it, but, in the case of Whirlwind, because of their fear, they looked for any reason to blame her, any excuse to hate her. They already had plenty of reason to fear her, or so they believed.

There was yet another problem. Whirlwind's father, Asquani, had been killed by his friend Young Puppy, and Young Puppy had stayed in the Peace Town for an entire year to avoid being killed by Asquani's Wolf Clan brothers. During that year, Young Puppy had been trained to be a priest, a leader of the ceremonies, and his name had been changed to Comes Back to Life.

Comes Back to Life had felt an obligation to the wife and children of the friend he had killed, and so Osa had become his second wife. Thus the young girl who was secretly hated and feared was also under the protection of the keeper of the ceremonies, one of the most important men of the town.

So there was nothing the people could do except give in to the whims of Whirlwind and grumble about it to themselves or, if they felt very brave, mutter quietly to one another about the way they felt.

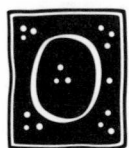

2

OUTSIDE the New Town council house, some men were playing the *gatayusti* game. A crowd was gathered there to watch and cheer on their favorite players. As usual, bets were made on the outcome of the game. Woyi and Striker, the two young men who had gone through the Friends Making Ceremony together and then had both married the same wife, were up to play against each other.

"This will be a hard one to bet on," someone said. "These two are closely matched."

"They're so close to each other, they're like one man," another agreed.

"Yes," said yet another, "they're close in many different ways."

The small crowd gathered there all laughed at the small joke. Then they made their bets. With Striker playing against Woyi, it really became a game of chance rather than skill, for the skills of the two men were just about equal. Woyi hefted his spear in his right hand for feel. Then he bent to pick up the stone disk with his left.

He looked ahead, then started to run. He drew back his left hand and, still running, tossed the disk with an underhand motion. Then, while the disk was still in the air and Woyi was still running, he raised the spear over his right shoulder and gave it a mighty toss.

The disk hit the ground and started to roll. The spear flew ahead in a high arc. Woyi hopped on his right leg a time or two, then stopped and stood straight, watching the path of the disk and the flight of the spear. The disk slowed down and started to wobble. The spear turned toward the earth. Then the disk fell over on its side, and the spear point jabbed itself into the ground a little ways ahead of the disk.

Some of the people groaned, and others cheered, depending on how they had placed their bets. Woyi waited and watched. The spear, its point not driven deeply into the ground, fell over. Its haft, about halfway up its length, was touching the disk. A loud roar went up from the crowd.

"That will be hard even for Striker to beat," someone said.

Striker stepped up in place and studied the score made by his closest friend. More bets were made.

About that time, Whirlwind walked up to join the crowd. She looked out over the field and took the situation in quickly. "Who made that toss?" she asked.

"Woyi made it," someone answered her. "It can't be beaten."

"It can be matched," Whirlwind said.

"I don't think so," someone else remarked. "Not today. Not even Striker. The toss was too good."

Whirlwind turned to see Daksi, or Terrapin, a young man she knew but casually. He was from the neighboring town of Coyatee and occasionally visited with his family at New Town. He was standing over a pile of trade goods.

"Did you win all that here today?" Whirlwind asked.

"Most of it," Daksi said. "I brought some of it with me so I'd have something to bet."

"And you don't believe that Striker can match the toss of Woyi?"

"No," Daksi replied, "I don't."

"Will you bet all of that?" she asked him.

"All of it?" he said. "Against what?"

"Against an equal amount," she told him. "I have it. Don't worry."

"I believe you have it," Daksi said. "You want to bet it all—"

"That Striker will match Woyi's toss," she interrupted.

"All right," said Daksi. "I say that he won't."

Whirlwind smiled, crossed her arms over her breasts, and turned again to face the field.

"Let's watch," she said.

Striker, his spear in his right hand, bent to pick up the disk. He balanced both objects, one in each hand, to get the feel of their weight. He looked out ahead at Woyi's spear and disk, studied the distance and the way they lay, then shouted and ran. He hurled the disk and, immediately after, tossed the spear.

Whirlwind's eyes narrowed into tiny slits as she stared hard at the spear in its flight. She concentrated with all her energy as the stone disk came to the end of its roll and fell over on its side. Then the spear seemed to take an unnatural downward turn. As had Woyi's, it stabbed into the earth, then fell, its haft touching the edge of the disk. A sound of unbelief went up from the crowd. Whirlwind turned to look at Daksi. He shrugged and smiled.

"All this is yours," he stated, motioning toward the pile of goods at his feet.

"Help me carry it to my house," Whirlwind said, and the young man bent to pick up his losses from the ground. His arms loaded, he meekly followed Whirlwind away from the council house and the crowd. Some pairs of eyes followed them.

"She made that happen," someone said in a near-whisper.

"Of course," another added. "She made a bet. Did you see all her winnings?"

"Did you see the strange way Striker's spear turned down? It would have gone farther out if she had let it alone. Well, you won the bet."

"No. I won't take your things. That toss wasn't fair. It was interfered with. We'll bet again on the next players. The witch has gone now."

Standing nearby, 'Squan' Usdi, the Little Spaniard, overheard the whispers about his sister. He said nothing and thought little about them; he had been listening to such talk all his life. He turned his attention back to the field where his mother's husband, Comes Back to Life, the peace chief of New Town, was about to make a toss. Everyone was interested in this match. Comes Back to Life was pitted against Oliga, the war chief.

❧

WHIRLWIND walked ahead of Daksi without talking, and she walked with a swagger. These people in New Town wondered about her relationship with men. Ha! She could get any man she wanted—if she wanted any—and what was more, she could get anything she wanted out of them. She had gotten this man's goods, had she not? And she had even made him carry them to her house for her.

Daksi, too, was enjoying the walk, even though he was loaded down with all the goods he had lost to Whirlwind on the bet. He was enjoying the walk because he was walking behind her and watching the rhythmic swaying of her slender hips. She was a tall girl, almost as tall as he, and her legs were long and shapely. He imagined that she could run like a deer. Black, straight, shiny hair hung down to her waist in back, and it, too, swayed as she walked. She wore only a buckskin skirt that covered her from her waist to just above her knees. In warm weather, it was the common dress for women of the Real People. Walking behind her, he could see her bare arms and shoulders, and her skin was smooth, a lovely light brown. He thought that he would like to know her better. She raised an arm and pointed to a house just ahead.

"This is my mother's house," she said.

He followed her up to the house and stepped inside behind her. She pointed to a spot beside the wall, and he put the pile of goods on the floor.

"*Wado,*" she said. "We'll have to do it again."

"I don't know," he replied, smiling at her. "If I bet more with you, I'll become a poor man."

She laughed. It felt good to hear such a confession from a man.

"You're Daksi," she remarked.

"Yes," he said, "and you're Whirlwind."

"We've never met before," she told him.

"No," he said, "but I know who you are."

"How do you know?"

"There aren't so many people in New Town," he replied, "or in Coyatee. After all, you knew my name."

"Yes," she said. "I did. So what do you know about me?"

"Just that you live here," he answered. "Your father is the peace chief of this town."

"He's not my father," said Whirlwind. "He's my mother's husband."

"Oh. Well, that's all I know."

"Have you heard people talking about me?"

"I suppose I have," he said.

"Did they tell you that I'm a witch?"

Daksi looked at the ground. "I guess I heard some things like that," he replied, "but people say lots of things about other people."

"You mean you didn't believe them?"

He shrugged.

"You should believe them," she said. "I'm dangerous. How do you think I won the bet with you?"

"I guess you used your power on Striker's spear," he answered her, but he was smiling.

"I did," she said. "So I cheated you. You can have your things back."

"I'd better leave them with you," he stated. "What would I say to people? They saw me lose the bet."

This time Whirlwind shrugged.

"What's your clan?" Daksi asked.

The question was abrupt, and it startled Whirlwind. She tried not to show it. "Why do you ask?" she said.

"I like you," he told her. "But if you and I belong to the same clan, I'll just have to put you out of my mind. Although that would be a very difficult thing to do."

Whirlwind bristled a little. *Who does he think he is,* she asked herself, *to express an interest in me like that?* Yet in another part of her she was pleased. He was handsome, very pleasant, and, most interesting of all, wasn't afraid of her as were all the young men in New Town. She liked him.

"I'm a Bird Person," she said. "But I'm a Bird Person by adoption. My father was the man known as 'Squani, the Spaniard. His mother was Timucua, a captive of the Spaniards. He was adopted by the Wolf People, and by then he had met my mother. She's Catawba, and so the Bird Clan of the Real People adopted her."

"I see," Daksi, remarked and to himself he thought that this young woman was becoming more and more fascinating. "Well, I have nothing so interesting to tell about myself. My parents are both Real People from Coyatee, and so am I. I belong to the Deer Clan. That's all."

"Oh," said Whirlwind. "I think there must be much more than that. Why are you here in New Town today?"

"I came with my mother and her brother and sisters," Daksi said. "We heard that you were having games today, so we came to watch— and to bet."

He laughed and Whirlwind laughed with him.

"Are you going home today?" she asked.

"No," he said. "It's too far. I think we'll stay here tonight."

"Then I'll see you tomorrow," she told him. Then suddenly changing her mood, she ran out of the house. "Come on," she said. "Let's go watch the rest of the games."

Daksi's suspicions about Whirlwind's speed were confirmed, for it was all he could do to keep up with her as they ran back toward the council house and the playing field adjacent to it. When they got there, Olig' was making a final toss with his spear. It landed with its point just a little ways off from the disk.

"Comes Back to Life has won!" someone shouted.

Whirlwind looked out on the field to see where the spear of Comes Back to Life was lying across the stone disk he had thrown. All around, people were collecting and paying bets. Olig' turned from the field with a heavy sigh. Comes Back to Life walked up to him and clapped him on a shoulder.

"Well," Olig' said, "you've beaten me."

"It wasn't easy," Comes Back to Life replied. "Your last toss was a good one."

"But not good enough," said Olig'. He held up his hands above his head, asking for silence, and soon everyone quieted and turned to hear what he had to say. "Wherever you go," he shouted, "tell everyone that here at New Town we have a peace chief who can beat anyone at *gata-yusti!*"

'Squan' Usdi walked over to his sister's side. "Did you see Comes Back to Life throw his spear?" he asked.

"No," said Whirlwind. "I was collecting my winnings from Daksi here. Daksi, this is my brother. We call him the Little Spaniard, after our father."

" *'Siyo,* 'Squan' Usdi," Daksi greeted him.

" *'Siyo,* Daksi."

"Daksi lives in Coyatee," Whirlwind said.

Just then a man nearby picked up a bundle of goods he had won. On top of the pile was a long, gleaming blade. It flashed in the eyes of the Little Spaniard as the sun caught its surface just for an instant. "Look," he said.

"What?" asked Whirlwind.

"A Spanish sword," said 'Squan' Usdi. "Like our father must have had."

"Yes," Whirlwind agreed. "Our real father."

3

HIRLWIND dreamed of two things that night. She dreamed of Daksi. For the first time in her life, she had met a man she wanted for herself, not just to torment some other girl. And she wanted him—well, she just wanted him. That was all. He was tall, and he was handsome. He had the look of a great hunter and a great warrior. He was young, so perhaps he had yet to really distinguish himself in those ways but sooner or later, he would. She knew it. She knew it by his looks, and she knew it—well, she just knew.

She wondered if there was some other young woman interested in Daksi, someone over at Coyatee. If so, she would just have to deal with that. She could take him away from any other woman. She knew that she could. After all, she always got what she wanted and this time would be no different. She would have Daksi. No one would stand in her way. She had made up her mind.

And the other thing that occupied Whirlwind's mind before she slept, and in her dreams after, was the Spanish sword. Every now and then, over the years, she had seen some Spanish object. The people had gathered up some things from the few fights they'd had with Spaniards over the last few generations. Yet such things were rare.

She was interested in the sword and any other Spanish goods, because they were rare. Anyone who owned such things was envied and if anybody around New Town was to be envied, Whirlwind thought that it should be she. She wanted the Spanish sword. No. Not really. She did not want the Spanish sword they had seen that day. She wanted other swords and Spanish goods. She wanted more Spanish goods than anyone else had. They were so rare and so much desired that she wanted to have a wealth of them. Then there was the strain of mysterious Spanish blood that ran in her veins, which made her feel that she had a right to the Spanish goods, more than anyone else. After all, her father had been named Asquani, Spaniard, and her twin brother was called the Little Spaniard, Asquani Usdi. Who else had more right to the Spanish goods? She fell asleep thinking about ways in which she might acquire those things.

Thus far, the Real People had experienced nothing but unpleasantness with the Spaniards. They hated and feared the hairy-faced men. There were other white men who had come into the country of the Real People, the ones who called themselves Française, and they had gotten along well enough with the Real People. In fact, the Française had actually fought alongside the Real People, including her father, against the hated Spaniards.

Whirlwind had never seen a Spaniard or a Frenchman; at least she had no memory of ever having seen one. She wondered what a meeting with these men would be like. If one walked up to a Spaniard and greeted him, would he simply strike out with his sword? That didn't seem reasonable to her yet the tales told by the Real People, some old enough to remember the actual events, maintained that there was nothing reasonable about a Spaniard.

Still, she wondered. Even though she had never seen a Spaniard, she knew that she could talk to them, for her mother had learned the language while she was a captive and Whirlwind had learned it from her mother. The more she thought about it, the more anxious she was to try out her linguistic skills.

❦

WHEN she woke up the next morning, it was as if she had never slept, for her thoughts picked up exactly where they had left off the night before. And she completed the process. She knew what she was going to do. She got up from her bed and went to the water to start a new day. She was lighthearted, excited about her plans and anxious to put them into motion. The first thing she had to do was talk to her brother.

Osa and Guwisti, Comes Back to Life's first wife, were busy helping their husband in his preparations for the next major ceremony to come. It was easy for Whirlwind to catch the Little Spaniard alone. She found him just outside the house.

"Come and walk with me, Brother," she said. "I have something to tell you."

"Of course," he agreed, and he followed where she led. He always did, of course. She walked toward the nearby creek without speaking, and he walked along with her, patiently waiting for what she would have to say. The last few people were leaving the creek to go back to their homes. At the edge of the water she sat down. No one else was around. The Little Spaniard sat beside her.

"I want to go on a trip," she said, "and I want you to go with me."

"Where will we go?" he asked.

"First," she said, "I want to get some others to go with us. Seven is a good number. I think we should be seven."

The Little Spaniard nodded his assent.

"And before we leave, we should gather up a great many trade goods."

"A trading trip?" asked the Little Spaniard. "Our grandfather, Carrier, was a trader."

"Yes," she said. "Except he wasn't our real grandfather. Some Spaniard was our grandfather. He may even be still alive."

"He'd be an old man by now," said the Little Spaniard.

"He's probably dead," she stated. "Anyhow, we need lots of goods, and we need several *caballos.*"

She had used the Spanish word deliberately, for the Real People called the great beasts *sogwilis,* indicating beasts of burden. The Little Spaniard was not as adept at languages as his sister, but he did know a few Spanish words, and he knew what she had said.

"I have a *sogwili,*" he said, "and so do you. Our father, Comes Back to Life, owns several."

"Maybe the others I choose to go with us will have their own," she said. "We'll need seven for the seven of us to ride, and we'll need more to carry our goods on their backs. Maybe four more."

"Eleven *sogwilis,*" said the Little Spaniard, musing as if trying to figure out where the horses would all come from. Then he remembered that his sister had never answered his first question. "Where will we go on this trip?" he asked again.

"We're going to the Spaniards," she replied, "in La Florida."

The Little Spaniard's eyes opened wide in disbelief. "We'll all be killed," he said.

"I don't think so," Whirlwind disagreed. "I know that everyone says the Spaniards are all monsters, but do you feel like you're part monster? Your grandfather was a Spaniard. Your father was half Spanish. How could they be monsters?"

"Well, I—"

"Besides," she continued quickly, "I can talk to them in their own language. We'll go to La Florida with trade goods, and we'll return with all sorts of Spanish goods. We'll be the richest people in New Town. Everyone will envy us for what we have."

The Little Spaniard didn't really want to be envied. He could see no advantage in that. He was well liked and that was plenty good for him. But if Whirlwind was set on this trip to the land of the Spaniards, he knew already that he would go along with her. He always did what she wanted. It had been like that all his life.

Besides, if it was to be a dangerous journey, he would have to go along to protect her. Even as he had that last thought, he considered its irony. Whirlwind didn't need protection, she had her own. He wasn't sure that he liked it when people called her a witch but he was aware that she did really have some kind of unnatural power. She always got her own way. She always came out of any scrape unscathed.

"When do we start?" he asked.

"Right now," she said. "Gather up all the trade goods you can. And all the *caballos*. I'm going to get five more companions to go with us."

Without another word, Whirlwind stood up and left. The Little Spaniard noted that she was gone in almost an instant. She hadn't seemed to run away, it was almost as if she had just vanished. Almost. She was like that, though. She had her ways.

He got up and walked back to his mother's house to begin the process of gathering the goods and other things necessary for the journey. They would need lots of trail food, extra clothing, and weapons. They would need weapons for hunting and for protection from any enemies they might encounter.

While he was thus engaged, Osa came into the house, her arms loaded with freshly broken off cedar boughs, material she had been gathering for Comes Back to Life.

"What are you doing?" she asked. "It looks as if you are preparing for a journey."

"Yes, Mother," he said. "That's what I'm doing. My sister told me that we're going on a trading trip. We're going south to the land the Spaniards call La Florida, and we'll come back home with lots of Spanish goods."

Osa put down the boughs she had brought in and turned to face her son. "Did you tell her that's a crazy idea?" she asked, her look accusing her son.

"I did," he said, "but you know how she is."

Osa recalled with horror her own days as a captive of the Spaniards.

"You can't go," she insisted. "It's much too dangerous. The Spaniards will either kill you or take you captive and make slaves of you. You don't know them. Whirlwind doesn't know them either. She thinks she knows everything, but she doesn't know the Spaniards. You should believe all the stories you've been told. And she should believe them. The Spaniards are cruel. They're more cruel than you can imagine. Your own father and I helped to drive them away, far away from our own country. We did it for your safety, for the good of all the Real People. No, you can't go on this foolish trip to the Spaniards."

"Mother," said the Little Spaniard, "I believe you. But I'm going to get all these things together because I told her I would. If you tell my sister that we can't go, that will be all right. I don't care so much about going there. I'll do as you say, gladly, but only if you tell Whirlwind that we can't go."

AT just about that same time, Whirlwind spotted Daksi standing alone beside the entrance to the council house. She walked casually over to stand beside him, and she gave him a quick smiling glance.

He returned the smile. " 'Siyo,'" he greeted her. "I've been looking for you this morning."

"Oh?" she said. "I've been busy. I just happened to see you over here."

"I know that your father is planning a big ceremony," Daksi remarked.

"That's not what I've been busy with," she said. "That's his business. I have my own business to deal with."

She waited for a curious question from Daksi, but it didn't come. She realized that she would have to be more open with him, more direct, if she wanted any reaction.

"I'm preparing for a long trip," she began.

"You're going away?" Daksi asked.

Good, she thought. *He's showing some interest.*

"Yes," she said. "For a while."

"I hope you won't be gone too long," he told her. "I've only just met you, and I was hoping to get to know you better."

"Well," she said, "you can if you really want to."

"I can?"

"Of course. You could go along with me."

"Tell me about this trip," Daksi said.

"I'm going to La Florida, to the south, where the Spaniards live, to trade with them," she explained, "for Spanish goods. My brother is going with me and I want five more men to make us seven."

"Is this a wise thing to do?" Daksi asked. "I've heard that the Ani-'Squani are very dangerous people."

"Only if one doesn't know how to deal with them. I can speak their language. We'll come home with many Spanish things, swords, shields, knives, pots—all made of the hard metal they use. Saddles for *sogwilis*. Guns even."

"Guns?"

"Their thunder sticks," she said. "Surely you've heard of them."

"Yes," he replied. "I've heard some tales."

Daksi seemed to be in deep thought and Whirlwind knew that she almost had him. Her two goals were coming together beautifully. She wanted the Spanish goods, and, if she could only get Daksi out on the long trail with her, she knew that she would be able to make him hers somewhere along the way.

"Did you see the Spanish sword yesterday?" she asked.

"Yes," he said. "I saw it. It's a strange and beautiful weapon."

"It's made of a very hard and shiny metal," she told him. "We can get lots of them. And lots of other fine things that everyone here will want." She paused, waiting for some comment from Daksi, but he was silent. "Well," she said, "I have much to do and I'd better get going. I have to find some brave young men who aren't afraid to go with me."

She started to walk away from him, and then Daksi spoke to her back.

"Whirlwind," he said.

She stopped and looked back at him over her shoulder. He thought again how beautiful she was.

"If you'll have me along," he said, "I'll go on this trip with you."

She smiled. As usual, she had gotten her way.

4

T TOOK four days for them to get everything together but, on the morning of the fifth day, they started out. The Sun had only just come out from under the eastern edge of the great Sky Vault when the seven riders rode away from New Town leading four heavily loaded packhorses.

Whirlwind rode at the head of the group. A little behind and to her right rode her brother, the Little Spaniard. Even with the Little Spaniard, riding to Whirlwind's left, was Daksi. Behind them rode four other young men: Groundhog and Atsila, or Fire, from New Town and Slow Walker and Wrinkle Sides from Coyatee. All the young men were unmarried. All were anxious for adventure.

Each of the seven young people was armed with a long bow and a bundle of flint-tipped arrows, a knife, a river cane blowgun with a supply of darts, a war club, and a spear. They also carried lines, hooks and nets for fishing, and, of course, extra clothing.

The four pack animals were burdened with a wide variety of goods: ginseng root, beautiful baskets made of river cane, oak splints, sugar maple splints and hickory bark, clay pipes with river cane stems, sheets of pounded mica, skillfully prepared beaver, muskrat, deer, and bear hides, clay pots, freshwater pearls, and other valuable trade items. They were also loaded with an ample supply of *gahawista*, or dried, parched cornmeal, and a variety of dried meat.

There had been protests from Osa and from the parents of some of the young men, but in the end Whirlwind had gotten her way. The young people were all old enough to make their own decisions anyway, and so there was really nothing for the older people, the parents and maternal uncles and aunts, to do but complain and wheedle and advise. The young people would make their own decisions and, of course, they decided to go along with the wishes of Whirlwind. They always did.

The sixteen-year-old Whirlwind rode proudly at the head of her small trading party. This was the first major leadership role she had ever undertaken. Before, she had only been the leader of her small group of peers around New Town, mostly just playing games. This journey to the Spaniards in La Florida, however, was a great undertaking.

She rode with confidence, for she was convinced that her goals would be accomplished. She had never really known failure or disappointment and she did not expect it now. And she rode with excitement and a great sense of anticipation. She was leading these six young men on a journey of great adventure, into lands none of them had ever seen before, to meet people they had never met and do things they had never before done. Every day there would be new scenery. All along the way there would be new people and new experiences.

And she, the only female in the group, was the leader. Women among the Real People were used to leadership roles, but their leadership capacity was usually exercised quietly, almost behind-the-scenes. The visible town government was male. The women met without ceremony and then told the men what they thought should be done. The male government would then meet and make their decisions, often, if not usually, just the way the women had advised them.

But Whirlwind had assumed an open leadership role as the head of a trading party. She had taken on what was ordinarily a male role, and that in itself made her a remarkable woman. She was delighted about that, as she was always glad of any opportunity to show the others that she could do anything she wanted to do, no matter what the common practice might be.

❧

THEIR first few days on the trail, they were still within the boundaries of the country of the Real People, and they stopped for the night in different towns, including Kituwah, the original home of Asquani, Osa, and their twin babies. At each stop, the townspeople fed them and so their supply of trail food was not much diminished.

At last they left the safety of their own land and moved into the disputed territory between the lands of the Real People and those of their southern neighbors, the Ani-Gusa, the people of the great Muskogee Confederacy. Whirlwind didn't say anything but rode a little straighter in the saddle, a little more alert to her surroundings.

"We'll have to watch out here," said Groundhog. "Some Ani-Gusa could be around."

"That's true," Atsila agreed.

"Any Gusa who comes near us," Whirlwind snapped back over her shoulder, "had better be careful."

"Yes," said Daksi. "I hope none among us is afraid of any Gusa. If they want a fight, we'll give them a fight."

There was no more talk about the Ani-Gusa, but each rider watched all around as they continued south. Each rider checked to make sure his or her weapons were within easy reach.

That night they camped beside a clear stream, and Daksi and the Little Spaniard caught fish for their meal. They cooked over a small fire. Even so, some of the other men worried quietly that the camp might be spotted by a sneaking enemy. None appeared, however, and they started on their way again early the following morning.

❧

IT was about midday, the Sun had almost reached her daughter's house just overhead, when they saw the men waiting for them up ahead. Whirlwind stopped her mount and the young men behind her did the same. For a moment they studied the men ahead in silence. The two groups were still too far apart for a good bow shot.

"Ani-Gusa?" the Little Spaniard asked.

"Probably," said Whirlwind.

"There are twelve of them," said Daksi. "If we have to fight, it will be a good fight."

"They won't fight us," said Whirlwind. "They're on foot, and we're on *sogwilis*. We could ride into them and trample them easily."

"What will we do?" Groundhog asked.

Whirlwind urged her mount forward. "Follow me," she said.

The seven Real People moved at a slow pace toward the twelve waiting men. As they got closer, they could see that the men were, indeed, Ani-Gusa, and they were heavily armed. They stood deliberately with scowls on their faces, looking as if they meant to bar the way—or to fight. They were more than close enough for bow shots. Whirlwind said nothing but kept riding. They rode close enough for a spear toss and the men behind Whirlwind began to get nervous. At last she stopped. A man with a good arm could have thrown a war club and hit his target.

"Are you trying to make us stop or turn back?" Whirlwind asked. She spoke in a loud, clear voice, using the common trade language.

One of the Muskogees stepped forward. He looked at Whirlwind. "You're Chalakees," he began, using the trade jargon word for the Real People.

"Yes," said Whirlwind. "Of course."

"You're on Muskogee land."

"I believe that the rights to this land are in dispute," Whirlwind replied boldly. "Until there is a ball play or fight to bring the matter to some conclusion, the matter is unresolved."

"Are you here to fight for this land, then?" the Muskogee asked.

"Right now, we're just traveling through," said Whirlwind, "on our way to trade with the Spaniards in the south, but if you really want to fight, we'll fight with you."

"You're going to trade with the Spaniards?" asked the Muskogee.

"Yes. I said so."

The Muskogee turned to his companions and spoke to them in their own language. Then he burst into raucous laughter and was joined by the rest of his group. Whirlwind's face flushed. She didn't like being laughed at. She waited until the laughter had subsided a bit so that she would be heard.

"What do you think is funny?" she asked.

The Muskogee spokesman looked back at her. "We had thought to kill you," he said, "and take your animals and your goods, but if you're going south to the Spaniards, they'll either kill you for us or make you slaves. We'll be rid of you, and no one among us will even be hurt. Ride on, Chalakees. We won't bother you."

Whirlwind stared hard at the man for a moment, and in spite of the numbers of the two groups, the Muskogee began to get nervous.

"Go on," he said. "Ride through. We won't stop you."

"I'd like to know your name first," Whirlwind said.

The big Muskogee warrior stretched himself and puffed out his chest.

"I'm called the Big Warrior of Tamatly Town," he said. "Do you not know my name?"

Whirlwind deliberately ignored his question. "I'm Whirlwind of the Bird Clan of New Town of the Real People," she said. "I and these men are going south to Florida to meet the Spaniards, whose language I speak and whose blood runs in my veins. When we return, we'll be burdened down with many Spanish goods, including hard, sharp knives and swords and guns. I want to meet you again on our return trip. Will you be here?"

"If you don't see me," the Big Warrior said, "you can call for me at Tamatly Town."

Without another word, Whirlwind kicked her horse in the sides, sending him forward with a jump. The six men behind her followed, and the Muskogees scurried to either side in order to avoid being run over. They turned around to watch the riders racing south and only when the Real People appeared to be small dots on the far horizon did they speak.

"Huh," said the Big Warrior, as if to dismiss the incident as insignificant. "They weren't much more than children anyway. Children led by a girl."

"She called herself Whirlwind," one of the others mentioned.

"Yes," said the Big Warrior. "That's what she said. Whirlwind."

"I think I've heard about her," another added. "Did she say New Town?"

"Yes," said the Big Warrior. "New Town of the Chalakees."

"That's what I thought," the other muttered, and his voice and facial expression both betrayed worry.

"What's wrong?" asked the Big Warrior. "Is something bothering you?" He kept it to himself, but something was bothering him. It was something about the Chalakee girl, something that he couldn't quite define.

"That New Town is a town on their far northern frontier," said the other. "They built it there because of the Shawnees, I think. Anyway, my cousin visited up there once not long ago. They say that she's a powerful witch, this Whirlwind. They say she can change shapes and she can swim through the earth as if it were water. Her own people are all afraid of her. She has a twin, and both of them lived. The girl, Whirlwind, was raised by an old woman from Kituwah."

A look of dark dread came over the solemn face of the Big Warrior. "Uyona?" he asked.

"Yes," said the other. "I think that was the name. Uyona. It's what the Chalakees call a horn. Did you know that old Chalakee woman?"

"Yes," the Big Warrior answered. "She was well known, even among us. I think we did well today not to fight with these children."

"But they'll be coming back."

"Maybe," said the Big Warrior. "But the Spaniards aren't afraid of anything. Maybe the Spaniards will kill them all, in spite of Whirlwind and her powers."

"Or make slaves of them," another added.

"Yes. One or the other," said the Big Warrior. "Maybe."

WELL away from the Big Warrior and his group, Whirlwind slowed the pace of the horses again. She knew better than to run them for too long a time. Behind her Groundhog spoke to Atsila, but Whirlwind could hear what he was saying.

"That was dangerous back there," Groundhog said. "There were too many of them for us to fight."

Whirlwind raced her mount forward a few paces, then turned him quickly to face the others. They all reined in abruptly.

"Could you have handled the situation any better than I did?" she snapped.

Groundhog ducked his head.

"I'm not afraid of the Ani-Gusa," she continued, "no matter how many of them there are. I'm not afraid of anyone or anything. If you're afraid or if you don't trust my leadership, you can go home. I don't need you. But the pack animals and all the supplies stay with me."

Atsila became suddenly bold. "You kept us out of a fight," he said. "That's good. But you provoked the Big Warrior, and he'll be waiting for us on our way back, maybe with more men. We'll have to fight with him then."

"Yes," Groundhog added, gaining courage now that he had an ally. "He'll probably be waiting for us to come back with the Spanish goods so he can kill us and take them for himself."

"I don't like this," said Atsila.

"I don't either," Groundhog agreed.

"Go back home then," Whirlwind said. "I don't want you."

"We know about you," said Groundhog. "We know what you can do."

"I won't do anything to you," Whirlwind responded. "If you don't want to go with me, you can go home. I won't hurt you. Go on."

Atsila looked at Groundhog. Groundhog suddenly jerked the reins of his mount, turning it and heading back north. Atsila followed him. Slow Walker looked at Wrinkle Sides for a moment.

"I'm going home, too," Wrinkle Sides said, and he and Slow Walker both turned their horses to follow the other two deserters.

Whirlwind turned on Daksi, her face flashing anger. "You, too?" she said. "Go on. Go with them if you want to."

Daksi smiled at her. "Not me," he said. "If you're going on, so am I."

"And me," said the Little Spaniard. "I stay with you, Sister."

"All right then," said Whirlwind. "Let's ride south."

5

HE RACED her horse ahead far longer than she should have done with the Little Spaniard and Daksi following, leading the packhorses and keeping pace with her as best they could. She knew better than to run the animals so fast for such a distance, but she was angry. She didn't care so much about the loss of the four who had turned back to go home. She really did believe what she had told them, that she didn't need them. But still she was angry, angry that they had not simply followed her without question. She was used to being followed without question, and the four had broken the pattern.

When at last she slowed to a sensible pace, the other two galloped up beside her again, one on either side, as before. They rode along like that for a while, no one speaking. All three riders just looked straight ahead. At last Whirlwind broke the silence.

"You think I was foolish to let them go?" she asked.

The Little Spaniard only gave a shrug.

"You said we don't need them," Daksi said. "I believe you. They say that Carrier went all the way to La Florida by himself. I guess then we three can do it."

Whirlwind's mood changed again, as suddenly as it had before. She looked at Daksi and smiled.

"That's right," she said. "My only mistake was in bringing so many in the first place. This is the way it should have been to begin with, just the three of us. Let's find a place to camp and eat."

They were on an old, well-traveled road that for the most part paralleled streams of running water. Good campsites were plentiful, many of them showing signs of recent usage.

Daksi pointed ahead to a place where the road curved to the right around a grove of trees. To the left of the road, a wide and level spot of ground lay between the road and the stream. "Up there, I think," he said.

It was Whirlwind's normal pattern to disagree with almost any suggestion made by someone else and supply her own in its place. She surprised her brother with her response.

"Yes," she agreed. "That looks good."

They rode the short distance to the designated spot and dismounted. Daksi and the Little Spaniard busied themselves with unburdening the animals, while Whirlwind gathered sticks for a fire. Soon they had a comfortable camp for a rest. They boiled some water from the stream over their campfire, mixed some *gahawista* in it, and had hot cornmeal mush with dried meat for their meal.

"I wonder how long we'll be in this land of the Ani-Gusa," the Little Spaniard said.

"A few days," answered Whirlwind, although she didn't really know.

"I wonder if we'll have any more trouble with them," he said.

"Ha," said Whirlwind. "That was no trouble. We'll probably see some more of them before we get through their country. Maybe they'll see us."

Daksi wondered what she meant by that last remark, but he didn't say anything. She was a very interesting young woman. She had more confidence in herself than did most men and he wondered if that confidence was merited. He thought that it probably was.

❧

THEY had been in camp long enough to be well rested and well fed. The horses were rested and had been grazing contentedly. It was about time to be on the way again, but Whirlwind made a sudden gesture with her hand.

"Be quiet," she said, "and be absolutely still. Someone is coming."

Daksi wondered if he should get his weapons ready, just in case, but he did what Whirlwind said. He wanted to ask which way the noises were coming from. He wanted to look. Instead, he sat still, staring at the small fire that burned between him and Whirlwind. To his right, the Little Spaniard sat. All three travelers were as still as if they had been carved from stone.

Then Daksi heard the noise of someone coming along the road. It was all he could do to keep himself from turning his head for a better look, but Whirlwind had given her instructions. Out of the corner of his eye he could see some men walking along the road. He could hear them talking with one another. He couldn't tell how many they were, and he couldn't understand their language. He thought that they were Ani-Gusa, and he estimated at least half a dozen.

He wondered if they would come over to the camp and start some trouble. Surely they would approach the camp to talk at least. They would be curious about the three travelers.

The strangers walked on, still talking among themselves. Their talk was relaxed and friendly. One chuckled at something, and then they all laughed together. They moved on.

Daksi could no longer see them, but he could still hear their talk. He sat still as it faded away in the distance. Still, he did not move.

"They're gone," Whirlwind said. "Let's be on our way."

They put the Spanish saddles, which they called *gayahulos*, back onto the riding horses and reloaded the pack animals. Daksi was wondering about what they had just experienced. Those men, likely Ani-Gusa, had walked right past them. One man might walk down the road and not notice three people sitting over by the stream. It was not likely, but he might. But six men or more could hardly keep from noticing the three people, the small fire, and the horses.

He wondered about what Whirlwind had done. Surely she had done something. He recalled something she had said earlier. "Maybe they'll see us," she had said.

As they remounted and moved back onto the road, Daksi looked back at their campsite. He thought there was no way he could pass by there and not see people sitting there, not see the fire and the horses.

Whirlwind had done something. *The things that people said about her back home must be true,* he thought. *She really is a witch. She really does have unnatural powers.* He had heard all his life that there were some among the Real People who could make themselves invisible but this one—she had made them all invisible: three people, a campfire, and seven horses.

Daksi asked himself if he should be afraid, traveling through strange country with such a woman. He was not afraid, but he wondered why he was not. Most of the people were afraid just knowing, or believing that they knew, what she was and what she could do, just having her around. Why, he wondered, was he not?

But he was not. Rather, he was fascinated by this mysterious young woman and he felt safe in her company. He was confident enough in his own powers, but they were natural powers. He was not afraid to fight any man, but he knew that somewhere there was a man who could beat

him. He knew also that he could not fight several men alone and expect
to win.

But in the company of this young woman, this Whirlwind, this . . .
witch, his own strengths and abilities were fortified by her mysterious
powers. Just a short while ago, he had actually been invisible—he
thought. For, try as he might, he could come up with no other explanation for the Ani-Gusa walking right past them. Yes. He had been
invisible, and she had done it.

He was overcome with a powerful passion he could not quite define.
It was a feeling for Whirlwind, but a strange feeling, unlike any he ever
felt before. He had seen other beautiful young women, and he had wanted
to make love to them. He had even thought of marriage a time or two.
But this feeling was different. It was like a feeling he might have for a
great leader, someone he would follow into any battle without question,
but it was also like the feelings he had experienced toward other women.
It was like that but more powerful.

He had another thought. He had heard that there were people who
made medicine to capture the affections of someone. Could it be, he
wondered, that this young woman had made such medicine and used it
against him? That would explain his unnatural and overwhelming feelings for her, for if those feelings were caused by medicine, by spells and
charms, they would of necessity be unnatural feelings.

He wondered but, of course, he could not tell. Finally, he told himself
that he really didn't care anyway. The feelings were there and they were
good feelings. He would simply accept them, live with them, and wait
to see what each new day would bring.

Riding slightly ahead of her two male companions, Whirlwind was
filled with pride. The journey was just begun, and she had dealt with
two different groups of Ani-Gusa. The first ones, had they pressed a fight,
would have been a match for them, even though she'd had six men with
her. It would have been a fairly even fight—they might have come
through it victorious or might have all been killed. At best, they'd have
had some casualties.

But she had dealt with the Ani-Gusa verbally and had backed them
off. She was proud of herself for that. Then she had sent the other four
men home, because they had been afraid and because they had dared to
question her behavior.

Originally, she had thought that seven was a good number for her
group, but now she was glad the four had gone back. Now they were
only three, but one of them was her brother, whom she dearly loved, and

the other was Daksi. She liked Daksi. She liked him a great deal. In fact, she had never liked any man so much. She was even beginning to think that Daksi might be the one she would marry. Of course, it would take some time to be sure, but this long trip was just the way to find out about him.

So far, Daksi was living up to her expectations. He had not shown fear when faced with the possibility of a fight and on the other hand, had not been rash. He had remained calm and allowed Whirlwind to deal with the situation. She had no doubt, though, that if one of the Ani-Gusa had started something, Daksi would have rushed headlong into the action.

When the four had said that they wanted to go home, Daksi had not wavered. He had said right away that he was going to stay with her. He had been as loyal to her as her own brother was. Then, when she had told them to be still back at the camp, he had done so. Many men would have turned to see who was coming. Many would have insisted on arming themselves and going out to the road to meet the ones who were coming. But Daksi had listened to her, he had done as she had told him to do, and she liked that about him. Of course, she always liked for anyone to do what she said. But with Daksi it was different. She had a feeling that Daksi was not afraid of her. Others gave in to her out of fear but Daksi gave in to her wishes willingly. He made his own decisions and, so far, he had decided to go along with her. She liked that. She did wonder, though, just how far he would go. At what point would he decide that she was wrong or that he was tired of following her orders, indulging her whims?

She thought about pushing him to discover his limits, telling him to do ridiculous things, one after the other. She could tell him that she wanted the feathers of a small red bird that lived on top of a mountain, and when he had brought them to her she could send him on some other errand. Then she told herself that those were foolish thoughts. He was already following her on a long and perilous journey, and so far he had done everything her way. She would keep things the way they were—for a while.

❧

IT was almost evening, and Whirlwind was thinking about a camp for the night. She had no idea where they were, other than somewhere within the boundaries of the Ani-Gusa country. She thought that there were no towns nearby, for they had not seen any other people since having left their small rest camp earlier in the day. The Sun was low in the west and they were watching carefully for a suitable place to camp when Daksi spotted six riders coming toward them from the south.

6

HE TWO groups of riders stopped, each group single file across the road, blocking the other's way. Three Real People faced six others. All were heavily armed. The six on the other side did not appear to Whirlwind to be Ani-Gusa, but she did not know who else they might be. She was fairly certain that they were still well within the boundaries of the Ani-Gusa. She kicked her mount easily in the sides to urge him forward slowly a few paces. Then she stopped again.

"Hello," she said, using the trade jargon. "Do any of you speak the trade language?"

One of the opposing riders moved his mount forward a little.

"I do," he replied. "I'm called Flies in the Night. We're Appalachee People. Who are you?"

"We're Chalakees," said Whirlwind, "from north of here. I'm called Whirlwind, and this is my brother, the Little Spaniard. We're from New Town on the Shawnee border. This other is Terrapin from Coyatee. We're traveling south to trade with the Spaniards. Are we not still in the country of the Muskogee People?"

"Yes," said Flies in the Night. "You're right. We are in their country. My friends and I are going to a meeting with some Muskogees. Will you stop and rest with us for a while?"

"Yes," Whirlwind agreed. "Thank you."

She turned to tell the Little Spaniard and Daksi what she and Flies in the Night had said, and the Appalachee did the same for his companions. Then they rode off the road to the side near the creek and dismounted. Two of the Appalachees gathered wood for a small fire while the others unsaddled their horses. At the same time, the Little Spaniard and Daksi unsaddled their own riding horses and unloaded the pack animals. Soon the six Appalachees and the three Real People were seated around the fire smoking together. Whirlwind and Flies in the Night talked with one another.

"We had some trouble with some Muskogees recently," Flies in the Night said. "We're going to their Tamatly Town to talk about peace. We were invited there for that purpose by the Big Warrior."

"We met the Big Warrior along this road," Whirlwind remarked. "He wanted to fight with us until I told him that we were going to the Spaniards. Then he laughed at us and said that he'd just let the Spaniards kill us and save him the trouble."

"He likes to brag," said Flies in the Night. "I know him. But he doesn't know the Spaniards very well, not nearly so well as he likes to pretend. I know that when they first came to this land from across the big water they killed and enslaved a great many people. But lately they've changed. They've withdrawn to their settlements in the south, and they seem to be trying to get along with most of the people around them now."

"That's good to know," said Whirlwind. "I hadn't heard that."

"I think that it's because of the other white people who have come among us," the Appalachee replied. "I think they're afraid that if they don't make friends of us, we'll join with their enemies, the French or the English, those most recently arrived." He gave a shrug. "I don't know," he continued, "but these Spaniards aren't like the ones who came among us at first."

"Some Real People and some Catawba People already joined with some French to drive the Spaniards south from the country of our neighbors, the Catawbas," Whirlwind said. "My own father was among them. Maybe you heard about it. He was called Asquani in our language. That means 'Spaniard.' "

"Ah," Flies in the Night replied, "yes. I have heard that tale. Many times. It's a good one. The Spanish were on an island, and they meant to stay there. Your father and the others whipped them good and drove them away."

"Yes," she said. "And they've never come back either."

"I'm glad to become acquainted with the daughter of so great a man," said Flies in the Night, and he glanced at the Little Spaniard, "and the son. But now you want to trade with them?"

"Yes," she answered. "I thought that perhaps enough time has passed since the fight. It happened before I was born. And we'd like to have the goods we can get from the Spaniards. What you've just told me about them is good news. It should be even easier to accomplish than I thought."

Flies in the Night took out his pipe and tobacco. He filled the pipe bowl and reached for a burning faggot in the fire.

"Yes," he said. "You should have no trouble." He puffed at his pipe to get the tobacco lit, then tossed the stick back into the fire. A thick cloud of heavy smoke rose around his head. He held the pipe toward Whirlwind, who took it, puffed four times, and gave it back to him. "The Spaniards still have some slaves they took from the tribes who live just by them," Flies in the Night continued, "but they're trying to be friendlier with the rest of us, I think. I think they'll welcome you. They'll want to make friends with your people and I think they'll trade with you."

Whirlwind mused for a moment. She was getting good information from this Appalachee, and she thought that she should give him something back.

"When you get to Tamatly," she said, "tell the Big Warrior that you met with me along the way. Tell him that you're my friend."

LATER, riding along in silence, the Little Spaniard and Daksi on either side of her, Whirlwind contemplated the things she had just heard from Flies in the Night. So the Spaniards were no longer the terror they had been in past years. There were now at least three different kinds of white people in this land, and they did not get along well at all with one another. When the Spaniards had been the only ones around, they had not worried about making friends. They had tried to get their way by terrorizing the native people. But now those same Spaniards wanted friends and allies against their own kind, and so their attitude had changed. Whirlwind thought that her father had been at least partially responsible for that change in attitude. The Spanish had suffered a stunning defeat at the hands of Real People and Catawbas allied with the French.

If it was now important to the Spaniards to have allies, she might be better off presenting herself not as a trader but as an emissary. Perhaps the Spaniards would give her gifts in exchange for a pledge of friendship. Then she would have the Spanish goods as well as her own trade goods.

Or, if they did not give her enough gifts to satisfy her, she could always trade with them afterward.

She decided that she would do that. She would leave the pack animals behind before they went in to actually meet the Spaniards. Perhaps she would leave Daksi or the Little Spaniard with the animals and goods while she presented herself to the Spaniards. That, she decided, was the best idea.

Even though she had never met a Spaniard, she could speak their language, and she had Spanish blood running in her veins. For those reasons and more, she was anxious to meet them. She was curious about their appearance and their manners. Of course, she had heard tales. She had heard that they were very ugly. Their skin was pale, like the under-belly of a fish and hair grew all over their bodies, it was said. She wanted to see them for herself. She had heard also that they never bathed and, therefore, stank. Their language sounded harsh and gruff, and their man-ners were rude. And, of course, she had heard many tales of their extreme cruelty, of how they casually lopped the heads off people with their long swords or set their vicious dogs on people to tear them to pieces for little or no reason. She did believe the stories, for some of them had come from Osa, her own mother.

Even so, she also believed that she would be able to deal with these men. She had absolute confidence in her own skills, abilities, and, yes, powers and something had told her that this was the right thing to do. Now having heard the new information from Flies in the Night, she was even more confident.

And now she wondered about the other white men: the French and the English. What were they like? She knew from the stories that her father and other Real People had made friends and allies of a Frenchman and they had fought together against the Spaniards. According to the stories, this Frenchman was not a bad man. He had peculiar ways about him, of course, but he had been a good friend to the Real People. There was another story, though, about how some of his people had engaged in violence in the Peace Town, Kituwah.

So apparently there were good and bad men among the French. Were there then also good and bad Spaniards? And what about the English? She knew nothing at all about the English except that they were yet another kind of white man from across the big waters. She knew of no one among the Real People who had ever met an Englishman, nor had she heard any stories about them.

The Spanish and the French both hated the English, from all she had heard. She wanted to meet all of these people and get to know what they were like. She wondered what kinds of trade goods each would have. She knew that these strangers had brought the *sogwilis* across the waters with them. She had not known life without *sogwilis* and would not want to know it that way. She loved riding the magnificent animals, and of course it was much better to haul things on the back of a *sogwili* than on one's own back.

She did not bother to share all of these thoughts with her male companions. She did tell them what Flies in the Night had said about the Spaniards and of her new plan to leave the trade goods behind, at least initially. That, she thought, was all they needed to know for now.

When they camped that night, Whirlwind's thoughts swirled in her head, but when at last they settled down, she thought about Daksi lying there just on the other side of the fire. She pictured his strong, young, beautiful body and thought about going to him, but she couldn't quite bring herself to do it. For one thing, she wanted him to come to her, and then, too, she wasn't at all sure that the time was right for such things. She decided to wait a while longer. She would know, she told herself, when the right time had come.

❦

WHEN she woke up the next morning, she saw her brother lying stiff, his eyes wide, staring at a large rattlesnake just beside him. The rattles on his back end were singing loudly. A short distance away, Daksi stood very still, his bow and an arrow in hand. His face wore a serious and worried look, and he was concentrating his gaze on the snake.

Whirlwind knew why Daksi was worried, and she also knew why he had armed himself. She would deal with that later. She sat up quickly.

"Don't do anything," she said. Then she got onto her hands and knees, and she moved slowly, almost imperceptibly, toward where her brother was lying so still. "Ujonati," she said, calling the rattler by name. "Grandfather Ujonati, we're not here to bother you. We're just traveling through your country."

She stared straight at the great snake as she crawled, still barely moving, not seeming to move at all, and she spoke in a low and calm voice. "Don't be angry with us," she continued. "If you leave us alone, we'll go away from here right away. You won't see us again."

She crept closer. The Little Spaniard was sweating profusely. He tried to hold his breath to keep from moving even his chest. Daksi still stood ready with his bow and arrow, the arrow nocked but the string not drawn. He, too, stared at the snake.

Whirlwind crept closer. "Ujonati," she said, "I'm talking to you. I'm over here. Look this way. Look at me."

She moved closer yet, and the rattlesnake turned to look directly at her. Still he stood up straight. Still his tail made terrible music.

"Ujonati," said Whirlwind, returning his stare and looking into his eyes, "we're not going to hurt you. Now, 'Squan' Usdi, roll away quickly." She had not looked away from the snake and had not changed the tone of her voice.

The Little Spaniard rolled away from the snake as fast as he could roll. Ujonati did not strike. He stared back at Whirlwind, who still returned his stare. The big snake swayed hypnotically from side to side, and Whirlwind swayed with him. By this time she was very close and the snake could easily have struck her. She stopped crawling and began raising her left hand slowly, almost imperceptibly.

"Ujonati," she said, "I'm going to take you a little ways away from this place, because I don't want us to bother one another. You don't want to hurt me, do you?"

Her hand was very close to the snake and, continuing to move slowly and deliberately, she closed her fingers around his body just below his head. Had he tried, he could not strike. He could only have wrapped himself around her arm, but he did not do even that. She did not squeeze him hard. She just held him firmly, and she stood up. She held the snake's head just in front of her face and continued talking to him as she walked away from the camp.

A safe distance away, she bent and placed the rattler on the ground. She moved back from him slowly, then straightened up.

"*Wado,* Ujonati," she said. "Now, let's you and I not meet each other again this year."

The big rattler looked back at her, then began to slither away, moving toward the thick underbrush beneath the trees.

7

OU KNOW the story of the rattlesnake and the hunter?"
Whirlwind asked Daksi.

"Yes," he said. "I know the story, but I was ready to shoot
the snake even so, rather than let him strike your brother."

Whirlwind stopped and looked at Daksi. She had not been prepared for that answer. She had thought that Daksi was on the verge
of foolishly shooting the rattlesnake because he did not know any
better, and she was about to give him a lesson in proper behavior.
But he did know, and yet he had been willing to sacrifice himself in
order to save her brother.

The Real People knew that it meant certain death to kill a rattlesnake.
The old story ran through the mind of Whirlwind.

> Once long ago, a hunter was alone in the woods when suddenly
> he found himself surrounded by rattlesnakes. He stopped still,
> afraid to move. Then a very large snake, the chief of the rat-
> tlesnakes, stood up tall on the tip of his tail and looked directly
> into the eyes of the hunter.
>
> "Your wife," the snake said, "has just killed my brother. I
> want you to go home now and tell your wife to go outside for
> water. When she does that, I'll be waiting for her, and I'll kill
> her then to balance things for my brother. If you refuse me,
> we'll just kill you right here and now."
>
> The hunter went home and, just as he'd been told, sent his
> wife outside for water. The chief rattlesnake was waiting out
> there, as he said he would be, and when she stepped close enough
> he struck, quickly and surely, and the woman was killed.

All of the Real People knew the story of the hunter and the rattlesnake, and they all knew that killing a rattlesnake would result in certain untimely death. Whirlwind realized that she had come awake at exactly the right moment, for both young men had been in terrible danger. The Little Spaniard might have been bitten by the snake or, if Daksi had chosen to shoot the snake in order to save the life of her brother, he would have sealed his own fate by having done so. There was no way of knowing just how or when it would have happened, but if he had killed the rattlesnake, he would have died soon after.

Whirlwind felt a deeper, warmer feeling for Daksi than before. What he had been about to do was selfless and brave, and it would have been an act of profound love, either for herself or for her brother. Whirlwind had wanted Daksi to become completely devoted to her. Perhaps he had. But, she now realized with some slight discomfort, she was suddenly completely devoted to him. Always before, people had done things for her because they were intimidated by her or because they were afraid of her, never, she thought, because of any fondness for her.

She had never before experienced a feeling from outside her own influence move in to take over her life. She had always been in control. This feeling was from outside her control. She had not made the choice, and she could not make a choice. She was in Daksi's debt, and it was a debt she could never repay. But the worst, or the best, of it was that she did not mind. She would be in his debt for the rest of her life, and she would like it. She was thankful for it.

She walked over to her brother and laid a gentle hand on his shoulder. Wet with perspiration, he was still trembling a little, and he was breathing deeply.

"Are you all right, Little Spaniard?" she asked.

"Yes," he said. "I'm fine. *Wado.*"

She turned to Daksi, cocked her head and looked at him for a moment, then walked up close to him. She put her hands on his shoulders.

"I thank you," she said, "for what you were about to do."

"You saved me from having to do it," he replied. "*Wado.* And what you did, well, it was amazing. I've never seen anyone do anything like that before."

She smiled and turned away. She was still ahead of him, it seemed, and that was good. She would try to leave it like that for at least a while longer.

"Let's get packed and get on our way," she said. "I'm anxious to meet the Spaniards."

THAT night, after a long day of traveling, they camped again. Whirl-wind estimated that they were either already out of the land of the Ani-Gusa or very close to its southern boundary. The next town they came to, she thought, would be an Appalachee town. When they got there, she decided, they would stop to visit and take advantage of Appalachee hospitality. A break from trail food would be more than welcome.

They unloaded the animals and set them out to graze, then built a small fire and cooked their meal. They ate, talked a little, and then made their beds for the night. Whirlwind deliberately stayed awake, though. She waited until she knew that the Little Spaniard was asleep, and then she got out from under her cover, and she was naked.

She walked around the fire and stood over the prone form of Daksi. Saying nothing, she looked down at him. In a moment, he opened his eyes wide and looked up at her in astonished wonder. She was beautiful standing there in the darkness, the light from the tiny fire illuminating the curves of her body. She was like a vision of all things beautiful and lovely.

He moved his cover aside, and she knelt beside him. He touched her thigh, and a thrill went through his body. She smiled and moved down on top of him, and he was engulfed in her warmth and sweetness. Then he drew the cover back over them both, and they made love together, softly and gently. It was beautiful, and it was good, and it was right.

"If you like," she said, lying still by his side, "I'll be your wife."

"I'd like nothing better," he replied. He knew, of course, that marriages were arranged between the clans of the two people who wanted to be married, but he also knew that Whirlwind always got her way. He couldn't imagine that anyone at home, in either clan, would voice any real objections. Even if they did, elopement was always an alternative among the Real People. So they had just eloped. They were married.

FROM the time he woke up the next morning and saw the couple to-gether under the same cover, the Little Spaniard noticed an amazing change in his sister. She was not quite so arrogant as before. For the first time in her life, she seemed to consider the feelings of others before her own. She had become a wife, and she was acting like a wife. She was still confident and she still voiced her opinion, but it no longer sounded so much like she was giving orders. She seemed now to merely suggest. And if the Little Spaniard or Daksi made a suggestion, she would actually consider it. She might even follow it.

The Little Spaniard had always been devoted to his sister. Even so, he liked this change in her, and he was more than pleased to have Daksi for his sister's husband. He thought that Osa and Comes Back to Life would be pleased, too. He knew that they would. Daksi was a fine young man.

Then he wondered if this new attitude on the part of Whirlwind would have a bad effect on their mission. Perhaps it would have been better, he thought, had she waited until they were back home to become a wife. Her personality was softened, and it was her tough, self-assured character that had been their strength. He worried about that a little, but he kept his thoughts to himself.

The Little Spaniard's fears were somewhat allayed when they reached an Appalachee town later that day. Whirlwind rode boldly ahead of the two men to meet the Appalachee men who came out of the town to intercept their unexpected visitors. She spoke out confidently to the man who seemed to be in charge, and then she told the Little Spaniard and Daksi to follow her.

The Appalachee men led them into the town, and soon a feast was laid before them. Whirlwind did all of their communicating with the Appalachees, for she was the only one of the three Real People with a command of the trade language. None of them could speak the language of the Appalachees, and none of the Appalachees in that town knew the tongue of the Real People.

She told the Appalachees that she was traveling south with her brother and her husband to trade with the Spaniards. She told them that she had met Flies in the Night and the others with him on their way to the peace mission with the Muskogees, and she told them that she had also met the Big Warrior of Tamatly Town earlier on the same road.

The people of the town were very much interested in all of that. They told her that she was visiting in the town of Flies in the Night. Naturally they were concerned about his well-being, and they were interested in any news about his travels. They also wanted to know about the disposition of the Big Warrior. Whirlwind told them that from all she had seen, she expected Flies in the Night to be completely successful in his mission.

That night the Appalachees held a dance in honor of their guests, and more food was laid out before them. Whirlwind, Daksi, and the Little

Spaniard all ate until they could eat no more and, far into the night, the Appalachees at last showed them where they could sleep. All three slept soundly, almost until the middle of the next day.

Whirlwind at first thought to resume the journey immediately, but the Appalachees urged her to stay one more night.

"Our next town along your way," said their jargon talker, "is another day's journey on your horses. It would be better for you if you stayed with us another night so you could start early in the morning and arrive there toward the end of the day."

While Whirlwind was considering the alternatives and talking them over with Daksi and the Little Spaniard, dark clouds suddenly welled up in the distant west.

"Look," said Daksi. "They're coming this way and moving pretty fast."

"Perhaps we should stay here after all," Whirlwind remarked. Then she turned back to the Appalachee jargon talker to tell him that they had decided to accept his invitation. They ate again, but everyone was quiet, watching the sinister-looking clouds as they kept moving closer. It wasn't long before the people began to hear thunder and see flashes of lightning in the now fast-approaching clouds. The Sun was hidden and the middle of the day became as dark as late evening.

"It's a big storm," someone said, "and it's coming right at us."

"It will be here soon," another added.

People began gathering up their things and taking them into their houses. Some mothers, grandmothers, and aunts began gathering up children and hustling them inside, but some of the children ran, preferring to stay outside and watch. Dogs howled or whined and ran for cover. Many people went inside their homes and stayed there. Others stood outside to watch the progress of the storm as it moved closer and closer. Its path was straight and it seemed determined to attack the town.

"Well, we're going to get wet, I guess," the Little Spaniard said.

"Worse than that," said Daksi, pointing toward the storm clouds. Whirlwind, the Little Spaniard, and others nearby looked to see what he was pointing at, and there they saw a tiny dark queue protruding downward from the bottom of the heavy clouds. As they watched, they saw it grow into a large funnel and dip down toward the earth. And still it moved toward them.

Now suddenly desperate, women grabbed the bolder children or ran frantically looking for them and calling their names. The children, now frightened, screamed and cried in terror.

"It's coming here. It's coming here. It will blow us all away!"

Whirlwind stood in the middle of the street and watched her terrible namesake bearing down on them. Rain started pounding down on the town, and the roar of the wind became almost deafening, and yet the funnel had not even arrived. Whirlwind grabbed her brother by the arm to get his attention.

"*Tsola,*" she said.

"What?"

"Tobacco," she repeated. "Get me some tobacco. Hurry."

The Little Spaniard turned and ran toward where their packs were stashed and a moment later came back to her with a twist of ancient tobacco, that special variety grown by the Real People.

Whirlwind almost jerked it from his hand. "Stay here," she said. Then she ran hard toward the approaching terror, heavy rain now slashing viciously at her face.

"What's she doing?" the Little Spaniard asked. "She's running straight into it."

"I don't know," said Daksi. "She's your sister."

"She's your wife," the Little Spaniard answered.

Daksi hesitated only an instant longer, then ran after her. The Little Spaniard stood still and shouted.

"Stop!" he called. "Daksi. Stay here. She said stay here!"

But Daksi could not hear the Little Spaniard for the noise of the storm, and even if he had heard, he would likely have kept going.

He ran, but Whirlwind was well ahead of him. He ran through the town to its far edge, and it looked to him as if he were going to run headlong into the raging whirlwind that was, by this time, almost on the town. The winds ahead of the swirl were strong, and Daksi found himself almost blown back. He stopped and looked ahead, trying to find Whirlwind. He had to shield his face from flying debris with his arm. Then he saw her.

She was standing not far ahead, arms outstretched, looking up. The great monster was almost upon her. In another instant she would be swallowed up and carried violently away, and he would never see her again. He couldn't move. He couldn't shout or scream. He could do nothing but watch in fascinated horror.

Then, just as Daksi thought that the end of the world was upon them, the great wind turned and slashed its way across an open field adjacent to the town. Halfway across the field, it took a mighty leap back up into the sky, and then it was gone.

8

NY DOUBTS that the Little Spaniard had entertained about his sister's softening personality were gone. He had known her all his life, but even he had been astounded by the magnificent way in which she had dealt with the giant tornado. He had often heard people say that she was a witch, that she had astounding and unnatural powers, but because she was his sister and because he had always known her, he had never really thought much about those comments.

Of course, he knew that she always got her way. He himself always gave in to her. But he had never given much thought to all that. It was just the way things were, just the way she was. But here he had watched her turn the terrible wind. He had felt the power of the smaller winds that ran ahead of it. He had seen the awesome power coming straight for them, and he had watched as his sister ran right at it, right into its path as if she would collide with it, defiantly challenging its awesome power.

He had stood there frightened and astonished as she raised her arms and spoke to it. He had no idea what she had said, for the noise of the great storm itself had been much too great, but he had watched as it came close to her, ready to suck her into its great swirl, then abruptly turned and went away, doing no harm to her or to the town in which they were visiting.

Now suddenly, the stories about his sister he had heard all his life had new and real meaning for him. She was indeed someone special. Not just because she was his sister, whom he loved, but because she was really someone special, someone special to all of the people. She had real and meaningful and useful powers. She had powers that were awesome and, he at last admitted to himself, even frightening. She could, he now believed, do absolutely anything she wanted to do.

❧

FOR the next several days, the three Real People rode without seeing any other human beings. They passed no more towns. Nevertheless, the traveling was pleasant enough. The weather was calm and each new day brought new scenery. The land opened up and flattened out around them. Each day was a new experience and each day brought them that much closer to their final destination and their planned meeting with the Spaniards.

And each new day brought the three companions that much closer to each other. The Little Spaniard was now in constant awe of his sister and was very proud. Daksi, too, was proud. He had a wife like no one else could boast of. Whirlwind's mind was occupied equally with her mission and with her new husband and the joys of her new status as wife. There was more excitement in her life than there had ever been before. At sixteen, she had her own man, her husband, and he was beautiful, brave, and honorable. He did anything she wanted him to do without question, but he did so, she was convinced, out of love rather than out of fear or intimidation. And yet she was equally devoted to him. She believed that there was nothing she would not do to keep him safe and happy.

Every night they made wonderful, passionate love together. In spite of what she had told Tobacco Flower that time, she had really had no idea then how lovemaking was for other people, but she knew now that hers with Daksi was the best. She knew that there could be no better.

Never before had she given any thought to the idea of being a mother, but now, with Daksi, she began to think about that likelihood and she liked the thought. She and Daksi would be parents. They would have their own children to raise. She would have her own house there in New Town where Daksi would live with her, and they would raise their children there. In her dreams now, round-faced babies suckled at her breasts and small children ran naked around her house.

And it was especially exciting to Whirlwind that she was embarked on a major trading venture to the strange people of her unknown grandfather in the company of her new husband. She was thinking that this would prove to be only the first of a lifetime of adventures the two of them would share.

Daksi, too, had a mind swirling with thoughts. He had paid a casual visit to New Town with his mother and sister and had become acquainted with the beautiful witch girl everyone talked about. She had invited him on a crazy journey, and he had accepted the invitation. Or had it been more of a dare? At any rate, he had accepted.

Now he was traveling with her and her brother somewhere in the middle of the land of the Appalachee People. He was in a land he had never seen before, in the midst of people he had never before met. He had watched the girl stand up to Muskogee warriors who seemed bent on fighting with them, and he had seen her actually turn away a raging monster storm.

Having seen all those things, he supposed that the things people said about her must really be true, but he didn't care. So what if she was a witch? She was also now his wife, and he was happier than he had ever been in his life. He was happier now than he had ever before even thought about being.

TOWARD the end of the day, they saw rain clouds approaching, and Whirlwind looked ahead for a good place to camp. She selected a tree-covered hillside not far ahead of them. It wasn't much of a hill, just a small rise in the prairie, and it was just off the right side of the road. A stream ran along on the left.

They rode their horses into the trees and quickly constructed a shelter of boughs for themselves and for their animals. They built a small fire under the shelter and waited for the rain to come. It was a steady, gentle rain when it arrived, and it lasted throughout the night.

In the morning the sky was clear again. They packed up their belongings and rode on. It was midday when they arrived at the wide river and found it high and running fast.

"There was more rain upstream, I guess," Daksi said.

"Can we get across?" the Little Spaniard asked.

"We have to get across," said Whirlwind. "There's no other way to go."

They rode up and down the riverbank in search of a good crossing but there did not seem to be one. Everywhere they rode, the waters rushed swiftly past them and the river was deep.

"We may have to wait a day or so," said Daksi, "for the waters to get low again."

Whirlwind was aggravated. She did not like the idea of having to wait for the river, but she knew that Daksi was right. It would be foolish to try to cross the river as it was. They would do well to get themselves and their riding animals across safely. The packhorses would almost certainly be lost in the swift waters. At last she agreed with Daksi, and again they sought out a good spot in which to make their camp.

When they were well settled in on a wide flat between the edge of the water and the slope of the small hill, there was still plenty of day left. Daksi decided to look for some fresh meat for them to eat.

"I'll go, too," said the Little Spaniard.

"Someone should stay here in camp with Whirlwind," Daksi mentioned.

"Oh. Yes," the Little Spaniard said. "Of course, you're right. I'll stay."

Daksi took his long bow and a few arrows and soon disappeared into the wooded slope behind their camp. Whirlwind watched him go. When she could no longer see him, she turned back to the small fire. The Little Spaniard moved to the other side of the fire from her and sat on the ground.

"He's a good man," he said. "Your new husband. I like him very well. You made a good choice, I think."

"Yes," Whirlwind replied. "He is. And I'm glad you like him."

"When we get back home to New Town," he said, "I'll go hunting with him sometime."

"Many times, I expect," Whirlwind declared.

Whirlwind was pleased with the relationship she saw developing between her husband and brother, and she was secretly amused that Daksi had thought it necessary to leave the Little Spaniard behind with her, as if she needed protection. *Protection from what?* she asked herself. Could either Daksi or the Little Spaniard or the two of them together have done the things that she had done? Could either of them have turned away the Big Warrior or the big storm? Still, she liked it that her husband had not wanted to leave her alone—unprotected.

"Sister," said the Little Spaniard, "these white men, these Ani-'Squan', what do you think they'll be like? When we actually meet them, what will they be like?"

"I don't know," Whirlwind replied. "Like you, I've never met a 'Squani. All I know is what we've heard about them from some of the older people, from our mother and from some of the others. They say that the Ani-'Squan' are brutal men. They kill without warning and with no feelings, even without anger. They kill calmly and brutally. They also say that the Ani-'Squan' have no manners. They're gruff and rude. So we'll have to be prepared for that when we get ready to meet them."

"They say that the Ani-'Squan' have no women," the Little Spaniard said.

"No one has ever seen a female 'Squan'," Whirlwind mentioned. "Maybe that's why they're so rude and brutal."

She laughed at that thought and her brother joined in. Then he got serious again.

"If they have no women," he said, "how do they keep making more of themselves?"

"That's why they go around the world in search of other people," Whirlwind responded. "They have to make their little ones off of the women of other people."

"Like our father was made?"

"Yes," she said, "but he fooled them. He didn't stay with them to become a 'Squan'. Instead he returned to the Real People."

The Little Spaniard was silent for a moment. He stared into the fire, seemingly concentrating on the flames. His brow was deeply knit.

"Whirlwind," he said at last, "I'll go where you lead us and I'll do what you say, but I must admit to you that I'm afraid. I'm afraid of the Ani-'Squan', and I'll be glad when we get back home."

Whirlwind stood and walked over to where her brother was sitting. She dropped down on her knees beside him and placed a hand on his shoulder.

"That's all right," she declared. "We should all approach these strange men with caution. Sometimes a little fear is a good thing. It's nothing to be ashamed of. Giving in to that fear is the only thing to be ashamed of. What would you do if you were walking in the woods and you met a bear? Would you be afraid of *yona?*"

"Well," he said, "yes. I suppose I would be."

"And what would you do?"

"I don't know," said the Little Spaniard. "If he was not too close, I might turn and run. Or, if I had a long bow and some arrows, I might fit an arrow and shoot him. But if he came up suddenly, very close to me, and there was no time to shoot or to run, I guess I'd pull my knife and fight him."

"It's the same with the Ani-'Squan'," Whirlwind said. "We'll see just what the situation is, and then we'll react to it. All right?"

"All right," he said.

"And remember one more thing," she added.

"What's that?"

"Remember what the Appalachees told us. The Ani-'Squan' may be rude and brutal, but right now they want to make friends. If that's true, then we have the advantage over them."

"And if it's not true?"

"Then remember what you just said about the bear."

She stood and walked over to where the packs were lying on the ground and dug into one of them. Soon she brought out two pieces of dried venison. She walked back to her brother and held one out toward him.

He smiled and took it from her. *"Wado,"* he said.

"It'll help until Daksi returns with some fresh meat," she mentioned.

They gnawed at the meat and occasionally fed the small fire, listening to the swift waters of the nearby river rushing past. Somewhere in the edge of the woods a blue jay called out in his rasping voice. A squirrel chattered. At last Whirlwind slept.

The Little Spaniard thought about trying to sleep but Daksi had left him behind to watch over his sister, so he decided that he should stay awake. When he had finished his dried meat, he walked back over to the water's edge and watched the river race by for a while. He looked across to the other side, thinking how far it looked across the swift water. He wondered what it would be like to try to cross it. When would it slow down? When would they be able to cross?

He squatted there beside the river and listened for the words of Long Man, but the words were not clear. The river was racing too fast, and he could not understand what it was saying. It occurred to him that this river might not speak his language anyway. Perhaps it spoke only to the Appalachees. At last he stood and turned to walk back to the fire, back where his sister napped. As he looked up, he saw Daksi come out of the woods, a freshly killed deer slung over his shoulders.

9

HEY FEASTED that night, and they saved a little fresh meat for meals the next day. The rest of the venison they cut into strips and hung out to dry in the hot sun. They made small talk and tried to make serious talk about their plans, but they had really already talked all that out. At the end of a seemingly endless day, they went to bed.

Whirlwind did not know if she slept and dreamed or if she was just drowsy and mused, but her mind was occupied with thoughts of her father. 'Squani, the Spaniard, had been killed before Whirlwind and her twin were born, so she knew him only from stories she had heard, mostly from her mother and from Comes Back to Life, her adopted father, the man her mother had married.

Whirlwind's grandfather, known as Carrier, had made a trip to La Florida to trade with the Calusa and Timucua People. He had been a young man at the time, and it had been his first major trip alone. In La Florida, Carrier had run afoul of the Spaniards, who had only recently arrived. During the conflict that followed, he had met a Timucua woman called Potmaker, and he eventually brought her home with him to be his wife.

But Potmaker had been pregnant as a result of the forced attentions of an unknown Spaniard during her captivity. Carrier had accepted that and when the child was born, he looked upon it as his own. That child had been Asquani, the Spaniard.

As a young man, 'Squani had felt out of place. When he heard that Spaniards had established a colony on an island off the coast, not too far from the land of the Real People, he had gone to live with them, to learn to become a real Spaniard. It was on the Dark Island, as the Real People had later called it, that 'Squan' had met Osa, a Calusa woman so named by her Spanish captors.

When 'Squani had at last decided that his place was with the Real People and not with the Ani-Asquani, he had taken Osa away with him. Some other Real People in the company of some Frenchmen went looking for the Dark Island, and with the help of Asquani and Osa they drove the Spaniards away, and the Spaniards had never come that close to the land of the Real People again.

'Squani had married Osa but, while awaiting the birth of his first child by her (he had no way of knowing that it would be twins), he had gone to the aid of his young friend Young Puppy, who had been ambushed by some enemy along a northern trail. When 'Squani came up behind Young Puppy in the heat of battle, Young Puppy had struck blindly, killing his friend by mistake.

In order to avoid retaliation from 'Squani's clan, the Wolf People, Young Puppy had stayed for an entire year inside the walls of Kituwah, the Peace Town, where no one could be killed for any reason. At the end of the year, all things from the past are forgiven, and so Young Puppy was free to go.

But during that year, he had been trained to become a ceremonial leader and, because he had survived the year, he had also been given a new name: Comes Back to Life. He had killed his own friend, although accidentally, and so he had decided to provide for his friend's family. Finally, at the urging of his first wife, Guwisti, he had married Osa. She had become his second wife.

All of these past events, as they had been related to her, swam through Whirlwind's mind, but mostly she thought about her father. She wondered what he had looked like. She wished she had known him. And, although she knew that Comes Back to Life had not meant to kill Asquani and had married her mother and cared for her and for Whirlwind and the Little Spaniard and all of the past was forgiven annually, Whirlwind still harbored a secret resentment against Comes Back to Life for having deprived her of her real father.

Would meeting the Spaniards bring her closer somehow to her lost father? She would at least experience for herself some of what he had experienced. She would meet them and talk to them. She would know some of what he had known. She was also following in the footsteps of her grandfather, Carrier, for it was he who had first gone to La Florida, first encountered the Spaniards.

She considered again the irony of her situation, for she had never known anything other than the life of a Real Person. Her home was with the Real People, her language was that of the Real People, and the only people she really knew well were Real People. Her mother had been adopted by the Bird People so she and her brother had been born into the Bird Clan. That made them Real People. But her mother, Osa, was a Calusa by birth, and her father 'Squani, had been half Timucua and half Spanish. No drop of blood of the Real People ran in her veins.

She was different in every way from all of the people she had grown up with. There was none other like her. It made her feel special but sometimes it also made her feel . . . alone.

It had made her feel alone until she had met and married Daksi. Now she knew she would never feel alone again.

THEY woke up early the next morning, all three of them, and they went right away to the water's edge to see if the level had dropped and the current had slowed, but if it had, it was not enough to be noticeable. The three stood side by side staring at the fast-moving waters in silence, disappointed looks on their faces. At last Daksi broke the silence.

"How do we pass this day?" he asked. "In laziness?"

"Let's say in rest," Whirlwind said. "We do have a long journey yet ahead of us. We'll need all of our strength."

"In rest then," Daksi agreed.

"I can't sleep anymore," said the Little Spaniard. "Maybe I'll ride along the river and see if it has gone down in any other places."

"Yes," his sister agreed. "But don't be gone too long. At the latest, be back when the Sun is at her daughter's house."

"All right," he said. "I will."

Then the Little Spaniard saddled up his horse and rode west along the riverbank. Daksi watched until he was out of sight, then turned to face his wife.

"I know how we can pass some time," he said.

They made love, hotly at first, then gently, for half of the morning, and then they bathed in the swift-running waters, careful to stay close to the edge amid large rocks that afforded them protection from the current. They lay side by side and naked in the sun to dry, and then they dressed. Daksi put some small branches on the fire to keep it going.

"We have some company across the river," Whirlwind said.

Daksi straightened up to look, and on the south side of the still swift-running river were four riders leading two extra horses. They didn't look like any people he had ever seen before. Their skin was dark, and their hair was long and straggly. Hair grew on the faces of two of the men. They wore greasy buckskin leggings and shirts of ragged cloth. Both Daksi and Whirlwind had seen European cloth before, even though they had not yet met the people who brought it.

Two of the men, Daksi could see, carried the long Spanish swords. The other two had war clubs at their sides, and all of them carried guns. The two with Spanish swords had long guns, and their two companions had short ones tucked in their belts. All four of their heads were tied around with dirty rags.

The four men stopped at the edge of the water and, sitting there on their horses' backs, seemed to study it for a while. Daksi and Whirlwind walked together to the riverbank on their side. Daksi waved at the men across the way. From the other side of the river one of the scruffy men casually lifted an arm. The hand he raised was holding a long gun.

He shouted something, but neither Daksi nor Whirlwind could hear him over the roar of the water. They watched as the man lifted a coil of rope and handed one end to one of his companions. Then suddenly he kicked his horse's sides, and horse and rider plunged into the water. The rider shouted and kicked and lashed at the struggling animal, and about halfway across the river he lost his seat.

For an instant he disappeared under the water, but he came up again sputtering, and he grabbed hold of the saddle horn. The horse continued to swim valiantly across the strong current. At last it found its footing near where Daksi and Whirlwind stood, and horse and man struggled onto dry land. The man looked up at the two Real People and grinned. He spoke, but the language was strange to the ears of Whirlwind and Daksi. They looked at one another.

"Is it Spanish?" asked Daksi.

"No," Whirlwind said. "I don't know it. I've never heard that talk before."

The man reached over and tied his long rope to a rock. Then he turned and waved to his comrades across the way.

"Watch them," Whirlwind said. "I don't like their looks." Then she shifted to the jargon. "Do you speak the trade language?" she asked.

The man looked back at her and grinned again. He showed uneven, discolored teeth. He stood up dripping and took a couple of sloshing steps in her direction.

"Ah, yes," he said. "I speak it well. Who might you be?"

"I'm Whirlwind, and this is my husband, Daksi," she replied. "We're Chalakees from north of here. We're on our way to La Florida to trade with the Spaniards."

"Oh, traders," the man said. He looked back across the water in time to see one of his companions plunge into the river. He shouted some kind of encouragement, again in the language that was strange to the Real People. This second rider was holding the rope the first had brought across. Like the first rider, he lost his seat; and he would have been swept away had it not been for the rope. He held tight, and soon after his horse stepped ashore he followed it, pulling himself out of the water by the line. He was coughing and spitting water, and he sank down immediately on his hands and knees.

The third rider went into the water riding one horse and leading another. Desperately he kicked and splashed and shouted. Midway across, he lost the extra animal, and its terrified neighing was awful to hear as it was swept away down the river. The rider and his saddle horse made it across safely. The fourth rider crossed successfully, along with the extra horse he had brought.

With everyone at last safely across the river, except for the one lost horse, the rider who had been the first to cross turned toward the one who had lost the horse. He slapped the man's face and shouted at him. Then he turned slowly back toward Whirlwind and Daksi with a sheep-ish grin on his face.

"I had to chastise him," he said in the jargon, "for losing the beast."

Daksi was tense. His war club dangled at his side, but his other weapons were some distance away. Like his wife, he did not like the looks of these men and a closer look at them only served to reinforce his initial feeling of distaste. They were dirty and they were rude. They were just his idea of what the Spaniards would be like but Whirlwind had said that they did not speak Spanish. Also, their skin was as dark as his own and he had always heard the Spaniards called white men.

"Who are these men?" he asked his wife.

"May we know who you are?" Whirlwind asked the man.

"Oh, yes," he said. "I'm called Gap Tooth, and these men here are Three Bears García, Wild Pig, and Marcos."

Two of the names sounded Spanish to Whirlwind, but the others did not. She wasn't at all sure what she was facing with these men.

"Are you Spanish, then?" she asked.

Gap Tooth said something to his companions in the strange language, and they all laughed. Then he turned back to Whirlwind.

"No," he said. "Like you, we're traders. See. We've just come from the Spanish colonies. We have new guns and swords and some other things. We had six horses until Wild Pig lost one."

"I see," said Whirlwind, "but are you then—" She hesitated before using the Spanish word. "—Indios?"

"Well, you see, little woman," said Gap Tooth, "we're a bunch of mongrel bastards, you know? A little of this and a little of that. We just roam around and do what we can to survive."

"We have some good deer meat," said Whirlwind. "Will you eat with us?"

"Of course," Gap Tooth replied, and he repeated the invitation in the language his companions could understand.

Soon they were all seated around the small fire eating. Whirlwind tried to decide what to do about these men. She couldn't quite bring herself to just tell them to go on their way. The Real People were always hospitable to guests. On the other hand, she didn't like these men at all or trust them. She fully expected trouble from them before much longer. If she or Daksi made a move toward their weapons, though, the strangers would be alerted, and they all had their weapons right at hand. She decided that it would be smart to just wait and watch and react when the time was right.

One of the men said something to Gap Tooth, and Gap Tooth looked across the fire at Whirlwind and grinned. He wiped the grease off his mouth and chin with his sleeve.

"We're all traders here," he said to her. "Right?"

"Yes," she agreed. "We're traders. But we have nothing to trade with you. We're going to the Spaniards."

"You have something to trade, all right," said Gap Tooth. "We want you. Just for a while. Ask your husband what he wants for that, little woman. Ask him."

10

EMAIN CALM," said Whirlwind, speaking in the language of the Real People to Daksi. "Do not show your anger. These men want to know what you'll take to let them use me for a while."

Daksi took a deep breath and exhaled slowly. "I don't think they'll want to pay us anything," he said, "no matter what I say. I think we're going to have to fight them."

"Yes," said Whirlwind. "I think that you're right about that. Well, you have your war club. I have my fire. Wait for my move before you do anything."

"Well? What's he say?" asked Gap Tooth.

"He wants to think about it some more while we eat," Whirlwind said.

"We've eaten enough," said Gap Tooth. "We'll eat again afterward. Right now, let's make our trade."

Whirlwind leaned casually forward toward the fire.

"I want some more of this cornmeal mush," she said. "I'm still hungry. Are you sure you won't have some more? Ask your friends."

"I don't need—"

Gap Tooth didn't finish his next sentence, for Whirlwind had grabbed the edge of the pot that was on the fire and flipped it, sending the hot *gahawista* flying in the face of Gap Tooth. He screamed in pain and swiped at his face with both hands. At the same instant, Whirlwind lashed out with the pot and smacked Three Bears García hard on the side of the head. García fell over sideways slowly and lay still.

Marcos stood quickly and reached for the long sword at his side, but before he could draw it out, Daksi's ball-headed war club smashed into his face, crunching bone on his lower forehead and between his eyes. He fell over on his back with a thud.

Wild Pig was on his feet, too, and he held his arm out straight in front of himself. His dirty hand clutched a Spanish pistol. His thumb pulled the hammer back. The barrel was pointed at the bare chest of Daksi. Wild Pig's finger pulled the trigger. It snapped, but there was no fire—his flint and his powder were wet. His face registered panic.

Just then, an arrow drove itself deep into his chest. He looked down at the offending missile, his eyes wide with horror and disbelief. His outstretched fingers relaxed, and the pistol fell to the ground in front of him. He moaned, dropped to his knees, and fell forward, the weight of his body driving the arrow through his back.

Daksi and Whirlwind turned to see the Little Spaniard behind them.

"Did I come back in time?" the Little Spaniard called out.

"Just in time," Daksi answered. Then he stepped over to retrieve his war club. He picked it up and moved in front of Gap Tooth, who was just sitting there holding his scalded face in his hands. Daksi raised his war club and bashed in the top of Gap Tooth's head.

The Little Spaniard rode on into the camp. "Who were these men?" he asked.

"You've heard of the slave catchers?" Whirlwind asked. "I think these were like them. Anyway, we have more goods now. We'll take their weapons and their *sogwilis*. Look in the pack on that one *sogwili* and see if we want anything from it. We'll pack up and get started again. If these men could cross using that rope, so can we."

ONCE again they rode south, this time with five more horses than they'd had before; one of the newly acquired horses was wearing a pack on its back.

"We haven't even traded yet," Daksi said, "and already we have more goods than what we started with."

The Little Spaniard laughed. Whirlwind was really feeling good. First the meeting with the Big Warrior, then the rattlesnake, the storm, and now the fight with the slave catchers or whoever they were. She felt absolutely invincible. Even without her extraordinary powers, she thought, the three of them were formidable foes. Add her powers and they were unbeatable.

Over the next several days, they rode by some abandoned towns and stopped at one inhabited Appalachee town. Other than that they saw no one. They passed no other occupied towns and encountered no one on the road.

At last they came to another town. This one had a slightly different look to it from the others. Some people came out of the town to meet them, men, women, and children. An old man carrying a staff, his wrinkled body covered with tattoos, walked in front of the others.

"Welcome, friends," he said in the jargon. "Come in and eat with us and rest."

"Thank you," said Whirlwind. She dropped down from the back of her horse and stepped forward to introduce herself to the old man. "I'm called Whirlwind," she said, "and these are my husband, Daksi, and my brother, the Little Spaniard. We're Chalakee People from north of here, on our way to trade with the Spaniards."

"Ah," said the old man, a smile spreading across his face. "I remember another young Chalakee who came through here a long time ago. He was called Carrier. We fought together against the Spaniards, and I went home with him and visited in your country."

"Carrier was my grandfather," said Whirlwind. "He's no longer with us."

"Well," said the old man, "he was my friend. I'm glad to know his grandchildren. I'm known as He Goes at Night. We're Timucua People here."

⌒

WHIRLWIND, Daksi, and the Little Spaniard were feasted and entertained well into the night but the best part of the visit for Whirlwind was listening to He Goes at Night tell the story of his adventures with Carrier. It was exciting for her to hear firsthand stories about her illustrious grandfather.

"The Spaniards in those days were attacking every town they could find," the old man said. "They asked for gold which, of course, we did not have, and then they took people to use as slaves. They also killed many people, anyone who resisted them. Sometimes they killed for no reason at all. We were very much afraid of the strange white people in their hard metal clothes riding on the backs of large animals we had never seen before.

"Your grandfather came among us to trade just as we got into a fight with the white men, and we and some Calusa friends and Carrier fought together against the Spaniards. He was a brave man and a good fighter."

"And he met my grandmother, Potmaker, among your people," Whirlwind said.

He Goes at Night grinned broadly. "Yes," he agreed, "and so you are our relative."

"Yes," said Whirlwind, smiling. "I guess that's true."

They spent the night there at the Timucua town and slept late the next morning. As before with the Appalachees, their hosts invited them to stay another day and night. If they left so late in the day, their traveling day would be short. Whirlwind's thoughts were divided. She knew they were getting close, but she was enjoying her visit with the Timucuas, especially He Goes at Night.

She thought that she was probably enjoying the stay more than were Daksi and the Little Spaniard, because neither of them could talk to anyone. None of them spoke Timucua, none of the Timucuans knew the language of the Real People, and she alone of her small group could speak the trade language. Even so, Daksi and the Little Spaniard seemed to be having a pretty good time.

At last she decided that one more night in the town would be all right. She accepted the invitation through He Goes at Night and told her companions that they would leave the following morning.

The rest of that day was spent in feasting and visiting, and Whirlwind pressed He Goes at Night for more stories about her grandfather. Toward evening, six Timucua men who had been traveling came home. Whirlwind soon discovered that they had just returned from the Spanish colony in La Florida. She was anxious to hear what they had to say and was thrilled when He Goes at Night called her over to meet one of the men.

"This is Panther Skin," he said. "He speaks the jargon, too, so you can talk with him. He and these others just got back from the Spanish towns.

"Panther Skin, this young woman is our relative. She's a Chalakee, but her grandmother was a Timucua woman. She and her husband and brother are going to see the Spaniards to trade."

"What can you tell me?" Whirlwind asked. "Are they friendly?"

"Just now, they are friendly," said Panther Skin. "In my grandfather's time, they were killing us and taking our people for slaves but they've changed. They want to make friends now."

"I've heard," added Whirlwind, "that it's because of the other white men, the ones called Frenchmen and the others called English."

"Yes," said Panther Skin. "That's true. Across the great waters, where they come from, the Frenchmen and the English are both enemies of the

Spaniards. They're afraid that if they don't make friends of us, we might ally ourselves with their enemies."

"That's good for us," whispered Whirlwind, out loud but more to herself than to Panther Skin.

"Yes," he said.

"Do you think that they'll trade with us?" she asked. "I want swords and guns, maybe other things, maybe some more horses."

Panther Skin studied the question for a moment, then slowly nodded his head. "I think they will," he said. "I don't think they want anything from us. They get all the food they need from the people who live near them. They don't seem to care about anything except gold. But I think they'll trade with you just to make friends of your people."

"Well," she replied, "I don't care why they trade, just so I get the things I want from them."

"Be careful, though," Panther Skin said.

She shot him a questioning glance.

"Their leader is a man called Bernardo Calvillo," Panther Skin continued. "He'll try to talk you into making some kind of alliance between your people and his. He'll want you to speak for all of your people."

"I can't do that," she said.

"But he'll try to make you do it."

"I won't do it."

"I just thought you should know."

"Thank you," said Whirlwind. "I'll be ready for him. Bernardo Calvillo, you say?"

"Yes," said Panther Skin. "Bernardo Calvillo. They call him 'Commandante.'"

❧

THAT night Whirlwind and the others went to bed early. She wanted to be sure that they'd get an early start the next morning. The end of her journey seemed near, now that she'd reached the land of the Timucuas and especially now that she had just met and talked with a man just returned from a visit to the Spaniards.

She and Daksi made quiet love that night, and then she slept deeply. She woke up in the morning feeling fresh, strong, and ready to go. They packed and saddled their horses, leaving the extras with the Timucuas. They would pick those horses up on the way home. Then they said their good-byes and headed south.

They traveled throughout that day and spent the night alone on a vast plain. Again the next morning, they were moving early and, about midday, they had to cross another river. The crossing was easy, however, compared to the previous one. By nighttime, the landscape was beginning to change again. There were more trees and they camped in a small grove.

The next morning, they rode south again, and it was evening when they came to the great water. None of them had ever before seen the great water, and they stood for a long time in awe, watching the big waves break on the sandy beach, staring out over the waters and wondering how far they went. They knew, of course, that the white men had come from across the great waters. Even so, it was hard to imagine that there was any other land out there somewhere. It was even harder to imagine anyone crazy enough to try to cross the great water.

The Real People believed that their world was flat and suspended from the heavens by long cords. The entire world was covered over by the Great Sky Vault, a giant dome made of stone, which rotated daily. At night, in the west, the Sun crawled under the edge of the Vault. All night long she traveled across on the other side. By morning she reached the bottom side of the edge of the dome on the east, and when it rotated again she came out from under that edge. Then she crawled along the underside of the Vault, and it was day. In the middle of the day, she stopped briefly at her daughter's house for a visit, directly overhead.

But Whirlwind knew from her mother that the Spaniards claimed that the world was a ball. She had thought long and hard about the two views of the world and decided that they might both be right. If the ball was huge, as it must be, then the land that the Real People lived on would be small in comparison to the whole, and it would seem flat. She looked out over the waters, and she imagined that she could indeed see a slight curve at the far horizon. Out there somewhere were whole other worlds that she could only begin to imagine.

11

T LAST they reached a part of La Florida where the landscape was changed utterly. There were plants, birds, and animals that the three Real People had never seen before. The bird-songs and the chatterings they heard from the woods were strange to their ears. The air was thick with moisture, and inland the ground was wet and swampy.

They came to a town of Calusa People where they stopped to rest and visit, and the people there told them that they'd had no trouble with the Spaniards for some time now. The white men still had slaves, but they seemed to be getting them from someplace else. They were courting the friendship of their native neighbors, looking for allies in case of trouble with the French or English.

The Spanish town, they said, was only two days' ride farther south. They assured Whirlwind that she and her companions would be welcomed by the Spaniards. Whirlwind asked if there was another town between this place and the Spanish town, and the answer was negative. She thought for a moment.

"May we leave our goods here while we go to meet with the Spaniards?" she asked.

"Of course."

After resting and being fed well, the Real People moved on. They traveled light now, having left their extra burdens behind.

They had not traveled far from the Calusa town when they met some people on the road. They were native people, carrying Spanish goods. Whirlwind took that as a promising sign.

Later they met other travelers. Traffic on the road was heavy. Whirlwind and the other two Real People agreed that they had never before been on such a well-traveled road.

They had talked with the first two groups they met, but after that they simply exchanged greetings. There were just too many people passing by to stop and talk with everyone who came along. Besides, Whirlwind wanted to get on into the Spanish town as soon as possible. That night, they camped beside the road.

In the morning, they dressed themselves in their best clothes. Daksi and the Little Spaniard each wore new moccasins, leggings, breechcloths, and fringed shirts, all finely decorated with porcupine quills. Whirlwind wore a new fringed skirt and a matchcoat, which was tied over her left shoulder and draped under her right arm. Her right breast was thus still exposed, a fashion common to the women of the Real People.

They were saddling their horses when they heard the clatter of horses' hooves accompanied by the clanking of metal coming up behind them. Whirlwind turned to look, and there was no mistaking what she saw.

"Ani-Asquani," she said.

Daksi moved up to stand just by her right side, the Little Spaniard to her left. They looked in amazement at the group of riders coming toward them from the north. Below their noses, their faces were covered with coarse hair. They wore metal breastplates and helmets, and each had a sword swinging at his side. Even the horses wore metal on their heads.

A thrill running through her body, Whirlwind raised an arm in greeting, and she was answered by a wave from the man riding at the head of the group. He then turned his big *caballo* and led his men off the road and right over into their camp. He stopped his own horse and halted his troop. Then he dismounted and stepped toward Whirlwind, a wide and friendly smile on his bearded face.

"*Buenos días, senorita,*" he said.

"*Buenos días,*" Whirlwind answered, excited to at last be making practical use of her knowledge of the Spanish language.

"Ah," the Spaniard said, "you speak my language."

"*Sí,*" said Whirlwind. "I learned it from my mother. This is the first chance I've had to use it. I'm called Whirlwind. This is my husband, Daksi, and this my brother, 'Squan' Usdi."

Deliberately, she had used the Real People's pronunciation of the Little Spaniard's name. She didn't want to bother with an explanation of his name just then. Perhaps later.

"We're Chalakees," she continued, using here the trade jargon word for her people, "from north of here, beyond the Appalachees and beyond the land of the Muskogees."

"Ah, Chalakees," said the Spaniard. "The *commandante* will be glad to see you. *Me llamo Santos Cristóbal.* I'm a captain."

"We've come all this way to meet with your *commandante,*" Whirlwind said.

"If you'll allow me," said Cristóbal, "my men and I will accompany you on in to the colony. We're just returning from a routine patrol. When we get back there, I'll personally take you to meet the *commandante,* Bernardo Calvillo."

"We'd be honored, *Capitán,*" Whirlwind said. She turned to her companions and told them most of what the captain had said. Then they finished saddling and packing their horses, mounted up, and turned south. Whirlwind rode beside Cristóbal, with Daksi, and the Little Spaniard just behind them and then the rest of Cristóbal's patrol.

"I've never met any Chalakees," Cristóbal said as they rode. "Of course, I've heard of your great nation."

"And I've never before met an Español," Whirlwind replied, "but of course I have heard of them."

Cristóbal laughed out loud. "I'm glad to be the first one," he said. He looked at her and smiled, and his eyes roamed down to study the exposed breast, which bounced nicely, he thought, as she rode along. "You're a lovely young woman. Are all Chalakee women as beautiful as you?"

"I don't know about that," she said, "but do you talk to every woman you meet that way?"

She was glad that Daksi could not understand the Spanish words they were speaking, and she hoped that he was unable to see the looks the *capitán* was giving her. She didn't want any trouble with the Spaniards, at least not yet. She decided to change the subject of conversation.

"You're not at all like the tales I've heard about the Spaniards," she said.

"Oh?" asked Cristóbal. "And what, then, have you heard?"

"I've heard that Spaniards are brutal and cruel," she said. "They want nothing but gold, and they kill everyone they meet—or make slaves of them."

Cristóbal stiffened in his saddle. "We make cruel enemies," he responded. "That much is true. But we also make good friends. The tales you've heard—they probably came from the time Don Hernando de Soto went through this country, and that was over forty years ago. Don Hernando began his last journey in 1539. Many of the Indios remember that time." He shrugged. "Some of my own people even think that Don

Hernando was too harsh. Anyhow, those days are gone. I hope we can be friends, you and I. Uh, your people and mine."

"We should be," Whirlwind said. "After all, we didn't make this long trip to fight with you. There would be more than three of us if we had."

Again Cristóbal laughed. "And if you had come to fight, little Chalakee," he said, "how many more would you have brought?"

"At least four more," Whirlwind replied.

Cristóbal roared with laughter, rocking back and forth in his saddle.

THE SUN was low on the far western edge of the Sky Vault when they at last reached the Spanish settlement. It was a busy little place, with Spaniards and Indios alike walking here and there. There were many horses, and there were other, smaller animals like the horses but with long ears. Swine were running loose, like the ones that had become wild, even in the country of the Real People, since the Spaniard de Soto had brought his large herd through that country.

The Spanish settlement was loud to the ears of the Real People. There was laughing, talking, shouting, and singing. There was the neighing of horses, the squealing of pigs, and the barking of dogs. A powerful, unpleasant odor hung over the entire place. There were numerous small huts, thatched, similar to native houses, and there was one small house built of stacked stones. But the things that most impressed the three Real People were the walls of the partially constructed large stone house.

Cristóbal dismissed his men, excused himself for a moment, then went inside the small stone house. He came out again soon and walked over to where Whirlwind, Daksi, and the Little Spaniard were still standing patiently beside their horses.

"I spoke to the *commandante*," Cristóbal said. "He told me to see that your *caballos* are tended to and that you have food to eat and a place to stay for the night. It's late today but he said that he'll meet with you in the morning. He told me to say that he welcomes you and he's glad that you're here from the great nation of the Chalakees."

Cristóbal looked around and shouted to a corporal who was walking nearby. Then he ordered the man to feed the three horses of the visiting Real People and put them into a corral for safekeeping. With a sweeping gesture, he then said to Whirlwind, "Follow me, please."

Cristóbal led the way to a small but tidy thatched hut and stopped beside the doorway. "You may consider this your home while you're here," he said. "I'll send some food over for you right away. Will there be anything else I can do for you before morning? Anything at all?"

"When we've had something to eat," Whirlwind replied, "we'll be just fine. We'll sleep and be ready to meet with your *commandante* in the morning. Thank you for all your kindness."

Cristóbal looked into Whirlwind's eyes, causing her to duck her head. His right hand twitched. He had almost reached out for her, but he caught himself just in time. He straightened himself up, as if coming to attention for a superior officer. "In that case," he said, "I'll say good night to you until tomorrow."

Whirlwind watched as Cristóbal walked away. When he was well beyond hearing, she spoke to Daksi and the Little Spaniard.

"These Ani-'Squan' are not so bad," she said. "They don't seem like monsters to me."

"They are ugly, though," Daksi put in.

"I don't like it here," said the Little Spaniard. "It smells bad, and it's too loud."

"I don't like that one," added Daksi. "I don't like the way he looks at you."

"Oh," Whirlwind said, "don't worry about him. He's not even important. The *commandante* is the important one. We'll meet him in the morning."

"What was that one talking to you about?" Daksi asked.

"He said that he'd send some food," she said.

She knew, of course, what Daksi had meant. She knew that he had seen Cristóbal's interest in his face, had heard it in his voice, but she didn't want to talk about that. She could handle Cristóbal, and she didn't want any problems. She would only tell Daksi and the Little Spaniard what she thought they needed to hear. Then the woman came with the large basket.

She was a native woman, an Indio, and the basket was filled with a wide variety of things to eat: several varieties of fish, variously prepared, smoked oysters, breads, beans, plums, grapes, nuts, and other things. The three Real People ate, mostly in silence, until they were well satisfied.

"Whirlwind," the Little Spaniard said, "we left all of our trade goods back in the Calusa town. We're not prepared to trade in the morning. So what will we do in the morning when we meet this Spanish chief?"

"The *commandante*, they call him," she replied. "We'll see. I want to meet him first and find out what he's like. When I've talked to him, then I'll decide about the trading."

"I wish we could just trade our stuff and then get out of here," the Little Spaniard said. "I don't like this place."

"We've made a long trip," Whirlwind answered. "You don't need to be in such a hurry to start back. We'll visit for a while with these white men, and then, probably, we'll trade with them. When that's all done, we'll start on our way home."

She glanced at her brother and saw that he was sitting, slumped, with his head hanging between his knees. He looked unhappy, not just tired. She moved close to him and touched his shoulder.

"Don't worry," she said. "It's easier for me, probably, because I can talk to them. But I'll tell you what they say. They're friendly. They're not like the Spaniards in the tales we've heard. Everything will work out just the way I want it to. The way we want it to work out."

The Little Spaniard gave a shrug but said nothing more. It was the way of the Real People. If one did not agree with what was being said but was ready to give up the argument, then one just kept quiet. She looked over at her husband.

"And you," she said. "How are you feeling?"

"Much like your brother," he replied. "I don't especially like that one who rode with you. But I agreed to make this trip with you, and I'll see it through. I'll go along with whatever you decide."

"Well," she said, "both my men are pouting. I hope that you'll both put on better faces in the morning when we go to meet the *commandante*."

"You don't need to be concerned about that," Daksi said. "I'll play my part. I only said what I did because you asked me."

Whirlwind looked at the Little Spaniard.

"I'll be all right," he told her.

"We all will," said Whirlwind, "after we sleep."

12

HE KNEW what Cristóbal wanted from her. It was easy enough to tell from the way he looked at her, from the tone of his voice. She thought about her own grandmother and the way in which her father had been conceived. And there were her own mother's stories about her life with the Spaniards before she ran away with 'Squani. She wondered, then, if that was all the Spanish men ever thought about. Were they, in fact, men without women? Were they wandering the world in search of women?

She knew that they were also interested in gold, and she knew that they were seeking allies because of the presence of their enemies, the French and the English. Then she wondered if the French and English had women. She had not heard of any. The stories about the Frenchmen who visited the Real People and fought with them against the Spanish did not include any Frenchwomen. As far as the English were concerned, she knew absolutely nothing beyond the fact that they were enemies of the Spanish.

She could understand why men without women searched for women, and she could understand the Spaniards having enemies and seeking allies, but she did not understand the Spanish lust for the yellow metal. Of course, she had not seen evidence of this lust. She had only heard tales.

The yellow metal was a thing that the Spaniards supposedly prized. She could understand that. There were things that the Real People prized highly, too: food, tobacco, animal skins. All these things were useful. Even the scales of *uk'ten'* and the crystal that grew between his eyes were useful to a person who knew how to control their power. But Whirlwind knew of no real use for the yellow metal. Perhaps the Spaniards knew of some use for it. She thought that she would like to know what that was.

❧

THE next morning the Indio woman came again with more food, and the three Real People ate. They dressed again in their best clothing, for they were going to meet with the *commandante*. All three of them were conscious that this was the day for which they had made the long trip. This was the day in which they would either accomplish their mission or fail. Whirlwind, of course, was completely confident.

They were ready and waiting when Cristóbal appeared. Whirlwind noted right away that he was not wearing metal. He was wearing clothing that covered his entire body, and it was made of cloth. She had seen some of the white man's cloth before, but not much. She was amazed that on a hot day the Spaniards should cover themselves so completely.

"Follow me, please," Cristóbal said, and he led the way to the small stone house.

Inside, a small man sat behind a table. He looked up and smiled as Cristóbal and the three Real People walked in. He stood and bowed. "Ah, welcome," he said.

"*Commandante*," said Cristóbal, "these are the three Chalakees. The woman speaks Spanish. She's called Whirlwind."

"I am Commandante Bernardo Calvillo," said the short man. "I'm pleased to welcome representatives from the great nation of the Chalakees."

"We're pleased to be here to meet with you," Whirlwind replied.

"You speak excellent Spanish," said the *commandante*. "Please. Sit down."

Cristóbal pushed some chairs forward, and everyone sat.

"This is my husband," said Whirlwind. "He's called Daksi."

"Daksi," repeated Calvillo, grinning and nodding in Daksi's direction. Daksi nodded in reply, his expression blank.

"And this is my brother," Whirlwind said. She hesitated, then continued in Spanish. "The Little Spaniard."

Calvillo's eyes opened wide. "The Little Spaniard?" he said. "May I . . . may I enquire where he got such a name?"

"Our grandfather was one of your people," Whirlwind explained. "When my father was born, they called him Spaniard, and so my brother is known as the Little Spaniard."

She stopped there, thinking it best to leave out the more unpleasant details. Calvillo stood up, unable to keep his smile from broadening. He walked around from behind his table to approach the Real People more closely, and he held out his hand to Whirlwind, who took it in hers. Then he pumped her hand vigorously.

"Welcome again," he said. "Doubly welcome."

He moved to the Little Spaniard and took his hand to pump up and down. "Welcome," he said. "Welcome, indeed." Then he moved to Daksi and shook his hand, again repeating his welcome. At last he moved back around to his chair and sat down again. He leaned back smiling widely at his visitors.

"Ah, well," he said, "so we have already a connection between our two peoples, and you and your brother are that connection. I want to make friends with your people. I want to make a peaceful alliance between the great nation of Chalakees and my own country."

"I'm sure," said Whirlwind, "that all Chalakee people desire peace with the Spaniards."

"Yes, well, I hope that we can make that desire into a more formal relationship," the *commandante* said. "But we can talk of that later. You came to see me because—"

"We came to meet you," said Whirlwind. "That's all. Because of the Spanish blood that runs in my veins, I wanted to meet you, to know what you're like. I also like your swords and knives and other things. I thought that maybe we would be able to trade with you."

"Yes, of course," said Calvillo. "Make yourselves at home in our settlement. Come back to dine with me at noon. Cristóbal, you'll see to it."

"*Sí, Commandante,*" said the captain.

The three Real People stood up to leave, and the *commandante* shook hands with each of them again. As they moved out the door, Calvillo stopped Cristóbal.

"And bring some gifts for them before noon," he said. "Get them each a sword and a knife. Whatever else you think they will like. And, Cristóbal, this is marvelous. Two part-Spanish Chalakees. Oh. We'll get an alliance out of this."

❦

THEY spent the rest of the morning looking over the Spanish settlement. Whirlwind was especially curious about the large unfinished stone structure. Cristóbal told her that it was a church, a place where the Spaniards, who also referred to themselves as *Cristianos,* went to worship their God. There was a priest among them, he said, and certainly, if the Real People were interested, they would be welcome at tomorrow's morning mass.

"The one for today has already taken place," he said.

Whirlwind noticed that people were busy at work on the church, moving and stacking the large stones. The workers were all dark-skinned people. Some appeared to be natives, Indios, as the Spaniards called them, but most of them were even darker, black almost. Spaniards stood around shouting and cracking whips.

Later in the morning, Cristóbal excused himself, telling Whirlwind that she and her companions were free to roam around the settlement as they wished. He would find them again to take them to their meal with the *commandante.* He still looked at Whirlwind with longing in his eyes.

As he left them, Daksi stared hard after him. "I'd like to kill that one," Daksi said.

Whirlwind gave her husband a hard look. "But you won't," she warned. "We won't start any trouble here. This is too important." Then, although she wasn't afraid herself, just to impress her husband she added, "And it would be much too dangerous. We are badly outnumbered here."

She couldn't tell if that all too obvious fact had an effect on Daksi or not, but it certainly did on the Little Spaniard.

"Yes," he said. "We're badly outnumbered. There are so many Ani-Asquani here, I can't even count them. And these others, they seem to be their allies."

"Or their slaves," muttered Daksi, a scowl on his face. "I don't like anything about these people or this place."

"Do you remember the tales about the Ani-'Squani?" Whirlwind asked suddenly. She looked from Daksi to the Little Spaniard. "Do you remember the horrors that were told to us?"

"I remember," said the Little Spaniard.

"And you?" she asked her husband. "Do you remember?"

"Yes," he said stubbornly. "Of course I remember them. They're terrible stories. One doesn't forget things like that."

"Then don't you both think that we'd be better off having these people as friends than enemies? Would you want them to march on our towns and kill our people the way the stories tell us they killed others? Can't you see how important this meeting could be? Not just to us. Not just to get goods for ourselves. But for the good of all our people. Can't you see that?"

Daksi looked at the ground and kept silent.

"Yes," said the Little Spaniard. "I suppose you're right about that. But I'll still be glad when we get back home."

"I'll be glad when we leave this place," said Daksi. "I'll be happy even to be back with the Calusa People or the Appalachees."

Whirlwind stepped up close between the two young men and put a hand on a shoulder of each. She softened her look and her voice.

"And so will I," she said. "But first we'll get our business here taken care of. Be a little patient. It won't take long."

A long table was set outside, just in front of the small stone house, with places for the *commandante,* Whirlwind, Daksi, and the Little Spaniard. The table was laid with a sumptuous feast: various kinds of meat, fowl, and fish, a variety of vegetable foods, and breads. And there was drink, a sweet-tasting drink that made one's head feel light and dizzy.

"Eat; drink," said Calvillo. "Eat and drink your fill."

"This drink is good," said the Little Spaniard.

"What does he say?" asked Calvillo.

"He likes your drink," Whirlwind said in Spanish. Then she spoke to her brother in the language of the Real People. "Be careful of that drink," she said. "Drink it slowly and don't drink too much. I don't trust it."

The Little Spaniard wrinkled his brow and looked at the glass in his hand. He shrugged and took another gulp. "Well," he said, "it's good. I like it."

She worried about her brother, but she didn't want to make a scene in front of the *commandante.* They ate until they could eat no more, and the food was good, but Whirlwind was careful to only sip a little of the drink. She noticed that Daksi, too, was cautious. He, at least, had taken her advice. It was her first experience with Spanish drink, but she recalled some stories about it: a strong drink that sometimes made men act crazy.

When they had at last finished their meal, Calvillo called out loudly for Cristóbal. The captain appeared, followed by another man who had his arms full of swords and knives. Whirlwind's eyes lit up at the sight of the long swords, three of them.

The *commandante* stood up. "I have some gifts for my new Chalakee friends," he said. "Cristóbal, present them."

Cristóbal stepped over to Whirlwind, and she stood. He took a sword from the other man and handed it to her. Then he laid a knife on the table there at her place. He moved on to Daksi and then to the Little Spaniard and did the same with each. The three Real People immediately strapped on their new weapons. Whirlwind and the Little Spaniard beamed with pride. Daksi's face, however, retained its sullen look.

"Gracias, Commandante," said Whirlwind, "and now, *con su permiso,* we'll take our leave for a short while. We have some gifts for you and some other goods that we would like to trade, but we left those things two days' ride from here. We'll go get them and bring them back."

Calvillo looked disappointed for an instant, but he quickly covered his feelings and once again smiled his broad smile.

"Of course," he said. "We'll wait for your return in four days. Then we can trade, of course, but we can also resume our talks of alliance between our two peoples. In the case of you and your brother, the Little Spaniard, I should say 'between your two peoples.' Eh?"

"Yes," said Whirlwind. "We'll talk some more."

The Real People left to return to their assigned hut and gather up their few belongings, but Calvillo kept Cristóbal behind. "Follow them," Calvillo said. "Don't let them out of your sight. I think they mean to return, but I don't want to take any chances. This alliance is much too important for us, for Spain. Don't fail me, Cristóbal."

"Have no fear, Commandante," Cristóbal said. "I'll know everything they do. I promise you."

13

RISTÓBAL was delighted that his *commandante* had ordered him to follow the Chalakees, for he had no intention of letting Whirlwind ride out of his life. He was absolutely smitten by her beauty. He felt foolish, like a schoolboy—after all, she was a savage and not much more than a girl.

But there was something about her. She was beautiful, of course, perhaps the most beautiful woman he had ever seen, but that was not all. There was something more, something mysterious about the young Chalakee woman. More than that Cristóbal could not say, but he knew that he had to have her for his own.

He knew that she had a husband, but if they had actually been married, he thought, it would only have been in some savage ceremony, not recognized by the Holy Church. So it wouldn't matter a bit. Even if they had been married in the Holy Church, Cristóbal admitted to himself, it would make no difference to him. To hell with it all, he would have her anyway. He must have her. With her consent or without it. With her husband's consent or without it. He would kill the husband if need be.

He took seven men with him, making a patrol of eight counting himself, and he made the men wrap their swords and anything else that would clank as they moved. He didn't want to stay too far behind the Real People, but he didn't want them to know that he was following them. He couldn't afford to be seen, and he couldn't afford to be heard.

He waited until the three riders were out of sight; then he ordered his men to mount their *caballos,* and he climbed up onto his own saddle.

"*Sergeanto!*" he called.

Sergeant Morales rode out in front of the other men.

"*Sí, Capitán?*"

"I'm going to ride ahead, Morales," said Cristóbal. "You keep a safe distance between me and the rest of the patrol. It's important that we keep sight of these people, yet they must not know that they're being followed. If I need you, I'll come back for you. Understood?"

"Sí, Capitán," Morales said. "I'll stay back, but if I hear you yell, I'll come running with the troops."

Cristóbal pointed ahead to a curve in the road. "Wait until I'm beyond that place," he commanded. "Then move out."

Cristóbal rode easy. He figured that with two days' ride, the Chalakees would not be in a hurry, and he didn't want to ride up on them unexpectedly. The worst part of the assignment for Cristóbal was keeping his distance from Whirlwind. He wanted to ride on ahead and declare his intentions, fight and kill her husband and even her brother, and have her for himself. He would like for her to be willing, but he would take her by force if that turned out to be necessary.

That was what Cristóbal wanted to do, but he had his orders, and he was a good soldier. He had never yet disobeyed an order from a superior officer, but never before had he wanted to disobey one so much as he did now, following the trail of this haunting young Chalakee woman, this savage.

Taking advantage of the terrain, Cristóbal moved ahead when he could to get a look at them. He would ride ahead fast to the top of a rise to look over it or to a stand of trees where he could keep his cover and still see ahead. The Chalakees kept to the road.

Toward the end of the day, they made a camp and built a small fire. When Cristóbal was certain that they had settled in for the night, he rode back to his patrol and ordered that they, too, camp for the night. He would get up early in the morning to make certain that the Chalakees would not get away from him.

❧

"I feel better already," said Daksi, sitting by the small fire, "just being out of that place."

The Little Spaniard was hefting his new sword in one hand and his knife in the other. "These weapons are good, though," he said. "I wonder what else we might get from them."

Whirlwind could see that her brother was softening toward the Spaniards. He wanted more Spanish goods, and, unfortunately, he probably wanted more of their drink. But Daksi was as obstinate as ever.

"Husband," she said, "do you like your new sword and knife?"

"They're good weapons," he replied, "but so are my old weapons. I don't need these from the ugly white men. I don't know how to use this long thing, but I know my old weapons well. I can fight any man with them."

☙

THEY started out early the next morning, and Whirlwind rode with an uneasy feeling. At first she thought that it must be because of her husband's attitude. It was midday before she realized what it really was. They were being followed. She said nothing to her two companions, but she kept herself alert, and soon she knew that Capitán Cristóbal was behind them.

She didn't think there was any danger, for Cristóbal seemed to be alone, and he was keeping well back. He was just watching them, it seemed. She thought that probably he was just making sure that they would actually return. But she wasn't sure. There could be another reason. She would watch him closely and carefully, of course. If Daksi knew, there would surely be a fight. She kept quiet.

But Daksi was surly, and she knew that this business with the Spaniards had come between them. She tried to tell herself that it would pass, that when they had completed their trade and were on their way back home everything would be all right; everything would be the way it had been between them. But two nights had passed, and they had not made love, had not even slept close together, touching one another. She had not thought much about that the night they had spent in the Spanish hut. She figured that Daksi had not been comfortable in those surroundings. Well, perhaps he was not yet comfortable, still so close to the Spanish settlement. She told herself that when they reached the Calusa town they would sleep there. Perhaps that night with Daksi would tell her something.

☙

CRISTÓBAL still kept watch, still from what he thought was a safe distance. He did not think that he had been discovered by the three Chalakees. His patrol still kept their distance behind him. It was all he could do to keep himself from riding fast ahead to catch up with Whirlwind. He knew that he could whip the two young men by himself and, if he did that, could have his way with her.

He was out from under the watchful eye of his *commandante* and could accomplish his purpose if he would only do it. The soldier in him caused him to hesitate, and the fact that he would eventually be discovered absolutely held him back. Calvillo had sent him to keep an eye on the Chalakees. If they failed to return to the settlement in four days, he would ask Cristóbal what had happened.

The *capitán* told himself that, as painful as it was, he would just have to be patient. He would have to bide his time. If he waited and watched long enough, surely he would get his chance and, when that golden opportunity made itself known to him, nothing in heaven or hell would be able stop him. He would have his way.

❦

THE CALUSAS were glad to see Whirlwind and her companions again and were sorry to hear that the three travelers would be around only for the one night. Whirlwind told them that they had come for their extra horses and their goods. The Spaniards were agreeable to trading with them, and so they would take their things in the morning and ride back to the Spanish settlement. Whirlwind and the Little Spaniard showed off their new swords and knives. Daksi was quiet.

Once again, the Calusas fed them well and they all sat up late visiting. Even so, early the next morning Whirlwind had her company ready to travel. They led nine packhorses behind them, the four they had brought from home and five they had acquired from the slave catchers along the way. The trade goods had been redistributed evenly among the nine animals.

Whirlwind was puffed up with pride. Their second appearance in the Spanish settlement would be an impressive one. They would ride in with a bold display of wealth, and their trading would be successful. She even thought ahead to their triumphant return to New Town. She would ride in with a new husband, leading nine packhorses loaded with Spanish goods. Everyone would envy her for what she had and for what she had accomplished.

The only thing dampening her otherwise high spirits was Daksi. He still sulked and the closer they got to the Spanish settlement, the surlier he became. Even in the Calusa town he had slept the night with his back to her. Again she told herself that he would change back into the old Daksi as soon as their trading was done and they were on the way back home.

The Little Spaniard, on the other hand, seemed to share Whirlwind's enthusiasm on this return trip. He had been uncomfortable at first but now he seemed anxious to be back among the Spaniards in the settlement. She was glad of that. She thought briefly about his newly acquired taste for the Spanish drink, but she dismissed that thought. The drink would be left behind when they were done with the trading.

They stopped for the night in the same place they had stopped before, and they built a small fire and made a camp. After they had eaten, Whirlwind sat down close beside her husband.

"You've changed toward me," she said. "I don't like that."

"I've not changed toward you," Daksi replied. "I just don't like these Spaniards, and I don't like this place. When we're done here and on our way home, I'll be all right."

She looked across the fire and saw that the Little Spaniard was already lying down for the night. She put an arm around Daksi and pulled him to her.

"Lie down with me," she said. "Close to me."

And he did.

CRISTÓBAL left his patrol in their camp. He also left his armor and anything else that would make unnecessary noise as he moved through the night. He rode his horse a little ways, then tied it beside the road. He walked the rest of the way, moving carefully in the dark.

He felt foolish. He did not know why he was doing this. He only knew that something was compelling him. Something seemed to be pulling him, drawing him ahead. Reason told him to stay back, to wait for the right time, to think only of his role as soldier, and to obey orders, nothing else.

But there was this other thing, this compulsion. He was losing control. He was following orders from somewhere else; from where he did not know. He stumbled once but kept himself from falling. He cursed under his breath, then moved cautiously ahead.

He kept close to the edge of the road and that made the footing a little less sure, but it also afforded him more protection. If he had to, he could slip into the cover of the brush just off the road. He felt a need for absolute secrecy. He was doing something for which he would be ashamed if he was discovered. He did not want to be discovered.

He knew that he was getting close to the camp of the three Chalakees. He had watched them when they stopped for the night, then had ridden back to meet his patrol and issue orders for their camping. He should be spotting the small Chalakee fire at any time now.

He cursed the *commandante* for his policy of placating the natives. Since when, Cristóbal asked himself, did Spanish soldiers need such allies? They could fight the French and the English at the same time and still come out ahead. In the old days, if a Spanish soldier wanted one of these native women, he just took her.

Cristóbal longed for the old days. He envied men like de Soto, who had ripped through the country doing whatever struck his fancy. Cristóbal wondered how many men would follow him if he chose to ride away from the settlement and separate himself from the command there.

But such an act would be desertion, mutiny, treason. He thought of the people back in Spain and what they would think of him. He thought about what would happen to him if he were caught in such an act. Still, he longed for the return of the old days and the old ways.

Then he saw the small fire, and he crept closer. He could see the outlines of sleeping forms around the fire. *They feel safe and secure,* he thought. *They have no watch. They're all asleep.* He moved closer. He could make out the form of a man alone on the ground. There was another form on the other side of the fire.

It seemed to take forever, but Cristóbal made his way around the camp to the far side. He moved in as close as he dared. He moved in close enough to see that the form on that side of the fire was actually two people lying very close together, and he knew that they were Whirlwind and her husband.

Cristóbal stayed there watching for some time. He knew not how long. At last, he left and made his slow way back to his horse and on back to his own camp. The sentry acknowledged him. No one asked where he had been. He crawled into his bed, and he lay there awake staring up into the starry sky above.

14

HEN THE three Real People rode back into the Spanish settlement, throngs of people came running to see what they were bringing in. Spanish soldiers, Indios, and mestizos, people of mixed blood, all came running to see the nine packhorses and what they were carrying. It was evening, but the Sun had not yet crawled under the western edge of the Sky Vault.

Whirlwind told Daksi and the Little Spaniard to unpack and lay out the goods and, once the wares were properly displayed, the trading was hot and heavy. The finely wrought pots, pipes, and baskets of the Real People and the beautifully prepared pelts of beaver went quickly. Whirlwind was thrilled at the way in which she was fast acquiring Spanish goods: more swords and knives, fine colored cloth, even guns and shot and powder.

Whirlwind knew that the Spanish guns were practically worthless as weapons, for they could only shoot one time without reloading, and the loading process was slow and complex. A good man with a bow could shoot arrows much faster. In addition, the gun was no good unless its target was close. But she also knew that they were impressive, and she was glad to have them. She made sure that a Spanish soldier showed her how to load and fire the loud weapons.

As the Sun crawled farther down the western edge of the Sky Vault, some of the Spaniards built a large fire for light and the trading continued. The *commandante* even made an appearance. He did not seem to be interested in the trading beyond making sure that Whirlwind was pleased. He told her that he would like to speak with her again in the morning, then took his leave and disappeared for the night.

The Little Spaniard did some trading of his own. Off to one side of the main action, he bartered with a mestizo for Spanish drink, and the drink he got was stronger than that he'd had in the *commandante*'s house.

The mestizo called it *ron*. The Little Spaniard did not like its taste at first, but he did like the way it burned its way down to his stomach, and he very much liked the way it made him feel. He decided at last that the *ron* was even better than the wine. He traded for some to drink and for a good supply to take home with him.

It was fully dark when Capitán Cristóbal returned to the Spanish settlement riding at the head of his small patrol. The only way in took him right by Whirlwind and the trading. As he rode by, Whirlwind greeted him. He acknowledged the greeting curtly, then rode on. In the center of the settlement Cristóbal dismissed the troop, with instructions to his sergeant to see to the horses. Then he stood and stared in Whirlwind's direction. There was something about the look he had seen on her face as he passed her by.

"She knows," he said to himself. "She knows everything. She knows how badly I want her, and she knows that I followed her. She knows that I've been watching her. She knows all there is to know about me. She has seen into the depths of my very soul. There is something mysterious about this young woman, something bewitching. God damn her to hell."

WHIRLWIND was at the *commandante*'s house early the next morning. She left Daksi and the Little Spaniard to load the horses. She was ready to go, but she had promised the *commandante* she would visit with him one more time. He greeted her with his usual broad smile.

"So the trading was good for you?" he asked.

"It was good," she said. "And now we're ready to go back home."

"But we were going to talk more about the alliance between our two peoples," Calvillo protested.

"Commandante," said Whirlwind, "I cannot make an alliance with you. I do not have that authority. No one person among the Chalakees has such authority. There would have to be a meeting of the town, and the people would have to all agree. Then the war chief of the town could speak with you about such an alliance and, if you and he agreed, even then you would have an agreement only between your people and the people of New Town, the town where I live. If you want further alliances with other Chalakee towns, you would have to deal with each of them separately."

Calvillo scratched his head, trying to take in the sense of what Whirlwind had just said. So each Chalakee town was autonomous. That would make things much more complex. *How many such towns are there?* he wondered. He was disappointed, for he had hoped to come to some agreement with this woman. He shrugged. At least he knew what the process would be.

"When you get back to your town," he said, "will you talk to your people about an alliance?"

"Of course," Whirlwind agreed. "I'll talk to them."

❦

WHIRLWIND found Daksi loading the horses alone. "Where's my brother?" she asked.

"He's asleep," said Daksi. "When I tried to wake him, he grumbled at me. He moaned and groaned and said that he was sick."

Whirlwind hurried to the small shack that had been provided them, and she found the Little Spaniard lying in his rumpled bed.

"Brother," she said, "are you awake?"

He moaned.

"What's wrong with you?"

"I'm sick," he said.

She could smell the strong drink all around him, and she knew what was wrong. She did not know what to do about it. She did not want to linger in this Spanish place but had no idea how sick her brother might really be. She did not know the effects of the Spanish drink.

"Can you get up?" she asked.

"No."

"We're packing to travel," she said. "We're ready to go home."

"Go on," he muttered.

"We can't go and leave you here."

"Go on," he said. "I don't care."

There was laughter behind Whirlwind just then, and she turned to see Cristóbal standing in the doorway. In spite of his laughter, he did not appear to be happy or amused. The expression on his face was strange. "Perhaps I can help," he said.

"We were going to leave," said Whirlwind, "but my brother's sick."

"He's not sick," Cristóbal told her. "He got drunk last night and now he has a bad head. That's all."

"I don't understand," Whirlwind said.

"Well," said Cristóbal, trying to think how to explain such things, "the drink makes one drunk. As the stupor wears off, one feels bad. One's head hurts."

"How long will he be like that?" she asked.

Cristóbal shrugged. *"Quién sabe?"* he said. "Maybe half the day. Maybe all day. Perhaps if he drank just a little this morning, it would help. But either way, he can travel. He won't like it, but he can ride."

They gave the Little Spaniard a little rum and loaded him groaning and complaining onto the back of his horse. Whirlwind said her good-byes, and the three rode out of the settlement. Cristóbal stood and watched them leave. He had helped her with her brother because he wanted them to leave. There was nothing he could do as long as they were the guests of the *commandante.* He waited until they were out of sight, and then he hurried off to find the man known only as Cruz.

Cruz was a mestizo, a sometime slave catcher and full-time soldier of fortune, a kind of land pirate, and he would do anything for a price. Cristóbal knew about him and had need of his illicit services, for he had something to do that he could not do with his soldiers. He had something to do that his *commandante* must not know about. He had something to do to keep himself from going mad.

⊄ᵔᵕ

THE LITTLE SPANIARD finally quit moaning out loud, but he was miserable. His head throbbed with a pain he had never felt before, and his guts felt terribly uncertain. There was a vile taste in his mouth and an uncomfortable dry feeling.

Each lurch of the horse beneath him sent racking pains shooting through his body. He was angry at his sister and her husband for having put him on the back of this beast. He wanted to get off the beast and crawl over off the road to lie down on the still, solid ground and be left alone to sleep.

"They tried to kill me," he said.

Whirlwind was riding ahead of him, so she heard him speak, but she did not understand his words. She looked over her shoulder at him.

"What did you say?" she asked.

"Those Ani-'Squan'," he said. "They tried to kill me with that awful *ron.* I'll never drink any Spanish drink again. Never."

"Good," Whirlwind declared. She slowed the pace of her horse, dropping back to ride beside him. "You'll feel better tonight when we stop to camp," she said. "Cristóbal said so. Maybe half the day or maybe all day, he said. Then you'll be all right again."

He did feel better by the time the Sun had reached her daughter's house. He did not feel good, but he felt better. The throbbing in his head had been replaced by a dull ache, and his stomach no longer felt as if it would erupt at any moment. He was almost at ease with the rhythm of the horse beneath him. For the first time since leaving the Spanish settlement, he knew that he would, after all, make it through to the end of the day.

That night, when they reached their same campsite, halfway between the Spanish settlement and the Calusa town, the Little Spaniard actually helped Daksi unsaddle the riding horses and unpack the others. By the time they were done, Whirlwind had already built their small campfire. They sat around the fire and ate in silence. At last they talked.

"Neither of you liked it," Whirlwind said, "while we were with the Ani-Asquani, but now it's all over with, and we were successful. We have everything we thought we would get. Even more."

"I feel much better," said Daksi. "Not because of the things we have, but just to be away from those white men. The others in their settlement—they're just as bad. Anyhow, I feel better just being away from there."

"It wasn't so bad," the Little Spaniard said.

"Oh no?" said Daksi. "Would you have said that this morning?"

Then Whirlwind and Daksi laughed at the Little Spaniard, and he politely joined in their laughter.

Soon they all went to bed. The Little Spaniard, however, did not sleep. He was thinking. He had been sick, terribly sick, that morning. He had felt so bad that he thought that he would die somewhere along the road. He had never known anything to hurt so bad or any sickness to make him so miserable. It had been terrible.

He thought about the drink that had done that to him, the Spanish *ron*. He recalled how vile it had tasted at first, but then he remembered that he had grown used to the taste. He had even decided that it was good. And it had felt good as it burned its way down his throat.

Then he recalled with pleasure the warm feeling that had come over him from drinking the *ron*. He had begun to like the men he was with, those who were drinking with him. He had not liked them before. The *ron* was good in that way. It made men who might otherwise be enemies get along well with one another.

The more he thought about it, the more he felt that the good points of the *ron* outweighed the bad ones. The good feelings and the fellowship were worth the suffering of the next day. He remembered the light-hearted good times more than he remembered the wretched suffering of the next morning.

Whirlwind had warned him about the Spanish drink, but even Whirlwind did not know everything, he told himself. She knew many things, and she did have her powers. But she had no experience of the Spanish drink. She had no more experience of the Spaniards than he or Daksi did.

Daksi didn't like the Spaniards because of the way in which the one soldier had talked to Whirlwind and looked at her. They hadn't said anything to him, but the Little Spaniard was no fool. He knew what the soldier had been thinking and why Daksi had been so surly.

He knew as much about it all as they did, he thought. He knew more about the drink, for he had tried it. They had each had only a little bit of the first drink, the weaker one that the *commandante* had served them with their meal. If they talked against the *ron*, they didn't know what they were talking about. They had no experience of it.

He waited until he knew that they were asleep, both of them. Then he got up as quietly as he could and made his way to the goods piled there on the ground beside the pack animals. Stealthily he rummaged until he found his own goods, until he found his supply of *ron,* and he took out a jug and uncorked it, and he drank.

15

HE LITTLE SPANIARD was sluggish the next morning. He did not feel as bad as he had the morning before, but Whirlwind could tell that something was wrong with him. She figured that it was the Spanish drink. He must have brought some with him, and he must have had some after she and Daksi had gone to sleep the night before.

She didn't like it that her brother was drinking the Spanish drink, and she didn't like it that he had not taken her advice. She knew, though, that there was nothing she could do about it. Among the Real People, individual behavior, as long as it did not infringe upon the rights of others or the rights of clans, was a matter of personal choice. She could do no more than let him know how she felt, and she had already done that. In the past, that had been enough.

He did his share of the work that morning and did not even moan or groan very much. It was just that he was a bit sluggish. They got packed up and started on the road again. By evening they would be at the Calusa town, and the Calusas would feed them well and give them a place to sleep for the night.

CRUZ RODE alongside Cristóbal. Behind them rode four other rugged and rascally looking men of ambiguous physical characteristics, all of them heavily armed.

"We could easily catch up with them and take them," Cruz said.

"Not yet," Cristóbal commanded. "We have to be well away from our headquarters. Calvillo must not find out about this."

"When then?" asked Cruz. "And where?"

"They'll be stopping at the town of Indios up ahead," said Cristóbal, "sometime this evening. They'll spend the night there, I'm sure, and leave early the next morning. We'll let them travel another half-day from there and then take them at noon."

Cruz grumbled but didn't argue. He and his men would help Cristóbal kill the two Indio men and capture the woman. Then, for their pay, they would get the horses and goods. Cruz thought that Cristóbal was either crazy or stupid to give up all that loot just for a woman but that was OK with him.

She was a pretty fine woman, though, he thought, and perhaps after they had killed the two men and captured the woman they would kill Cristóbal and take the woman for themselves. They could have a good time with her and then sell her for a good price.

The more he thought about it, the better this new plan seemed to him. He decided to keep it to himself and not even tell his band of ruffians. He might wait until they had accomplished their purpose and then surprise even his own men by just killing Cristóbal with no warning. Yes. He liked that plan. He was so well pleased with himself for thinking this one up that it was just about all he could do to keep himself from laughing out loud.

THE CALUSAS welcomed them back, just as Whirlwind knew they would. They made much over the loaded packhorses that attested to the success of Whirlwind's trading and brought out an abundance of food for their guests. Then Whirlwind opened up some of the packs and gave gifts to the head men of the town.

The Little Spaniard found some new friends, too, and shared with them some of his strong drink. Whirlwind knew what he was doing. She told herself that his supply could not last forever. She hoped that he and his temporary companions would drink it all that night. Then that would be the end of it.

Late that night Whirlwind and Daksi went to bed. She did not know where her brother was—likely he and his companions were still drinking—but at least Daksi was in a much better humor now that they were two days away from the Spaniards. When they lay down, he moved close to her and held her, and they made love again that night. Once again everything was all right between them. Everything was as it should be. Everything was good.

BUT in the morning, things were not so good. Whirlwind had meant to get an early start, but the Little Spaniard was nowhere to be found. It took them about half the morning to locate him and two Calusa men. They were lying on the ground outside of the town. Whirlwind knew that, as Cristóbal had said, they were drunk. She and Daksi had a difficult time getting the Little Spaniard awake and on his feet. The day was wasting away.

When it became obvious that the Little Spaniard was going to be no good that day, Whirlwind decided to take drastic action. The Calusa town chief had offered hospitality for another night, and she accepted the offer. She knew, though, that her brother would do again what he had done the night before and she and Daksi together could barely keep him on his feet. She told the town chief her plan, and he agreed.

In the center of the town was a pole set hard in the ground. The chief led the way, and Whirlwind and Daksi half dragged the groggy Little Spaniard to the pole. With the help of a couple of Calusa men, they held him on his feet against the pole and tied him there.

"He'll be ready to go in the morning," Whirlwind said.

As he came out of his stupor, the Little Spaniard started to yell. He shouted at Whirlwind and Daksi, and when they ignored him he screamed and shouted at everyone who walked by. Even when he could see no one, he called for someone to come and rescue him. But no one did. No one dared.

"GOD damn it, they're staying another night," Cruz said. "You said we'd take them today at noon."

"I thought we would," Cristóbal replied. "I thought they'd stay just the one night. They have a long way to travel."

"They think they have a long way to travel," Cruz said. "But really it won't be so long."

"No," Cristóbal agreed. "Not so long."

"Well, we'll wait another day then," said Cruz. "No more."

EARLY the following morning, Whirlwind and Daksi saddled and packed their horses. When they were ready to go, they untied the Little Spaniard. Sulking, he climbed into his saddle and rode fast ahead of them.

"How long will he be that way, do you think?" Daksi asked.

"I don't know," Whirlwind said. "I think he'll be all right later in the day. We'll see."

They rode north along the same well-traveled road they had taken before. Daksi felt better about it this time, though. He was glad to be on the road and headed back toward home. Even Whirlwind had to admit to herself that she, too, would be glad to finally have this trip over with. It had been more than successful. She had met the Spaniards and learned something about them. She had tested her command of their language and had acquired a wealth of Spanish goods and horses. She had also gotten herself a husband. All that was good.

But her husband had been surly while among the Spaniards, and so, for a time, had her brother. Now her husband was all right, but her brother had acquired a taste for the Spanish drink. She was anxious to get him home and for his drink to be used up.

She worried a little about the safety of the Little Spaniard when he first rode off ahead of them, but he had slowed down and, though he still rode alone and ahead, was not really very far ahead. She could see him. Now and then he looked back, a surly expression on his face, as if to make sure that they were still following him and that they knew that he was still very much upset with them.

❦

BACK in the Calusa town, Long Hair, one of the young men who had gotten drunk the night before with the Little Spaniard, was sitting alone just outside of town. Like the Little Spaniard, he was not feeling well. He had decided to get away from everyone for a while to avoid questions and teasing. He was not hurting as badly as he had been earlier in the day, but he was still feeling slow and heavy.

He was not too interested or surprised, at first, when he saw the six riders go by. His town was on a well-traveled road, and the Spaniards sent out regular patrols. Usually, however, people stopped at the town when they were traveling. That was the first thing that made him curious. These six seemed actually to be avoiding the town.

He looked more closely at them as they rode on, and he recognized the one in the lead, the one the Spanish soldiers called Capitán. But the *capitán* was not wearing his uniform. That was unusual. And the others with him, the one he rode beside and four riding behind, were not soldiers. They were the other kind, the renegades, bad men who were not Spanish soldiers and did not belong to any tribe.

Long Hair wondered what the *capitán* could be doing so far from home with these men. Then he recalled that the three Chalakees with all of their wares had ridden out just that morning on that very road. These men were behind them, and they were in too much of a hurry to stop and take advantage of the town's hospitality. It was a long ride to the next town, and the men had already been on the road for two days.

Taking all of this into consideration, Long Hair decided to seek wiser counsel. He got up and, in spite of his sluggishness, hurried back into town. After a quick consultation with the town chief, Long Hair and six other young men armed themselves and rode after their Chalakee friends.

❧

THE LITTLE SPANIARD was not quite so far ahead as he had been earlier, but Whirlwind had a new worry. She was sure that someone was following them. She had not yet seen anyone, yet she knew. The feeling had been with her for a while, but she had not said anything yet. She had waited to be sure.

"Daksi," she said, "don't look back."

"Is someone back there?" he asked.

"Yes," she said. "I think so."

"Do you know who it is?"

"No."

"Up ahead where the road curves," he said, "I can hide and wait a little to get a look at them."

"Do that," she agreed.

Just then the Little Spaniard disappeared around the curve. It was a sharp curve to the right around thick vegetation. Daksi would be able to wait there in secrecy and watch to see who was coming behind them.

"Just don't wait too long and get caught," Whirlwind said. "See who it is and hurry back to me."

"Don't worry," he said.

When they reached the curve, Daksi eased over to the side of the road. Whirlwind could see the Little Spaniard up ahead again. She continued on her way, not looking back at her husband. The Little Spaniard glanced back over his shoulder and saw what was happening. He turned his horse and rode back to his sister's side, his sulk suddenly replaced with serious concern.

"What's happening?" he asked her. "Why is Daksi back there?"

"Ride on," Whirlwind said, "but stay right beside me. Someone's following us. Daksi is looking to see who it is."

"I should get my weapons," he said.

"Yes," she agreed. "Get ready. We don't know who it is yet, but we should be ready."

Whirlwind and Daksi were both armed, but the Little Spaniard had been unceremoniously loaded onto his mount that morning, so he alone was not prepared for possible trouble. He dropped back beside one of the pack animals, found his weapons, and armed himself. Then he rode back up beside Whirlwind.

"I'm ready for them now," he said, "whoever they might be."

"Good," she said. "We'll just continue straight ahead as if there's nothing wrong. We'll wait for Daksi to come back and tell us what he saw."

They were just topping a small rise, and ahead of them the landscape opened wide onto a vast prairie. If there was to be trouble, there would be no place to hide or seek cover. If there was to be a fight any time soon, it would be out in the open.

BACK at his hiding place, Daksi saw the riders come into view. He waited until he could count them, six men on horseback, two riding slightly ahead of the other four. He waited a little longer, and then he recognized Cristóbal. He wasn't sure about the others. They looked like any number of wretched-looking men he had seen in the Spanish settlement. He could tell that they were all armed, and as he watched, they kicked their horses into a faster gait. Daksi turned and rode hard to catch up with Whirlwind.

16

ONG HAIR had a fast Spanish pony, and he had to force himself to hold it back to keep from running away from his companions. He didn't want to ride alone into the midst of Cristóbal and his hard bunch. He had six men behind him, making them seven. It would be foolish to rush alone against the six men ahead.

But it wasn't easy to hold the little horse back. It was fast, and it loved to run. Long Hair loved to ride it, too, when it raced against the wind. It was frustrating to both of them, then, to allow the others to keep up with them but, Long Hair told himself, they must.

He hadn't quite figured out his strategy either. His three Chalakee friends were riding ahead, going home, as they thought. But they were being followed by Cristóbal and his band of outlaws: six very tough men. Long Hair and six other Calusa men followed even farther back.

So the Cristóbal outlaws were outnumbered, six to ten. But would all ten be together at the right time? Or would Cristóbal catch up to the Chalakees and overwhelm them before the Calusas could arrive? Long Hair wanted to race ahead for more than one reason, yet he felt he must be cautious.

Racing wildly ahead, Long Hair could give himself away to Cristóbal before he himself ever even managed to catch sight of the Spaniard. He could unwittingly turn the element of surprise back on himself. He thought hard as he rode, trying to come up with a plan. He had gotten drunk with the Chalakee known as the Little Spaniard and considered him a special friend. Long Hair liked the other two as well. He meant to rescue them from danger but he couldn't afford to make any mistakes. He suddenly slowed his pace and allowed the next rider to come up beside him.

"Keep moving as you are," he said. "I'm going to race ahead and try to get a look at them. When I know something, I'll come back."

The other nodded, and Long Hair let his little Spanish pony go. Rider and horse felt a sudden wonderful sense of freedom as they surged forward, leaving their companions behind. But Long Hair knew that he couldn't go at that speed for long. He would have to slow down soon and look for a vantage point from which to scan the area ahead. He raced ahead, though, until he had left his companions far behind and out of sight; then he pulled the pony back to a walk.

He rode into the dark shadow cast by the thick woods at the far right edge of the road and, thus hidden from sight, moved slowly ahead, alert to any movement around him, but especially in front of him. Not far ahead was a slight rise, a place that could afford him some range of vision. He rode toward it at a steady pace.

CRISTÓBAL'S heart was pounding. He was getting closer to his goal with every passing second. The beautiful young Whirlwind was just ahead. Soon he would have her for his own. He wasn't at all sure what he would do once he had taken his pleasure. Obviously he could not take her back to the settlement and keep her there as his woman. Calvillo would find out what he had done and most likely have him shot.

He wondered if he would be able to take her to some village of Indios and live with her there as man and wife. He wondered if he could live that kind of life. All he knew was the life of a soldier. Could he throw that away for a woman? A woman who would probably hate him for the way in which he had taken possession of her?

So what was left for him to do? He could take her and ravish her until his lust was sated, and then he could kill her. Both Chalakee men would already be dead, killed by Cruz and his sorry lot of no-good renegades. There would be no one left to tell Calvillo what he had done. He would make some excuse for his absence, and that would be the end of it.

Cruz and the others would have all the loot, and that would satisfy them. They would keep quiet about the whole affair, for if they said anything, they would give themselves away.

But he hated to think of killing her. He tried to make himself think only of the pleasure he would experience with her and not of what must happen afterward. It would be much easier if he did not allow himself to think about it beforehand. But his mind kept calling up an imaginary scene where she sat glaring at him, like a wounded animal. His lust was sated, and he was hating himself and her. Then he reached for her lovely throat to strangle her.

He shook the horrible scene from his mind only to have it replaced by another, one in which he sliced at her with his sword and her blood was splattered all around, even on his chest and face. Maybe he could just tie her to a tree and leave her for the wild animals, he thought, and then his mind was filled with scenes of her beautiful body being ripped by wolves or bears.

He asked himself if he was losing his mind. Why had he gotten himself into this untenable position with these men who were little more than beasts? To what depths had he descended? And would he ever be able to feel any sense of manly pride again? He thought that he would not. And there was a strange and terrible uneasiness within him that told him that in some sense, in one way or another, his life was coming to an end.

And it was all because of that witch. *For she must be a witch to have done this to me,* he told himself, no mere woman could possibly reduce him to what he had become. This was not even a Christian, not white. A brown-skinned savage, and a child at that.

Just behind Cristóbal rode Cruz. He had no such thoughts. He had thoughts of satisfying his lust, of course, but they were nothing like those of the soldier. Cruz would take the woman and be done with her, passing her along to the others. Then he would take her, along with the goods and the horses, somewhere to sell. That was all there was to it. He had no feelings for her, no feelings about her. He had no feelings for the men who followed him. If he shared with them and treated them halfway decently, it was only to assure that they would continue to follow him when he had need of their services. Cruz's only feelings were for his personal profit and personal pleasure. Beyond that, he did not feel. He certainly had no feelings for the pompous soldier who had sought him out for this chore. He could tell that Cristóbal found his company distasteful. He knew what Cristóbal wanted and how desperate he was to get it. For Cristóbal Cruz had only contempt.

Earlier, he had considered murdering Cristóbal. Having considered it for a while now, he was sure that he would, in fact, do it. He had even formulated a plan of sorts. He would allow the foppish soldier to lead the charge. Of course, the battle would be over in an instant. It would not really even be a battle. *Slaughter* would be a better term for it.

There were six of them, and they were well armed. They would sweep down upon the naked Indios and slice the two men to pieces. That would be all. Then Cristóbal would go for the woman, and Cruz's men would go after the goods on the backs of the packhorses. At that precise moment, Cruz himself would stab Cristóbal in the back. It was that simple.

⸙

WHIRLWIND knew that a fight was coming. She had faith in her own abilities and in her charmed life. She also had faith in the abilities of her brother and of her husband. But she was wise enough to know that just having faith was not enough. She had to be prepared, and she had to be ready and willing to fight.

She wished for a better place in which to make their defensive stand, a place with some cover of some kind, a rocky or brush-covered hillside, a depression in the ground, anything. But all around them she saw nothing but flat plain. Well, they'd have to make do with what they had. Perhaps if the attackers, whoever they might be, did not come upon them too soon, the landscape ahead would change. She would keep watching. Without looking over at him, she spoke to her brother.

"I'm watching ahead," she said, "looking for a place to fight. You watch behind us. Tell me if you see anyone coming."

⸙

AT his vantage point Daksi sat very still and watched the road behind him. Glancing ahead, he noted that he was about to lose sight of Whirlwind and the Little Spaniard. Looking behind, he could not yet see Cristóbal and his roughnecks coming. That was good, he thought. There was still a long distance between the two groups. Then he saw them. Cristóbal was in the lead. Five others followed. He moved out onto the road and turned his horse to race after his companions.

⸙

"DID you see that?" Cristóbal asked.

"What?" said Cruz. "See what?"

"A rider just on the top of the rise there," Cristóbal said. "Indio. He was just sitting there, and when he saw us coming he turned and rode away. It was one of them. The Chalakees. He was watching for us, and now he's going to tell the others. They know we're coming. They're waiting for us now."

"So what?" Cruz said. "There are three of them only. We're six. They're children, and we're men. One of them's a woman, a girl really. What do we care if they know we're coming? Huh? What do we care?"

Cristóbal kicked his horse in the sides, sending it ahead in a sudden leap.

"Come on!" he shouted. "Let's get them."

"Ah, hell," said Cruz, then over his shoulder to the others, "come on then."

The five men rode fast after Cristóbal, and as they rode, they screamed and yelled.

❧

LONG HAIR saw the bandits led by the soldier as they raced ahead screaming and waving their weapons. They were attacking the Chalakees already. With a sudden sense of wild desperation, he turned his own mount around to hurry back for his own companions. He kicked and slapped at his little Spanish pony, urging it on faster and faster, and when he saw his friends he reined it in just a bit, shouting at them.

"The white men are attacking the Chalakees!" he called. "Follow me. Quickly."

He jerked the pony around once again, and once again he made the game little animal race for all it was worth. He didn't bother looking back to see if the others were catching up with him or falling farther behind. He knew they couldn't catch him. He just raced ahead, hurrying to the aid of his friends.

❧

"DAKSI'S coming," the Little Spaniard said. "He's riding fast, too."

"That means that we're being attacked," Whirlwind said. "Do you see anyone else?"

"I don't see anyone but Daksi."

Whirlwind turned in her saddle to look back at Daksi, and she saw him riding hard. Like her brother, she saw no one else, but she knew that if Daksi was hurrying back to them, others were on the way. She looked around for the best spot from which to make a defense, but no spot seemed any better than any other. All was the same. All was flat and wide open.

She stopped her horse and dismounted, calling out for the Little Spaniard to do the same. Jumping down off the back of his horse, he watched his sister as she made her horse lie down on its side. He pulled his own down. She was by then pulling the first of the packhorses over, and he ran to help her. By the time Daksi arrived, Whirlwind and the Little Spaniard had a curved line of horses on the ground. Daksi added his own to the line. The three Real People stood behind the animals and watched the road behind them.

"Who is it?" Whirlwind asked.

"That Spanish friend of yours," Daksi said. "It will be a little while yet before they get here. They were not very close to me. I started back to you as soon as I saw them, but I think they saw me."

"Let's get the guns," Whirlwind said.

"They're no good," Daksi protested, but Whirlwind and the Little Spaniard were already pulling guns, shot, and powder out of one of the packs. So Daksi went to help them in spite of his scorn for the white man's weapons.

"Do you remember how to load these things?" Whirlwind asked.

"Yes," said the Little Spaniard.

"I remember," added Daksi.

"Let's load them all," she said. "We'll get down behind the *sogwilis* with these guns, and when they come close to us, we'll shoot with the guns. Maybe they won't kill anyone, but they'll frighten the white men's, *sogwilis,* and they'll probably surprise the men, too. They won't expect us to shoot guns at them. Then we'll grab our own weapons to really fight with."

Daksi smiled then, realizing the worth of Whirlwind's plan, and went on about loading the Spanish guns with more enthusiasm.

"That's good," he said. "That will surprise them."

17

AKSI, the Little Spaniard, and Whirlwind, each armed with a long bow, stood behind the curved line of lying-down horses waiting for Cristóbal and his hired bandits to come riding down the road. Two loaded Spanish guns leaned against horses just in front of each of the three Real People.

"We'll see them soon," Daksi said.

"When they start coming," Whirlwind said, "we'll shoot at them with our bows. We can shoot an arrow farther than their guns will shoot. If they get past our arrows and come riding down on us, get down behind the *sogwilis* and wait for them to get real close. Then shoot the Spanish guns at them."

"All right," said the Little Spaniard.

"That sounds good," said Daksi.

Whirlwind felt a thrill run through her body. Not many women were warriors, but a woman of the Real People could do just about anything she wanted to do. There was nothing to say that a woman could not fight beside a man, most women just didn't want to. They wanted to stay home with children and work their gardens and prepare food. Whirlwind had never thought that to be a very interesting way to spend her life.

Now, as she waited for Cristóbal and the others to attack them, her heart pounded with excitement. She was ready for a good fight. *Six white men against three Real People are fairly decent odds,* she thought. *That's two of them for each of us.*

But waiting for the attack, she began to wonder about Cristóbal. He was only a *capitán*. Calvillo was the *commandante,* and Calvillo had wanted to make friends with her and, through her, with all of the Real People. Now Cristóbal was about to attack them.

She wondered if Cristóbal was acting entirely on his own, if Calvillo knew what his *capitán* was up to. She thought that he probably did not. She considered whether she should go back to see Calvillo again, once this fight was over and done. Perhaps it would be a good thing to do. The foolish *commandante* might be inclined to give even more gifts by way of apologizing for what his *capitán* had done. The more she thought about it, the better it sounded to her mind. She knew that Daksi wouldn't like the idea, but she figured that she could talk him into going along with her.

Then she saw the white men riding quickly over the rise. Daksi and the Little Spaniard saw them, too. They were shouting and waving their weapons over their heads.

"Here they come," the Little Spaniard said. "Six of them."

They looked at each other. Then each of the three Real People nocked an arrow.

"Wait until they're close enough to get a good shot," Whirlwind said.

"Let's knock down three at once with our arrows," the Little Spaniard said. "Then we'll each have only one more to deal with."

❦

AT the top of the rise and on the edge of the vast plain, Cristóbal, riding hard, saw the Chalakees waiting for them down below. He reined in his mount and whipped out his sword. He looked over the situation below, then glanced over his shoulder at Cruz and the others.

"What the hell are you stopping for?" Cruz asked.

"Don't hurt the girl," said Cristóbal. "Do you hear me? She mustn't be harmed."

"We know. We know," said Cruz. "Now let's go get them."

"Come on then!" shouted Cristóbal. "Follow me. Charge!"

He kicked his horse in the sides and raced headlong toward his prey. Cruz and the others behind him joined in the attack, screaming and shouting oaths. Two of them discharged guns harmlessly into the air.

On the plain, some of the downed horses, frightened, started to neigh and struggled to get to their feet.

"Hold them down!" Whirlwind shouted.

Daksi looked ahead at the attackers. They were almost close enough for a bow shot, but the horses were getting out of control. He ran to one of the struggling animals to try to hold it down. Frantically he looked up at the riders coming fast in his direction.

LONG HAIR topped the rise just then, and he looked out over the plain ahead. He saw the Chalakees, their horses down. He saw them struggling to keep the animals under control, and he saw, about halfway between himself and his friends, Cristóbal and the ruffians racing forward on the attack.

His mind raced. Should he attack the white men from the rear, or should he race back for his comrades and bring them to join in the fight? He decided that he could do both. He nocked an arrow, screamed a shrill war cry, then let the arrow fly at the back of one of the white men. One of them heard his cry and looked back, just as the arrow stuck in the thigh of another. Both of them started shouting, and the whole attacking group became suddenly disoriented, scattering in several different directions, looking ahead at the Chalakees and back at the Calusa, wondering now just where to concentrate their attention. Having caused this confusion, Long Hair turned his horse and started back for his companions.

"NEVER mind the *sogwilis!*" Whirlwind shouted. "Loose your arrows."

The three Real People stood up and drew back their bows almost at the same time. As they did, the horses they had been trying to control scrambled to their feet and started to run. Three arrows flew.

CRISTÓBAL was looking ahead as the deadly missiles were released. He turned his horse to his left to escape their path, and he shouted as he turned.

"Watch out!"

One arrow buried itself in the dirt behind him. Another tore into the neck of a horse. It screamed and reared, unseating its rider, who landed hard on his back on the dusty plain. The third ripped the left bicep of Cruz. He looked down to see his own blood and flesh fly, and then he screamed and cursed and kicked his horse hard, riding directly toward the Chalakees.

❦

LONG HAIR spotted his people coming, and he waved and shouted at them to follow him, to ride harder and faster. As soon as he knew that they understood what he wanted, he turned again to hurry back toward the fight. He glanced back over his shoulder only once to make sure that his six companions were riding hard on his trail. He knew that he would arrive at the battle scene before they would, for their mounts could never catch up with his fast Spanish pony, but he also knew that they would come along shortly behind him.

❦

DAKSI saw Cruz coming at them. He remembered what Whirlwind had said, and he picked up one of the Spanish guns there before him. He looked at Cruz, racing toward him. He looked at the gun and found it distasteful. It also offended his sense of pride to be hiding behind a packhorse. He threw down the gun, pulled loose his war club, and leaped over the horse, running toward Cruz and gobbling like a wild turkey.

Cruz had expected the Indios to run or, at the very most, to huddle up snug behind the barrier of horses and wait there for the fight. The last thing he expected was for them to charge. His horse was also surprised. As Daksi came close, the horse shied and veered to his right. Cruz twisted in the saddle and fired a short gun, but the shot went wild, and Daksi grabbed Cruz by his hurt arm and jerked him from the saddle.

Cruz screamed in pain and rage, like a wounded beast, and hit the ground hard, but he rolled quickly to his feet and, roaring, slung Daksi around, sending him flying through the air. Daksi landed, rolled, got to his feet, and caught his balance, and the two men stood facing one another. Daksi held his war club ready. Cruz drew out the saber that had been hanging at his side.

❦

CRISTÓBAL rode toward Whirlwind in a frenzy of passion. There was fighting all around him, but he had only one thing on his mind. As he rode close to the living barricade, he spurred his *caballo* and made a leap over the horse that was lying in his way. The Little Spaniard suddenly stood up from behind the same prone animal and fired one of the Spanish guns he had hidden there. The explosion frightened the Little Spaniard and the loud noise made his ears ring, but through the stinking smoke and fire of the shot he watched in horrified amazement as Cristóbal's face burst into a mass of bloody splotches.

Cristóbal's *caballo* was in midleap as the rogue *capitán* opened his mouth wide to scream and reached for his lacerated face with both hands. The horse finished the leap, but his rider was no longer on his back. Cristóbal had fallen almost at the Little Spaniard's feet. The frightened horse ran away.

The Little Spaniard stood stunned for a moment, looking at what he had done. He had never before fired a gun, had never seen what a gun could do. Cristóbal was rolling on the ground, moaning, holding his bloody face in his hands. The Little Spaniard recovered, pulled loose his war club, stepped forward, and smashed Cristóbal's skull. The *capitán* was still.

Whirlwind's second arrow drove itself into the chest of one of the land pirates. The man's horse kept running, as the wounded rider looked stupidly down at the stick protruding from his body. He turned loose of the reins and reached for the offending missile with both hands. As he did so, he fell off the back of the running horse. He did not get up again.

Another rider leaped the barricade of horses, and Whirlwind fired a gun. The rider screamed and ducked, falling off his horse. His sleeve was burned and smoking, but he was up on his feet, snarling and moving toward Whirlwind. She had nothing with which to fight except the now-useless gun. She threw it at his head, but he managed to ward it off with a forearm. He stepped closer and reached for her.

Just then the Little Spaniard came up close behind the renegade and rammed a Spanish sword all the way through his body. The man stopped and looked down at the bloody blade poking through his stomach. He shivered and twitched. Then his knees buckled, and he fell forward on his face.

The mounted man with the arrow in his thigh hesitated, turned his horse, and rode back out to where the other had fallen early from his horse. The unseated one stood up on uneasy feet. He was only just getting his wind back after the hard fall he had taken.

"They've killed two of us," said the mounted one, "and that damned fool Cristóbal."

"Catch me a horse," said the other.

"Catch it yourself," said the rider. "I'm getting out of here." He kicked his mount in the sides and, without looking back at his stranded companion, headed back the way they had come.

"God damn you!" shouted the one on foot. "You son of a bitch. Come back here. Coward. Bastard."

When he saw that his cursing would do no good, he turned to look for a loose horse he might be able to capture. There was no horse near. Ahead of him Cruz was facing one of the Indio men, and a little farther ahead the other Chalakee man and the woman were still behind the barricade of horses. He decided that he would run after his cowardly companion and, when he next caught up with the man, kill him for having abandoned him in such a way. He started to run.

☙

CRUZ took a vicious swipe at Daksi with his sword, and Daksi ducked under it as the sharp blade whistled, slicing the air over his head. He tried to run in close to Cruz, but Cruz quickly recovered from his swing, jumped back, and prepared to try again.

Daksi stepped back. Unless he could get in under the long blade, Cruz had the advantage. He had a longer and more dangerous reach with the sharp blade. Cruz lunged, stabbing at Daksi, and Daksi stepped quickly to one side. Then he jumped in to deliver a blow to the side of Cruz's head with his war club, but Cruz ran forward, and the blow only grazed the side of his head, tearing his ear a little and making the blood run freely down his neck and onto his shoulder. They squared off again.

As the mounted man who had abandoned his horseless companion approached the rise ahead of him, he saw the Indio on the small *caballo* riding toward him. He heard the rider scream his war cry.

The white man hesitated, pulling back on his reins. Then he drew out his sword and started riding again, ready to slice the man off his horse, but as they passed each other the Indio ducked, avoiding the slash of the blade. Both horses turned. They charged again. This time the Indio delivered a hard blow with his war club to the man's chest.

The land pirate doubled over in the saddle, all of the wind knocked out of his lungs. His horse slowed, then stopped. The rider sat slumped in the saddle. Long Hair rode up beside him and delivered a powerful death blow to his head.

☙

BACK down on the flat plain, the man on foot saw what had happened to his fleeing companion. He stopped in his tracks. He looked over his shoulder at the scene behind him. It had not changed much. There were three Indios down there, and the only one of his companions alive was Cruz. He looked ahead again. The mounted Indio was being joined by others. His only choice was back down on the plain. Maybe he could catch a horse. One was milling around on the far side of Cruz and the Indio he was fighting. He headed for that one.

❧

AS the other Calusa men rode up to join Long Hair, they looked on the scene below. They saw the one white man on foot running toward where Daksi and Cruz faced each other. They saw Whirlwind and the Little Spaniard behind a line of horses, some lying down, some standing. They looked at the bodies of the rest of the white men who had followed Cristóbal.

"Our Chalakee friends are doing well by themselves," Long Hair said.

"Yes," said another.

Just then Cruz lunged again at Daksi with the sword, and Daksi neatly sidestepped the blade. He swung hard with his club, bringing it down on Cruz's sword arm. Cruz bellowed in pain and dropped his sword. Daksi swung again, aiming for the face, but just as the blow landed, Cruz straightened up. The stone head of the war club smashed his larynx.

He clutched at his throat and fell to his knees, gagging and gasping for breath. Daksi stepped in to deliver the death blow, but just then the man on foot came up behind him. Daksi raised his arm. The man pulled a short gun out of the sash around his waist and fired.

Whirlwind saw it coming, but there was nothing she could do.

"Daksi!" she screamed, and she ran toward him. As she ran, she saw the surprised expression on his face. She saw him as he fell forward, the life seemingly gone from his body. She saw as he landed hard on his face and did not move.

Still she ran. She wanted to stop by his side and lift up his body. She wanted to cradle his head in her arms. She wanted to doctor his wounds and keep the life from running out of him. She wanted to sit with him and cry. But she had no time for any of those things. As she passed him by she slowed down only long enough to sweep up the war club from his hand, and she continued running, straight toward his killer.

The man at first thought to keep running after the nearest loose saddle horse, but he saw Whirlwind coming toward him. He saw the swiftness with which she ran, he saw the war club she brandished, and he saw the intense anger on her face.

He turned to face her. She would be upon him in an instant. But she was only a woman. He could kill her quick, get the horse, and be on his way. He reached for his sword only to discover that he had lost it. He had already fired his short gun. It was useless. He pulled out his knife and braced himself.

Whirlwind did not slow her long strides as she came close to the man. Two more steps and she would run right into him. She saw the steel blade in his hand. She ran one more step, then leaped high into the air, and her next step was a kick that smashed the nose on the man's face.

He screamed, blind with pain. He slashed at the wind, for he could not find his target. The Little Spaniard came running to his sister's aid. She saw him out of the corner of her eye and shouted.

"Stay back!"

The Calusas, led by Long Hair, rode toward her, but Long Hair heard her when she spoke sharply to the Little Spaniard. He pulled up his horse, and his followers did the same. They dismounted and joined the Little Spaniard as he went to the fallen Daksi to see how he was.

The blinded pirate still slashed at the wind and growled. Whirlwind moved around quietly behind him. She raised Daksi's war club and bashed the man between his shoulder blades. He howled, dropped his knife, and fell on his knees. She moved around to pick up the knife, and she stepped close to him.

"I'm Whirlwind," she said. "I want you to know who is killing you."

Then she calmly slit his throat.

18

AKSI was dead. He was dead, and there was nothing she could do to bring him back. She kept thinking that there should be something she could do, but she knew there was nothing. She was helpless, and she was angry. She had never before felt such total defeat. Here was a situation in which she could not have her way. For the first time in her life, she could not have what she wanted, and she had never wanted anything as much as that which she could not now have. It was a hard lesson.

The Little Spaniard grieved both for Daksi and for his sister. He had liked Daksi a great deal and had been delighted to have Daksi married to his sister, and so he was greatly saddened at the sudden loss. But he also saw how Daksi's death was affecting his sister, and he wept bitter tears for her. He wondered if she would ever be the same again.

Long Hair and the other Calusa men stayed with them. They didn't like to leave their new friends alone after such a loss. Besides, there were now only two of the Chalakees left, and they might not be safe on the road. Long Hair decided that he and his Calusa companions would travel back to the Chalakee country with Whirlwind and the Little Spaniard. He told the other Calusas, and they agreed. He would tell Whirlwind later.

They stayed on the plain for four days while Whirlwind mourned the loss of her husband, and then they headed north. The body of Daksi was wrapped and loaded onto the back of a horse. The Calusas had rounded up all of the horses, and so the company was now Whirlwind and the Little Spaniard, followed by Long Hair and the other six Calusas. All were mounted. Whirlwind and the Little Spaniard had their original four packhorses and thirteen more. Had they not lost Daksi, the trip would have been counted a tremendous success.

But Whirlwind's mind was only on the loss. She had looked forward to a long life with Daksi. He was the only man in whom she had ever had any interest. Now she knew there would never be another. If she lived, she thought, and she wasn't at all sure that she wanted to, she knew that she would wind up like old Uyona, the woman who had made her what she was.

She did not remember Uyona, the old woman who had died while Whirlwind was still an infant, but she had heard the tales, and now she thought that was the way she would be. She would grow old alone, and she would be hated and feared by all of her own people. They would talk about her behind her back and call her names, but when they wanted some help, they would come to her with their heads down and ask her to use her powers for their benefit. That would be her life without Daksi.

❦

FOR the first several days of their ride hardly anyone spoke. It was a solemn journey. Along the way, when the appropriate time came, they cleaned the bones of the body they bore. It would not be possible to take the decaying flesh all the long way home. Daksi's family would get back a bag of bones.

They rode on. Eventually the Calusa men began talking to one another again, and a day or so later the Little Spaniard joined them. Still Whirlwind kept to herself and kept quiet. Her brother worried about her.

At night when they camped, he got into his supply of *ron* again, and he and the Calusa men drank together. Whirlwind knew, but she didn't care. She didn't care about anything anymore, and the Little Spaniard could tell that about her. That worried him more, and the more he worried, the more he drank.

❦

BACK home at New Town, the reception came in stages. At first the people were amazed at the safe return of Whirlwind and the Little Spaniard. They had been gone a long time, and many had believed that they would never see them again. But then when the people heard of the death of Daksi, they were saddened. Some were angered. They said that it was Whirlwind's fault. The trip had been her idea and she had talked the young men into going with her.

They were gracious hosts to the Calusa men. After all, Daksi's death had not been their fault, and they had tried to come to the rescue of the three Real People. Then the Calusas had accompanied them on their long journey home. For that the people were grateful, and they showed their gratitude by hosting the visitors lavishly.

Then there were the horses and the Spanish goods that Whirlwind and the Little Spaniard had brought home with them. Whirlwind showed no interest in them, and so the Little Spaniard distributed gifts generously, both to their new Calusa friends and to the people of New Town.

Gradually the animosity toward Whirlwind faded, and the people began to think more about her amazing accomplishments. As they looked at their newly acquired and now cherished goods, the steel knives and pots and other things, they thought about further trade with the once hated and feared Spaniards. Whirlwind, it seemed, had opened up that possibility. Some of the rest of them could go down there now, or maybe Spanish traders would bring goods to them.

They had lived so long with frightening tales of horror about the Spaniards that it was good to hear that they could actually be friends with them now. They no longer had to fear the Spaniards. They no longer would have to worry about the Spaniards trying again someday to invade their country. This, too, was due to the bold efforts of Whirlwind.

Some of the men drank the *ada yuhs desgi* with the Little Spaniard, and as they drank it they knew that his supply would not last. They talked then about more trips south to trade. They would have to trade to get more of the Spanish *ron*. Maybe Spanish traders would bring *ron* to them. For this, too, those who drank the *ron* were thankful to Whirlwind, for had she not proposed the trip, they would not have the *ron*, the *ada yuhs desgi*.

And Long Hair, the Calusa, told the people of New Town what he had seen at the fight with the renegades. He told them how he had come to help the three young Chalakee people in their desperate fight, but he had been late. The three, he said, had already killed four of their enemy. He told how he had watched as Daksi killed his foe, only to be struck down from behind in a cowardly manner.

Then he told how Whirlwind, who had already killed one enemy, ran furiously to the side of her fallen husband and picked up his war club. He told how she had run straight toward the hateful enemy, kicked his face and blinded him, clubbed him to the ground, and then calmly cut his throat with his own weapon. He told this amazing story again and again, and it spread from New Town to other towns of the Real People.

When Long Hair and the other Calusa men at last left New Town to return to their own home, the Real People still told the story of Whirl-wind, the young woman, not much more than a girl really, who had seen her husband killed, then picked up his weapon and avenged him, killing the foe herself. They called her a brave woman, a fighter, a warrior.

At last, there at New Town, with many visitors present from other towns of the Real People, they had a great ceremony that lasted for four days, and during this ceremony they made all the talk official. They gave her a new exalted status, and with it they gave her a new name. She would no longer be called Whirlwind. Now she was War Woman.

WAR WOMAN accepted her new status and new name with graceful dignity, and most people probably thought that her new solemn manner was a result of maturity and position. The Little Spaniard, however, knew different. He knew that she was not enjoying her new position. He knew that had all this come her way before the death of Daksi, she would have been delighted with all the attention and all the praise. She had lived for such things. She had wanted nothing so much as to be known and respected, and when she had not felt as if she was getting enough respect she would settle for fear.

Now she had the kind of status she had always craved, and it was based not on fear and suspicion but on genuine admiration and respect. And now she did not care. The loss of her husband had taken all the joy out of her life. The honors, the respect, the fame meant nothing to her anymore, not without her Daksi.

She had thought to come home with her new husband and announce to everyone that they were married. She had thought to build a new house for her husband and herself. She had thought that she would be-come acquainted with her new mother-in-law and all of Daksi's family.

Instead, in spite of all the honor and respect she was getting from others, Daksi's family kept their distance. They did not accept her as his widow. They did not acknowledge the elopement as a real marriage, and they obviously blamed her for Daksi's death. They said nothing. They did nothing. But they stayed as far away from her as they could.

Everything that she planned had worked out the way she had wanted it, except that she had not planned to fall in love and marry. Once that happened, she had certainly not planned to lose her new husband. Every-thing had worked out just right except for that one thing, and the loss of that one thing had made the achieving of all the rest of it worthless.

Osa knew that her daughter was miserable, and Comes Back to Life could tell that all was not well, but it was the Little Spaniard alone who knew the source and the extent of her misery and pain. He alone knew what she had wanted and how she had felt before, and he alone had seen her hopes dashed with the cutting down of Daksi.

The Little Spaniard alone knew as well that his sister had been used to having her own way and that it was terribly painful for her to be taught in such a way and with such a loss that she could not always have it so. He knew also that except for himself, his sister had always really been alone. She'd had no friends.

The Little Spaniard alone, aside from War Woman herself, knew all of these things. Perhaps because he was her twin, he even knew more. Perhaps he felt some of what she felt. Her pain was his pain.

He thought at first that she would get better, that time would heal her pain and she would once more be as she had been before. He longed to see her run and laugh, play pranks even, the way she had before. He longed to see her once again force her own way on those around her, even if she forced her way on him.

But he watched her day after day and could see no change, see no signs of the old Whirlwind in the new War Woman, and gradually he came to believe that he would never see her again. He suffered for her deep inside, and for solace he drank the Spanish *ron.*

2

War Woman

1600

19

E WAS STILL called the Little Spaniard, for he had never earned another name, although he was thirty-six years old. His sister, his twin, the War Woman, was one of the most important people in all of the towns of the Real People, the people who were more and more being called Chalakees or Charakees.

The name came from the Choctaw language through the widely used trade jargon, and when Ani-yunwi-ya, the Real People, talked to anyone else, they had to use it, too, to designate themselves. Some of them were even beginning to use it themselves even when speaking their own language to one another. But when they did so, they put the word in their own form: Tsaragi or Tsalagi, depending on the dialect of the speaker.

The Little Spaniard's sister was renowned and respected, but he was not. He was known far and wide as the worthless twin brother of the War Woman. He and his group of friends did nothing but drink the strong drink of the Spaniards, the drink the Spaniards called *ron* and the Real People now called *ada yuhs desgi,* meaning, "I'll get drunk with it." When the young men drank too much of the *ron,* they were just called crazy or sometimes the Spanish word, *borracho.*

The Real People by this time had been engaged in trade with the Spaniards to the south for twenty years, ever since that time the Little Spaniard and his sister had gone to Florida, that long ago time he did not like to think about, for she had gotten herself a husband and then lost him. Nothing had been the same since that time. For much of that time, he had been drunk, crazy, *borracho.*

After so many years, the people, many of them, had become utterly dependent on the trade with the Spaniards. When he thought about it, if he allowed his head to become clear enough to think, he thought that his sister with her grand scheme had done their people a tremendous disservice. There were actually many young ones among them, twenty years old and less, who did not know anything about life without a steel pot or steel knife or horses or guns.

When they had first acquired those things, he could remember, they were nice luxuries. It was fun to have them, but no more than that. Now, with many of the people, those things had become absolute necessities. The people could no longer live without them, and that meant that they could no longer live without the Spaniards.

When he thought about these things, when he let his head get clear because he was out of *ron,* he laughed at himself. He laughed at himself because he knew that there was no one more dependent on the Spaniards than he and his friends, for they needed the *ron.* They needed it every day and every night and could no longer live without it. And the only way to get it was through the trade with the Spaniards.

He knew what people thought of him, his own people as well as the Spanish traders, even his own sister. He knew the things they said about him, and he didn't care. He had his own friends, the other men who drank the *ron* with him. They were like a family. They cared for each other and looked out for one another. They understood each other without bothering to talk about the things that gave them pain. He didn't care what any of the others thought. No. Not even her.

He was with his friends. Each of them had some things they had begged from some member of their families. The Little Spaniard had some beaver pelts his mother, Osa, had given him. The Spanish traders were coming, and they were going to meet them. They were going to trade for *ron.* Their supply was almost gone, and they were anxious to replenish it, for the thought of running out completely was frightening to them.

"Someone said they were coming," said One-Eye. "Do you think they're coming?"

"Yes," said the Little Spaniard. "It was Swift Deer who said that he saw them. If we hurry we'll meet them on the road before they get to New Town."

The Little Spaniard and his friends did not like to trade with the Spaniards in town, when everyone else was trading. They didn't like the way people looked at them when they asked the traders for *ron.* They didn't like the feeling that they were skulking away with their drink, so when they heard that the traders were coming they got their trade goods and hurried down the road to meet the Spaniards early. That way they could get their business done in private.

WAR WOMAN saw the Little Spaniard and his friends leave New Town, their bundles in their arms. She knew where they were going and why they were going. Everyone knew it. This had been going on for years. She had gotten over the feeling of being ashamed of her brother, and she scorned the pity she knew that most of the people felt for her because of him.

But they could not know how she felt about him. He was her brother, and they were even closer than were most brothers and sisters, for they were twins. She loved him. And she knew that he was in some kind of deep pain. But as close as they had once been, she could not talk to him about this problem.

She was known far and wide as one of the most powerful of the Real People. It was often said that she could accomplish anything, that she could have anything she wanted. She had even believed that herself one time—years ago. But the truth was that she could not have the two things she wanted most in life. She had lost her husband, and in another way she had lost her brother. If her powers could accomplish anything else in the world but could not save her husband and her brother, then those powers, she thought, were worth nothing. She was thirty-six years old, and she lived in a house alone. She had never remarried. She had never wanted another man after the death of Daksi. And she'd had him for such a short time.

She was dressed in her best clothing, for she was going to meet the Spanish traders just outside the town walls. It was expected of her, for she was an important person. She did not particularly care that she was such an important person, but the role had been thrust upon her and she had accepted it. She would play the role with dignity as well as she could.

She knew, too, that she was responsible for the trade with the Spaniards. She had started it twenty years ago; therefore, it was up to her to keep a watch on it, to make sure that the traders were treated well when they came to New Town and to make sure that the traders were fair with her people. In short, she was expected to keep everyone happy with the trading, and she readily accepted the responsibility.

Juan Morales and Miguel Urbanez, the two Spanish traders, knew her well and respected her. She spoke their language well, and they much preferred that to having to try to manage with the trade language common to the tribes in the area.

In a way, War Woman looked forward to her meetings with Morales and Urbanez. It provided her with a break in her routine. It allowed her to speak Spanish for a change, and it gave her a chance to look for any new goods from Spain and to ask for any news of interest. The only thing she did not like was the fact that they carried the hateful *ron* to New Town.

She had thought about asking the council to forbid the Spanish traders to bring their *ron* to New Town for trade, but she knew that if she did that, if she succeeded, her brother and the others would simply leave New Town and go to another town where they could get the drink. If they had to, she knew, they would go all the way to La Florida for it, and they would stay there. So she let it go. What else could she do?

In front of the town house, the two town chiefs, Olig' and Comes Back to Life, were waiting for her. They, too, were dressed in their best clothing. She walked over to join them.

" '*Siyo,*" she said.

"Shall we go to meet our friends the Spaniards?" Olig' asked.

"Yes," War Woman said. "Let's go."

They walked to the place where the two ends of the fence around the town almost came together but instead overlapped and ran parallel to each other for a distance, creating a passageway in or out of town. They walked through the passageway and stood just outside the wall as the traders approached. Morales and Urbanez were in the lead, accompanied by two soldiers. When they saw the welcoming group, they smiled and waved.

"Hello, War Woman!" Morales called. "It's good to see you."

"Hello," said Urbanez. "Please tell the others that we greet them."

"Greetings to you," War Woman replied, speaking Spanish, "and welcome to New Town. Please come in with us."

They went back through the passageway, followed by the Spaniards, and led the way to the town house. There the traders unpacked and spread their wares, but before the trading began, food was brought out and laid before the guests. The Spaniards ate voraciously.

For the rest of the day trading was almost frantic. War Woman stayed apart from it, almost aloof, yet she sat and watched. Morales waited for his chance, then said something to Urbanez to excuse himself and walked over to her. He took off his cap.

"War Woman, my old friend," he said, "may I join you?"

"Yes," she replied. "Please do."

He sat beside her on the bench.

"The trading is good?" she asked.

"Oh, yes," he said. "As usual. It's always good here in your town."

"Better than in other towns of my people?"

"*Sí*," he said. "Much better."

They were silent for a moment, like two old friends who could sit together without talking. Then, "You saw my brother," she asked, "and his friends?"

"Yes," he said. "They met us on the road."

She didn't ask any more about the meeting, and he said nothing more about it. He knew how she felt about her brother and the others and the trade in *ron*. He wished that there were something he could do for her about it, but he knew that there was nothing. If he did not bring the *ron*, someone else would. If no one brought it, the men would go where they could find it.

"So," she said, "what news do you bring with you this time?"

"We have a new *commandante*," he replied.

"Again?" she said, and she smiled.

He liked it when she smiled. It happened so seldom.

"Yes," he said. "The administrators don't last long these days."

"But you last," she reminded him.

"I'm nothing," he said with a shrug. "A trader. I'm not important enough to be replaced. I'll be around for a long time, I expect."

"You keep watching me grow older," she said.

"Perhaps," he replied, suddenly growing bold. "All I know is that each time I see you, you're more beautiful than the time before."

The comment took her by surprise. She looked at the Spanish trader, but only for a moment. She looked at the ground in front of her feet. "You're just being polite," she said.

"No," he said. "Bold, perhaps. I had no right to be so familiar with you. Please accept my apology for that. Maybe I should not have said anything. Nevertheless, I meant what I said."

"*Gracias*," she said, and in spite of herself, she felt a warmth that she had not felt for years. No man had spoken to her like that since—well, no man had spoken to her like that for many years. Were they afraid of her? Did they just know that she wasn't interested? Or did they not find her attractive? She didn't know. She hadn't thought about it. Hadn't wondered. She'd had no interest in men for all these years.

Now all of a sudden, this Spanish trader had told her that she was beautiful. At thirty-six, a twenty-year widow, she had begun to think of herself as an old matron and this Spaniard had said that she was beautiful. It had given her a warm feeling, and that feeling of warmth made her think of Daksi and made her feel guilt.

She stood up abruptly.

"I'm going now," she said, and she walked away.

Juan Morales came to his feet quickly. He reached out as if to try to stop her, but he did not. He opened his mouth as if to speak, but he said nothing. She was gone. He had offended her. He would have to apologize in the morning, the first chance he got. He could not afford to offend the War Woman. It would be bad for the trade, and the *commandante* would want to know what had happened. Morales would be in trouble. Perhaps, after all, he would be replaced, like an administrator.

But he was upset with himself for a much more important reason than that. He liked the War Woman. He liked her very much. He even thought that he could love her, and he had made a fool of himself because of that. He had blurted out a bit of his feelings. But if he could not love her, if he could never ask her to be his wife, he at least wanted to keep her as a friend. He valued that, and he desperately hoped that he had not spoiled it.

20

HE DAY THAT the traders came to New Town was always a special one. The people feasted, traded, and visited late into the night, and, at last, the day came to an end. The visitors were shown where they could sleep, and the townspeople began making their way to their own homes. The town, which had been bustling, suddenly became quiet.

NOT far downstream from New Town, the Little Spaniard and his associates had constructed a rude shelter. A lean-to made of poles tied to two trees with cross poles and thatching, it had been built originally to shelter them from the rain while they drank their *ron* outside of town, away from disapproving eyes. Gradually it had become their home.

They returned individually to town and to their families when they needed something, some food or clothing or something to trade with the Spaniards for their *ron*. The families clearly disapproved of the lifestyle these men had developed. They were ashamed of them and hurt by the condition they were in. They worried about the men and were concerned about their welfare but never turned them away, never refused their requests for help.

The Little Spaniard, One-Eye, and four others were sitting around a small fire under the shelter drinking from a jug of *ron*. They smiled, made crude jokes, and laughed with one another. It was almost like any other domestic scene—almost. There were no women, no children, no old people. There was a dog; it slept just at the edge of the shelter.

One of the men was already lying down next to the dog in a heavy sleep from the drink. Another was nodding regularly, but he was still sitting up and still taking his turn when the jug came around to him. He had stopped talking, though, and he no longer laughed at the jokes.

The Little Spaniard laughed, though. He laughed at almost everything that anyone said. As long as he had *ron* and friends to drink it with him, everything was funny to him. One-Eye only looked at him and he laughed. When the jug came to him, he drank greedily. He loved the way the *ron* burned his throat as he swallowed, and he loved the fuzzy feeling it brought to his brain. He handed the jug to One-Eye.

"Drink," he said. "Nothing else matters."

"*Ron*," said One-Eye.

"*Ron, ron, ron*," said the Little Spaniard. "Good Spanish *ron*."

"I like the white men," said One-Eye, his speech slurred just a bit, "because they bring us the *ron*."

"Our good Spanish friends came to see us today to bring us some *ron*," said the Little Spaniard.

"I like the white man's *ron*," said Meadowlark, who was sitting to One-Eye's right. "Give me some."

One-Eye passed the jug. "Here's *ron* for you. Drink all you want. Drink until you fall over. I'm going to fall over before long."

The Little Spaniard laughed. "Fall over," he said. "All of you. Soon I alone will be sitting up. I'll have the *ron* all to myself."

"That's because you're part Spaniard," said Meadowlark. "You're the one who first brought us the *ron*, and so you know more than we do how to drink it. Because of you these other Spaniards now bring it to us. Oh, you Little Spaniard, we're glad for your Spanish part."

They all laughed heartily at that, and the jug went again around the circle. Soon only the Little Spaniard, One-Eye, and Meadowlark were still sitting up. The Little Spaniard drank again and handed the jug to One-Eye. One-Eye held it up as if to drink, thought better of it, and offered it to Meadowlark. Then he discovered that Meadowlark, though sitting up, was asleep. He offered it back to the Little Spaniard, who took it and drank. One-Eye turned and lay down deliberately on his side.

The Little Spaniard had been right, for all of his companions were now asleep and he still sat up, still drank. He was not even nodding. But he did not laugh. Not anymore. Not alone. He did not even smile. Alone he was sullen and morose. Alone with no one to watch, he could think of nothing that was funny, nothing to smile at, nothing to make him laugh. Sometimes he wished that the *ron* would put him to sleep as fast as it did the others, for though he drank it to make him forget things, he did not forget, not even when he was drunk.

◈

JUAN MORALES lay awake late that night. In the darkness of the small house the Chalakees had given him for the night he could hear Urbanez snoring on the other side of the room. The two *soldados*, their military escort, were in another house. The accommodations were good. Morales was perfectly comfortable. He was actually more comfortable here than in his quarters back at the Spanish colony in La Florida. Lack of comfort was not what was keeping him awake. Morales liked the Chalakees—he liked their hospitality and their lifestyle.

That was the real reason he had proposed to the *commandante* that he be stationed permanently at New Town. He could be a representative there at all times, he had argued, a Spanish presence to ward off any possible inroads the French might try to make—or the English. From what he had been hearing, the English were getting closer all the time.

He could keep the Chalakees working all year round to gather up the goods the Spanish needed back in the colony or to ship back to Spain. If he lived with the Chalakees, if he was a resident in one of their towns, he had argued, he could hold their confidence and their friendship more effectively. Urbanez could continue to travel back and forth, carrying the trade goods and making reports.

He had won the argument. The *commandante* had given him permission to set up residency at New Town or any other Chalakee town he might choose. Now Morales was only waiting for the right moment to mention the plan to War Woman, for he did not want to try to live in New Town without her permission and her blessing. But now he was afraid that he had ruined his chance. He might have to try for another town. But he wanted to live at New Town. He wanted to live if not with her, at least near her.

He wondered if he would be able to salvage the situation with some kind of apology, and he called himself one hundred kinds of a fool for having spoken so plainly, so boldly, to a woman of such status among her people. He was no one. Not even a soldier. A simple trader. Nothing more.

◈

WAR WOMAN went to her house and sat alone in the dark. She considered her life. She had spent much of it alone, even though she had been surrounded by people. She had never had friends. She had been close to no one except her mother and her brother, and because of her mysterious powers, she had not told them everything that was in her mind. She had always kept much to herself.

Then she had met Daksi and she had loved him. She'd had him only for a short time, though. Daksi was gone, and now, in another way, the Little Spaniard, too, was gone. War Woman, in spite of her status among the Real People, was very much alone.

For years that had been all right with her. She had even considered that it enhanced her position as someone special among the Real People. It set her apart physically as well as in the minds of the people. She had accepted that as her role.

Then Juan Morales had come into her life and they had become friends. Months passed between his visits to New Town, but they always greeted one another as old friends, they visited, and they both enjoyed the visits. She looked forward to his visits and, she admitted to herself, missed his company when he was gone.

Now he had said something to her that she had not expected, something warm and personal, something that had made her think of things she had not thought of for years. This Spanish trader, this Juan Morales, had told her that she was beautiful. He was a man thinking of her as a desirable woman.

She thought about her empty house and her empty life, and she wondered if it really was supposed to be that way. She reached back in her mind to Daksi, and she found that she really could not remember just how he had looked. It had been a long time.

She had told herself there would never be another, and for twenty years she had not wanted another. Juan Morales had made her question that state of mind. Was she being disloyal to the memory and the spirit of Daksi? Was twenty years long enough? Must she be alone forever? Or would it be all right for her, at her age, to take another man? She wondered what the people would think, and that thought almost made her laugh.

And wasn't it strange, she asked herself, that it was a white man making her think these thoughts? A Spaniard? But perhaps not. After all, her own grandfather, though unknown to her, had been a Spaniard. Her father had been half Spaniard, and therefore she herself was Spanish. At least, a part of her was Spanish.

But her father, who was even called Spaniard, had hated the Spaniards and fought against them and helped to drive them back down into La

Florida. He had made friends with their bitter enemies the French and the Real People had been taught to hate the Spaniards. She had grown up with that hatred.

Thinking back to her youth, she wondered if that had been the reason she had made that ill-fated trip to La Florida. Because her people all hated and feared the Spaniards had she, just to show them all that she could do anything she wanted to do, gone to make friends with them? Probably so, she thought, and she chuckled at herself.

She wondered, too, as she had wondered many times over the years, if the trip had been a mistake. If she had not made the trip, her people would still hate and fear the Spaniards. They might fight with them again and people would be killed. Had she not made the trip, she and her people would not have the advantage of the trade and would not have the Spanish goods that they so valued. If she had not made the trip, the Spanish traders would not be coming to visit them, and she would not have met Juan Morales. But then, if she had not made the trip, Daksi might still be alive, and the Little Spaniard would not be a drunk.

War Woman still had these thoughts, but they no longer tormented her as they had for a few years. What was done was done. Nothing would be accomplished by brooding over it. She believed, as did all of the Real People, that usually, at least, things happened because they were supposed to happen.

Was something supposed to happen now, she asked herself, between her and Juan Morales? She would just have to wait and see. If it was supposed to happen, then it would not matter what she did. She could not make it happen, nor could she prevent it. But would she like it, if it happened? That was an entirely different question.

She thought about the trader. She couldn't always tell about the white men, but she thought that he was a few years older than she, probably about forty years old. He was a big man with broad shoulders and a thick chest. Like most of the Spaniards, his face was partly covered by hair. And his hair was a light brown color. There was even hair on the backs of his hands. His eyes were green.

He was a handsome man, she thought, and she marveled that she could so easily recount his features. She saw him but seldom and then for brief visits, and, of course, she never stared at his face. Yet she could recall his features easily. His voice was smooth and low, pleasant to listen to, and his words to her were always kind and respectful. In fact, his entire manner was polite, easygoing, and calm. She liked that about him. She liked—

What did she not like about him, she asked herself, and she could not think of a thing. Perhaps if he stayed around, if she had to live with him day after day, then she would find something to dislike. Perhaps. But she couldn't imagine what it would be. She believed that she would not find such a thing about Juan Morales.

She wished for a moment that there were someone she could talk to, someone she could tell her feelings to, someone whose advice she could seek on this weighty matter. But there was no one. Her mother had almost never given her advice—in fact, had always given in to her wishes and whims. She could no longer talk with the Little Spaniard, and the rest of the people—well, they came to her for advice. There was no one to whom she could go.

So she would keep it to herself. She would wait and watch and see how things turned out. If her life was to remain as it had been, she could accept that. She had thought all along that it would be so. On the other hand, she at last decided, if it was to be otherwise, she could accept that, too. She thought that she would even be able to enjoy it. At last, she slept.

21

HILE HIS business partner, Urbanez, still slept, Juan Morales got up and dressed early. He knew from his previous visits to the Real People that they arose early and went to the water each morning. He had thought before that he would like to join them in that daily ritual, but he had never done so. Now, thinking of the possibility of staying at New Town as a resident, he decided that he would try. He hung around the town house until he saw Comes Back to Life, now an old man, walking by, and he approached the peace chief of New Town.

"Is it allowed for a visitor to join you when you go to the water?" Morales asked.

"Of course," said Comes Back to Life. "You're welcome to go to the water with us."

At the edge of the water the people gathered in two separate groups, the men and women keeping apart from each other, and they stripped off what few clothes they wore. As Comes Back to Life chanted ancient, sacred words that Morales could not understand, they all walked into the waist-deep water.

Morales shivered. The water was cold. It was cold and clear and swift. Comes Back to Life was still talking. Even so some of the men close to Morales were smiling, chuckling, and speaking to one another in low tones. He knew that they were laughing at him, the white man shivering in the cold water.

Then the people all bent their knees and leaned forward, ducking their heads under the cold water, and Juan Morales did the same. Before going into the water, he had wondered if he would be able to see War Woman among the women, and he had felt just a little guilty at having had such thoughts. Now, shivering in the cold water, the men around him laughing at him, he had no such thoughts to worry about.

HE saw her later in the day. There, outside the town house, there was still trading. Some of the young men of New Town were engaged in the *gatayusti* game in the nearby field and others were gathered around watching, placing bets on their favorite players. He had not seen her approach, but when he glanced casually over his shoulder she was there. She smiled. He smiled back and stepped over to speak to her.

"I wanted to see you this morning," he said.

"And I wanted to see you," War Woman replied. "I was rude to you last night."

"Oh no," he said. "I spoke out of turn. I didn't mean to offend you. I apologize for my words."

"Por favor," she said. "Stop apologizing to me. I was planning to make my apology for walking away from you. I'm not offended by your words."

Morales smiled, a relaxed smile, and he had to force himself to not stare at her lovely face. He knew that among the Real People such a thing was rude. He looked at the ground between them.

"Well," he began, "I'm very glad that you're not upset with me, for I have a thing to ask of you."

"Let's walk," she said.

Casually, side by side, they strolled down the streets of New Town.

"I would like very much to live here," Morales said. "I have permission from our *commandante* in La Florida, but I would like to have your opinion before I say anything to anyone else."

"Such a decision would not be mine to make," War Woman said. "It would be for Olig' to decide after a council of the people."

"Yes," said Morales. "I understand that, but if you do not approve of the idea, I won't even go to Olig'. I want your approval first. If you agree, then I'll speak to the war chief."

"Why do you want to live here with us?" she asked.

"It would be good business," said Morales, with a casual shrug. "It would be good for the trade, and it would be good for relations between our two peoples."

She glanced sideways at him as they walked, and she smiled.

"And you could keep a better watch on us," she commented, "in the event any Frenchmen or Englishmen should come among us."

Morales blushed slightly and ducked his head. *Damn,* he thought, *this woman is amazing. She reads my mind.* He shrugged.

"It would put me in a good position to—"

She laughed, interrupting his hesitant speech. "That's all right," she said. "Speak to Oliga. I think it would be good. Besides, I enjoy your company."

⌒⌒

MORALES was astonished and greatly relieved at the decision and at how easily it had been arrived at. He had anticipated some argument against granting his request, but if there had been any, it had been little and quiet, for he was totally unaware of any opposition at the council. Olig' consulted in private with his own advisers, with Comes Back to Life and with War Woman. At last Olig' had reported the decision to Morales.

"You're welcome to stay here with us for as long as you like," he had said.

Morales lived in the house that he and Urbanez had stayed in before as guests. It was unusual among the Real People for a man to live alone. Men lived with their mothers until they married, then lived with their wives. Morales already knew that, and he knew that the reason for that practice was that the women owned the houses.

As soon as Urbanez and the two *soldados* left to return to La Florida, Morales began to settle into the rhythms of New Town. Each morning he went to the water with the rest of the residents. For a while, some of the men continued to chuckle at him as he shivered, but slowly they stopped chuckling. Slowly he grew used to the cold waters and stopped shivering.

At the ceremonies, he joined in. He watched the games, and he joined in the betting. He developed friendships, and he improved his command of the language of the Real People. Still, when he visited with War Woman, they spoke Spanish, for she wanted to use that language, but he talked with the others around him in their own tongue.

He began to hunt with some of the men, and when he did, he made himself go through the same preparations as did they. The first time he killed a deer, he brought it back to New Town and presented it to War Woman. Graciously she accepted it. And people began to talk about War Woman and the Spanish trader, Wani.

Morales also conducted his business. As people brought him furs and other goods, he kept a ledger, and he told them that when Urbanez returned they would receive an equal value of Spanish goods. The people accepted the system and readily took part. They knew that by following Morales's new way they would receive more goods when the time came than they had before. They were building credit with the trader. It was a new thing in their lives, but they took to it easily.

Some discovered that the credit could work the other way. The Little Spaniard knew that Morales had a good supply of *ron,* which Urbanez had left behind with him, and when he and his companions had run out, he sought out the trader.

"Wani," he said, "give me some *ron.*"

"What do you have to trade?" Morales asked.

"I have nothing right now," said the Little Spaniard. "Write it in your book."

"My book is a record of the things your people have given me," Morales replied. "When Urbanez returns, they will receive goods from him to equal the value of what's written in the book for them."

"You take their goods and pay them later," said the Little Spaniard. "Let me take your goods and pay you later. I need *ron.* Me and my friends need *ron.*"

So Morales had given *ron* to the Little Spaniard and written it down in his book. He felt bad about that, for he knew how War Woman felt about the drinking of her brother and his friends. And the Little Spaniard was not looking healthy. The color of his skin and of his eyes was bad, he had the look of death upon him, Morales thought. He went to find War Woman.

"Your brother came to see me," he said.

"He must have wanted some *ron,*" she responded.

"Yes. He asked me for credit."

"Did you give it to him?"

Morales hesitated a moment before answering.

"I didn't know how to avoid it," he said. "He told me that if I took goods on credit, I should allow credit the other way. I should also let him take goods on credit. I did not want to give him the *ron.* It's bad for him. I know."

War Woman stared silently into the distance for a long while. Morales felt bad for her. He knew what she was thinking, knew that she was hurting for her brother. He wished that he could do something for her, but he also knew that when the *ron* got hold of a man, there was nothing another could do for him. He had seen it before, in La Florida, in Spain.

At last she spoke. "There was nothing else you could do," she said. "If you had not let him have it, he and his friends would probably have stolen it from you. And he was right about the credit, of course. If it works one way, it should work the other. You had no choice."

"I shall be eternally grateful to you for your understanding, War Woman," Morales said. "I never before knew a woman who . . ."

His voice trailed off. He was dangerously close, he thought, to over-stepping the bounds again. War Woman found it a convenient time to change the subject. "You never married?" she asked.

"No," he said. "I was too poor. That's why I came to this country. To make my fortune."

"Too poor?" War Woman asked, her brow wrinkled in puzzlement.

"Yes, well, in España," Morales said, trying to find the right words to explain, to answer her question, "things are not as they are here. Here you women raise your crops. Your men hunt and fish. You have plenty of wild berries and nuts and other foods to gather. The way you think of wealth and poverty is very different from our way in Spain."

"How can you be too poor to marry?" she asked.

"In España," he said, "one must have money."

"Money?"

"Well—gold."

"The yellow metal?"

"Yes."

"What good is that?" she asked.

"Well, it—why—"

Suddenly Morales realized that he did not know what good the yellow metal was. He considered that any explanation he might offer would sound foolish indeed to this woman of the Real People. Yet he must try to answer the question.

"It's not worth anything, really," he said. "Not in itself. Oh, beautiful things can be made of it, of course, but that's not the real reason for its value. It's valuable, I suppose, because it's rare and, beyond that, because we have agreed among ourselves that it has a certain value.

"Suppose we agreed, you and I, that a piece of gold, say this big, would be equal to the value of one *caballo.* Then if you had a piece of gold and I had a *caballo,* you could buy the animal from me."

"Then I would have a good horse," War Woman said, "and you would have a rock. What good is that?"

"If all the people agree with each other," Morales replied, "then I could take my 'rock' and buy something else that I wanted."

"But why bother with the gold?" she asked. "Why not just take your *caballo* and trade it for the thing that you want?"

"Well, I—well, perhaps the person who has the thing that I want does not want a *caballo*. Or perhaps I want something else, something that is worth more than one *caballo*. I can save my piece of gold and sell something else later and work for some gold and eventually have several pieces of gold—enough to buy the thing I want. Do you understand?"

She thought for a moment. "And the one with the biggest pile of rocks then is the wealthiest," she said.

"Yes," Morales affirmed. He laughed. "Exactly."

"I think I understand," War Woman said, "but it seems unnecessarily complex to me."

"At just this moment," Morales agreed, "it does to me as well. Your way of life, here in New Town, seems to me to be much superior to that I have known before."

"Be careful," War Woman said. "Soon you'll be wanting to speak the language of the Real People with me and not Spanish, and before you know it, you'll no longer be Juan Morales. You'll be just Wani."

Morales laughed again, but he thought, *Would that be so bad?* He did not think so. He did not think that he ever wanted to return to Spain or to the colony in La Florida. He liked his new situation very much, and he had no idea how long it would last. It was certainly possible that he would be called back one of these days.

He wondered what he would do when that day came. Would he just pack his things obediently and go back to his old life? Back where? La Florida? España? He would not want to go back to either of those places. He knew that much. But would he dare to defy any orders coming from La Florida, from the *commandante*? He did not know. He hoped that such a day would be a long way off or that he would never be faced with such a decision.

22

ORALES had lived in New Town for a full year, and he had participated in all of the ceremonies and the annual buffalo hunt. He had modified his dress into a combination of his own European style and that of the Real People, wearing buckskin leggings and breechcloth with a linen shirt. He wore moccasins and wrapped a cloth around his head into a turban. In cold weather, he wore a jacket over his shirt.

He adapted quickly and well to the lifestyle of the Real People, yet, of course, he did not become one of them. He was still a Spaniard, still a trader with a business to run, books to keep, and a *commandante* back in La Florida to whom he must answer. His business partner, Urbanez, made periodic trips to New Town, and the two of them together would balance the books of the Indios with Spanish trade goods from La Florida.

Having found his niche in New Town society, Morales grew a bit more bold. It was time, he decided, to make his move. Dressed in his best, he sought out War Woman at her home one spring morning. It was a nice day, just a little cool. She stepped outside to meet him.

"I've come to speak to you," he began, "about a very important matter."

"Then let's sit here together," she said, indicating a bench by the front wall of her house.

Morales waited until she was seated, then sat down beside her. He looked straight ahead as he spoke.

"War Woman," he began again, "I've known you for a long time now, and we've been friends."

"That's true," she said.

"Now I've lived among your people for a year."

"Yes."

"I think that things have been going well," he said. "I have friends here."

"You get along well with everyone," she agreed.

"I try to," he said, "and it's not difficult. I like your people, and I like the lifestyle here. It's easy to get along, I think. I'd like to stay. I'd like to grow old here . . . with . . ."

War Woman waited for him to finish his statement, but he fell silent. She thought that she knew what he had wanted to say. She thought that she knew why he had not finished what he was saying.

"There were no conditions placed on your request to live here," she said. "You're free to stay here for as long as you like."

"I'd like to stay here for the rest of my life," he said, "if you would consent to be my wife."

War Woman did not look at him. She sat straight and continued looking forward. She did not react in any visible way. She had wondered already when he would ask her. She had known that the question was on his mind, and she had wondered also, for a time, what her answer would be. But, because she had known, she had also given the matter much consideration.

She had no one to whom she must go for advice or for permission. She was one who gave advice to others, and she was a mature woman and a widow. She would make her own decisions. She had done so her whole life. No one among her people had ever married a white man. She was not at all sure how the people would react to such a thing. She was sure that she didn't really care what they thought. She still retained some of her youthful spite. She would do what she wanted to do, and if it bothered others, she might actually enjoy it just a little more because of that.

"I'll be your wife," she said.

❧

MORALES moved into the house of War Woman, and the house with which he had been provided became a storehouse and office for his business. He began teaching her to read and write, and she began to help with the books. She took an immediate interest and then an active part in the business. Before long, she had acquired a taste for the acquisition of wealth in the European style.

Juan Morales and War Woman built themselves a larger house, they developed a large herd of horses, and they saved, from Morales's pay, a goodly amount of Spanish gold coins. Eventually War Woman even acquired cloth skirts and blouses, and soon other women of New Town began to trade for the same things. Some of the men, too, began to trade for Spanish shirts and jackets.

Gradually the people of New Town took on a slightly different look from that of the people in other towns of the Real People. In the other towns, people traded with the Spaniards, too, but they did not acquire as much from the trade as did the people of New Town. That was due, of course, to the constant presence and influence of Juan Morales in New Town.

War Woman had a child, a son, and she named him Asquani, after her own father, but Juan Morales called him Paco Morales. A year later, they had a second child, a girl. Morales named her María. If War Woman gave María another name, she didn't bother telling it to her husband or to anyone else. When speaking her own language, she called the little girl Meli, as did the other Real People in New Town.

When Urbanez showed up one day, he brought with him a woman with black skin, and when the trading was over and Urbanez left, the black woman was left behind. Morales told War Woman that he had purchased this black woman. He called her a slave, and he said that he had purchased her to work in their house. She was called Consuela, and she would cook and wash and keep the house clean and look after the children. War Woman, Morales said, was much too important a person to be bothered with those kinds of things. War Woman did not object.

❦

WAR WOMAN'S life with Juan Morales was pleasant. There was nothing of the youthful passion she had experienced with Daksi, but then, she was no longer a girl. She did not expect that. She was well beyond it. Morales was good to her, and he was nice to have around. He even, she thought, actually added something to her already high and unique status among the Real People.

Then Urbanez came again. After the initial excitement of his arrival and the first frenzy of trading had calmed somewhat, Urbanez sought out his partner for a quiet conversation.

"How are things with you, *amigo?*" he asked.

"My life has never been better," Morales answered.

"I'm glad to hear it," Urbanez said. "The *commandante* is glad too to have you here and married to this *importante* Chalakee woman."

Morales cocked his head to one side and looked at his partner. "Oh?" he said.

"*Sí, amigo,* he's very glad of it. It's been good for business, you know."

"Yes," said Morales. "I know that."

"It might be good for even more important things," added Urbanez, suddenly almost conspiratorial.

"What are you trying to get around to, Miguel?" Morales asked.

"There's gold in the Chalakee country, Juan," Urbanez said, leaning forward and speaking in a harsh whisper.

"Gold?" Morales repeated. "Are you sure? They've been looking for gold since de Soto's day and never found any in this land."

"I've seen it," Urbanez said. "But it's not there just for the picking up. It needs to be mined. I've told the *commandante.* He said we should mine it, but I told him that it's not that simple. Unless he wants to come with *soldados* and be prepared to fight, we need the permission of the Chalakees."

"And what did he say to that?" Morales asked.

"He said, 'Then get the permission,' of course."

"And have you done so?"

"No. It's not so easy, Juan. The nearest town to the gold is called 'Yellow' in their language."

"Dahlonega," Morales said.

"Yes," said Urbanez. "That's the one. The war chief there is hesitant to agree to allow us to dig for the gold."

"What's his name?" Morales asked.

"They call him the Raven of Dah—that yellow town," Urbanez said, stumbling over the Chalakee word.

Morales stroked his chin in deep thought. He was still Spaniard enough that the thought of gold made his eyes glitter.

"I don't know him," he said.

"But does your wife know him?"

"I don't know."

"Even if she does not," Urbanez said, "surely he knows of her. Surely he knows her at least by reputation."

"Yes," Morales agreed. "I would imagine so. I'll talk to War Woman tonight about this problem. You and I will speak of it again tomorrow."

THEY were lying side by side that night, War Woman and her Juan Morales. He had built them a large bed. He had ordered a mattress from Spain through Urbanez, but it had not yet arrived. In the meantime they made do with woven mats laid on top of a tightly stretched net of rawhide ropes. It was a comfortable bed, in all respects.

Morales lay on his back staring up. War Woman could sense that he had something he wanted to say. She spoke to him in Spanish.

"Something is on your mind," she said.

"Yes," he replied. "It's business."

"Oh? Business is good, isn't it?"

"Yes," he said. "Our business here is good. This is larger business, business of the colony that Miguel brought to my attention just this evening."

"You're not going to be called back there, are you?" she asked, worry apparent in her voice.

He chuckled softly. "No. No, my love," he said. "Nothing so serious as that. Besides, I don't want you to ever worry about that. I'll stay here with you no matter what they say."

War Woman rolled over to lean across him and kiss him tenderly on the lips. He had never said that before. She had known that it was a thing that worried him. He had wondered what he would do should such a thing happen. Now he had made up his mind.

"I'm glad," she said. "So what is this important business that's troubling you?"

Morales told her about the gold. He told her that the *commandante* had ordered them to make some kind of deal with the Raven of Dahlonega to start mining operations. The Raven, Urbanez had said, was hesitant. Some diplomacy was required.

"Do you know this Raven of Dahlonega?" Morales asked.

"Casually," she said.

"But he'll know you," Morales responded, and she understood the implications of that statement. She knew what was wanted of her. At the same time, her mind called up the old stories of Spaniards and gold, tales of the horrors they had perpetrated on people in their frenzied search for the yellow metal.

"Tell me about this mining," she requested.

Morales shrugged. "I don't know much about it myself," he said. "I've never worked in a mine. The gold is in the ground, and so they must dig it out. They dig a large shaft into the side of a mountain, and the men go in there to get the gold."

"What men?" she asked. "The Spaniards?"

"I don't know," he said. "Probably slaves. Spaniards would oversee their work."

"No Indios," she insisted. "Especially no Chalakees."

"I would say that you could negotiate the terms," he said, "and that could certainly be part of the agreement."

"And if the Spaniards dig out the gold," she asked, "what do the people of Dahlonega get in return?"

Again he shrugged. "What would they want?" he asked.

"Trade goods," she said. "Trade goods for the whole town in exchange for the gold the Spaniards take."

"That sounds reasonable to me," Morales replied. "Could you make it all sound reasonable to the Raven?"

"Perhaps," she said.

They were silent for a moment, lying side by side. Then War Woman spoke again.

"If I can persuade the Raven of Dahlonega that this arrangement would be beneficial to his people," she asked, "what would I get for my efforts?"

"Ah," said Morales, "you have indeed become a woman of business."

"Yes," she stated. "What would I get?"

"I would think that, perhaps, it would not be unreasonable for you to expect a commission from the *commandante*," Morales said. "A percentage of the gold taken out of the ground maybe."

"Yes," she agreed. "A percentage."

"Shall we go to see the Raven?" Morales asked.

"No," War Woman said. "We'll go to La Florida to see your *commandante*. If he agrees to my terms, then I'll offer my services, and then we'll go to Dahlonega and talk to the Raven."

Morales smiled. This woman he had married was really amazing, he thought. She could deal with anyone and come out ahead. He recalled when he had first explained to her the European concept of wealth. Now she was on her way to becoming a rich woman.

"When will we go?" he asked.

"We'll go with Urbanez," she said, "when he goes back."

"Good," he agreed. "Consuela can stay here with the children."

"Consuela and the children will go with us," War Woman said. And that was the end of the discussion.

23

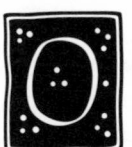VER the next four days, War Woman talked with Comes Back to Life, the peace chief of New Town; Oliga, the war chief; and Osa, her mother. War Woman told them what the Spanish *commandante* wanted from her, and she told them what she was planning to do. She might have been asking their opinions on the matter or seeking their advice. She got neither from any of them. They each only nodded and thanked her for informing them. During that same four-day period, Consuela was busy getting together all of the things they would need for a long journey.

Urbanez had been accompanied, as usual, by two soldiers, and so on this, her second trip to La Florida, War Woman, with her slave and children, was accompanied by four Spaniards: her husband, his partner, and the two *soldados*. That made it a much safer trip than the one she had taken years before. They met people along the road, but no one threatened them in any way. The trip was long and tiring and, for the most part, uneventful.

The Spanish colony, in the same location as before, had changed much since War Woman's last visit. It had grown larger. The church was finished, and there were other stone buildings, including houses. There were houses made of logs and a few made of planks that had been split from large logs. The population was larger than before and at least as diverse. War Woman took it all in as they rode into the town.

It was still loud, still smelly, still busy. In fact, it was more of all those things than it had been before, simply because it was larger and more populous. War Woman recalled how distasteful Daksi and the Little Spaniard, too, had found it to be, at first. She understood more this time than she had then why they had thought it so. On that first trip she had been young, she had been excited with the spirit of adventure.

She had been—she surprised herself at her choice of words—drunk with anticipation. The two young men had gone along only because she had asked them. On this, her second trip to the Spanish colony in La Florida, she was older, more mature, and she approached the Spaniards this time with the cold eye of business. Because of that, she understood better the feelings of the two young men those many years ago.

She had been impetuous and she had been aggressive and arrogant. Thinking back on those days, she wondered that anyone had wanted to be around her at all. Of course, not many had. Her brother had been the only one, really, up until she had met Daksi. Her musings were interrupted when Urbanez called a halt.

He had led them through the chaos of the Spanish colony directly to a small stone building, which he identified for them as the headquarters of the new *commandante*. War Woman tried to decide if the headquarters was in the same spot as it had been years before, but things had changed so much that she could not be sure. It was certainly not the same old building.

Urbanez said that they should report to the *commandante* immediately upon their arrival. Then, he said, they would be able to get settled into some quarters for the night. He expected that they would talk business early in the morning. He knew the *commandante* was anxious to negotiate with War Woman in order get the mining started as soon as possible.

Urbanez went in ahead of the others. He was followed by Morales and then War Woman while Consuela waited outside with the two children. The soldiers had already been dismissed. Inside the office, a large man with gray hair and beard sat behind a desk. He looked up as Urbanez stepped in.

"Ah, Miguel," he said. "You're back in good time."

"*Sí, Commandante,*" said Urbanez.

"I trust you had no problems along the way."

"It was a good journey," said Urbanez.

"And you've brought someone back with you."

The *commandante* was new to his post and so had not yet met Morales face to face. He knew, of course, of the partnership of Urbanez and Morales and knew where Morales had been living and why. At least, he knew the official reason.

"*Sí,*" said Urbanez. "May I present my partner, Juan Morales, and his wife, the War Woman of New Town of the great nation of the Chalakees."

The *commandante* stood up with a broad smile, arms opened wide, and walked around the desk to shake hands first with Morales, then with

War Woman. "An honor and a great pleasure," he said. "Welcome. I am Emiliano Vásquez Huelga. My house is yours. Please be seated."

As Huelga's guests seated themselves, the *commandante* poured glasses of wine and then distributed them. He sat on the edge of the front of his desk. War Woman accepted the wine, though she found it distasteful because of what the drink had done to her brother. She knew, though, that she could sip the one glass with no ill effects. She had done so before, and that in her youth. To refuse, she thought, might be considered rude.

Huelga held up his glass for a toast. "To everlasting friendship," he said.

Yes, thought War Woman, *and to gold, which is much more important to a Spaniard than friendship.* They all drank, but War Woman took only a tiny sip.

"Now, my friends," said Huelga, "I know we have serious business to discuss, but all of you have just completed a long and tiring journey. I'll give you some time to unpack and settle in your quarters. Then, if it meets with your approval, you'll be my guests back here for supper. We can save all business talk for tomorrow."

"That sounds most agreeable," said War Woman, and Huelga took note of the fact that the woman had answered for the trio. The two Spanish men had simply nodded in agreement. That was all. Urbanez had told Huelga that this woman was the power, that she would be the one to bargain with. Already he could see that the trader had been correct.

War Woman, her husband and children, and Consuela were settled for the duration of their visit into a nice stone house just down the street from the *commandante's* quarters. It was small, but it had everything they needed and it was clean. They unpacked and relaxed a little, and then Urbanez called for them. Morales and War Women went with him to dine with the *commandante*. Consuela and the children were served at the little house. The evening meal with the *commandante* was filled with small talk; then everyone went to bed for the night.

❧

SHE had known it would happen. She had thought that she would be prepared for it, but she learned that she had not been. There must be, she thought, some things that one can never really prepare for. The memories that came flooding her mind were from long ago, yet they were painful. She had not been in this place since her youth. She recalled with longing the youthful and passionate love she and Daksi had shared, and she recalled their wedding vows to one another. And, of course, she recalled that deadly blow to her youth, the terrible loss she had felt when he had been killed so violently and so unexpectedly. Even more, she felt the loss anew, almost as if it had just happened.

The old and agonizing memories rushed at her with a clarity she had not seen in years. She saw almost as if it were happening again right in front of her eyes the splattering blood and the lifeless, falling body. Again she saw him lying there, the beauty of his youth terrible in death. Once again she felt the helplessness, the hopelessness, and the devastating emptiness of soul.

For the first time in years, she missed Daksi—terribly, almost as much, perhaps as much, perhaps even more than she had missed him those first days and weeks and months after his untimely death. She felt a heavy sense of guilt because of the man lying beside her, a Spanish man. She felt as if she had betrayed Daksi. And then she thought of the goodness of Juan Morales, and she felt guilty again. She felt as if she were betraying Morales, too, with her thoughts of Daksi.

Had she known just how painful this would be, she asked herself, would she have made this trip? Would she have put herself through all this pain?

She considered the diplomatic significance of the trip, both for the Spaniards and for the Real People. She pondered its importance to her husband's career and the possibility of her own increased wealth, and at last she gave herself an answer. Yes, she thought. Of course. It was like enduring anything else for a reason. If the reason was sufficient, if the goal was desirable enough, the thing could be endured.

She told herself that she would sleep, that she would rest, and that in the morning she would be refreshed. She would be rested from the journey, and she would have put all the pain of the past behind her once again. She would be ready to deal calmly with the Spanish *commandante* Huelga, and she would negotiate a deal that would be beneficial to the people of Dahlonega, to the Spaniards, and to herself and her family. Then she slept.

WAR WOMAN bargained shrewdly at the meeting with Huelga the next morning. The *commandante* wanted so much to start mining the gold in the Chalakee country, and to avoid any trouble with the Chalakees at the same time, that he readily agreed to paying her a percentage of all gold taken out of the mine. He also agreed to allow War Woman and her husband the right to inspect the mine and its records at any time. They could also oversee the entire mining operation from its inception to the end of its life.

All of this, of course, was contingent on her securing from the Raven of Dahlonega the right for the Spaniards to dig out the gold. In order to secure that right, War Woman said, she would have to be able to make certain assurances to the Raven, and those assurances would have to do with the amount of goods to be paid to the people of Dahlonega, the timeliness of those payments, the number of people the Spaniards would bring into the country to work the mine, and the behavior of those people. With Huelga she drew up mutually agreed upon limitations. She learned how much she could offer the Raven, how far she could go with promises in certain areas.

Huelga promised to have a document prepared and copied, with the understanding that War Woman could change certain details in the document during the course of her negotiations with the Raven. Once she had reached an agreement with the Raven, she was to have him sign a copy of the document and then sign it herself. It would also be signed by Morales and Urbanez as witnesses. Then, Huelga said, they could bring it back to him for his own signature to seal the bargain.

"Let Urbanez bring it back to you," War Woman said. "My husband and I will remain with the Raven."

"Very well," Huelga agreed. "When Urbanez brings me the signed document, I'll sign it and send a copy back to you for the Raven. Then we'll all know that we have all come to an agreement."

War Woman stood up. "Good," she said. "Then if everything is agreed upon between us, I'll be going back to my children."

"Good night, War Woman," said Huelga. "And thank you."

War Woman left the office, and Morales started to follow her out.

"Señor Morales," said Huelga. "A moment, please."

Morales turned back into the room. *"Sí, Commandante?"*

"I'm most pleased to have had this opportunity to meet you personally at last," said Huelga. "I've been hearing good things about you, and the trade with the Chalakees has been going well."

"Gracias, Commandante," Morales said.

"You know," the *commandante* said, "you have married a remarkable woman, this . . . War Woman."

Morales smiled at the *commandante. "Sí, Commandante,"* he said. "I know that. *Gracias."*

"Yes," Huelga mused. "Remarkable. A stunning beauty and a shrewd woman. She would triumph even in the court of Spain."

"Señor," said Morales, "I believe you're right about that."

"You made a very wise move, Morales," Huelga added, "when you married that Chalakee woman. A wise move for Spain. I think we could not have a better ally among those Chalakee people than your wife."

Morales bit his tongue. He wanted to tell the *commandante* that he had not married War Woman for the sake of Spain, for her high position and the benefits that might accrue to him as her husband. He had married her because he loved her as he had never loved anyone else in his life. He adored her, and he would give his life for her without hesitation. He wanted to say all those things to Huelga, but he did not. He just smiled diplomatically instead.

"*Sí, Commandante,*" he said. "Having her by my side has been a great advantage."

24

UELGA HAD been correct in his assumption that War Woman would smooth the way between the Spanish colony and the Chalakee town of Dahlonega. She had no trouble at all. The deal was made in a short time, and War Woman and Juan Morales had a temporary home prepared for them there in Dahlonega. War Woman meant to watch over the development of the gold mine and, of course, her interests in the gold that would come out of it. Everyone in the town was curious, but War Woman, Morales, and the Raven of Dahlonega took particular interest. When the Spaniards arrived and the laborers began the tedious work of excavation, those three were watching. They watched the miners dig into the side of the hill with their hard metal shovels and picks, watched as they shored up the entrance with timbers cut with hard axes and the strange many-toothed saws, and they watched as the tunnel probed deeper and deeper into the dark guts of the virgin hill.

"Will they find the yellow metal in there, do you think?" the Raven asked.

Juan Morales shrugged. "I'm not a miner," he said. "I guess they know what they're doing. They think that they'll find it in there. If they didn't think so, they wouldn't be digging so much."

"They'll find it," War Woman stated.

Neither Juan Morales nor the Raven of Dahlonega asked War Woman how she could know that gold would be found in the mine. Neither one questioned her confidence. Morales had grown used to her strange powers, and the Raven knew her reputation well.

The three of them stood side by side, close enough to watch but out of the way of the miners. Just behind them was a small crowd of curious Dahlonega residents. Morales seemed casual, War Woman aloof, and the Raven, like the crowd behind him, intensely curious and somewhat skeptical. As the miners took a break from their work to rest and drink water, the mine supervisor, Gregorio Alvarado, walked over to join them.

"How goes the work, Gregorio?" Morales asked, speaking Spanish.

"It's slow," Alvarado said. "This ground is rocky. Slow but steady. We're getting there."

"Are you convinced that there is gold in there?" Morales asked.

Alvarado waved his arms out to his sides in a grand shrug. "Ah," he said, "one never knows for sure, *amigo,* but the signs are very good. Very good indeed. The quartz on the ground has wire gold in it, and the vein seems to run into the hill. We can only dig and look for the large vein of gold that runs through the mountain. It should be there, but I have dug tunnels in my day that led to nothing."

"This one will lead to your . . . large vein," said War Woman.

Alvarado gave Morales a curious look. Morales gave a slight shrug, but War Woman still detected it.

"She's seldom wrong," Morales said. "About anything."

War Woman frowned at him.

"Seldom, if ever," he added.

"Well," Alvarado said, "I'll take any hopeful sign I can get. At any rate, we should know soon, for sure. Right now I'd better get the work going again. Excuse me, please."

Alvarado went back to the lounging laborers, both Spanish miners and black slaves, and shouted to them to get to their feet and back to their work. War Woman knew that the black men were slaves, and she knew that the Spaniards could be cruel to their slaves. She also knew that they were not being so cruel to these, because of her demands on Huelga. She had insisted that the slaves be treated humanely. She did not want the Real People at Dahlonega to be subjected to any scenes of Spanish brutality. All this was in the agreement Huelga had signed with her.

Day after day the digging continued. All day long, black men wheeled carts loaded with dirt and rocks out of the tunnel. Alvarado inspected each cart. *"Nada,"* he would say, and he would send the man on to dump the contents onto a large and growing pile off to one side of the mine's adit. From time to time he would take a torch and walk into the dark shaft himself to inspect its walls.

The miners settled into a routine existence there at Dahlonega. After a while most of the residents ceased watching the daily activities, but Morales, War Woman, and the Raven kept watching. The slaves were chained together at night to keep them from escaping, and at least one Spaniard always stood watch over them.

Alvarado was in charge of the mining operations, but he did not seem to be in charge of the handful of *soldados* that had come along. That authority seemed to belong to Capitán Martín Gros, called, behind his back, El Gordo.

Early each morning, about the time the people of Dahlonega were going en masse to the water to start their day, El Gordo raised his *soldados*. The one who had been watching was allowed to sleep, the others marched alongside the slaves to the mine. Then Alvarado began again to supervise the work.

Some of the women of Dahlonega fed the Spaniards and their slaves twice each day. For that they were to receive trade goods. The whole business settled in and became routine. The Spaniards were soon no longer even considered curiosities. They were accepted as slightly strange neighbors.

Every now and then one of the old-time residents of Dahlonega would make a remark such as, "I remember when we were very much afraid of these white men. They told us that they were monsters."

Another might add, "When I was little, I thought that they grew on the backs of their *sogwilis*." Then everyone would laugh.

Morales and War Woman kept watching the mining closely day after day. They watched the rock pile outside the mine grow larger and larger. And, as they watched, Morales began to feel discouraged.

"I don't know," he said one morning. "Maybe Alvarado's wrong. Maybe there's no gold here after all."

"They'll find it," War Woman replied.

She was standing there watching calmly when she noticed the young woman standing off to one side looking in her direction.

Morales, too, noticed then. "What does she want?" he asked.

"She wants to talk to me," War Woman said.

"Why doesn't she come on over here then?" asked Morales.

"She's afraid," War Woman said. "And she's being respectful. Go see her. Tell her it's all right if she wants to come over here."

Morales walked over to the young woman, and as he drew near, she ducked her head. He spoke to her in the language of the Real People.

"My name is Juan Morales," he said. "I'm the husband of War Woman."

"I'm Running Deer," said the girl, "of the Deer Clan in this town."

"Do you want to speak with the War Woman?" Morales asked.

"Yes."

"Then come with me," he said.

Morales walked with Running Deer over to where War Woman waited.

"Wife," he began, "this is Running Deer of the Deer Clan. She'd like to speak with you."

"All right," said War Woman. She did not look at the girl. Rather, she continued to stare at the mine entrance.

Morales turned and walked away a respectful distance to allow for private conversation between the two women. Running Deer stood quietly, looking at the ground.

"Well," asked War Woman, "what is it?"

"I don't know if I should bother you with this," Running Deer said.

"When I know what it is," War Woman told her, "I'll let you know about that."

"One of the Spanish soldiers came to me last night," the girl said. "He wanted me to go to his bed. I wouldn't go with him, and he took hold of me. I thought that I would have to fight him or call for help, but just then my brother walked up, and the soldier let me go and hurried away."

"No harm was done?" War Woman asked.

"No," Running Deer said. "No harm."

"It's good you came to me," War Woman told the girl. "I'll speak to the soldier chief and see that it doesn't happen again. I'll also speak to the Raven about what to do. I'll talk with you again."

Running Deer knew that the interview had come to an end, so she left. Morales walked back over to stand beside his wife. He looked at her with a questioning expression on his face.

"A soldier tried to get her in his bed," she said.

"Damn," said Morales.

"Get El Gordo," she instructed, "and Alvarado. Then see if you can find the Raven."

It wasn't often that War Woman issued abrupt orders to her husband, and when she did he knew that the matter was urgent. He did not resent her telling him what to do in such situations. She was on familiar ground, and even though he was becoming more and more comfortable living with the Real People, he was still an outsider. He would always be so. He hurried off to find the three men and send them to her. Soon they were gathered, and War Woman repeated the tale Running Deer had told.

The Raven's face grew long and solemn. Alvarado seemed concerned, but El Gordo gave a shrug.

"So?" he said. "It's not as if the girl was raped."

"*Capitán*," said War Woman, "unless you want to answer to your *commandante* for having this entire operation shut down, you'll see to it that your *soldados* stay away from the women of Dahlonega."

"I don't think there's any gold in there anyhow," El Gordo said.

"It's there," War Woman insisted.

"How would you know?"

"I don't know how she knows," Alvarado said, "but she's right. It's in there. All the signs are right."

"Well, I'll tell the men to keep away from the damned Indio women," said El Gordo.

Morales spoke to the Raven in the language of the Real People, interpreting for him what was being said in Spanish.

The Raven scowled, then spoke. "The girl must be paid," he said.

Morales turned to War Woman and started to speak, but her look told him that she had heard. She looked at El Gordo.

"Find out who the soldier was," she said. "Then make him pay the girl the value of a *caballo*."

"A *caballo*?" El Gordo blurted out. "She wasn't raped. She wasn't hurt. Why should she be paid? If she had gone with him, maybe she should be paid, but—"

A sudden piercing look from War Woman directly into the eyes of El Gordo shut him up. He wanted to look away from her, but he couldn't pull his eyes away. It was as if he was frozen in position. His mouth was opened as if he meant to continue speaking.

"Listen to me, El Gordo," she said. "You're not in España here. You're not even in your Spanish colony in La Florida. You're in the land of the Real People, the people you call Chalakee, and you're a guest in this land, in this town of Dahlonega. If you wish to stay, you'll behave yourself and see that all your men behave. The girl has been insulted, and the Raven of Dahlonega is letting you off easy. A payment from you will make things right. Of course she was not hurt. Had she been hurt, we would demand that the man be killed."

"Don't press our luck," Alvarado said. "Find the man and make him pay."

"I'll find him," El Gordo replied. "He'll pay."

El Gordo turned and walked away, feeling lucky to have escaped with—he wasn't sure, but he felt lucky.

War Woman turned toward the Raven. "It will be done," she said.

The Raven nodded, turned, and walked away.

"I apologize for my countrymen," Alvarado said. "Some Spaniards are very crude."

"Someone has to go back to the colony to see the *commandante*," War Woman said.

"What for?" asked Morales.

"First," she said, "the Spaniards have whores in the colony. Some of them must be brought here to make sure that these men leave our women alone."

"And second?" Morales asked.

"El Gordo must be replaced."

Morales stood in deep thought for a moment.

"Well," he said, "it will have to be you or I. The *commandante* won't listen to anyone else on this matter, I'm afraid."

Just then one of the miners came running out of the tunnel waving his arms and shouting.

"Señor. Señor. Come quickly!"

Alvarado turned toward the mine.

"What?" he called out. "What is it?"

"Oro. Oro. Mucho oro."

"They've found it," Alvarado said. He ran toward the mine.

25

LVARADO followed the excited miner into the dark tunnel, and right behind him were War Woman and Morales. The miner led the way cautiously, holding a flaming torch aloft. They went deep into the side of the mountain, and in spite of herself, War Woman had an eerie feeling, a nagging, troublesome thought that she was somehow violating the earth, prowling around there in its guts. She tried to dismiss the unpleasant notion from her mind and think instead of the wealth that this project would bring to her and her husband.

At last the miner stopped walking. He held the torch close to the wall of the tunnel on his own right. In the weird, dancing light the miner's eyes flickered almost like the shimmering ore on the wall. He reached out with his free hand and touched the golden streak, gingerly, as if he might bruise it.

"Here," he said, his voice now a whisper. "Here it is. You see? You see it? It's a rich vein, all right. Here it is. Right here. Right here."

Alvarado stepped up beside the miner and close to the wall. He put his hands on the gleaming yellow streak and stroked it lovingly. His eyes were wide and wild, and his mouth was hanging open as if he were preparing to bite into some delicious morsel.

"*Sí,*" he said. "*Sí.* You're right, *compadre.* This is a very rich one. A very rich one indeed. Oh, we've done well today. Juan, *amigo,* War Woman, you see it? This is what we were looking for. This is it."

Morales looked at his wife, his expression contrite.

"You were right," he said, "of course. There is gold in the mountain, and now they have found the gold. It's good."

War Woman did not speak aloud, but to herself she said, *I'm not so sure about that.* Her demeanor, however, betrayed no doubts. She stood in silent dignity and studied the rich rock of the tunnel wall.

BACK outside in the fresh air and daylight, the Spaniards danced and sang. Even the slaves rejoiced, for Alvarado ordered the day's work stopped for celebration. Rum kegs were tapped and cups passed around. Some of the people of Dahlonega joined in the celebration. The Raven stood apart looking stern. He wasn't at all sure, in spite of the gold, that he approved of the presence of the Spaniards, and he definitely did not approve of his people drinking their strong drink. War Woman was aloof. No one could read her thoughts.

In the midst of the joyous carousing, one Spanish soldier stood apart and scowled and grumbled to himself and occasionally to his friends when they came near and would listen to him. His name was Eugenio Romero, and earlier in the day El Gordo had made him pay an amount equal to a full month's wages to the young woman he had so rudely approached—the one who had complained about him and said that she had been insulted.

"But, Capitán Gros," Romero had said, "I got nothing from her. I did nothing to her. Why should I have to pay?"

Gros shrugged. "They say that you insulted her," he replied.

"But so much?" Romero asked.

"Because we want their gold," El Gordo said, "we have to indulge them. Like children."

"God damn them," Romero swore.

"Those are the orders of our *commandante.*"

"Then God damn him, too."

"Here," said Gros. "Hush now. You mustn't talk like that."

Romero hung his head like a child chastised. "I'm sorry, Capitán," he said.

Gros stepped in closer to Romero and lowered his voice. "You and I think alike, *amigo,*" he said, "but we must keep such thoughts to ourselves. You understand? If I was truly in command here, we'd have the gold and have our way, too. We would show these Indios who's in charge around here. We'd kill a few of them as examples, and then we'd have all of the women we want. We'd have the men working the mine."

"That's what the great de Soto would have done," said Romero. "But those were the old days. I'd like to have been with de Soto."

"He found no gold," said El Gordo, "and he died."

"I know that," said Romero, "but if he were here now—"

"Be patient with me," El Gordo said. "We may get our chance before this is all over. Eh? Come on now. Have a drink with me. Don't pout."

WAR WOMAN and Juan Morales lay quietly side by side that night in their bed in the temporary house provided for them in Dahlonega. They had made gentle love, and the night was quiet except for singing bugs and one lone whippoorwill.

"I'm going to see Huelga," War Woman abruptly told her husband.

He sat up, surprised. "When shall we leave?" he asked.

"Not we," she said. "One of us has to stay here to watch the mining. We don't want to be cheated of our share. And I don't trust that El Gordo to control his *soldados*. You have to watch him, too. And our children, of course. I'll go alone."

"It's a long trip," he remarked, "and dangerous."

"I know," she said. "I'll be all right."

Morales knew better than to argue further with War Woman. He didn't like the thought of her traveling alone to La Florida, but she would do as she pleased.

"Well," he said, "as long as you're going, you might as well take care of several things at the same time. I know you want to complain about Gros."

"El Gordo," she said.

"Yes. Then there's the matter of the . . . of the women."

"I'll tell the *commandante* to send their prostitutes up here," she said.

"And you can give Commandante Huelga a progress report," Morales said. "Take a sample of the gold we've found here. That will please him and make him all the more disposed to agree to everything you want him to do. I'll speak to Alvarado about it first thing in the morning. I'm sure he'll agree to letting you carry a sample back to the colony with you."

"Yes," she said. "A sample of the gold is a good idea."

"Yes," he agreed.

They fell silent, and Morales was amazed at how she could make such tender love to him and then, almost immediately after, turn so cold and businesslike. It was just one of the many things about her that kept her so fascinating to him. He loved her deeply, but she remained an unfathomable mystery to him.

"Juan," she said, the tone of her voice softened once again. "I miss our big house in New Town. It will be a long time before we get back to it."

"I'll build us another one—one just like it—here at Dahlonega," he said.

"Will it be ready for us to live in by the time I return from La Florida?" she asked, and now her voice was like that of an excited young girl.

"Yes," he said, still amazed again at her many moods and facets. "It will be ready. Waiting just for you. I promise."

"Don't wait for my return," she told him. "When it's finished, you and the children and Consuela move in. When I get back, I want to go right into my new house."

"All right," he said. Talking about the house, he had almost forgotten the trip. He wished that he could think of some way to make her change her mind. "When will you leave?" he asked, his voice a bit sad.

"In the morning," she said, and once again, she was all business. The tender lover, the young girl, both had been replaced by the stern administrator. Morales sighed heavily.

"Is there no one who can go with you on this journey?" Morales asked, making one last try.

"I don't want anyone," she said, and that was the end of the discussion.

OUTSIDE Dahlonega in the Spanish camp, some few men still sat and drank. They were no longer loud, for they were very drunk. El Gordo was one, and Alvarado was another. Although the two men were not friends, they were the two in charge. They were also two of the very few still awake. They sat together and talked, their speech slurred and slow.

"A great day," said Alvarado. "And you said that we wouldn't find any gold here."

"I did say that," Gros replied. "I admit it. I admit, too, that I was wrong. You've made a great strike."

"Huelga will be pleased," Alvarado said.

"Huelga," Gros repeated, and then he snorted.

"What's wrong with Huelga?" Alvarado asked, a frown on his face.

Gros lifted his eyebrows and spread his hands. "I didn't say nothing about Huelga," he said.

"No," Alvarado admitted, "but you snorted at his name. I heard you snort."

"So? What will you do? Go to Huelga and tell him that I snorted?"

"No," said Alvarado. "I don't tell tales. But I heard you snort."

"So I snorted. I snorted because I don't agree with our *commandante.* The way he coddles these damned Indios. In the old days they didn't pamper them so. De Soto didn't ask them for anything. He took what he wanted, and he told them what to do. If they even hesitated, he killed them. Without him, without what he did, we wouldn't even be here today."

"I don't know," said Alvarado. "But whether you're right or wrong, you'd better be careful what you say."

Gros struggled to sit up straight, and he tried to focus his red eyes glazed with drink on Alvarado. "What do you mean by that?" he asked. "Why must I be careful?"

"The War Woman wants you replaced," Alvarado said. "I heard her say so."

"Ah, who cares what she wants?"

"*Amigo,*" Alvarado said, leaning forward groggily, "the War Woman arranged for this mining operation. Now we have found a rich vein of gold here. Our *commandante* is already much taken with this woman, and once he knows what we have found here—well, he'll do almost anything for her; I'll bet you that."

"Shit," said El Gordo. "I don't like this damn duty here anyway."

"I'm not a military man," said the miner, "but it seems to me that it would be just fine if you asked to be moved or if you were recalled for some more important duty elsewhere. But to be recalled because of a complaint—from an Indian woman—I don't know."

Gros lay back and tried to appear unconcerned, but he was worried. It would be bad for him to be recalled because of a complaint against him. The miner was right about that. No telling what Huelga would do. He could take away Gros's rank or have him shipped back to Spain in disgrace. Huelga could even have him whipped in public. And all because of a damned Indio woman. The thought was almost too much to bear.

He tried to think of what he should do. He was in trouble because of his big mouth. He should have kept his thoughts to himself, but it was too late for that now. No use thinking about what he should have done—or should not have done. He had to decide what to do.

He could apologize to War Woman and the Raven for the things he had said. He could pretend to be sincerely repentant and swear that it would never happen again. They should believe him. After all, he had made Romero pay the woman. They would probably accept his apology, and then everything would be all right again.

Everything except his pride. He could not bring himself to apologize to the Indios. What would a man like de Soto think of such a thing? And if he could not apologize, then what? He had to do something. He asked himself what de Soto might have done under similar circumstances, and the answer was clear.

De Soto would have said to hell with the *commandante.* He would have killed the Raven and perhaps the War Woman and then taken over the entire town and the mining operation for himself, not for the glory of Spain.

But El Gordo wasn't ready for such a bold move as that. The idea was appealing to him, and he would keep it in his mind for some future date. When the time was right, he would make such a move. In the meantime, he had to make sure that he was not recalled. He wondered, too, if he had a sufficient number of men to succeed in such a venture, and he wondered if the men would follow him. After all, he was contemplating what some would call treason.

No. He had to think of something else, and it wasn't easy thinking with such a fuzzy head from so much rum. He tried to clear his head, but it was no use. He was about to fall asleep, too, but he felt a desperate need to get clear in his mind what he would do about this mess he had gotten himself into.

How would Huelga know that the War Woman was unhappy with him? Of course, someone would have to go to Huelga and tell him. That thought made El Gordo smile. He was perfectly safe until someone headed for La Florida—probably to take a load of gold. Why else would anyone make that trip? Would someone go there just to complain about him? Someone might. And someone might go soon. He would have to be on watch. He would have to make sure that he knew when anyone left Dahlonega going south. With that thought in his head, he drifted off into a deep and drunken sleep.

26

AR WOMAN left Dahlonega early the next morning. The Sun had only just made her initial appearance low on the underside of the Sky Vault in the far east. War Woman was riding her favorite *sogwili*, a small, fast Spanish paint pony she called Runner, and she led a packhorse behind her, loaded with all the provisions she would need for her trip south. It also carried a bag of samples of the rich gold ore from the mine.

Morales and the children had kissed her and held her as long as she would allow them to do so. Then she had mounted up and started riding without a look back. Her family stared after her, waving, until they could no longer see her, then Consuela took the children, and Morales went on about his business. He would be busy, for he had to watch over the mining (and their interests), and he now had to start building another house. He would have more than enough to do.

Off to one side of the town, another watched with interest as War Woman departed. El Gordo stared until War Woman was out of sight, then hurried off to find the disgruntled Romero. Romero had held the last watch over the slaves the night before, so Gros found him asleep in his tent. He shook the bleary-eyed soldier awake roughly.

"Romero," he said. "Wake up, Romero."

Romero half sat up, rubbing his eyes with the back of his hand. "What the hell?" he said. Then he saw who was there. "Oh, Capitán. Do you know that I just got off watch?"

"Never mind that, *amigo,*" Gros said. "I have something very important to discuss with you. A thing that no one else must know about."

Romero sat up on the edge of his cot, his eyes wide open now. "What is it, Capitán?" he asked.

"Not here," said Gros. "Someone might hear us."

AT El Gordo's suggestion, Romero dressed himself again, armed himself fully, saddled a horse, and rode out of town to the top of a high hill. There he found El Gordo waiting for him. The fat *capitán* was sitting in his saddle. Romero rode up beside him and halted his mount. He looked at El Gordo with anxious curiosity written on his face.

"*Amigo*," El Gordo said, "do you know that the War Woman rode out of town this morning?"

"No," Romero replied. "Where is she going?"

"She's going to La Florida to see our *commandante*," El Gordo said. "Do you know why?"

"No."

"She's going to tell the *commandante* that she wants to have me replaced. She doesn't like my attitude. She wants someone here like her sorry wretch of a husband. Someone who will do anything the Indios tell him to do. Someone who will kiss their brown asses. What do you think of that, *amigo*?"

"I don't like it," said Romero. "What do you think the *commandante* will tell her?"

"He'll tell her, 'Yes, ma'am,' of course. What do you think? He'll do anything she wants him to do. He wants the friendship and goodwill of these goddamned Chalakees so bad that he'll bow down to her and kiss her hand—or something else. Whichever. He's not a soldier. He's a goddamned clerk. That's all."

The features of Romero's face twisted into an ugly grimace. "That makes me sick to my stinking guts," he said. "It makes me want to puke."

"If you think that makes you sick," Gros continued, "just wait. When the damned War Woman returns, she'll have along with her a new *capitán,* and he'll be carrying orders from Huelga. Those orders will place him in charge, and they will send me God knows where. If you think I was unfair to you over that business with the Chalakee girl, just wait until you have to serve under the new *capitán*—the one War Woman will have approved, maybe even hand-picked. Why, they'll tie you to a post and have you whipped for insulting the girls."

"What are you going to do, Capitán?" Romero asked, desperation sounding clearly in his voice. "Are you going to let them get away with that?"

Gros shrugged. "What can I do?" he said. "I'm a soldier. I follow orders."

"God damn it," Romero cursed. "I wouldn't follow such orders. They're foolish orders. *Estúpido.*"

"Of course," Gros said, "if War Woman should never reach La Florida, never talk to Huelga, then none of this would ever come about."

He looked at Romero, who stared back at him with astonished eyes.

"You know, *compadre,*" Gros continued, "she carries a bag of gold with her."

"A bag of gold?"

"Yes. To show to our beloved *commandante.* To make him even more ready to do her bidding. Of course, if something should happen to her along the way, who would ever know what might have become of a little bag of gold? Just a little bag, but more, I bet you, than what a poor *soldado* makes in a whole damned month."

Romero leaned forward in his saddle. "Capitán, I—"

"No," Gros interrupted. "Don't say anything. I know that you'll do what's right and what's best. You're a good soldier and a good man. You don't need to tell me your intentions. You don't even need to tell me that you have any intentions. It's none of my business. I only asked to see you here because I knew of your interest in these matters and I thought that you deserved to be informed. *Adiós, amigo.*"

Gros started riding toward the slope of the hill, leaving a perplexed Romero sitting on top staring after him. He rode a short distance, then looked back over his shoulder.

"Oh yes," he said, "she only rode out at daybreak, and she took the main road south. *Adiós. Adiós.*"

ᗧ᠁

WAR WOMAN stopped for the night alongside the well-traveled road. There was a clear, fresh stream nearby. She unsaddled her pony and unburdened the packhorse, tethering them where the grass was lush underneath their hooves. She gathered twigs and small branches and built a thrifty fire. Then she went to the stream for fresh water. She ate *gahawista,* the trail food made from parched cornmeal, and then she prepared herself a bed on the ground.

Lying on her back, looking up at the clear, star-filled sky, she enjoyed her rare moment of aloneness. She took note of Ani-Tsutsa, "the Boys," the group of stars she knew the white men called the Pleiades, and she recalled the tale told by the Real People about its origin.

In the early days of the life of the earth, there were seven boys who played the *gatayusti* game all the time, the game that had been invented by Untsaiyi, Brass, the Gambler. It was all they did. Their mothers, afraid that they would grow up to be just good for nothing, fussed at the boys and scolded, but nothing they could say or do would make the boys stop playing the *gatayusti* game long enough to do anything else.

One day the mothers got together with a plan. That night, at the home of each of the seven boys, the mother boiled *gatayusti* stones in water. When the boy came home to eat, his mother gave him a hot stone in a dish.

"Since this is all you care about in the whole world, since you like it better than tending the cornfields," she said, "you can have it for your meal."

The angry boys all ran out of their homes. As late in the day as it was, they met at the town house near the *gatayusti* playing field. They soon discovered that the same thing had happened to each of them.

"Since our mothers are so mean to us," one of them said, "let's go somewhere they won't be bothered by us anymore."

They started to sing and dance around the town house, and their song and dance was also a prayer. They went around the town house again and again. They had been gone so long that their mothers came looking for them, and when the women found them at the town house they saw that the boys' feet were not touching the ground. They were still dancing around the town house, but they were dancing in the air just a little above the ground.

As the astonished women watched, the boys rose higher and higher. The frightened mothers ran to get their children but, by then, the boys were as high as the top of the town house and their mothers could not reach them. One of the women grabbed a pole and managed to reach her son with it, but when she pulled, he fell down so hard that he went down into the earth. The other six boys kept circling the town house and rising higher and higher.

Finally the six rose clear up into the sky, where they stayed. The Real People called them Ani-Tsutsa, the Boys.

The mother whose boy had disappeared into the earth grieved over the spot every morning, dropping her tears on the ground there where he had landed, until eventually a green shoot came up from there, and it grew up into a large tree that became the pine.

War Woman smiled, musing over the old tale, and she wondered who was right, the Real People and the Boys or the white men and the Pleiades.

She looked at the Trail Where the Dog Ran. That one, she knew, the white men called the Milky Way. She wasn't sure why they called it that and she had never heard a story to go with the name. But she did, of course, know about the dog.

There were some people who had a corn mill where they ground their corn. When they came in the morning with more corn to grind, they could see that someone had been eating the meal they had left the night before. They ground their meal and went off again at night, but this time they came sneaking back to watch.

Pretty soon a dog came and began to eat the meal out of the bowl. The people jumped out of their hiding places with sticks and began to beat the dog. He ran howling with meal dripping out of his mouth, and he ran so hard that he ran up into the sky, leaving the trail of meal behind him. The Real People called it Gili utsun stanunyi, or Where the Dog Ran.

Maybe there was never a dog that left that trail, War Woman mused, and maybe there were never six boys who danced themselves into the sky. It was difficult to imagine dancing around and around until one rose up into the sky or running so hard that one would run into the sky. Even if one could do one of those things, it was even more difficult to imagine that one would stay there and not fall back to earth. Perhaps these were just tales invented to entertain children. But then, she wondered, did the white man have explanations for what he called the Pleiades and the Milky Way, and if he did, were they any more plausible than the tales the Real People told?

Whatever the truth, the old stories were fun, and the bright stars in the clear night sky were beautiful. And they were keeping her mind off her business. That was restful. She was glad that she had made Juan Morales stay at home this time to watch over the children, to look out for their interests in the gold mine, and to build her a new house.

Again she smiled. Among the Real People, a woman built her own house. When she married, her husband came to live with her—in her house. If she tired of him for any reason, she could tell him to go away, and he had no choice but to obey. It was a good way, but War Woman's husband was a white man. She knew that she could have things both ways or either way, whichever way suited her best. So Juan Morales could build her a new house (he had built the other one at New Town) and still it would be her house. He was more comfortable in a white man's style home anyway, so he might as well have to build it. Never mind that she had also become comfortable in such houses.

She realized that she was becoming comfortable with a number of the white man's ways. She was also adapting well to the white man's notion of wealth. She and Morales were managing to accumulate a good deal of gold. She liked the thought of being a rich woman. That was the main reason she had helped Huelga, the Spanish *commandante,* reach an arrangement with the Raven of Dahlonega. She and Morales would get their percentage of everything that came out of the mine.

She also liked many of the Spanish trade goods, the steel knives and swords, the cloth, the paint. She liked the horses, too. She would have hated going back to a life without horses. And she had her Consuela, and she liked that, too.

While she was accepting more and more of the ways of Morales and his people, he was also adapting to many of the ways of the Real People. He talked to everyone except War Woman, and the other white men, of course, in the language of the Real People rather than in Spanish. He was gradually adapting his clothing, one item at a time. He enjoyed participating in the ceremonies and the games and the hunts. Yes, she thought, they were an interesting pair, the two of them.

She looked up again at the bright stars above her, and she spoke their names out loud.

"Ani-Tsutsa," she said. "Pleiades."

27

HE TINY FIRE was almost out. Had someone added twigs and small branches it would have grown again, but without some tending it would soon die. Even so, in the otherwise dark night its glowing embers cast a dim and flickering light over the campsite.

It made no noise, though, no longer crackled, so the only sounds were the night songs of whippoorwills and certain singing bugs and the hooting of owls. There was also a slight stirring of overhead leaves from the gentle breeze that wafted through the clear night air. Occasionally one of the two horses made some sound that intruded into the space of the night: a snort or a movement sound.

But on a nearby hillside, skulking in the cover of trees and brush, Eugenio Romero, ludicrously overarmed, looked down with beady eyes. Romero was a soldier. He had killed before. But this was a different kind of killing. A murder. He was planning to slip up on a woman alone and . . . what?

He had not yet thought it out thoroughly. She was sleeping there beside the fire. He could walk up and quietly slit her throat. She would never know what had happened to her, would simply never wake up. But it might be easier to shoot her. One well-placed shot at close range would do her in, and the result would be the same. She would never know.

It was comfortable to think that he could do the deed and never have to look his victim in the eyes. There was something unsavory, even to the seasoned killer, about what he was planning. Of course, he told himself, the great de Soto had killed women and children—Indios, naturally. But, when he had done so, it had been in the open and part of military action, not sneaking, nighttime murders.

Romero did not like to think of himself as a common cutthroat. He was a soldier, a proud soldier, but then good soldiers followed orders, followed them blindly, without question, and hadn't his *capitán* ordered him to do this deed? Of course, Gros had not really ordered him to kill War Woman, not directly. Rather, Gros had implied that killing her would be a good thing to do and left the decision to Romero.

But Romero knew that if he failed to do the killing, Gros would be disappointed in him, and Romero did agree wholeheartedly with Gros about the shameful way in which the Indios, these Chalakees, were practically lording it over Spanish soldiers. It was disgraceful, and War Woman was the main cause of it. She was also, if no one interfered, about to be the cause of the removal of his *capitán*.

There was also the gold she carried. A bag of gold that would more than replace the month's wages she had caused Romero to have to give up. There were good and ample reasons for killing this woman, and Romero, lurking in the darkness above her camp, reviewed them all carefully, not to steel his courage, but to convince himself that what he was engaged in was not a dastardly deed but, in fact, a patriotic one.

The more he thought about it, the angrier he became. Just who the hell did this so-called War Woman think she was anyhow? *Zerra. Puta.* God damn her to hell. A woman. A woman to treat a Spanish soldier the way she had done. Not just any woman, but an India. Not Spanish. Not even white. Not *Cristiana.* She needed to die, he told himself, for the good of Spain. As long as she was allowed to live and to dictate her whims to the *commandante,* there could be no glory for Spain.

He considered once again his own personal humiliation and financial loss. Everyone in the camp and all the Indios in the town as well knew that he had been made to pay the woman and that it was because he was said to have insulted her. Insulted her! *By God,* he thought, *I paid her a high compliment, offered her a high honor. For such a one as I, a Spanish soldier, to offer to lie down with such a one as her, a brown-skinned heathen, can in no way be construed an insult. Rather, it should be viewed as a privilege, something much to be desired by those goddamned women.*

My honor needs to be upheld, he told himself, *and my purse needs to be replenished. I both want and deserve recompense for my suffering and humiliation. My captain is depending on me. The glory and honor of Spain must be defended. For all of these reasons, what I am about to do, though it has the appearance of cowardly murder, is actually a deed of valor brought on by utmost patriotic fervor. I must do it, and I will do it.*

But how will I do it? He thought about the quickness of a single shot, but he rejected that method. As far as he knew, there was no one near but himself and his intended victim. Even so, he didn't like the thought that the report of a gunshot might bring someone running to investigate. There might be someone, unbeknownst to him, somewhere in the neighborhood.

He considered sneaking into the camp, kneeling quietly beside her sleeping body, and reaching out with his keen knife blade to slice her throat. But what if she should wake and see him there and reach out first with her sharp nails to claw at his face like the wild animal he knew she was? He could still kill her, of course, she was a mere woman. But she might scar his face. He might be discovered after the fact.

He decided, at last, that his long sword would be the proper weapon to use. He would walk up beside her and remain standing. She, of course, would be lying down, probably asleep, and he could easily dispatch her with one well-placed thrust of his trusty *espada*. Even if she were to wake up, he could still kill her easily, before she could rise. If his first thrust failed, he could stab again and again while he would be beyond the reach of her nasty nails.

He was ready. At last he knew that he would do it, and he knew how he was going to go about it. He came slowly out of his hiding place, and he began to move slowly and cautiously down the hillside, making as little noise as possible. He heard some leaves crunch beneath his foot, and he stopped still, watching the camp for any sign of movement, any sign she had heard the crunching noise that had seemed so loud to him. There was no reaction from the camp. He moved on.

One slow step at a time. Beads of perspiration popped out across his forehead, and his palms were wet with sweat. He couldn't figure out what it was about this killing that was making him react in this way. He felt like a coward, but he knew that he had never been a coward. Yet something was amiss.

Halfway to the camp, he stopped and slowly began to draw out his sword. To his ears, even the scraping sound of the keen blade sliding slowly and smoothly out of its scabbard was loud and rasping, and it seemed to take an especially long time to pull the weapon free.

For an instant he had the frightening sensation that the blade had grown longer, that his arm would not be long enough to draw it clear of its scabbard. But at last the weapon was out, and he felt foolish for having had that thought. Again, he stood still and watched to see if War Woman would spring up from her bed, alerted by his clumsy noises. She did not. There was no movement below. He moved on.

By the time Romero reached the small pile of glowing embers, he was almost exhausted. He was breathing heavily, and he was almost certain that the sound of his breath would wake her. He stared at her form there beside the embers, completely covered in a Spanish blanket, a blanket, he thought, that had no doubt been given her by the simpering *commandante*. She was only a couple of strides away from him.

He raised the sword high. A vicious snarl spread over his face, and he stepped quickly to the helpless form there on the ground.

"Ahh," he growled as he drove the long blade clear through the prone shape and into the ground beneath it. He jerked it out and drove it in again and again, and when his fury was spent he realized that something was very wrong. Something had not felt right when he made his thrusts; there had been no reaction from the form beneath the blanket. No twitching, no movement of any kind. A look of panic spread over his face. With the point of his sword he pricked the blanket and flung it aside.

There was no body there. A pile of leaves.

"Ah, hell," he said, and he slashed at the pile as if hoping to find hidden somewhere beneath it the ghastly, bloody thing he wanted to see. There was nothing, nothing but a pile of leaves. He stopped hacking and stood breathing heavily. Where was she? He felt the hair on the back of his neck begin to rise. He thought that he could feel someone behind him. He whirled, ready to fight. He saw no one.

"Where are you?" he shouted. "War Woman. *Puta.*"

"Why do you call me names?" she said, and the voice seemed to come from behind him.

He whirled again, but still he did not see her. "Where the hell are you?" he shouted.

"You came to kill me," she said. "Why? What have I done to you?"

"I have good reasons," he snarled. "Come out. Show yourself."

Romero turned again. He turned in a complete circle. He could not see her anywhere. Yet when she spoke, her voice was clear . . . and close.

"What good reasons?" she asked. "Because you had to pay the woman you insulted? Would you kill me for such a reason?"

"No," he said. "Not because of that. Not just because of that. And I didn't insult her anyway. Hey. Where are you?"

"Should I show myself so you can more easily kill me?" she asked. "Do you want me to help you?"

Every time she spoke, it seemed to Romero that her voice was coming from a different direction. Each time he heard her, he turned quickly toward the sound of her voice, and yet she was not there.

"Where are you?" he shouted.

"Here."

He turned again and saw nothing. He screamed and ran frantically away from the camp out into the darkness in the direction from which he had come. He ran toward the hillside. Up there on top, his horse waited for him. He ran blindly and stumbled over something, a rock, a fallen branch, he did not know, but he fell headlong onto the hard, rough ground, bruising himself painfully, and he groaned out loud. He had dropped his sword. He put his palms on the ground to push himself up, but before he could rise, he heard her once again.

"Have you hurt yourself?" she said.

He screamed again, for she was close, too close. She was right there with him. Still he did not see her. He scrambled to his feet and ran again. Reaching the base of the hill, he began to struggle up the rise. He ran into thick bramble, and he fought his way through, the tangles scratching and tearing at his hands and face. At last he broke through.

"Why are you running from me?" she said, and the voice seemed to be just there in front of him, but he did not see her. He turned to his right and ran. He fell again, struggled back to his feet, and started again toward the top of the hill.

"Run," she said.

He ran still harder, but he was not moving fast. The climb was steep. It would have been difficult enough in daylight, but in the darkness it was almost impossible for a man in a hurry.

"Run," she said.

Her voice was loud in his ear. He imagined that he could feel her breath on the side of his face.

"Run."

He stopped and slapped at her, but he was slapping at air. There was nothing there. Nothing to feel, nothing to see.

"Coward," she said.

He started again, struggling toward the top, toward his waiting horse. Surely his *caballo* could outrun her. Romero's legs were heavy. Each stride became more difficult than the last. But the top was near. He was getting closer to his mount. His legs would hardly carry him anymore. He put both hands on his forward knee to help himself up just one more step. Then again on the other knee. He could only just manage to stay on his feet, to take one laborious step at a time.

But he was so close, and he realized that she had not spoken to him now for some time. He had escaped her at last. Or she had satisfied herself and tired of tormenting him. He struggled with another step and then another, and then he was on top of the hill. He stood, leaning forward, hands on knees, panting.

He wanted to straighten himself up, but he could not. He sucked in gulps of fresh night air, rejoicing in the fact that her voice was no longer ringing in his ears, that she was no longer breathing against the side of his face. At last he could breathe a little more easily, and he managed to straighten himself up. He stood a moment like that. His legs still felt uneasy, as if they might betray him and give way beneath him at any moment.

He waited to make sure that he was steady enough on his feet, and then he started to move slowly but deliberately toward his waiting *caballo*. Ahead he saw a large shape looming in the darkness. The *caballo!* He was almost there. He almost smiled. He walked on. He could see its head in silhouette. He still sucked deeply and desperately for breath, and he staggered and stumbled, but he kept moving. The shape was becoming clearer.

Then he stopped—horrified. She was there, waiting for him, sitting in his saddle, on his horse's back. He felt transfixed with terror.

"What are you stopping for?" she said. "You wanted to see me."

Romero screamed, and in spite of his weak, numb, and shaking legs, he turned and fled. He ran he knew not where. He only ran away from her. He ran into the deathly darkness of the starry night, as if he were being pursued by demons from hell, and he ran headlong out and over the steep and sudden edge of the very hillside he had so recently struggled so painfully to ascend.

Then there was no ground beneath his feet, and arms and legs flailing wildly, he ran out into space and he fell. With the first bounce against the rocky hillside his neck was snapped. His worthless body tumbled awkwardly and grotesquely the rest of the way to the bottom of the hill.

28

UAN MORALES stayed so busy that some might have said that he didn't have time to miss his wife, but of course, he did miss her. He missed her so much that her absence was to him like a dull pain in his breast. Even while he was engaged in doing something physical—felling a tree, splitting a log, moving large stones, playing with his children—even at such times, he longed for her presence. He longed to know that she was safe, and he longed for her to be nearby.

He worried about her almost constantly, even though he kept telling himself that she was the most capable individual he had ever known—or known of. She could certainly take care of herself. There was nothing a man could do that she could not do, and there was much she could do that no man Morales had ever known could possibly do.

He reminded himself of all these things to try to keep himself from worrying so much about her. Even so, he worried. It was a long trip and it would take her through the lands of several different peoples. Morales knew that these local tribes of Indios could be friends for a while and suddenly become enemies. Much like the countries of Europe, he thought ironically.

Also, in that country between Dahlonega and the Spanish colony in southern Florida, there were renegades of various kinds: Indio refugees from towns that had been wiped out, Spanish brigands, land pirates, men who had come along with the military to the colony and then gone off on their own. Some were even military men who had deserted. Some of these brigands were from other Spanish colonies from lands farther south and west than La Florida.

The country itself could also be a danger—swift, swollen rivers, sudden thunderstorms, loose, rocky hillsides where one could lose one's footing and slide to serious injury or even death, and unpredictable wild animals.

Why did I allow her to travel alone for such a distance? he asked himself on more than one occasion, and each time he asked, he returned the same answer: *I did not allow her to go. There is no question of allowing War Woman to do anything. She does what she wants to do, and that is that. She tells me what to do, and that is also that.* But none of it helped. He missed her tremendously, he worried about her safety, and he felt guilty for not having gone with her.

So he kept himself busy. He watched the mining operation. It was not that he did not trust Alvarado. The miner was a good man, trustworthy so far as Morales knew, but Morales did not really know Alvarado well. And War Woman did not trust anyone. She had especially told Morales to watch out for their interest in the gold and to not allow Alvarado or anyone else to give them a short count or cheat them in any way. So he watched. He watched and, as he watched, the gold that was his share— his and his wife's—grew steadily. They were becoming a wealthy couple.

And he worked on their house, for War Woman would expect it to be ready for her when she returned. Morales did not want to disappoint her. He wanted never to disappoint her in anything, for he loved her beyond anything or anyone else he had ever loved in his life, and she knew that. He knew that she knew, and he knew that she took full advantage of the knowledge, and he did not care. Let her take advantage of him. Better him than some other man, for he loved her more than life itself.

So he worked every day on the house, and the house was not like one he would have built in Spain. One built a house of the materials at hand, and in the country of the Real People there were many trees. Trees were everywhere.

As he had done at New Town, he would build a house of logs. The Real People built their own homes of logs, but the logs were small. The houses were small. He had built a large log house at New Town, and he would build another here at Dahlonega.

He prepared the land for the house, then laid a foundation of stones. Next he cut trees and trimmed them, and he piled up logs. Some days he wondered if he would finish before War Woman returned, and then he redoubled his efforts. *The house must be ready for her to come home to. It will be ready,* he told himself.

He had other assignments, too. War Woman had told him to keep a sharp eye on El Gordo and the soldiers. The soldiers would not be a problem, were it not for their *capitán,* for a leader leads in many ways, and one of the ways he leads is with his attitude toward the people and things around him. El Gordo was disrespectful toward the people of Dahlonega, and therefore the soldiers were also disrespectful. That was one of the main reasons for War Woman's trip. She wanted to have El Gordo replaced as the *capitán* of the soldiers there at Dahlonega. In the meantime, she was worried that there might be more trouble. Morales had to watch for that.

During the first few days of her absence, Morales was curious to note that El Gordo and the soldiers were all pretty quiet. They kept to themselves. They bothered no one. They were not surly, nor were they gregarious. They were quiet and—well, formal.

Then Morales noticed that El Gordo began to appear nervous. He seemed to look south frequently, as if he were watching for someone or something to come from that direction. Morales wondered if the *capitán* had figured out the purpose of War Woman's trip and was watching for the messenger that would bring word of his transfer. But it was much too soon for that.

In the next few days, El Gordo became more and more restless, and Morales therefore became more and more curious. He spent more time watching El Gordo—discreetly, of course. He could tell that El Gordo was agitated about something. *What could it be?* he wondered. He thought about just asking, but then, he figured, if El Gordo wanted to share some concern with him, he would. If not, he would not answer a question put to him about it. So Morales just kept watching.

Early one morning, Morales watched as El Gordo sent out four mounted soldiers. They rode south from the camp. El Gordo stood staring after them as they rode off. Morales, trying his best to appear casual, strolled over to the side of El Gordo.

"*Buenos días,*" he said.

"Uh, *buenos días, amigo,*" El Gordo answered, but he was obviously still thinking of something else. He merely glanced at Morales and continued to look after the four soldiers.

"Where are they going?" Morales asked, still trying to seem casual about it, as if he really weren't interested but was just making conversation.

El Gordo shrugged. "Ah, just a routine scouting mission," he said. "I don't want them to get rusty, just sitting around here. It's nothing."

Morales did not believe El Gordo but kept that opinion to himself. Soon he took his leave and went back to watching the mine, but he was also watching Gros. In fact, he was watching Gros more than he was watching the mine.

THE *CAPITÁN* hardly moved from his spot, the same spot from which he had seen the four men away that morning. He had been there at noon, and he was still there in the middle of the afternoon. He was there, too, at dusk when the four men at last returned leading a saddled but riderless horse. Here was something Morales would not have to pretend about. Anyone would be interested in this alarming news. He ran to join El Gordo and meet the returning riders.

When the men were close enough for shouting, one of them called out the news. "It's Romero's *caballo,*" he said.

Morales looked at El Gordo. "Romero?" he said.

"*Sí,*" said El Gordo. "I didn't want to say anything before, but now I can't keep any secrets about it. Romero was gone. He took the *caballo.* It was unauthorized. I sent these men out to look for him."

Just then the riders arrived close to their *capitán.* They halted their mounts and climbed wearily down out of their saddles.

"It's Romero's *caballo,* Capitán," said one.

"Yes. I see," said El Gordo. "And Romero?"

"We saw nothing of him. This *caballo* was loose, and it was coming back this way. It was coming home."

"When did you meet the *caballo?*" asked El Gordo.

"It was about noon."

"All right. Take care of the *caballo,* then go take care of yourselves and your own horses. Get a good night's sleep. You're going out again in the morning. Be prepared to stay longer if you have to. Be prepared to make a camp for the night. I want you to find Romero and don't come back without him. He's a deserter."

"*Sí,* Capitán."

LYING alone in his bed that night, Morales thought about the incident with Romero's horse. Had the man deserted because of his chastisement? Because he had been forced to pay the woman he had insulted? And when had he deserted? Could he have ridden out just after War Woman had started her trip to La Florida? Was he blaming her for his own humiliation, and if so, was he riding out to wreak revenge on her?

But his horse had come back alone. That would seem to indicate something had happened to Romero. He might have met with some kind of accident. If so, it could have happened either before or after he had caught up with War Woman. If he had been pursuing her at all. On the other hand, perhaps he had gone after her and caught up with her and she had prevailed. That, Morales thought, was certainly a possibility.

He worried, but not much more than he had been worrying all along. Eventually he drifted off to sleep.

❧

THE four soldiers rode out again early the following morning, and El Gordo watched them go, but this time he did not stand and watch all day. This time he went back to his own tent. He went about his business for the rest of the day as if it were a normal day, a day like any other day. Was he relaxed, Morales asked himself, because of Romero's horse?

Morales considered what El Gordo had said and then considered El Gordo's actions and moods. The *capitán* had said that Romero was a deserter, and he had sent the four men out to look for him. While waiting for them to return, he had been nervous, worried. When they had returned bringing with them Romero's horse, Gros had relaxed. What could that mean?

El Gordo must have figured, as had Morales, that Romero had been either hurt or killed. Was that why the fat captain had relaxed? That didn't make much sense to Morales. He asked himself if there might be some reason that Romero alive was a problem for El Gordo?

Suddenly Morales wondered whether or not Romero had even really deserted. What if El Gordo had figured out that War Woman was going to La Florida to get Huelga to replace him? What if, in a cowardly attempt to prevent that from happening, he had sent Romero, already disgruntled for his own reasons, to stop her?

With something like that going on, El Gordo would naturally be nervous. Then when it seemed as if Romero was probably dead, El Gordo had relaxed because there would be no evidence against him. Now he simply claimed that Romero had deserted. Romero was a poor scapegoat.

Gros had not accomplished his mission but no one would ever know about his mission. He would still have to face the problem of War Woman's report to Huelga. Gros would still have to deal with that, but he would not be accused of murder or attempted murder.

Again Morales thought of the possibility that Romero had met with an accident and that it could have happened after he had met with War

Woman. In Morales's mind, his wife was not yet safe. He knew that he would not relax until she was safely back home, but all of this was mere speculation—Romero might have just deserted. Still, Morales slept fitfully another night.

◎ᵣ◯

IT WAS early evening of the next day when the four tired soldiers, riding slowly, once again returned to the Spanish camp outside of Dahlonega. This time they brought with them a body, the remains of Eugenio Romero. His neck was broken. Looking at the grisly corpse, El Gordo was remarkably calm.

"Where did you find him?" he asked the men.

"It was a full day's ride from here," answered the soldier in command of the group. "We found him just off the main road. He was lying there at the foot of a hill, a steep, rocky hill. It looked as if he had fallen from the top of the hill."

"Did you see anything else?" El Gordo asked. "Anything to indicate that there might have been a fight, for example? How did he fall from a hill?"

"I don't know how or why he fell, Capitán," said the soldier. "I can't even figure out what he was doing up on that hill in the first place. There's nothing up there. No reason that I can think of for anyone to be up there. We found a small campsite below the hill, but I don't think it was his."

"Why not?"

"It had a very small fire. It was an Indio camp, I think."

"All right," said El Gordo. "What else?"

"Just that Romero had been on the hill with his *caballo*. We found where the *caballo* had waited for him for a while."

Morales heard all this. The camp had been War Woman's, he told himself, and Romero had been on top of the hill to spy on her and to await his chance to attack. That much seemed clear. It also seemed obvious to Morales that El Gordo had been the instigator of all this, but there would be no way to prove it. But the main thing, to Morales, was the fact that the soldiers had found no evidence of a fight and had not found War Woman's body. Romero had not accomplished his mission after all, and War Woman was safe.

29

HEN WAR WOMAN rode into the Spanish settlement, she was greeted like visiting royalty. Servants were sent right away to unpack her horses (she first retrieved the bag of gold and held onto it) and to accompany her to the quarters of Huelga.

He rose to meet her with a wide grin and open arms. "Ah, War Woman," he said, "a great surprise and an even greater pleasure. Where is your husband?"

"Señor Morales is still at Dahlonega," War Woman said. "I made this trip alone."

"Alone?" Huelga echoed, an amazed look on his face. "You came all that way alone?"

"Yes," she said. "Someone had to stay and watch over things."

"But a woman alone on such a trip. Ay, me. You will always amaze me, War Woman." He gestured toward a chair in front of his desk. "Please," he said. "Please sit down. I'll have some food brought in for us."

War Woman seated herself while Huelga stepped to the door and yelled at someone out there to bring a meal for two. He hurried back to his desk and perched himself on its front edge. He looked down at War Woman, still amazed. He has not yet learned that it is rude to stare, War Woman thought, but since she knew that he was ignorant, she did not take offense.

"You amaze me," he said. "You're the most remarkable woman I have ever met. Juan Morales is certainly the most fortunate of men."

"Thank you, Commandante," she replied. She thought about presenting him with the bag of gold right away in order to change the subject, but then she didn't really want to talk about business matters until after they had eaten. She waited. She could handle him easily.

"Yes," Huelga said, "he is certainly a most fortunate man." Then he laughed nervously. "Uh, is your husband well?" he asked.

"He's quite well," said War Woman.

"And your children?"

"They are fine," she said.

"Well then," Huelga began, "may I know why you have made this trip?"

Just then the meal was brought into the room by a black woman, and War Woman was glad for the interruption. Huelga grew silent until the food was laid out and the servant had gone away.

"So," he said, "let's eat."

There was no more talk while they ate, but War Woman noticed that Huelga kept looking at her with what she could only define as desire. He was overweight and slovenly in his dress, and he was wet with perspiration. While he ate, she could see the food he was chewing in his mouth, and grease ran down his chin. She was in La Florida strictly on business, and even if she had been interested in such pastimes, she would certainly not have been interested in such a thing with him. The thought of it alone disgusted her.

When they had finished their meal, Huelga shouted again, and the servant came to clear away the dirty dishes. They waited in silence until she had gone.

"Now, Commandante," War Woman said, "I'll tell you the purpose of my visit. To begin with, the mine is doing very well."

Huelga's eyes lit up at the thought of gold. War Woman stood up, stepped forward, and dropped the bag of gold heavily on the desk in front of him. He stared at it wide-eyed for a moment, grabbed it up, pulled it open, and poured the contents out on his desktop. His hands drew back as if he had poured hot coals out there, and his eyes grew even larger.

"*Madre mía,*" he said. He reached down to touch it. Finally he picked up some nuggets to hold in his hands. "You have done well, War Woman. Very well."

"I brought this little bit to you just as a sample," she said, "to show you what we've found."

"*Gracias,*" he said. "*Muchas gracias.* You came all this way—and alone—to bring me this bag of gold. This sample."

"This small sample," she said. "And to ask a favor of you."

"Oh, lovely lady," he said, "your wish is my command. Tell me what it is you want, please."

"I want you to replace Capitán Gros."

"Consider it done," he agreed, "but may I know why? For my records, you know."

"May I just say that he does not relate well to the people of Dahlonega?"

Huelga shrugged. "Yes," he said. "Of course."

"When I return to Dahlonega," she continued, "I would like to be accompanied by his replacement."

"It will be done," Huelga said. "I have a man in mind. You can meet him in the morning to see if you approve of my choice."

"Thank you," she responded. "And now may I be shown to my quarters? I'd like to get a good rest before I start back in the morning."

"In the morning?" Huelga said. "So soon."

"Yes."

"You should rest for a few days," Huelga protested. "And you should rest your *caballos*."

"I had hoped," War Woman said, "that you would trade me some fresh *caballos* for mine. Mine do need a rest."

"Well, yes, of course," Huelga said. "We can certainly do that. Take all the *caballos* you want. Even so, you should rest yourself."

"I need to get back to Dahlonega as soon as possible," she replied. "I have no time for rest. My husband is a very capable man, but there are some things among my people that are beyond his capabilities. The mine is too important for me to be away from it for too long. Oh yes, I must keep my Runner. He's my favorite *caballo,* and I don't want to trade him off."

Huelga's face wrinkled in thought. "You're anticipating some trouble at Dahlonega?" he asked. "Aren't you? Because of Gros?"

"I need to go back," she said diplomatically.

"Yes, well, I think I understand. All right. All right. I'll have Capitán Lucien Arredondo ready to leave with you first thing in the morning, and I'll have fresh *caballos* as well as your own waiting for you. Consider the fresh ones a personal gift from me. Now if you'll come with me, I personally will show you to your quarters."

"Thank you," she said.

Huelga raked the gold nuggets on his desk back into the bag, pulled the drawstring, and stuffed the bag of gold into a desk drawer. Then he rose and headed for the door. War Woman stood up to follow him out of his office.

Outside, the settlement was still alive. It was yet early evening for the Spaniards and others who lived there with them. People walked to and fro, and War Woman wondered where they could all be going.

Soon she and Huelga arrived at a small house. War Woman wasn't sure, but she thought that it was the same one she had stayed in with Juan Morales on their last visit. Huelga opened the door and stepped aside.

War Woman moved into the darkness of the small room, and Huelga followed, then closed the door behind himself. He stood in silence, breathing heavily. War Woman waited for a moment, giving him a chance to say something, to explain himself. He did not. She turned to face him, and she could see where he was standing, but she could not see his features in the darkness.

"Good night, Commandante," she said, and her voice was cold.

There was another long moment of silence before Huelga answered her.

"Good night," he said, and he walked out of the house and shut the door again. War Woman did not know what disgusted her more—the thought of what Huelga wanted of her or the fact that he was too much of a coward to even say anything about it. She was glad that he was gone.

As she lay in bed that night, she was proud of herself. She was satisfied that she had made a successful trip. She had been attacked along the way, and she had prevailed. She had impressed the insipid *commandante* with the bag of gold from the mine that would not even be in operation had it not been for her, and she had gotten the troublesome El Gordo replaced. To top it all off, she had even repulsed the repulsive, though halfhearted, advances of Huelga, and she would have fresh horses in the morning. She drifted off into a deep and satisfying sleep.

WAR WOMAN woke up early feeling much refreshed. She washed herself as best she could from a bowl of water there in the house. She would much have preferred going to the water outside. There was a stream nearby, but it had been dirtied by the Spaniards. Besides, the white men did not understand the practice of the Real People in going to the water in the mornings. They only enjoyed ogling the naked women. She would not allow them to make eyes at her body and joke with each other about what they saw. She dressed herself and left the little house.

Outside, she was surprised by the sight of the horses, her own and two new ones, one loaded, another saddled. They were being held in readiness for her, along with four other saddled horses, by three soldiers. Off to one side, a young soldier stood. He stiffened as War Woman made her appearance, and he stepped forward to meet her.

"*Buenos días,*" he said. "I am Capitan Lucien Arredondo. I have been ordered by the *commandante* to greet you this morning."

"Good morning, Capitán," she said, and she smiled. He was a very pleasant young man. War Woman formed her impressions of people quickly, and she was proud of the fact that those first impressions were seldom wrong. This one would do, she told herself.

"Your *caballos* are ready to go," Arredondo said, "and I am to accompany you, along with these three *soldados,* to become the replacement for Capitán Gros—unless you have any objections to that. If you do, I'm to report them to the *commandante* and he'll find someone else."

"That won't be necessary, Capitán," said War Woman. "I'm sure that you'll do very well. But the other three men—"

"The *commandante* said that for such a long trip, and with such an important person as yourself, we should have protection."

"That was very thoughtful of the *commandante,*" War Woman said, again with a smile.

"Then," Arredondo said, "if everything meets with your approval, these men and I are at your disposal."

"The *commandante* is not coming out this morning?" War Woman asked. Even though he had said that he would see her off, she knew that he would not make an appearance, and she knew the reason. She found it all rather amusing.

"He sends his apologies," Arredondo said. "Some important matters came up, and he will not be able to bid you farewell in person. If there is yet some matter you need to see him about—"

"No," War Woman said. "There's nothing. Everything has been done, and I'm ready to get started. Shall we go?"

"*Sí, señora,*" said Arredondo. He turned to face the *soldados* and barked out an order. Two of the *soldados* moved forward, leading saddled horses. The young captain took the reins of War Woman's horse, then held the animal for her while she got into the saddle. Then he moved back to his own *caballo,* took the reins from the other soldier, and mounted up. The three soldiers then mounted. Each had another horse to lead: the resting packhorse, the loaded packhorse, and Runner. Arredondo moved up alongside War Woman. With a wave of his arm, he started the little caravan moving out of the Spanish settlement.

War Woman, feeling very smug, was on her way back to Dahlonega.

She thought about what her reception would be like. Juan Morales and her children would all make a fuss over her. They would be delighted just at her safe return. The children especially would care nothing for what she had accomplished. They would care only that their mother was home.

But Morales would also be concerned about the business of her trip. When he realized that she had successfully gotten El Gordo replaced, he would be very proud of her indeed. El Gordo, on the other hand, would not be pleased at all. She tried to imagine what the fat captain's reaction to the news might be.

She was fairly certain that El Gordo had been behind the crude attempt on her life. He would wonder just how much she had told the *commandante* and would be afraid of what was about to happen to him on his return in disgrace to the colony. Would he be desperate enough to resort to violence again?

The Raven would be pleased, though, along with all the residents of Dahlonega. None of them liked El Gordo anyway, and with good reason. They would all be happy to know that she was bringing his replacement and that El Gordo would be out of their lives for good.

❧

THE return trip was an uneventful, though tiring, one, and the entry into Dahlonega was just about as War Woman had imagined it would be. After she had hugged her husband and her children, she put her official manner back on to introduce Arredondo to the Raven and then to the others. El Gordo stood nearby but to one side. At last War Woman took Arredondo to him.

"Capitán Gros," said Arredondo, "I am Capitán Lucien Arredondo. I have been ordered here by our *commandante* to replace you in this command. You are to return with three *soldados* of my choice to our headquarters in La Florida and report immediately on your arrival there to the *commandante*."

War Woman was a little surprised at El Gordo. He stood stiffly, like the Spanish soldiers did when talking to their superiors. He seemed perfectly composed, perfectly . . . military.

"*Sí, Capitán,*" he said. "I will prepare myself for immediate departure. This command is now yours."

"Capitán Arredondo," War Woman requested, "may I speak with Capitán Gros alone for a moment?"

"Of course," said Arredondo, and he turned and walked away.

War Woman looked El Gordo in the eyes for a long moment. She had learned to do that from the white men. Pig eyes, she thought. Appropriate. His countryman had brought the pigs into this land.

"Capitán Gros," she said finally.

He looked at her warily.

"Sí?"

"I don't like you," she said. "I think you know that."

"I know," said Gros.

"And I know," War Woman continued, "what you think of me and of my people. I made this trip to see your *commandante* mainly to have you replaced, and as you have seen, I've succeeded in doing that."

"Yes," he said. "You have. Congratulations, Señora Morales."

"Furthermore," said War Woman, "I believe that the foolish *soldado* who attempted to murder me in my sleep along the road did so at your instigation. But as you know, he did not succeed in his clumsy attempt. He was easy for me to deal with."

"I—"

"Never mind," she said. "I just want you to know that in spite of what I think of you and what I believe you have done, I told your *commandante* only one thing about you. I told him only that you did not relate well to the people of Dahlonega."

War Woman turned and walked away without another word, without waiting for a response from El Gordo. The newly cashiered captain stared after her with his jaw hanging in disbelief.

3 0

ACK AT New Town, Comes Back to Life worried about the Little Spaniard. He had taken the widow of Asquani as his second wife and had taken on the responsibility of her children. He had done so with the blessing of, actually at the suggestion of, his first wife, Guwisti. For it had been Comes Back to Life, when he had still been known as Young Puppy, who had killed his own friend Asquani, the Spaniard. He had not intended to kill Asquani. He had been under attack, and he had heard a noise behind him. Thinking an enemy had come upon him, he had turned and struck, only to discover that it had been his friend coming to aid him. So he had left his friend's wife and two small children without a husband and father. He promised to provide for them, and then Guwisti suggested that Osa become his second wife. Guwisti and Osa got along well and were best of friends, and the Little Spaniard had never been a problem. War Woman, known then as Whirlwind, had been the one to cause them concern. She had been headstrong and selfish as a girl, but since then she had grown into a prominent figure among the Real People. The Little Spaniard, who had always been such a quiet and well-behaved child and young man, had become a drunk. He had become totally dependent on the strong Spanish drink. He would do anything, it seemed, to get it. He was totally worthless.

"Is there anything we can do for him, do you think?" Comes Back to Life asked his two wives one evening. They were sitting outside in front of the house. A small fire burned in front of them.

"There's nothing," said Osa. "Not even War Woman can do anything about him. If she can't make him stop what he's doing, who then?"

"It's that drink," said Guwisti, "that white man's strong drink, that makes him act crazy. Him and those others."

"Can we keep him from the drink?" Osa asked.

Comes Back to Life shrugged. "The trader brings it," he said.

"What if we were to tell the trader that he is no longer allowed to bring the drink in here?" Guwisti asked.

Comes Back to Life and Osa looked at Guwisti, then at each other.

"If there were no Spanish drink here," Comes Back to Life said, "then the Little Spaniard and his friends could not drink it, and if they did not drink it, they wouldn't act the way they do."

"I think that you should talk to Olig'," Guwisti said.

"I will," said Comes Back to Life.

❧

THE next morning, Comes Back to Life found Olig' still at his home. He announced himself and told the war chief that he had something to discuss with him. They sat together in front of Oliga's house and smoked their pipes. At last, Comes Back to Life spoke.

"I was talking with my wives," he said. "We were talking about our son, the Little Spaniard."

Olig' frowned. "That's a sad case," he said. "As a young man, he showed much promise. Now—"

"Yes," said Comes Back to Life. "We talked among ourselves, wondering if there was anything we could do."

"The relatives of all the young men who are like him are also worrying about them," Olig' said. "No one knows what to do about it."

"My first wife asked me if we could stop the trader from bringing the drink here," Comes Back to Life said. "You're the war chief. The trade is your business, not mine."

Now Oliga's brow wrinkled in thought. He put a hand to his forehead. Olig' had never been a deep thinker, and he did not like problems. He was a man of action, a good man in a fight, a good leader of men in a fight—those were the qualities that had elevated him to the position of war chief of New Town. Sometimes he wished that he had not been given such an honor and such responsibility or that his responsibilities had only to do with war. But they did not. They were more than that. Anything that had to do with outsiders was his business: war, treaties, alliances, trade. The internal life of New Town was the business of Comes Back to Life, the peace chief.

"Do I have such authority?" Olig' asked. "I don't think so."

Comes Back to Life puffed on his pipe and allowed clouds of blue-gray smoke to obscure his face from the vision of his friend. "No," he said. "I don't think so either, but you do have the authority to call a council. At a council meeting you could ask the people what they think of this idea. If they decide that the Spanish trader can no longer bring his drink in here, then he'll have to stop bringing it. That's all."

"Yes," said Olig'. "You're right, of course. I'll call a council."

ALL the people of New Town gathered at the seven-sided town house. Each of the seven sides was designated for one of the seven clans of the Real People, and the people sat in their clan sections. A fire burned in the center of the large room, and in spite of the smoke hole at the center top of the roof, much of the smoke stayed inside. That, combined with the smoke of many pipes, filled the town house air with smoke.

The atmosphere was also charged with anticipation, for the Real People had much personal freedom. Everyone knew that the meeting had been called to discuss curtailing that freedom. As Oliga stood up to address the crowd, all the talk ceased. Everyone looked toward Olig'. He opened with the proper formalities, then started to talk about the reason for the meeting.

"Several different people have talked with me about what the Spanish drink is doing to some of our young men," he said. "No one seems to know what to do about this problem. Mothers have talked to their sons. Wives have talked to their husbands. It makes no difference to them. If they have been captured by the drink, they don't listen. They are also becoming good for nothing. If they have anything of value, they trade it for the drink. Then, when they have nothing left to trade, they beg from their families for something of value, so that they can get more drink from the trader when he comes.

"Someone asked me if we can tell the trader that his drink is no longer allowed in here at New Town. If we tell the trader that he can no longer bring the drink, then our young men can no longer get it. They will no longer get drunk. Maybe they'll once more be the way they used to be. Maybe they'll be worth something again.

"I said that I alone do not have that kind of authority. I cannot take it on myself to tell the trader not to bring his drink in here. To do something like that, we need to have a meeting of the people. We need all of you, the whole population of New Town, to agree. If we all agree, then we can stop him from bringing in the drink, and we can stop our young men from ruining their lives."

When Olig' stopped talking, the Little Spaniard stood up from his place in the back row of the section for his adopted Bird Clan.

"It is no business of anyone else," he said, "what I drink. No one has a right to tell me or any other person of New Town what we can and cannot pour into our own mouths. This council should be ended. It was called for a foolish reason."

A woman in the Wolf Clan section stood up. "Of course he's talking that way," she said. "He's one of them. He's one of the drunkards. He's the one, in fact, who started it all. He got my son to drinking with him, and now I don't even know my own son anymore."

A man stood up in the Deer Clan section. "I don't drink the Spanish drink," he said, "and I am disgusted with those who do. I understand what this mother just said, but I cannot agree that we should try to control these young men by law. The problem is a problem of their behavior, and such a problem is the clan's business. Their mothers' brothers should find a way to straighten them out."

The meeting went on and on. It seemed as if every citizen of New Town had an opinion and wanted to voice it. After a while, the Little Spaniard and his friends left. They were impatient with the long meeting, with all the talk. They were disgusted by the proposition before the people and were tired of listening to arguments of those who would control their activities. They thought that no one could convince a majority of the Real People of any town to agree to such extreme measures, and so they left. They had expressed their opinions, their disgust with what some crazy people of their town were trying to do, and were confident that those few crazies would be laughed out of the town house. They went out to get drunk.

Back in the meeting, the arguments went on. Mothers cried or raged. Young wives told about throwing their husbands out of their homes. Mothers talked about having their worthless sons come back home to live off of them again after their wives had thrown them out. One by one, the opposition voices ceased. Some of the more liberal among them perhaps had been convinced. Others just tired of speaking out. It was late at night when no one was speaking anymore except those who wanted the Spanish liquor banned from New Town.

Olig' waited a respectable time, making sure that no one else wanted to speak the other opinion. Then he at last declared that since there was no longer any opposition, the council of New Town had passed a new law. No longer would the Spanish traders be allowed to bring their strong drink into New Town. Those who had opposed the measure were not visibly outraged by this action. They were quiet. Those in favor of the measure were elated. *Perhaps now,* the mothers thought, *we will have our sons back the way they used to be. Perhaps everything will be all right.*

❦

THE Little Spaniard and his friends were outside of town at the lean-to they had built for their gatherings, the place that had for all practical purposes become their home. They laughed and scoffed at the foolishness of Olig' and the old women who supported his position. No one in his right mind, they agreed, would ever think that a town of Real People could be convinced to adopt such a coercive measure.

"Olig' was once a good man," said the Little Spaniard, "and a good war chief, but now he's old. He needs to be replaced."

They drained a crock and opened another. There were three crocks left. They wouldn't last much longer.

"When is Urbanez coming back to town?" One-Eye asked.

"Maybe four more days," said the Little Spaniard. "I think four more days."

"I think maybe you're right," agreed Meadowlark. "Four days more."

The Little Spaniard took another drink, and then he looked at their stash of three crocks. A worried expression darkened his worn features.

"I don't know if we can make this last four more days," he said. "If we can't make it last, we'll all be hurting by the time Urbanez arrives with more."

Since they had left the council early, they could not know that Urbanez would not be allowed to trade with them anymore for his rum. They drank some more, until they had forgotten about any future worries, until all of them had passed out. Then they slept the deepest of sleeps the living can sleep.

31

 RBANEZ was nearing New Town when Oliga and some other men suddenly appeared on the road blocking his path. He was startled and nearly reached for his belt pistol, but good sense made him hesitate. Instead he forced a friendly smile.

"My friends," he greeted them, "what is the matter here?"

"We have a new law," said Olig'. "Your strong drink is no longer allowed in New Town. You must leave it here or turn around and go back where you came from."

"If I leave it here," Urbanez said, "what will prevent someone from taking it?"

Olig' wrinkled his brow in thought. That was a very good question. Of course, the Little Spaniard and his friends would do that. They would do almost anything to get the drink and, if they were to meet Urbanez in town and find out that he had no drink, would surely discover that he had been forced to leave it behind on the road.

"I'll leave these men here to guard it until you return," Olig' agreed. "You'll be on your way then, and you can pick it up and take it back with you."

Urbanez thought for a moment, trying to come up with some argument, but he found none. The trade in rum was lucrative for him, but he knew better than to try to defy a law of the Real People. He also knew what had become of the Little Spaniard and other young men from New Town. He really couldn't blame Olig' and the others for what they were doing. With a sigh, he swung a leg over his horse's back and dismounted.

"I'll unload it here beside the road," he said.

The rum business had been doing so well that Urbanez had brought two extra pack mules with him this trip, each carrying nothing but two kegs of rum. He unburdened the beasts and tied them there beside the kegs. Then he looked at Oliga.

"All right?" he asked.

"Let's go into town," Olig' said.

Olig' and Urbanez rode into New Town side by side, and the people, first noting the smug look on the face of Olig' and thereby deciding that he had been successful, smiled and prepared themselves for an exciting day of trading with the Spaniard.

The Little Spaniard and his surly friends lurked about the fringes of the crowd, craning their necks in vain attempts to locate the liquid they desired. They had somehow missed the trader on the road, so in order to get their *ron* they had to deal in town.

"I don't see any," one of them said.

The Little Spaniard then grew bold and shoved his way forward through the crowd. Rudely he stepped in front of someone to face Urbanez.

"Where is the *ron?*" the Little Spaniard demanded.

"There is none," Urbanez said.

"What do you mean, there is none?" the Little Spaniard roared. "You always bring *ron*. Where is it?"

Olig' appeared just then beside Urbanez. He drew himself up tall and puffed out his chest.

"There will be no more strong Spanish drink in New Town," he said. "It's our new law."

The Little Spaniard for a moment looked as if he would leap at Olig', strike him, or at the very least shout in his face. He leaned forward, trembling, holding himself back from violence. He made strange noises as if trying to speak—or trying to keep himself from speaking and saying something that would get him in trouble. He was dumbfounded and horrified. He could not believe what was happening. They could not thus tamper with his personal freedom. Suddenly he turned and rushed away. His companions all followed him.

ʕ₊ʃ

BACK at the lean-to they gathered. The Little Spaniard sat on the ground sulking, his knees drawn up to his chest, his arms hugging his knees.

"What did Olig' say to you?" asked One-Eye.

"Did he say there is no *ada yuhs desgi?*" Meadowlark asked.

The Little Spaniard did not speak. He pulled his knees up tighter into his chest. His sulk had become a vicious scowl. The others saw his expression and questioned him no more. He was angry, and he wanted a drink, and that, they knew, could be a dangerous combination. He wanted a drink badly, and he was outraged that Olig', or anyone, would dare to impose such an unfair and arbitrary law on him—on any Real Person. At long last he spoke.

"What Oliga said to me," he said, "is that there will be no more *ada yuhs desgi* in New Town. No more *ron.*"

"You mean the trader did not bring any with him on this trip?" One-Eye asked. "He always brings it. Why didn't he bring any this time?"

"They have told the trader that he cannot bring any," said the Little Spaniard. "Not ever again. They have made it against our law."

"Can they do that?" Meadowlark asked.

"It's not right," the Little Spaniard said, "but they've done it. They did it at the instigation of Oliga, our war chief."

"Oh-h," One-Eye moaned.

"I'm sick," said Meadowlark.

"What will we do?" asked yet another of the crowd. "Is there someplace else we can go to get some?"

"I'm thinking," said the Little Spaniard.

One-Eye lay down on the ground and rolled back and forth holding his stomach and groaning. Meadowlark paced. Another stood staring at the Little Spaniard.

Suddenly the Little Spaniard got to his feet. "Urbanez could not have known," he said.

"What?"

"The trader could not have known about the new law. They only just told him. He must have brought some *ada yuhs desgi* with him."

"Then where is it?"

"It's hidden somewhere."

Now the Little Spaniard paced, one arm across his chest, one fist against his forehead, deep in thought. He stalked the length of the lean-to, then back again.

"He must have brought some with him," he said. "When he came to town, Olig' told him that he can no longer trade the *ron* with us. But I didn't see any *ron* anywhere. Perhaps Olig' and some others stopped him before he got to town and made him leave it out there someplace."

"Let's go find it!" One-Eye shouted.

All of them were suddenly joyous at the thought that they might find the rum hidden along the road somewhere. Following the Little Spaniard through the woods, they raced off in the direction of the road.

THE guards Olig' had left with the rum ran all the way back to town. They had an important message to deliver, and what they would have to say might be interpreted as failure on their part. They were probably a little worried about that, but not too much. They felt like they had done the only right thing under the circumstances. They'd had no choice in the matter. In town, they found Olig' standing near the trader, Urbanez, and ran right up to him. Oliga's face registered astonishment, for he knew that they had been left to guard the rum.

"What's happened?" he demanded of them.

One of the men stepped forward.

"The Little Spaniard and the other drunks came," he said. "They said they wanted the *ada yuhs desgi.* We told them about the new law, but the Little Spaniard said that they didn't care about that. We said that we had been told to guard it, but then they were going to fight us for it. We didn't want to kill Real People over this white man's property."

Oliga was befuddled for a moment. He dismissed the former rum guards with a wave of his hand. Then he moved over close to Urbanez, who was busily negotiating with a woman over a mirror. Olig' leaned in close to the trader's ear.

"The drunkards have stolen your drink," he said.

"What can we do about it?" Urbanez asked.

"Let's go see," said Olig'. Then he called a temporary halt to the trading and led Urbanez away to find Comes Back to Life.

"Your adopted son has done a bad thing," Olig' said. "He and his friends have stolen the trader's *ada yuhs desgi.* I think that now that we have a law about it in town it's under your authority, but I'll go with you to investigate, if you want me to."

Comes Back to Life glanced at Guwisti and Osa, who were both standing nearby with worry wrinkling their brows. Without a word, he started walking.

"Let's go," he said.

THE Little Spaniard and his companions had broken into one of the rum kegs and were dipping the rum out with their cups. The kegs were heavy, and they had decided that they could drink right there. They could not carry the kegs off, and they did not want to bother strapping them on the backs of the waiting mules. Besides, they had rum now. Nothing else mattered to them, and one place was good as another to get drunk.

They felt wonderful as the first swallow burned its way down their throats, and then none of them felt sick anymore, as the liquor seeped all through their bodies. The Little Spaniard was no longer surly. He smiled as he drank. Everything was all right once again. He had no more animosity for Oliga or Urbanez or anyone else in the world. The world was a wonderful place to be. It would be—for a while.

"I'm glad the white men came," he said. "They brought us this fine drink."

They all laughed and all agreed with him and they all drank some more. Then the Little Spaniard straightened himself up, puffed out his chest, and put a stern and serious expression on his face.

" 'There will be no more *ada yuhs desgi* in New Town,' " he said pompously.

The others laughed uproariously. One-Eye laughed so hard that he fell right over on his back and rolled on the ground.

" 'This is not something to laugh at,' " said the Little Spaniard. " 'This is a very serious matter. Some of our young men have become no good for anything at all. They have become drunkards and it's all because of that drink the Spaniards brought, that *ada yuhs desgi, that ron.* It will no longer be allowed in New Town.' "

He tipped up his cup and emptied it, then staggered back toward the opened keg. His companions all laughed.

"In New Town," One-Eye said.

"Yes, of course, in New Town," the Little Spaniard agreed. He shoved his arm down into the rum, bringing out a full cup and a dripping arm. "I said that. There will be no more *ada yuhs desgi* in New Town."

"But we're not in New Town," said Meadowlark, his speech already slurring a bit. "We're out here on the road. We're not anyplace."

The Little Spaniard stopped and feigned a perplexed look. He touched fingers and a thumb on his forehead as if in deep thought.

"That's true," he said. "I hadn't thought of that. Well then, I suppose it's all right to get drunk out here. Even for a war chief."

He took a gulp from his cup, and again his companions burst into laughter. They were all enjoying the rum and their own jokes so much that the horses were upon them almost before they knew anyone was coming. Startled, they looked up to see Oliga, Comes Back to Life, and Urbanez, and they ran to the side to avoid being trampled by the big *sogwilis.*

"What are you doing here?" the Little Spaniard said. "Leave us alone."

Comes Back to Life dismounted and stepped up close to the Little Spaniard. He looked his adopted son hard in the face, and the Little Spaniard withered a little under the threatening look. Then he braced himself up and stared back.

"You're my son," said Comes Back to Life, "but—"

"I'm not your son," the Little Spaniard snapped. "I'm the son of Asquani, the Spaniard, whom you killed."

The cruel rebuff stung Comes Back to Life. He took a deep breath and continued looking hard at the Little Spaniard.

"I raised you as if you were my son," he said. "I've thought of you as a son. But I cannot condone your behavior. You've caused me and your mother much sorrow lately, but this thing you've done today is the worst yet. You know of our new law."

"Ha!" said the Little Spaniard. "We are not in New Town."

"That law was meant to govern the behavior of the citizens of New Town," Comes Back to Life said. "But even if it only applies to what you do inside the walls of New Town, you've done something else. You've stolen this man's goods."

"We found this out here on the road," said the Little Spaniard. "We assumed that it belonged to the Little People, and we told them that we were going to use it."

"Worse and worse," said Comes Back to Life. "Now you're lying, for there were men here guarding this, and they came into town and told us that you threatened to fight them for it."

"Maybe they're the liars," said the Little Spaniard.

Comes Back to Life heaved a heavy sigh and turned away from his adopted son. He stepped over to stand beside Olig', who had also by this time dismounted.

"I think there's been enough talk here," Comes Back to Life said. "I think this has become a matter for the council to consider." Then he turned toward Urbanez, who still sat in his saddle. "I myself will pay you for your loss," he said. Then he looked again at Olig'.

"We'll have to take them back to town," Olig' said. He stepped toward the Little Spaniard.

The Little Spaniard braced himself. "We're not going to town," he said. "We're not going anywhere with you."

32

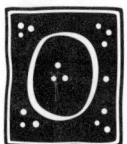LIGA TOOK another step toward the Little Spaniard, and the Little Spaniard struck out, smashing his cup on the side of Oliga's head. Olig' screamed, as much in surprise as in pain, and reached for the wounded spot with his right hand as he sank to his knees.

"What have you done?" shouted Comes Back to Life, running toward the Little Spaniard.

The Little Spaniard braced himself to take on his adopted father, but before Comes Back to Life could reach him, two others began pounding on him with their cups and then, as he fell, with sticks and rocks.

Urbanez kicked his horse's sides and raced forward, scattering the assailants momentarily. But the Little Spaniard picked up a fist-sized rock as the trader rode past him and turned and threw it with all his might and with fine accuracy. It bounced hard off Urbanez's head, and the Spaniard fell out of his saddle like a dead man. He hit the ground hard and did not move.

Then the Little Spaniard and his companions all began to beat and kick the three helpless men on the ground. At last, out of breath, the Little Spaniard stopped and backed away, realization of what he had just done sinking into his fuzzy brain just a little.

"That's enough," he said.

Some of his companions kept kicking.

"*Eliqua!*" he shouted, and they stopped and looked at him for further direction.

"Now," he said, "we'll have to load the *ada yuhs desgi* onto these stupid animals, these *digali-yanuh-hida,* and get it away from here. Others might come from New Town to see what's happened here. Come on."

None of these men had ever before even attempted to load kegs onto mules. They looked at the mules and the ropes and straps that they knew

Urbanez had used for that purpose. They wrestled the kegs over beside the mules. Then, exhausted, they each had another drink.

Urbanez came awake, but he was thinking clearly enough that he did not immediately raise his head. He chose not to call attention to himself. He lay still listening, and he could hear the drinkers over by his mules. Slowly and carefully, he moved his head to take a look. He located them in his vision, and he saw that they were paying no attention to him. He looked back the other way, and he saw, lying on the ground not far from him, both Oliga and Comes Back to Life. They looked a mess, battered and bloody. Neither one moved at all. Urbanez did not know if they were dead or alive.

He looked back toward the Little Spaniard and the other drinkers and decided to take a chance. He could probably get up and get to his horse before they would notice. Once in the saddle, he could get beyond their reach almost at once. He knew that he must hurry back to New Town and tell the people there what had happened. He wondered whom he would tell, with both town chiefs lying alongside the road unconscious, maybe dead.

He looked once more from the drinkers to his horse, and then he got himself to his feet, staggered once, quickly got control of himself, and ran to the waiting animal. At first it shied. He stopped and talked to it quietly, glancing over his shoulder, expecting to discover angry pursuit. Seeing none, he turned his attention back to the horse. He was able to get ahold of the reins, and he had just managed to get a foot in a stirrup when he heard a voice call out from behind him.

"*Ni!*" One-Eye cried. "Look. The white man is escaping."

"Ah, let him go," said the Little Spaniard. "We need to get out of here with these stinking *digali-yanuh-hida.*"

Urbanez lashed at his *caballo* and raced onto the road, turning back toward New Town as fast as he could go. His head pounded as he rode, from the bump he had gotten when the Little Spaniard hit him with a rock. Urbanez, of course, did not know what had hit him, just knew that something had. He only remembered riding into the fray in an attempt to save the two town chiefs and then waking up on the ground.

He lashed harder at the horse, hoping to reach the walls of New Town before he grew faint again. He could not recall a time when he had ridden a horse so hard, and he was afraid that he might be doing it irreparable damage. It wasn't far back to New Town, but it was far enough to be a long ride for a horse when it was a hard ride all the way. A *caballo* was only good for short distances if ridden hard. He knew that. Still, fearing for his own life, he drove it on.

Behind him were a half-dozen or so angry, drunken Indios. They might already have killed their own town chiefs, and surely after having done that they would think nothing of killing a Spaniard. He rounded a corner in the road, and ahead he saw the walls of the town. Still he did not slow down until had almost run up into the passageway that would lead him inside the walls.

He dropped off the horse, leaving it to fend for itself, and staggered into New Town. At first no one seemed to notice. Then a woman shouted something he could not understand. The next thing he knew, he was surrounded by Chalakees, all jabbering at him. He wished that his partner, Morales, hadn't gone off digging for gold. Morales could understand this gibberish. He could not. Not well. Only a few words.

And then there was that wife of Morales. She could always take control of a situation, it seemed. Oh, why were they not around at such a time? Then someone shouted and the people quieted a bit, and a woman edged her way through the curious and somewhat alarmed crowd to stand in front of Urbanez.

"Señor," she said. "Señor."

Urbanez could hardly believe his ears. "You speak Spanish?" he asked.

"Sí," she said. "But you're hurt."

"Not too badly," he said. "First, someone must go down the road to where my mules and my rum were left. The drunkards have beaten your two chiefs and left them lying beside the road. I ran away. I don't know if they're alive or dead."

Osa tried to ignore the painful fact that one of the drunkards—their leader, in fact—was her own son. She raised her voice and told the crowd in the language of the Real People what Urbanez had said. There was an immediate uproar and some wailing, and then several men went rushing out of town through the narrow passageway. Osa put an arm around Urbanez to help support him.

"Come with me," she said. "We'll tend to your wounds."

❧

THE Little Spaniard led the way through the thick woods. His muddled brain was working well enough for him to know that he and his friends were in deep trouble for what they had done to Oliga and Comes Back to Life. He was going through the woods, but not in the usual way. He was not headed for the lean-to that had become his home. They would look for him there. He wasn't at all sure where he was going.

The way was rough, and the undergrowth in this part of the woods was thick. Small branches and vines cut at his arms, legs, and face. He fought his way through them. Behind him his companions muttered and complained, but they followed, and they led the mules, rudely loaded with the rum kegs. The kegs bounced loosely on the sides of the abused pack animals, and the rum inside sloshed. The one keg they had busted open spilled its contents with every jog until the rum was down too low to do so anymore.

Then one mule, caught in a particularly troublesome tangle of brush, brayed and complained and balked. The man with the lead rope pulled and threatened the mule, and One-Eye got behind to push. The mule complained more loudly and kicked out with its hind legs, caving in the left ribs of One-Eye, who had been tormenting it from the rear.

One-Eye screamed and collapsed, and the mule broke loose, knocking the keg on its right side into the trunk of a tree. The keg fell and smashed, and all of the rum was spilled onto the ground. Everyone not holding a lead rope, except One-Eye, ran to try to get control of the errant mule and save the other keg, which by this time was dangling beneath the poor animal's belly. At last they calmed the mule, but of course they could not lead it anywhere, not with a large keg hanging under its belly.

"What are we going to do?" Meadowlark asked.

"Help me," said One-Eye, whining.

"Get that keg up on its back," the Little Spaniard commanded.

Two men started wrestling with it, one on either side. The mule started complaining again.

"It tried to kill me," said One-Eye from his position on the ground. "Don't leave me here to die like this. Give me a drink, at least."

The Little Spaniard looked at the two men who seemed to be getting nowhere with the dangling keg, then at One-Eye, still lying on the ground and whining.

"Let's all have a drink," he said, "and we'll think about these things."

COMES BACK TO LIFE had been badly beaten, but he was alive, and soon after having been carried back to town he was awake. He was cut and bruised and his left arm was broken, but the doctors of New Town treated his wounds, set his broken bone, and sang over him for a speedy return to health. Oliga was dead.

"I can no longer help him," Comes Back to Life said, lying on a cot in Guwisti's house. Guwisti was there, and so was Osa. Osa was not crying. Her face showed no emotion.

"You did everything any father could do for a son," she said. "Because I have no brother here, you did even more. It's not your fault. It's only his own. Not even War Woman could help him now."

"The people of Oliga's clan will demand a life," Guwisti said.

"Yes," said Comes Back to Life. "It's their right and their responsibility."

Osa only stared at the ground in front of herself.

In front of her own house, Tsiwon', the wife of Olig', sat in the dirt, her once beautiful long black hair cropped short. She picked up handfuls of dirt and threw them on her head as she wailed and moaned out loud for all the residents of New Town to hear.

THE funeral was done, and the four days after had passed. It was time. The elders of Oliga's clan had gathered to discuss the matter of retribution for his death. There were few options open to them, and the meeting was more a matter of form than anything else.

A death must be balanced by a death. Had it been accidental or in self-defense, something might have been arranged: a payment to the dead man's survivors perhaps. But, in the case of a deliberate killing, the only thing to do was demand a life in return, preferably the life of the killer.

In this case, there was no question. The Little Spaniard had struck the first blow. Whether that blow had been the one that killed Olig', it mattered little. For that blow was the cause of all that followed—it was the cause of death—and the entire incident had occurred because the Little Spaniard had been trying to circumvent a law passed by the New Town council. He had stolen the trader's goods and, when Oliga had confronted him, had struck Oliga, the war chief of New Town. The men all agreed. The Little Spaniard must die. They would demand it of his clan.

Since the Little Spaniard's mother, Osa, was not a Real Person by birth, she had been adopted by the Bird People, and because his mother was a Bird, the Little Spaniard, too, was a Bird. So these men would go to the Bird People and present their demand for the life of the Little Spaniard. The Bird People could then indicate that they would not interfere with the retribution or they could do the killing themselves. That much would be up to them. They could even offer a life other than that of the Little Spaniard, as long as it was the life of a Bird Person. They could do that if they so chose but it was unlikely they would make that decision in this case.

Probably the elders of the Bird Clan had already reached their decision, even though the demand had not yet been made of them. Like everyone else in New Town, they well knew what had happened. They would have been talking about it already. They would likely have decided already what their answer to the demand would be.

No one expected any trouble. The case was too clear. Oliga's clan would demand the life of the Little Spaniard, and the Bird Clan would agree. Certain members of Oliga's kinsmen would be designated to do the deed, and they would go off in search of the Little Spaniard.

A group of members of the Bird Clan stood waiting. They knew that it was time, and they knew who was coming. Their faces were all long. They stood still, patient, not lamenting, just serious. They watched as the others approached. They waited for the others to speak, and when they had listened to the demand, the oldest man among them gave the answer.

"Go," he said. "Take the life you demand."

In the back of the small group of Bird People, Osa stood. She watched, and she listened. Her face betrayed no emotion.

33

OR SOME unknown or unspecified reason, everyone in and around Dahlonega was testy. The women promised by Huelga had at last arrived, and for a while the soldiers and the free miners were elated over that new diversion. Soon, however, the women themselves became a major new source of trouble. There weren't quite enough of them to go around, and therefore the men argued with each other and fought over them.

The Spanish soldiers grumbled almost constantly, and they argued with each other, it seemed, over just about anything. One afternoon, two of them got into a terrible fight, first pushing and shoving, then scuffling on the ground, wrestling. At last blows were struck. One had a bloody nose. Then, knives had been drawn and before the new captain could separate the angry men, one of them had a bad cut on his right forearm.

The wounded man was lying in his tent moaning and groaning with high fever day and night. His arm was swollen, and the wound had become infected and was festering. His condition and the noise he made over it only exacerbated the already-truculent mood of the troops.

"Flies buzz around him, and he stinks," one of his former comrades said, none too sympathetically.

"He keeps me awake at night with his groaning," another said.

Capitán Arredondo was terribly frustrated with his new command, feeling, perhaps rightly so, that the very serious problems he faced at Dahlonega were not of his own creation but, rather, he had inherited a bad situation from El Gordo.

Then there was the mine. Alvarado was surly because production was down in the mine. It had dropped down to half overnight, then had gone down steadily from there to a trickle. At first, Alvarado had blamed the miners, the slaves, and others working the mine. He lashed out at them verbally and viciously, calling them lazy and worthless, accusing them of trying to undermine his success.

But as time went on and he himself went into the mine to examine the vein more closely, he saw that, indeed, there simply was not as much gold to bring out as there had been. The vein really was playing out on them, and he had not anticipated that, not so much and not this soon. He had to admit that he had seriously overestimated the value of the strike.

Even so, not yet quite willing to admit defeat, Alvarado was hoping that the vein would still get larger again as the tunnel reached deeper into the bowels of the mountain. In a near-frenzy, he ordered the men to dig farther and faster. He worked himself and the others as if they were working under an imminent deadline, in grave though unspecified danger should they fail to meet it. As a result, he and everyone connected with the mine became terribly edgy. They snapped at each other and others at any excuse.

Watching all of this with deep interest, the Raven of Dahlonega grew even more solemn and stern than usual. He had made an agreement, and he was attempting to live up to his word. But it was more and more obvious each day that he did not like what was going on around his town.

Not only were the Spaniards causing unrest, but the rewards to the town were diminishing. The trade goods had been distributed according to the value of the gold being taken from the mine. With less gold coming out, fewer goods were being distributed. The arrangement was no longer worth what it had been.

"It will get better again," Alvarado kept saying.

Of course, the percentage going to War Woman and Juan Morales was less and less as time went on. War Woman could sense that trouble was brewing, and this time she had no one on whom to place the blame. Young Lucien Arredondo seemed to be doing the best he could, and she wasn't at all sure that anyone else could do any better. Even so, it was not good enough.

In the beginning, she had been confident that they would find gold, and she had been right. Now, Alvarado kept saying that the vein would increase again but she wasn't at all sure. She could only hope that he was right as she had no feeling about it one way or the other. She only had a vague feeling that some kind of trouble was ahead, and therefore she worried.

Sitting under the overhanging roof of the big house Juan Morales had built for her, Morales beside her, the children playing nearby under the supervision of Consuela, War Woman mulled these things over in silence. At last she spoke.

"Juan," she said. "Has it been worthwhile for us? This gold mine? What do you think?"

"Well, I—what do you mean?"

"It's been quite a bit of trouble," she said, "and there will be more trouble, I think. I don't know the value of gold. With all the trouble, has it been worth it for us?"

"We're quite rich, my love," Morales replied, "if that's what you mean. So, yes, I suppose you could say it's been worth it."

"And if there's no more gold," she said, "if we've come to the end of it, will you still say so?"

"Yes," he insisted. "We already have much more than I could have earned just as a trader in—oh, five years or so."

War Woman opened her eyes wide in surprise. "So much?" she said. "Yes."

"Then it has indeed been worth it," she said, "and even if it comes to an end soon, it won't matter, at least not to us."

"It won't matter at all to us, my darling," Morales said. "It's been a valuable episode in our lives together. That's all. It needn't be—no, it shouldn't be our whole lives."

"When it is finally over, we can return to our home in New Town," she said. She took a deep breath and let it out as a long sigh. "I'm looking forward to that. I admit it to you. I miss my home. I miss my mother and my father—my adopted father, Comes Back to Life.

"And the Little Spaniard. In spite of what he's become, I miss him. He's my brother, my twin. He's the other half of me." She sat for a moment in silence. "And some others back home, too," she said. "There are others I miss. I'll be glad to see them all again. No, I won't be sorry when this gold-mining business is over."

"Well, it may be over sooner than we think," Morales said. "Alvarez believes that the vein will grow larger again as he digs deeper into the mountain. At least, that's what he says. I'm not so sure. Of course, I'm not a miner." He shrugged and paused for a moment. "Maybe he's right," he continued, "but I don't think so. I don't really think he even believes that himself. I think it's wishful thinking he's indulging in. But he may be right."

"I hope not," War Woman said. "I'm tired of this business, and I'm tired of this place."

❧

CHICO HERNÁNDEZ was a miner. He had been a miner all of his life. The hard work didn't bother him at all. In fact, he liked it, but this job was different from any he had ever had before anywhere, back home in España or in this so-called New World. With this job, he had soldiers all around him all the time, watching his every move, and his boss—the mine supervisor, Alvarado—was some kind of problem, too. He had seemed all right to Hernández for a while, but as soon as the mine's production had slowed, Alvarado had become damned irritable. He could lose his temper over nothing. Did he think it was the fault of the miners? All they did was dig where he told them to.

Then there were the damned Indios. They hadn't actually been any trouble. There had been no fights with them, no incidents, not even any threats or hostile gestures, but they were so damned inscrutable. Hernández couldn't make out what they were thinking, and that irritated him. They stood around stern-faced, watching every move, acting superior to the Spaniards. Especially that War Woman and the one they called the Raven. They didn't want the Spaniards going into their town and getting anywhere near their women. As if the Spaniards were a bunch of goddamned lepers. Ever since that little problem with Romero and the Indio woman . . . and look how poor Romero had been made to pay so dearly for his tiny violation of their etiquette. El Gordo, too, of course, but Romero had paid the ultimate price.

No, there had been no real trouble with the pompous Indios. All the fights that had taken place had been among the Spaniards. That much was true. Still, Hernández simply wasn't . . . comfortable living and working just outside a whole town of Indios. And paying them a share of the gold. They weren't even working for it. Lazy bastards. Hernández worked his ass off for pissant wages. No percentages. No shares.

In a way, he thought, *that's OK. That's just fine, because my wages stay the same, and now the percentage ain't so much.* That thought made him chuckle, but the good mood was momentary and fleeting.

Alvarez seemed to think that the mine would keep producing, would get better again. He could be right. Hernández had seen such things happen before. But this time he surprised himself by wishing secretly that the damned vein would play out completely, so that they would shut down the whole blasted operation and get the hell out of this Indio country. He was damned sick and tired of all the grumbling, all the surliness.

He had just put in an especially hard day's work, and he wanted a few drinks of *ron* and the cozy company of plump Josefina, one of the prostitutes so recently sent up from La Florida.

Back in his own tent, he cleaned himself up a little, took a couple of stiff drinks, then pulled a coin out from under the cot he slept on. He went outside, puffed himself up, and headed for Josefina's tent with thoughts of a joyous romp swimming in his head.

Hernández arrived at Josefina's tent almost simultaneously with Sgt. Jorge Quintana. The two men stopped and looked each other hard in the eyes. Hernández moved first, reaching out with his right hand for the tent flap.

Quintana grabbed Hernández's wrist and gripped it tight. "Me first," he said.

"I was here as soon as you," said Hernández. "A little sooner even. Why should I wait for you?"

"Because I'm a soldier," Quintana retorted, "and a sergeant."

"I'm not a soldier, so your rank means nothing to me," said Hernández. "I'm a miner."

"A soldier is a more important hombre than a miner," said Quintana, "a common laborer. Move aside."

"I've been working hard all day," Hernández said. "What the hell have you been doing besides taking siestas in the sun?"

"That's none of your damned business," Quintana snarled. "Step out of the way now. I'm tired of talking to you."

"All right then," said Hernández. "As you wish. No more talking."

Hernández suddenly swung his left fist low, driving it hard into Quintana's belly. Quintana doubled over, the wind knocked out of him. Hernández brought up his right knee, bashing the sergeant's lips and nose and knocking him over backward. Then the miner stepped back to wait for the soldier to get to his feet.

"Come on, Sergeant," he said. "Important hombre. You want to make me get out of your way? You want to make me wait for you? Come on. Let's see how goddamn tough you really are."

Quintana got slowly to his feet. Blood trickled from his nose and mouth, and he wiped it on his sleeve, smearing it across his face. He stood for a moment glaring at Hernández.

"Bastardo," he snarled. *"Hijo de puta."*

His right hand went for a knife at his waist, and Hernández lurched forward, grabbing Quintana's wrist. Grappling, they fell together to the ground, rolling over and over. A crowd began to gather around them, shouting, cheering them on, anxious to see more blood.

Hernández still held fast with both his hands to Quintana's wrist in an effort to keep the soldier from pulling the knife out of its sheath. Quintana reached for Hernández's face with his free hand, clawing and gouging at the eyes.

"Kill him!" shouted someone in the crowd.

Hearing the noise, Capitan Lucien Arredondo came out of his tent. He looked around quickly, saw the crowd gathered, and knew immediately what was going on. It had happened often enough already. He rushed toward the melee, shouting angrily as he ran.

"Break it up!" he yelled. "What the hell is going on here? Break it up, I say."

He forced his way through the crowd just in time to watch in helpless horror as Hernández, to protect his eyes from Quintana's probing fingers, released his grip on Quintana's wrist with one hand. Quintana wrenched his wrist loose of the other hand and drove the blade of his knife, all the way up to the haft, into the side of the miner. Hernández gasped, then groaned through clenched teeth and rolled away, clutching his bloody side.

Arredondo quickly stepped in between the two antagonists. "Stop it immediately!" he shouted. "This is shameful."

Hernández needed no such order. He was holding his wounded side and writhing in pain on the ground. Two soldiers in the crowd, their commanding officer now present, stepped forward to pull Quintana to his feet and hold him still from behind.

Arredondo took hold of the sergeant's wrist. "Drop the knife," he commanded.

Quintana allowed his bloody knife to fall to the ground. "He started the trouble," he grumbled.

"We'll see about that," said Arredondo. "You're under arrest." Then to the two soldiers holding Quintana, he said, "Take him away."

Off to one side the Raven stood, watching with stern disapproval.

34

 HE LITTLE SPANIARD woke up with a groggy head. He rubbed his eyes, then slowly sat up and looked around. The mules were grazing contentedly not far away. The keg that had been dangling beneath the belly of the one mule was on the ground. The other mule was still loaded. The Little Spaniard knew that he and the others should have unburdened the animal, but they had not done so. He shrugged it off mentally.

He got to his feet laboriously with a groan and stood there relieving his bladder. Then he moved to the keg they had broken open, found a clay cup on the ground, and reached in to dip himself a drink. He was delighted to see that there was still plenty of the stuff in there. He took a healthy swallow, and it cleared his head. Then he looked around some more.

His companions were all lying around on the ground still sleeping it off. Even One-Eye with his bashed-in ribs slept soundly. Slowly the events of the previous day came back into the Little Spaniard's mind, and he realized that he and the others were fugitives. They had beaten up both of their town chiefs and the Spanish trader. Someone would come after them, probably to give them a good beating. They would also try to take the *ada yuhs desgi* away from them and give it back to the trader.

He would have to rouse the others, load the two kegs, and move on— somewhere. They would have to find themselves a new home, a place where the others from New Town would leave them alone. He wondered how far they would have to go to find such a place.

It would also have to be a place from which they would be able to get more *ada yuhs desgi*. The Spanish trader would have to come to that place regularly. He could ask Urbanez where else they could go and still have him visit. But then, they had beaten Urbanez, and he might not

want to talk to them at all. He might not want to do any more business
with them.

Well, the Little Spaniard thought, *Urbanez is not the only trader around.
What about that other one? The one my sister married? Juan Morales. He can't
refuse to help me. Where did he go with my sister? Dahlonega. I wonder how far
it is to Dahlonega. Maybe we should go there.*

But there was a more immediate problem, he knew. He had to
get the others up and moving. They had to get a little farther away
from New Town before the people there came after them. He took
another swallow of the *ada yuhs desgi.* It was good, and he was
tempted to just sit down again and drink some more—until he fell
over again—but if he did that they would catch him and beat him too
easily.

He walked to one of the still-sleeping men and shoved him rudely
with his foot. The man moaned and rolled over. The Little Spaniard
nudged him again, this time a little harder.

"Wake up," he said. "We have to go."

It took a while, but he got them all up and got the mules ready. Then
they headed south—more or less. They avoided the road, because they
didn't want to meet anyone. Traveling was more difficult that way, but
it was safer for them. They had to stop periodically to rest and to have
a few drinks, but they kept going.

"Oh, I'm hurting bad," One-Eye said. He had already fallen behind
the others. He was hugging himself and walking doubled over with the
pain. "I can't go on walking like this."

"What do you want us to do about you?" asked the Little Spaniard.
"Do you want to go back to New Town to be mended? They'll beat you
up more."

"No," said One-Eye, whimpering. "I don't want to go back there."

"What then?"

"Let me ride one of the mules."

"You want to leave some of our *ada yuhs desgi* behind?" the Little
Spaniard asked.

"No," said One-Eye.

"Then quit whining, Broken Ribs," the Little Spaniard said. "Broken-
Ribs-One-Eye. You'll just have to keep up with us the best way you can."

They walked on a little farther and One-Eye fell down. The Little
Spaniard was aggravated, but he did not want to just abandon his
wretched companion.

"All right," he said. "We'll rest a little here. Give him a drink."

They all had a drink, and then they all had another.

"Are we far enough away from New Town yet?" Meadowlark asked.

The Little Spaniard looked around. A steep hill rose to their left. It was covered with trees and thick shrubbery. But there was one dark spot that caught his attention. It appeared to be some sort of depression in the hillside. A cave perhaps.

He wasn't sure how far away from New Town they had gotten, but then, he asked himself, how far would the people be willing to chase them just to give them a good beating—or to get the trader's *ada yuhs desgi* back for him?

"I'm going to look over there," he said.

"What for?" Meadowlark asked.

The Little Spaniard didn't bother to answer the question. He walked toward the hillside. The others stood around the mules and watched him go. He disappeared from their sight soon because of the growth around them, and then they all had yet another drink.

"Will he come back?" One-Eye asked.

"Of course he'll come back," said Meadowlark. "The *ada yuhs desgi* is here with us."

AFTER a difficult climb, the Little Spaniard found the cave. He had been right about the dark spot on the hillside. It would be some trouble to get the kegs and One-Eye up there, but the others shouldn't have much trouble. If they decided to stay, they could clean up a little around the cave and make the trail up the hillside a little more accessible.

It could make a pretty good home. He knew that the others were tired and wanted to stop. He himself wanted to sit down and relax and get drunk. He decided that they were far enough away from New Town. He went back down the hillside and back to the others.

"I found us a place," he said. "Let's go."

One-Eye groaned and complained and the others asked questions that went unanswered, but they all followed the Little Spaniard. He led them a short distance through thick brush to the bottom of the hillside. Then they started climbing. The way was steep. The brush was still thick, and the ground was rocky. The men complained mightily, especially the ones leading the mules, and the mules balked and brayed.

The Little Spaniard urged them on. "Come on. Come on," he said. "It's not far. Come on."

One-Eye again came up last. He moaned with each step. He was on the verge of tears, perhaps because of the pain, perhaps because he felt sorry for himself. No one was taking pity on him. At one point he looked up and saw no one. He had fallen too far behind. He was alone.

"Where are you?" he called. "I don't see anyone." There was desperation in his voice.

"You're OK," came an answer. "Just keep straight on. We're right up here."

He moved a little faster, even though it hurt, trying to catch up. "Wait for me!" he called. "Wait."

Up ahead the mule with the open keg strapped to one side suddenly rebelled. The way was too steep and too rocky. It stopped. The man with the lead rope pulled and shouted. Another man got behind and shoved. The mule brayed a loud protest and reared, but it had not counted on the steepness of the hillside. It fell over backward, barely missing the man behind it. He yelled and threw himself to one side, landing hard and rolling, picking up a number of fresh cuts and bruises.

The mule landed on one keg, smashing it to bits. It rolled over and began sliding down the hillside, the other keg loosening all the way. The poor beast kicked and twisted and finally got itself back onto its belly. It dug into the hillside with its front hooves and finally slowed and stopped. When it scrambled to its feet, the second keg dropped away and rolled down the hill into a thick tangle of brush where it came to a stop—unbroken. Two of the men yelled at the mule and ran after it, as it ran back down the hill.

"Let it go," said the Little Spaniard. "We don't need it."

He squatted down beside the broken pieces of keg and looked at the wet ground where the rum was slowly soaking in and disappearing, and he felt sad at the sight of such a waste. The two men who had started to chase the mule came back up and stood beside him panting.

Then One-Eye at last caught up with them. "What happened?" he asked.

"Never mind," said the Little Spaniard. "Let's go."

Meadowlark pointed toward the unharmed keg sitting down below. "What about that one?" he asked.

"Pick it up and carry it on your back if you want to," said the Little Spaniard. He walked ahead, not looking back.

Meadowlark looked down at the keg of rum on the hillside below.

He stared at it for a moment, then turned to follow the Little Spaniard.

Soon they found themselves in the cave. It was a good one. There was plenty of room, and it was dry. It was also fairly clean. With a minimal amount of work, it would make a good-enough home for them. At the mouth of the cave, they unloaded the other mule. They still had two full kegs, and a third was just down the hill. When they were desperate enough they would bring it on up to their new home. For the time being, everything was just fine.

Unloaded, the second mule began to stray away from the cave. Meadowlark said something about it, but no one made a move to stop it. The Little Spaniard said that they no longer had any use for the stupid animal anyway. Soon it was gone.

They broke open another keg and dipped their cups into it and drank deeply and greedily and gratefully. They had all just suffered the most physical exertion they had endured for months. They'd had a fight, a run, a long walk, and then a steep climb. Along the way, they had to load and unload heavy kegs and fight with stubborn mules. They were exhausted, and they were thirsty.

The rum was very good. There were certain things that should be done, but the good-tasting *ada yuhs desgi* made them forget about those things—or at least not let those things worry them. And they became better companions after a few drinks. When they were sober—or nearly so—as they had been earlier in the day, they snipped at one another. The Little Spaniard ordered them around, and though they usually did as he told them to do, they grumbled and complained.

After a few drinks, they were once again the best of friends. They laughed and joked with each other and had a very good time indeed. They never got angry with one another as long as they had plenty of *ada yuhs desgi.* They were companions, brothers. Yes. They were like a family. And it was a good thing, too, for there was no one else—not their parents or brothers or sisters or former best friends—who understood them as they understood one another.

There in the cave, the first evening in their new home, they drank until they were well relaxed. They joked easily with one another, and even One-Eye, though it hurt his bashed ribs terribly when he did so, laughed heartily at the jokes. They talked about the people in New Town being so stupid as to think that they could stop them from drinking *ada yuhs desgi* by passing a law. Then they laughed at the two old chiefs and the trader coming to try to take the kegs away from them.

"Did you see the funny look on the face of our great war chief," Meadowlark said, "when the Little Spaniard conked him?"

They all laughed.

"The great war chief was no match for us," another said.

One-Eye laughed so hard that the pain from his sides caused tears to run down his cheeks.

"And that other one," said Meadowlark, "he should know better than to try to fight. He's the peace chief. He should have stayed home to pray."

They laughed at that, too. Everything was funny. Everything was good.

"What about that white man?" asked One-Eye, holding his sides and grimacing. "Did you see how he fell from the back of his *sogwili?*"

"Yes," said Meadowlark. "What good is a *sogwili* anyway? It only makes you fall farther when you get hit."

They all roared with laughter at that one, even the Little Spaniard.

"I wonder," he said, "what the good people of New Town will think of their chiefs when they go back into town all covered with marks from the beating we gave them."

"Maybe they'll choose new chiefs," said One-Eye. "Maybe they'll say, 'You can't be our chiefs if you can't even whip those no-good drunks.' "

That line brought the biggest laugh of the whole evening. Tears of laughter ran down everyone's cheeks. Each man had to sit on the ground in order to keep from falling. One-Eye laughed so hard that he thought that his sides would burst open. The pain was terrible. Then his laughter became a choking and then a gagging cough, and he rolled over onto his side, hugging himself, his knees drawn up into his belly. He tried to catch his breath, but he couldn't. He was gasping and hacking, and then he began to heave, and he spit up great gobs of blood, while his comrades all around him continued to laugh at the last joke he had made.

$$35$$

HE LITTLE SPANIARD woke up the following morning the
way he usually did. He was groggy, and he wanted a drink.
He got up onto unsteady legs and carefully made his way to
the keg. The level was not down too much from the festivities
of the night before. He liked the kegs. They held so much that several
men could drink from them for a long time, and they still seemed to be
nearly full.

He found a cup and dipped himself a drink to start the day. It soon
made him feel alive again. He looked around the cave and saw his companions, all still asleep. He was usually the first one to wake up. He
stepped to the mouth of the cave and looked outside. It was a bright,
clear morning. The Sun was already well up toward her daughter's house
on the underside of the great Sky Vault.

Even so, there was a slight chill in the air. He thought casually that
they would have to gather some firewood for the cave. He took another
drink, and then he heard a loud rustling nearby. He looked to his right
and saw two squirrels running around and around the trunk of a tall tree,
one obviously chasing the other. He chuckled.

He knew that the one was female and the other, the one doing the
chasing, was a male. Eventually he would catch her, and then he would
ravish her. That was the way with squirrels.

"Catch her, *saloli*," the Little Spaniard said, and he laughed. He heard
someone stirring behind him in the cave, but he didn't bother turning
his head to see who it was. He didn't care. He didn't really like any of
his companions all that much. It was just that he could have no other
companions. These were men like him. These were the only people with
whom he could live anymore. They all had something very important in
common. It was their love for strong drink and their understanding of
one another.

He thought about his real family: Osa, his mother; Comes Back to Life, the only father he had ever known; and his sister, the one person to whom he had always been close. He thought of her as Whirlwind rather than as the War Woman she had become. Even though she had always had her way, even though she bossed him around, he had always felt as if she was a part of him. They had been that close.

He thought about the days of their childhood and youth and the times they had enjoyed together. He thought about the way in which he had always been so proud of her, almost as if her powers and her accomplishments were his own. Those had been good times, he thought. Then he considered that he had brought an end to those good times with his drinking. He tried to dismiss that thought, but he couldn't.

He did not want to take the blame, though, for his estrangement from his family, especially from his twin. So he thought some more. She was the one who had caused all the trouble after all. She had insisted on the trip to La Florida to meet the Spaniards. That was when he had first tasted the drink. That was also the trip that had cost him his first brother-in-law, a brother-in-law of whom he had been especially proud and fond.

She had then welcomed the Spanish traders to New Town and even married one. Juan Morales. The Little Spaniard did not like Morales. If she could not find another like Daksi, he thought, she should have remained unwed. A Spanish trader.

Even so, he was grateful to the Spaniards, for they were the providers of the *ada yuhs desgi,* the drink that they called *ron.* He'd had enough of this painful thinking. He decided that all he really needed was another cup of the good *ron.* He turned to go back inside the cave and almost ran into Meadowlark. Meadowlark stopped right in front of him and just stood there, still, wearing a long face.

"What is it?" asked the Little Spaniard, his voice betraying a little irritation. "Get out of my way. I'm getting myself a drink."

Meadowlark made a feeble gesture in the direction of One-Eye. The Little Spaniard glanced over that way. One-Eye was not moving. The Little Spaniard gave a casual shrug.

"Let him sleep," he said.

"He's not sleeping," said Meadowlark. "He's dead. Sometime in the night, One-Eye died."

The Little Spaniard looked again at One-Eye. Sure enough, he was lying awfully still. The Little Spaniard pushed his way past Meadowlark and walked over to the keg to refill his cup.

❦

THEY gave poor One-Eye a hasty burial and the best funeral they could provide. They even poured some *ada yuhs desgi* over the grave to help him along the way in his journey to the Darkening Land.

"Will he be able to get *ada yuhs desgi* up there?" Meadowlark asked.

"I don't know," said the Little Spaniard. "We could kill the trader so his Spanish spirit can take some up there for him."

They all laughed at that idea as they made their way back to the cave to have more drinks for themselves. Along the way, the Little Spaniard thought about how terrible his companions were looking. He had not considered it before, had not noticed, but looking at the emaciated body of One-Eye had made him realize that the others looked pretty bad, too. He had not seen himself in a long time, and he wondered if he, too, looked that bad.

He wondered how long it had been since any of them had eaten a meal. They had been living off the drink. He had not thought about that before. He could not recall his last meal—or theirs. But he was not hungry for food. By the time they reached the cave, he had dismissed those thoughts and dipped himself out another drink.

❦

IN New Town, a party of seven men had been formed to search out and bring in the murderer, the Little Spaniard. Their instructions had been clear: Bring him back alive, if you can. Kill him if you must and bring back the body. If it's convenient, beat his companions, but if not, don't worry about them. They don't really matter. According to the tale told by both Comes Back to Life and Urbanez, the Little Spaniard was the one who had dealt the first blow of the fight, and that blow had been the blow that had killed Oliga. The Little Spaniard was the one who would have to pay.

The party left New Town early in the morning. They were well armed, although their leaders said that the arms were unnecessary against the drunks. They could take care of them with bare hands. Even so, they had gone armed.

Their leaders were Woyi and Striker, two old men who had gone through the Friends Making Ceremony years before and had later both married the same woman. Closer than brothers, they had been almost inseparable all that time. They were old, but they were still strong and healthy and had much experience. The young ones would learn something from them. They knew where the killing had taken place, and they went there first. They stopped awhile at the site of the crime to study the signs.

"Right here," Woyi said, "Olig' was struck down by the Little Spaniard. Here he bled and died."

"They knocked him down and then knocked down Comes Back to Life," said Striker. "Here they beat and kicked them while they were down. The trader rode his *sogwili* into their midst right here, and they scattered."

"The mules were here, and the kegs," added Woyi. "The Little Spaniard and his friends put the kegs back on the mules and went off through the woods."

"That way," said Woyi, pointing. "Let's go."

The other five men kept quiet, waiting for the two best friends of forty years or more to make the decisions and give the orders. The young men watched with fascination as the two old men worked together, almost as one man in two different bodies. As Woyi and Striker moved into the woods, the others followed.

After traveling some distance through the woods, the two old friends stopped. The young men gathered around behind them, but not too close. Looking over the shoulders of the older men, the young ones could see what had stopped them: a smashed keg was lying on the ground beneath a tree trunk.

"The mule knocked it against the tree," said Woyi.

"And they stopped here to rest and probably to drink," Striker added.

They looked around closely at the ground for a while, and some of the young men wondered what they could be looking at. What more could be learned here? They had broken a keg, stopped, rested, and had a few drinks. Striker was squatted on his haunches studying the ground. Woyi saw him and moved over to his side.

"I think one was hurt here," Striker said.

"Yes," said Woyi. "When they left, he was moving slowly and dragging his feet."

They continued to follow the trail until it led them to the base of the mountain beneath the cave. What had happened there was even obvious to the young men.

"The drunks stopped here," said one of the youngsters. Then he pointed to the side of the hill. "Then they went up there."

"Good," said Woyi. "And now—"

"We're going up there after them," said Striker, finishing the sentence Woyi had begun.

They stopped on the side of the mountain when they found the abandoned keg, and soon Woyi and Striker had discovered the signs that indicated where the mule had fallen over and slid. They stood beside it and looked up the hillside.

"I think they won't be far from here," Woyi said.

"They wouldn't have left this behind," added Striker.

"Not far behind," Woyi said.

"Right up there," noted one of the young men. "Is that a cave?"

"Yes," said Woyi. "It is."

"You have good eyes," said Striker.

Woyi pointed up and to his left. "Let's go that way," he directed.

"The cave is there," said the young man who had spotted it.

"Yes," said Striker. "We don't want to approach it from in front. They'd be right above us."

"We'll come at them from the side," Woyi said.

They climbed until they were level with the cave, and there they found the fresh grave of One-Eye.

"The one who was injured back there," said Woyi.

"Where they broke the keg," Striker added.

"Come on," they both said together, and they started moving toward the cave's entrance. The five young men followed. It was only a short walk. They could hear the voices of the men inside the cave. They were talking—joking and laughing. Woyi stopped just beside the entrance. He looked back at Striker and the others and gave a nod toward the cave. Then he stepped quickly inside.

Striker stepped in quickly and stood just beside Woyi. Then the other five moved in and spread out, standing just behind their leaders. All seven faces were stern. The drinkers inside the cave stopped drinking, stopped talking and laughing. They stared at the invaders of their new home.

"What do you want here?" the Little Spaniard asked.

"We came for you," said Woyi.

"To take you back to New Town," Striker added.

"You go back to New Town," said the Little Spaniard. "I don't want to go. I don't like it there anymore."

"We were sent to take you back," Woyi said.

"This is my new home," said the Little Spaniard.

Meadowlark made a sudden break for the opening, trying to dodge between the invaders who stood guarding it. Woyi and Striker ignored him, letting him through to the line of young men. The young men cuffed him to the ground and then kicked him until he rolled out of the mouth of the cave and on down the rough hillside. Seeing that, the others backed away from the invaders.

"Get the rest of them out of here, too," Woyi said.

"All but the Little Spaniard," Striker said.

The young men moved into the cave, chasing down each of the remaining companions of the Little Spaniard, beating them as they caught them, dragging them to the mouth of the cave and throwing them out, causing them to roll down the rough mountainside. Only the Little Spaniard remained. He stood still, his arms crossed over his chest, and he stared hard at the two old men.

"I'm here," he said. "You can give me my beating now. All seven of you."

"We're not going to beat you," said Woyi.

"We're going to take you back to New Town," Striker added.

"Why do you want to take me to New Town?" asked the Little Spaniard. "No one wants me in New Town anymore."

"We're taking you back to New Town to be killed," Woyi said.

The Little Spaniard's face registered a momentary surprise, but he quickly regained his composure. There was no escape for him. He could see that.

"Why not just kill me here?" he said.

"We're to take you back," said Striker.

"To be executed," Woyi finished.

"For beating two old men and stealing a white man's *ada yuhs desgi?*" the Little Spaniard asked. "Are there yet more new laws at New Town?"

"You're to be executed for the killing of Olig'," Woyi said.

The arrogance suddenly drained out of the Little Spaniard's expression, leaving him a sickly pale. Amazingly, it had never occurred to him until that moment that anyone might have been killed. So Olig' was dead, and the Little Spaniard had done the deed. He was a killer and, of course, he must be killed. He knew the law. He let his hands fall limply to his sides.

"I'll go back with you," he said.

36

UINTANA received a brief military trial at the soldiers' camp outside Dahlonega, and he had been sentenced to die for the murder of the miner, Chico Hernández. Quintana had protested mightily, that it had been a fair fight, that the miner had started it, that it had been self-defense, but all to no avail. Capitán Lucien Arredondo was unmoving. He had to get control of his troops—the lack of discipline was appalling. Quintana's execution was an absolute necessity.

The trial had been concluded, and the time of execution had been set for the following morning, Quintana having been given the night to make his peace. Early the next morning, two soldiers brought Quintana out of his tent, each holding him by an arm. At first, he stepped out boldly and stood for a moment looking at the world on his last day. Then the soldiers urged him forward and he balked. He wouldn't take a step. They pulled, and he struggled with them.

"Come on," said one of the soldiers. "Come on. It's time."

"No!" Quintana shouted. "You go to hell. Both of you. I'm not going quietly, by God. I'll fight you."

His legs were chained together and his arms were tied behind his back, so he wasn't fighting very effectively, but he was causing them problems. He pulled and jerked, trying to tear himself loose from their grasp.

"Untie my hands and give me a sword!" he screamed. "I'll fight you all. At least let me die fighting. Let me die like a soldier."

Finally the two managed to pull hard enough to jerk Quintana off balance, and they began to drag him forward. Suddenly he changed again.

"No," he said. "No. Don't do this to me. I don't want to die. I didn't do anything wrong. He started it. It was self-defense, I tell you. I didn't mean to kill him." He was blubbering, and tears were streaming down his face.

The soldiers stood in stiff formation, and on the other side of Quintana the miners and the slaves were gathered. This was all according to Arredondo's orders. Off farther to one side, but close enough to see what was going on, most of the people of Dahlonega watched. War Woman and Morales stood side by side. Near them was the Raven, solemn as ever.

They watched as the two Spanish soldiers dragged the sniveling Quintana to a place where they had built a scaffold. From the crosspiece a rope was dangling, a noose at its end. Beneath the noose was a wooden box. War Woman felt sick with disgust as she watched the soldiers half help, half force the mewling and trembling Quintana to step up onto the box. Then a third soldier stepped up behind him and pulled the noose over his head, tightening it around his neck.

War Woman couldn't decide what it was about this gruesome spectacle that was most disgusting to her. The way in which the Spaniards had decided to kill the killer was disgusting enough in itself. It was a horrible, sickening way to kill a man. But, just as bad, was the cowardly way in which the man was facing his death. No Real Person, she told herself, would allow himself to be seen behaving in such a way, especially just before he was to make his journey into the Darkening Land, the land of the spirits.

"I've seen enough," she said, and she turned to walk away. Morales thought to follow her, but something kept his eyes glued to the morbid scene playing itself out there ahead of him. He hesitated. He watched, fascinated, as the third soldier backed off the box and listened as Quintana screamed obscenities, as Arredondo read the orders for execution. Morales winced as a soldier kicked the box out from under the feet of the condemned man and as Quintana swung back and forth, kicking and gagging, slowly strangling to death. Then he turned and hurried to catch up with his wife.

"I'll never get used to the ways of your people," she said, still walking, not looking at him.

"He was a murderer," Morales protested. "He had to be executed."

"But in such a manner?" War Woman said. "I've never seen such a thing before. It's not human."

"Killed is killed," Morales said. "Is it better to push a sharp stick into his heart? Crack his skull with a rock? He's dead no matter how he's killed. Who cares how it's done?"

"I've heard the tales of the horrors your people have committed," she said. "They never meant much to me until now."

Morales began to feel as if he were being accused personally of having committed atrocities, and by his own wife.

"War Woman," he said, "I didn't do the deed."

"No," she said, "but they're your people."

He stopped her, taking her by the shoulders and turning her, forcing her to face him.

"And yours," he reminded her. "What is the name of your brother? Who was your father? And who was his father before him?"

War Woman turned her face away from her husband and looked down to keep him from seeing the pain in her expression. He was right. She knew. And she knew further that she was almost personally responsible for the presence of these Spaniards at Dahlonega.

"Juan," she said, "take me home."

❧

WAR WOMAN sat alone smoking a short clay pipe. Her mood was somber. Part of it was the execution she had witnessed—or almost witnessed. She knew that, but she also knew that it was not the whole explanation for the way she was feeling.

Morales had tried to join her, to keep her company, to comfort her, and she had sent him away saying that she wanted to be alone. She was not comfortable in her aloneness, yet she did not want company. Something was very wrong, and she couldn't define what it was. The Spanish execution had been ghastly, but that was not it. That could not have been it.

She didn't know Quintana, but she knew his type, or at least she thought that she did, and she knew what he had done. She had no sympathy for him, especially having seen the way in which he met his death. He had been a bully and a coward, and she was just as glad that he was gone. No. It was something else. It was as if the manner of Quintana's going had drawn something else up from inside her, something that had been smoldering there.

Was it simply that the presence of the Spaniards there in the country of the Real People was an affront to her sensibilities, and the more so because of her own complicity in the business? Daily they were gouging more and more deeply into the bowels of the earth, the mother of all living things. And for what? For yellow rocks.

Her Spanish husband believed in the value of the gold, and so she had agreed to help the Spaniards get it—for a share, so that she and her husband would be rich, rich in the way the Spaniards judged wealth. And in order to accomplish this goal, she had brought these people into her own country.

They had brought with them a rudeness and a smugness that was almost unbearable and a contentiousness that led easily to senseless violence. They had made life at Dahlonega uncomfortable for everyone and had brought ugliness into the world of the Real People. She was ashamed of the part she had played.

But War Woman still carried with her a tremendous pride that made it difficult for her to admit to any shame or any blame. She dismissed this last thought to dwell on the general unpleasantness of the Spaniards. She cataloged their bad habits, their bad characteristics, and then she added to the list their drunkenness. They brought with them wine and rum, and when they drank those drinks they became even crazier than usual. They had also gotten some of the Real People using the drinks, making them crazy, too. There were several around Dahlonega—

Her thoughts stopped abruptly, as definite a stop as if she had been speaking out loud and suddenly stopped speaking midsentence. Her brother was a drunkard. She had not been thinking about the Little Spaniard. She had left him at home, left him with his problem, left Osa and Comes Back to Life to deal with it as best they could. Of course, she knew that there was nothing they could do.

She knew also that her mood was all really the result of her twin. They had always been close, she and the Little Spaniard. He was tormented about something, and therefore he drank the horrible Spanish drink. She was feeling his torments, she was hurting for him. She had managed somehow to suppress those feelings, pushed them somewhere deep inside her, and the horrible Spanish execution had pulled them out again.

She recalled the time she had made the Little Spaniard go with her to La Florida to meet the Spaniards. He had been so young and handsome then and, though he was always a quiet one, a brave young warrior. She had been proud of him then. Had she ever told him so? She couldn't remember.

He hadn't really wanted to go to La Florida that time. She knew that and had known it then. But she had made him go. Of course, she could say that he had been free to do what he wanted to do, but she knew better than that. He had never been able to refuse her.

And Daksi. Her first lover and her first husband. The Little Spaniard had liked him, too, had been very proud to have him for a brother-in-law. She remembered the Little Spaniard talking about going hunting with his new brother-in-law. He had never gotten that chance.

Then he had tasted the Spanish wine, and he had liked it, and then he had tasted the *ron.* He more than liked the *ron,* it had taken over his life. It had an evil spirit of its own, and it was a strong spirit. War Woman had always had confidence in her own powers, but faced with the power of the *ron* she had been helpless, even though it meant the life of her brother.

She wondered where he was at that very moment, and then she was afraid that she knew. He would be with his drinking companions in the shabby lean-to they had built outside of town. They would be drinking, or they would be lying around in the dirt in a heavy, drunken sleep. It hurt her to think of him thus. It made her sad, and it disgusted her.

Now that she had faced the real source of her moodiness, she wondered what she should do. Should she abandon the gold mining at Dahlonega and go back home to New Town? She had made a commitment to Huelga and to her husband. She had never before walked away from something she said she would do. The thought of people talking about her behind her back, saying that she had failed, was something she couldn't bear.

And what about Morales? In view of the things she had been thinking about the Spaniards, should she tell this Spaniard to move out of her house and out of her country? Would that help her brother? She knew that the Little Spaniard had never really approved of her second marriage but she was fond of Morales. He was not like the other Spaniards. He had a gentleness about him, and he loved her deeply. He would do anything for her.

And she—she couldn't quite bring herself to say that she loved him. She knew herself too well for that. She loved only herself, really. She loved others, if she loved them at all, exactly in proportion to the good they would do her.

She asked herself if she had even loved Daksi. She had wanted him, because he was young and handsome. He had been a brave and a good fighter and had been a bit aloof to her. She had wanted to prove that she could have him. She had wanted to show him off. But had she ever actually loved him? Or anyone else?

She wasn't even sure if she could say that she loved the Little Spaniard, her own brother, not in the way one person loves another. She couldn't say that because she had never really felt like her brother was another person. He was more like another part of herself. It had always been that way.

She was still trying to sort out these thoughts, trying to make some sort of decision about what she would do—or what she should do—when Morales walked up to stand beside her once again. He put a hand on her shoulder.

"I know you sent me away earlier," he said, "but I don't want you to sit alone for so long. Not when you're feeling like this."

She turned her head to look up at him, and this time her expression was not stern. It was soft, and her eyes were wet, though tears did not run. She reached up and put a hand on his.

"When you need someone," he said, "when you're feeling bad, when things don't seem to be going right—those are the times that I'm here for. If you need a shoulder to put your head on, or if you need someone to shout at—either one—that's me."

She smiled.

"You're a good man, Juan," she said, "and I always treat you badly."

"That's not true," Morales said. "Are you all right now?"

She stood and looked at Morales, a smile on her face.

"Yes," she said. "I'm all right. I was just sitting here thinking about my brother. That's all."

37

HE EXECUTION of Quintana did not have the effect on the rest of the troops and the miners that Arredondo had hoped for. He had expected that he only needed to be more severe, to show them that he was in control and that he insisted on military discipline. Quintana had killed a man and had been tried, sentenced, and executed, all legal and all very military.

But it had not worked. The soldiers and the miners were all disgruntled. Among themselves the soldiers complained bitterly about their new *capitán*. He had sided with a miner against a soldier. A soldier has to be able to depend on his commanding officer, they said, he has to be able to trust him and believe in him. He has to know that he will always be able to depend on that officer, otherwise the officer is ineffective, no good.

One man tried halfheartedly to defend Arredondo. "He's young," he said. "Maybe he'll get better with experience." But the others groaned and made fun of him, and he never again tried to defend Arredondo. In fact, he added his voice to those of the others and complained vociferously.

The hanging had not done anything to satisfy the miners either. A soldier had killed a miner. In their mutterings to one another, they seemed to simply ignore the fact that the killer had been tried and executed. "The soldiers think they're better than us," they said. "They think they can do anything."

It didn't help their moods any that very little gold was coming out of the mine each day or that another of their number lay moaning in his cot with a slashed arm that was festering more each day. His moans and occasional screams annoyed them and set their nerves on edge. "Which one of us will be next?" they asked each other.

One morning, a particularly frustrated Arredondo walked to the mine looking for Alvarado. He found the mine superintendent pacing back and forth nervously just in front of the entrance to the mine.

"Alvarado," he said, "we need to talk."

Alvarado stopped pacing. He looked at Arredondo, and his face was furious. "What?" he snapped. "Can't you see we're busy here?"

"I only see you walking back and forth," the captain said. "I see nothing else going on."

"I'm waiting here for the next cartload of ore to come out of the mine. It should be coming out any minute now. What do you want?"

"The morale here is terrible," Arredondo said. "My soldiers and your miners. All of them. We have to do something to improve the situation here."

"There's nothing wrong with my miners," Alvarado disagreed. "If you would keep your soldiers in line, we'd be all right here. As soon as more gold starts coming out again, we'll be all right."

"How do you know there's any more gold in there?" the captain asked, but it sounded more like a challenge than a question.

"I know my business," Alvarado said. "Do you think we just dig anywhere and hope to find gold? That would be stupid. We know where to dig."

"And you found some gold," said the soldier. "How do you know you haven't gotten it all? What makes you think there's any left in there?"

"Tend to your soldiers," Alvarado said. "Leave me alone to do my work."

Arredondo felt a sudden urge to whip out his sword and slash at the arrogant mining man. He trembled, restraining himself. He turned abruptly and walked away, stiffly but fast. *I'm doing it myself,* he thought. *I almost did what I hanged a man for doing. There's a sickness here, and I'm catching it.* He walked straight back to his own tent and went inside, pulling the flap shut, shutting himself in, attempting to shut out his troubles.

◈

BACK at the mine, the cart came out shortly after Arredondo had disappeared. Alvarado looked frantically at its load.

"Rocks," he said. "Nothing but goddamned rocks."

He stalked into the mine, deeper and deeper, until he came to the place at the far end of the tunnel where the miners should have been digging. He found them, instead, sitting or leaning against the walls of the shaft. Not even the slaves were working. The men all were dirty, sweating, and exhausted. That did not matter to Alvarado.

"What the hell are you doing?" he shouted. "Get back to work. Dig."

"There's nothing here to dig for," a miner said.

"Nada," said another. "It's played out."

"It's not played out!" Alvarado shouted. "We have to dig farther. That's all."

A big, burly miner stepped up close to Alvarado and stared him hard in the face.

"There's nothing more to be found in here," he said. "It's all gone. We're not digging in this tunnel anymore."

"I tell you there's gold."

"I've been in more gold mines than you have," said the husky miner, "and I tell you we've sucked this one dry."

Alvarado grabbed the larger man by his shoulders and attempted to spin him around and shove him back toward his abandoned tools.

"Get back to work, I say."

The miner shoved back and sent Alvarado sprawling on the hard mine floor, bruising and scratching his back. Alvarado shouted in anger and pain, started to get up, and stopped in a half-sitting position. He winced at his aching back. Then he got slowly to his feet, turned, and walked back toward the mine's entrance, hanging his head dejectedly.

The big miner watched as Alvarado disappeared from sight, then spoke to his companions without bothering to turn and look at them. "Let's go," he said. "We're finished here." And the miners walked together toward daylight and fresh air.

❦

WAR Woman and Juan Morales sat in front of their big house on chairs that Morales had built with his own hands. Morales was smoking a pipe. War Woman watched her children at play, under the supervision of Consuela. She looked up to see the Raven walking toward them.

"Consuela!" she called.

The slave woman looked toward her mistress.

"Bring some *kanohena* for the Raven."

"Stay right here," Consuela said to the children. "I'll be right back."

She hurried into the house for a bowl of the hominy drink traditionally served to visitors. By the time the Raven had reached the house, Consuela had come back out. She handed him the bowl. He took it and drank. Morales stood up from his chair and offered it to the Raven. The Raven sat down. For a long moment he sat in silence.

"Those white men are making me crazy," he said at last. "If I had not given my word to this project, I think I'd just kill them all."

"I think it would not be a good idea to kill them," Morales responded. "If you were to kill them, the *commandante* in the south would send many more up here to get even."

"I'm not afraid of the Spaniards," the Raven said. "But I did give my word."

The three fell silent again, the silence interrupted mainly by the laughing and chattering of the children at play.

"We haven't been getting paid, though," the Raven said.

"That's because they haven't been bringing out any gold for a while," Morales said.

"But if they don't pay us," the Raven asked, "does that mean that our bargain is no longer any good?"

"Well now," said Morales, "I don't know. That would be a question for the lawyers, I think."

"What's this—lawyer?" the Raven asked.

"Among my people," Morales said, weighing his words carefully, "we have specialists. When there is a question of law, when there are ambiguities in the law or in the language of an agreement, they decide the question."

The Raven nodded his understanding. "I have advisers for that purpose," he said. "Perhaps I should call them together and present them with this question. Then they could decide."

"Well—"

The Raven stood up suddenly. He had a smug, self-satisfied expression on his face.

"Good," he said. "I'll call my lawyers together for a conference on this matter."

He slurped down the rest of the *kanohena* and put the bowl down on the ground. Then he walked away.

"I'm not at all sure how the *commandante* will react to a legal opinion from the Raven's advisers," Morales said.

"We're in the land of the Real People," War Woman said. "Whose legal opinion should we listen to?"

Morales gave a slight shrug and sat down again in his chair beside his wife.

"That's a very good point," he said. "Yes. A very good point indeed."

❧

WHEN the miners stepped out of the tunnel, they stopped, standing in a cluster, Sandoval, the burly one who had shoved Alvarado, in front. None of the men carried mining tools. They had left them all in the tunnel at the far end where they had stopped working.

"Sandoval," said one, "what are we going to do now?"

"We're going to get some food," he replied, "as bad as it is, and we're going to get some rum, and then we're going to get some *caballos* and head back to La Florida. That's what we're going to do."

"What will Huelga say to us when we get back?" asked one.

"We're not going to wait to see what Huelga has to say," Sandoval said. "When we get back, we'll go straight to him, and we'll tell him what's been going on here. He'll hear the tale from us first."

"Will he believe us, though? When Alvarado and Arredondo both tell a different tale?"

"Haven't you noticed, you blockhead," said Sandoval, "that those two hate each other? Even if they both contradict what we say, they'll also contradict each other. They'll never agree with each other on anything. Huelga won't have any choice but to accept what we say."

The others weighed that argument, and it sounded good to them. When Sandoval started walking, they followed him. They would follow him to the food, to the drink, and all the way back to La Florida.

❧

"WHAT are those miners up to?" a soldier asked. He was lounging in front of a tent with a few companions.

"I don't know," said another. "Aren't they supposed to be working this time of day?"

"I thought so."

"Of course they are," said a third soldier.

"The lazy bastards," the second muttered.

"Well," said the one who had first spoken, "someone should go tell their boss what they're doing."

"That Alvarado?" said the second soldier. "Hell, I saw him go to his tent a little while ago."

"To sulk? To pout?"

"Like our *capitán*?"

They laughed at the thought of both their leaders, the military and the civilian, sulking in their tents, but the laughter was not raucous. It was wry, and it was short. The one who had spoken first stood up slowly and hitched his pantaloons.

"What are you going to do?" asked one.

"I'm going to send those lazy bastards back to work," he said.

Another one laughed and stood beside the first. "I'll go with you," he said.

"You'll just get into a fight," added a slightly more cautious one. "They won't want to take any orders from us."

"We won't ask them what they want," said the first. He started walking toward the miners, and his companions joined him, all but the cautious one, who stayed behind watching until they had gone about half the distance to the miners. Then he jumped up and ran toward the tent of his *capitán*.

"Capitán Arredondo!" he called. "Capitán!"

"What is it?" snarled Arredondo from inside his tent.

"There's going to be trouble," said the soldier.

"There's nothing here but trouble," the *capitán* answered.

"Big trouble, Capitán," said the soldier. "You'd better come."

Arredondo drew on all his military training and patriotic upbringing and forced himself to come out of the tent. He looked at the soldier standing there.

"What is the trouble?" Arredondo asked.

The soldier pointed. "The miners came out of the mine," he said. "Some *soldados* said they're going to make them go back to work."

"Oh, God," said Arredondo, "come on," and he ran alongside the common soldier toward the brewing melee.

38

RREDONDO stopped in his tracks when he saw what was about to happen. He felt helpless. There were too many of them—on both sides—and neither had any respect for his rank or for him as a soldier or a human being. He knew that he wouldn't be able to stop the fight. He would not be able to prevent more horrible bloodshed. He turned to the soldier beside him.

"Saddle my *caballo,*" he said. "Quickly."

The puzzled soldier gave the captain an inquisitive look, but the captain just snapped back at him, "Quickly, I said."

The soldier ran toward the rope corral where the horses were kept, and Arredondo ran back to his tent. He had turned his back on two very angry groups of men who were facing each other as if for an impending battle. Inside the tent he dressed and armed himself fully. Then he hurried toward the corral and his waiting horse.

"Capitán," said the puzzled soldier, "where are you going?"

"I'm riding to Huelga!" Arredondo shouted. His horse reared, and he doffed his plumed hat, swinging it around over his head in a magnificently dramatic gesture. Then he raced away. The poor soldier stood dumbfounded for a moment, then ran over to join his companions.

"Hey!" he called. "Hey! The *capitán* has run away."

"What? Run away?"

"That's right. Just now. He made me saddle his *caballo,* and he rode away as fast as he could make the poor beast run."

"What did he say? Did he say anything?"

"He said that he was going to Huelga."

The other soldiers stood befuddled for a moment. Then one started to laugh, and the others all joined in.

"To Huelga?" one said. "That's going to take him a while."

They all laughed again. All except the one who had saddled the captain's horse.

"Is he going to ask Huelga what to do to make us stop what we are doing?" said one.

"Does he think we're all going to just stand here and wait until he gets back?" added another.

They laughed some more. Then even the miners started to laugh. The riotous laughter was contagious. Soldiers and miners held their sides and their bellies. Some sat on the ground. Some rolled on it, roaring their laughter. Tears ran down their cheeks.

Alvarado heard the commotion and came out of his tent to look. For a brief moment he thought about going over to the crazy-acting men and demanding to know just what the hell was going on, but he was still smarting from having been pushed down in the mine by Sandoval. Alvarado wondered where Arredondo was and why he was allowing this nonsense to go on but then decided that Arredondo was a fool and that was explanation enough. He decided to seek out Morales and War Woman for help and advice.

ᦔᦲ

CONSUELA answered the door at the house of War Woman. She asked Alvarado to wait and went back inside. In another moment Morales came out.

"What is it?" he asked.

"There's trouble," Alvarado said, "between the miners and the soldiers."

"What kind of trouble?"

"They're all facing each other at the camp, squared off for a fight."

"Where's Arredondo?"

"The last I saw of him," Alvarado said, "he was sulking in his tent. He's not worth anything. He's hiding from it all."

"I don't believe that," said Morales. "Come on. We'll find him."

The door opened again, and War Woman stepped out. "What is it, Juan?" she asked.

"Trouble at the mine, my darling," he said. "I'll take care of it."

Morales hurried off with Alvarado. At the Spanish camp they checked Arredondo's tent, but he was nowhere to be found. Then they looked toward where the men were gathered. By this time they had been joined by the women, the *putas* Huelga had sent. They were all sitting around together drinking rum—miners, *putas,* and soldiers. Morales gave Alvarado a stern look, and Alvarado, a puzzled look on his face, shrugged.

"Come on," said Morales, and he led the way over to where the men were gathered.

"Morales," said Sandoval, "have a drink with us." He gave a scornful look to Alvarado. "And you, too, even," he added. "Sit down."

Alvarado stood stiffly, but Morales sat and gestured for Alvarado to do the same. He did.

"Why aren't you miners working?" Morales asked.

Sandoval shrugged. "There's no more gold," he said. He gave Alvarado a hard look, and the mining superintendent sat closemouthed.

"I see," said Morales. "I heard there was trouble here, but I don't see any trouble. Was there trouble?"

A few of the men laughed a bit nervously.

"No," said Sandoval. "No trouble."

"There was about to be a fight," said Alvarado. "I saw you. All of you."

"Oh, that," said one of the soldiers. "We saw these men come out of the mine early, and we thought they should go back to work. But we didn't know there was no more gold in the mine. If there's no gold, why should they work?"

"So we all sat down to have some rum," Sandoval said. "That's all."

Morales took a sip of rum. "Where's Captain Arredondo?" he asked.

Everyone was silent for a moment. At last the soldier who had saddled the captain's horse spoke up.

"He thought there was going to be a fight, too," he said. "He told me to saddle his *caballo,* and he said he was going to Huelga. He rode off."

"Why the hell would he go to Huelga?" Morales asked.

"Because he's an incompetent," Alvarado said. "He saw a little trouble ahead, and he rode for help, even though help is so far away. *Estúpido.*"

"Where are the slaves?" Morales asked.

"They're over there where they belong," said Sandoval. "Chained up as usual. Everything's under control here. There are no problems."

BACK at his wife's house, Morales sat in one of the chairs out front and stared ahead, lost in thought. War Woman came out and sat beside him.

She waited a moment for him to volunteer information about what had been going on. When he did not, she spoke.

"So," she said, "did you take care of the trouble?"

"Most strange," he replied. "I found no trouble."

He fell silent again, and this time War Woman waited for him. At last, he spoke again.

"Alvarado came here," he said, "because he saw the miners facing the soldiers, all ready for a fight. He had seen Arredondo go into his tent, and the captain did not come out to interfere in this trouble. So he came here and I went back with him. But there was no trouble. There was no fight. The soldiers and the miners were all getting drunk together, along with the *putas*. And Arredondo? He was not in his tent. According to one *soldado,* he had mounted his horse and ridden for La Florida."

War Woman said nothing.

"Well?" he said.

"Well what?" she said.

"What do you make of all that?"

"They're all crazy," she said.

❧

BARBARO was half African and half Indio. He had no idea what kind of Indio his father had been and had known his own mother but a few years of his life. The Spaniards had sold her away from him. His entire life had been lived in slavery. He knew no language other than Spanish.

But he did know, or at least he thought, that there must be some better life somewhere. There were free men. There were masters even. Not all were slaves. He sometimes wondered if it was all planned by some higher power or if it was a simple matter of determination. He was inclined to think the latter, for he could not imagine why some god would decide that he, Barbaro, would spend his life in slavery.

Today, he had decided, would be the day on which he would test his theory. He would put his determination to work and find out once and for all if he was a slave because he had no choice or because he had no guts. When the free miners had quit work earlier that day and walked out of the mine, they had abandoned the slaves. The slaves, chained to one another, had walked out and gone to the same place they always went after a day's work.

The miners had dropped their tools, however, and Barbaro had bent to pick up a long, sharp chisel. He had it with him still. Now, the soldiers and the miners were all drunk, the *capitán* had ridden away, and no one was paying attention to anything like duty or obligation. It was a good time to try to break the chains and escape from the Spaniards.

Barbaro had mentioned his desire to escape once before to another slave, and the other had asked him where in the world he would go and how he would live. Barbaro did not know exactly where he would go or how he would live, but he knew that he would be able to manage somehow. This was a vast land. There were lots of places to go and be far away from the Spaniards. There were plenty of Indios with whom one might live happily, and if not, if a number of slaves were to escape together, they could simply establish their own town and live as the Indios lived, by hunting, trading, and planting. It was all very simple.

As soon as Barbaro was sure that none of the Spaniards were paying any attention to him, or any of the other slaves, he began chipping away at a link in his chain very close to the iron band around his ankle. It was slow and tedious work, but he could see that the chisel did actually do damage to the chain. Each time Barbaro struck the chain link with the chisel, it made a small dent. If he could strike it enough times, the link would be cut.

At first he was cautious. He struck the link once and waited to see if anyone would come running to find out what had made the metallic sound. No one had. He struck it again and waited again. Still there was no reaction from the Spaniards. He struck harder and faster, and every now and then he would stop and wait and watch before continuing. No soldier or miner ever seemed to notice the sound. No one came over to check on the slaves.

He had seen the time earlier when the Spaniards had been on the verge of fighting among themselves, and he had seen the *capitán* ride away. No one was in charge. No one was taking care of any of the jobs they usually had assigned to them. Other nights, at least one *soldado* had been assigned to stand guard over the slaves. Not this night.

He beat away at the chain link. The slave next to him in line was watching him intently.

"That will take you all night," he said.

"Maybe," Barbaro replied.

"Then what will you do? Run away by yourself?"

"Maybe. Or maybe you and the others could come with me."

"How will we get out of our chains? There won't be time."

"You should have picked up tools in the mine the way I did," said Barbaro. "When I get free, you can follow me if you want to. You can do your best to keep up. That's all I can say." He hammered away at the chain link.

"Wait," said the other. "Wait a minute."

Barbaro stopped and gave the other a disgusted look. "What for?" he muttered.

"Look."

The other nodded toward the soldiers. One man was walking away from the group. He was walking toward the slaves. Barbaro recognized the man. He was the one who had been on duty guarding the slaves the night before. He must have suddenly remembered that he was the last one with that duty. He still had the keys, and he knew that no one had bothered chaining one end of the chain to the nearby post. He would be coming over to take care of that little chore. The man came closer. Barbaro sat still. He slid the chisel underneath a leg.

The soldier stopped just beside Barbaro and looked down. He grinned. "You thought you would get away tonight, didn't you?" he said.

Barbaro felt his heart pound in his chest. The man had discovered him. The soldier bent over and picked up one end of the chain, the end near Barbaro, and carried it to the post, lapped it around, and snapped the big lock shut. Then he looked at Barbaro and laughed again.

"You thought that I forgot. Well, don't look so sad. You wouldn't have gone far anyway, all of you chained together like that."

He turned away and, laughing, started to walk back to the group of rum drinkers, but Barbaro shot out a leg and tripped him. The startled soldier landed hard on his face. Barbaro was up in an instant. The chain was barely long enough, but he scrambled on top of the soldier's back and, with one hard plunge, drove the chisel through his body, pinning him to the ground.

39

HE SOLDIER was not dead. Barbaro could hear him gurgling. The slave held a tight grip on the end of the chisel with one hand, and with the other he pressed the soldier's face hard into the ground.

"They'll skin you alive," said the slave next to Barbaro.

"Shut up," Barbaro hissed. He felt the soldier beneath him kick a little with both legs. Then he was still. There was no more gurgling. Barbaro relaxed the pressure on the back of the man's head just a little, then more. Convinced that the soldier was dead, he got off of the body and made a quick search around the waist for the keys. They were hooked to the belt, and he pulled them loose. Soon he had himself free. He glanced at the others.

"You coming with me?" he asked. "Or you afraid of getting skinned?"

"Unlock us," said the next man, and Barbaro did. He unlocked them all. They stood, crouched, and looked at the group of soldiers and miners across the way. No one was watching them.

"Follow me," said Barbaro, and he ran toward the dark woods, the others close behind.

⁊

IT was the next morning before anyone discovered the dead body and that the slaves were missing. One of the miners was walking off to the side of the camp to find a convenient place in which to relieve himself and saw the body. It took him another moment to realize that the slaves should have been there chained to the post. They were not. The needs of his body were momentarily forgotten as he ran screaming back into the camp. Soon everyone was up, talking and shouting. Everyone was armed and looking around, as if the murderous slaves might be lurking anywhere.

Soon the once surly and rebellious soldiers and miners realized that they were sorely in need of leadership and, since Arredondo was gone, Alvarado was the only one left among them with any kind of authority. They found him standing in front of his tent, and they gathered around him suddenly quiet.

Sandoval stepped forward. "What are we going to do about this, señor?" he asked.

"Why are you asking me?" said Alvarado.

"Capitán Arredondo is not here," Sandoval replied. "You are the only one here with any authority."

"Yesterday you scoffed at my authority," Alvarado said. "You made your own decisions then. Make them now."

A soldier stepped up close to Sandoval and spoke low in his ear. "Let's go to Morales," he said.

They walked to the edge of Dahlonega and stopped. Dahlonega was off-limits. They knew, though, that they had to talk with Morales. Sandoval agreed to be the one who would take a chance and go into the town. He took off his hat and carried it in front of him in both hands. He hadn't gotten very far when he was stopped by the Raven.

"Please," Sandoval said, "I must speak with Morales."

The Raven did not understand Spanish, and although Sandoval could not understand the language of the Raven, he easily caught the meaning of the words the man was uttering. He was not wanted inside the town.

"Morales," he said. "Morales. *Por favor.*"

The Raven did understand the name. He held a hand out to indicate that he meant for Sandoval to wait right where he was, then turned to a passing young man and spoke to him. The man nodded and trotted away in the direction of War Woman's house. It wasn't long before Sandoval was joined by Morales.

☙

BACK at his wife's house, Morales was getting himself outfitted as quickly as he could.

"I have to take charge," he said to War Woman. "There is no one else. The men are back in their camp getting ready. They'll be waiting for me."

"What will you do with the slaves when you catch them?" War Woman asked.

"If we can determine which one is the murderer," Morales said, "he alone will die. If not, they must all be killed."

"Of course," War Woman said.

THE trail left by Barbaro and the others was easy to follow. They had crashed into the woods like so many wild animals, tearing and trampling the underbrush in their desperation to escape. But they had been running all night and would be well ahead of their pursuers. The Spaniards, riding on horseback, would, under other circumstances, have had a good chance of catching up with them quickly, but the horses were almost a hindrance in the thick woods.

Once Sandoval even questioned the wisdom of having brought the *caballos* along in the first place. "They're just slowing us down," he said. "Why don't we leave them behind?"

"The slaves are too far ahead of us," Morales replied. "We'd never catch them on foot. Sooner or later, they'll have to come out of these woods. When that happens, we'll be glad for the *caballos.*"

So they kept fighting their way through the thick woods, following the clumsy trail left by the escaping slaves. By noon the men were tired, hungry, and sweating. They had been bitten, it seemed, by every imaginable kind of vile insect and were still in deep, thick woods. The band of righteous men who had begun their pursuit so enthusiastically were turning back into grumblers.

"Who cares if they get away?" one of the soldiers said. "Let's go back before we get lost in this goddamned forest."

"We won't get lost," Morales said. "We have a clear trail behind us all the way back to our camp."

"Stop grumbling," Sandoval ordered. "They killed one of your comrades."

"I never liked that one anyway," said a soldier. "He cheated at cards."

Morales was grateful when he came across a small clearing. He called a halt for a short rest. They ate a meager meal, and some of the men managed to get themselves short naps. Others sat around complaining.

Sandoval moved over to sit beside Morales. "What do you think?" he asked.

"About what?" said Morales. "What do you mean?"

"Will we catch up with them?"

"I don't know," Morales said, "but we have to try. They're not only escaped slaves, they committed a murder. We can't allow Spanish soldiers to be murdered, especially by slaves."

"No," Sandoval agreed. "I suppose not. But what if we can't find them at all?"

"So far," Morales said, "we're on their trail."

"Yes, I guess so. But if it takes too long to catch them, I'm afraid the men will rebel."

"Then they'll have to kill me," Morales said, "for if they rebel and leave me alive, they'll all be reported to the *commandante* as rebels. I promise you that."

Sandoval heaved a heavy sigh. *"Sí, señor,"* he said. He put a hand on his knee to get himself back up on his feet. Then he stood looking down at Morales for a moment. *"Señor,"* he said, "I'll help you all I can."

"Gracias," Morales said.

After a short rest, Morales, with the help of Sandoval, got all the men up and moving again. The trail of the escapees was still clear. They were still moving through a troublesome tangle of undergrowth. Morales thought the half-naked slaves must be cut to ribbons by all this wicked bramble.

At last they came out on a plain, and the Spaniards felt as if they could breathe again. They welcomed the openness as a sailor long at sea welcomes the sight of land. They rejoiced as had the wandering tribes of Israel at the sight of the Promised Land.

"Let's mount up," shouted one of the soldiers, "and chase the bastards down!"

"Which way will we chase?" Morales asked.

"What?"

"Which way?" Morales said. "Do you see the trail?"

The loudmouthed soldier looked around. The grassy plain looked the same to him everywhere. "Well, no," he said. "I don't see it, but—"

"But what?" Morales snapped. He was getting tired of the gross insubordination of these men. He was tired of their grumbling and complaining and their loudmouthed braggadocio. "Do you want to ride off in just any direction? Do you want to ride off on a damn fool's mission?"

The soldier looked at the ground. "No," he said.

"It's late evening anyway," Morales told the man. "We wouldn't get far before we'd have to stop and make a camp. So let's make it here. We'll get a good night's rest and have a fresh start in the morning."

They made their camp, and although there was some grumbling, the men were all soon asleep. They'd had a long, hard day, and so sleep came quickly. Morales was glad of that, even though he himself lay awake. He wished that Arredondo had not ridden off. Morales longed for the presence of a real military commander for this mission.

But without such a man, he would have to do. He, it seemed, had been chosen. Well, he would do the best he could, would do everything in his power to maintain some discipline and hold the men together to keep them on the trail. He would try everything he could think of to bring back the escaped slaves and discover the identity of the murderer.

He was feeling all of this with such intensity that he had a sudden revelation about himself. He had just about begun to believe that he had become one of the Real People. He had told War Woman more than once that if the *commandante* should send him someplace else, he would not go. He would stay with her. He would stay among her people and live as one of them. But how could he be so driven to catch these slaves and punish them and discover the killer of the Spanish soldier if not because of his loyalty to España? What were his present feelings if not patriotic?

These thoughts were puzzling to Morales, and they were uncomfortable. He tried to push them out of his mind and concentrate on what he would do in the morning. Where had the fugitives gone? How would he decide which direction to take to follow them? When he had asked the fool soldier, "Which way will we chase?" he had not known either. He had also asked, "Do you want to ride off on a damn fool's mission?" and he certainly did not want to lead them on such a mission.

He wondered if one direction made more sense than others. He tried to think like a desperate fugitive. Faced with tenuous freedom and this vast land, where would one run? Away from the Spaniards, of course. Beyond that, he did not know.

IN THE morning they ate. Then Morales had his men saddle some horses, but not all of the horses.

"Do we break camp, *señor?*" a soldier asked.

"No," Morales said.

When the horses he had called for were ready, he gathered the men around him.

"Listen," he began. "We don't know where they went from here. The trail ends. We can't track them across this grass. I want two men to ride straight ahead, two more to ride that way, and two that way." He indicated directions to his right and left. "I want you to ride until midday. When the Sun is high in the sky, turn around and come back here. Look for any sign of the slaves."

"What if we don't find any sign?" asked one.

"I think you will," Morales said. "One of the pairs will. Remember, they're on foot. They can't be that far ahead of us."

"What if we see them?" asked another.

"Just ride back here and tell the rest of us," Morales said.

"Two of us could take them," the soldier said. "They're slaves, they're naked, and they have no weapons."

"Perhaps two of you could take them," Morales said, "but in order to do so, you might have to kill them. I don't want them killed if we can avoid it. I want them brought back alive and properly punished. Besides, how do you know they're unarmed? They killed one Spanish soldier already, did they not?"

He stood silent for a moment looking over the faces of the men in front of him, waiting to see if there were any more protests, any questions. There were none. Quickly he selected six men and assigned them their directions.

"Remember," he said, "when you find them, or when you see any sign of where they have gone, get back here as fast as you can."

40

AR WOMAN had a bad feeling. It was a feeling of impending disaster. She tried to set it aside by playing with the children, but it didn't work. It nagged at her constantly, almost like a physical pain. Something was very wrong somewhere.

Juan Morales had gone off leading a bunch of armed Spaniards in pursuit of escaped slaves, at least one of whom had murdered a Spanish soldier. If the slaves themselves were not a danger, the soldiers and miners certainly could be. They had been fighting among themselves for some time now. There had been one killing, and another man might die. And Morales was not a soldier, he was a trader, a businessman.

Yet War Woman knew somehow that her uneasy feeling had nothing to do with Morales and his possibly dangerous mission. Morales, she knew, would come home safely. She wasn't sure if he would be successful or not, but he would be safe. So what was it? Where was the danger or the tragedy or whatever bad thing it was that was causing this feeling?

She had been trying to play with the children, but her mind was elsewhere, and so she was just as glad when she saw the Raven walking toward her house.

"Run along," she said. "Play with Consuela. I have to talk to the Raven."

She walked to the front of the house where the two chairs sat. The Raven arrived there at just about the same time, and the two sat down.

"I have some news," the Raven said.

War Woman waited to hear it. In a moment the Raven continued.

"My advisers met," he said. "My lawyers. We talked about the agreement I made with the 'Squanis about digging for the gold. I told them I don't like having the Spaniards here, but I made a promise. I said that they could dig for the gold in our mountain.

"But I told them they, too, made a promise to me. They said that we would receive certain trade goods once every month. Now they're not getting any more gold out of their hole, and we're not getting our trade goods.

"They thought about it, talked about it for a long time, then went home. They came back the next day and talked some more, and then they called me. I went to them, and they said that they had decided that the Spaniards had broken the agreement. Therefore, they said, I no longer have to keep my promise. My promise has been blown away by the Spaniards.

"So I asked them if I can kill the Spaniards now, and they said that I probably should not. They said that I should not do anything without a council decision. So I'm calling a council for four nights from now.

"When the council meets, I'll ask them to decide to tell the Spaniards to get out of here. I'll tell them what my lawyers said. We can kick the white men out of here without breaking our promise. I'll ask the people to decide to do that."

War Woman had sat in silence listening to what the Raven had to say. When he stopped talking, she still kept quiet. A moment later, he glanced at her. Then he spoke again.

"Well," he said, "what do you think about that?"

"It was I who brought the Spaniards here," War Woman replied.

"Yes," said the Raven, nodding his head. "I know."

"It was I who negotiated the terms of the agreement between the Spaniards and the people of Dahlonega," she said.

"Yes, you did," the Raven agreed.

"Now you're talking about bringing that agreement to an end."

"Yes, I am."

"And you should," she said. "The time for the arrangement is past. The agreement is no longer any good for anyone. The Spaniards are no longer getting any gold, and you are no longer getting paid with trade goods. There is bad feeling between the Spaniards and the people of Dahlonega. There is even bad feeling among the Spaniards. There is no longer any reason for them to be here. If you want me to, I will speak at the council in favor of your proposal."

The Raven stood up. "*Wado,*" he said. "I'm glad that we agree on this matter, and I'll be glad of your help at the council." Without another word, he turned and walked away.

War Woman considered the end of an episode in her life, her venture into business with the Spaniards, the gold-mining business, a period of life away from home. She had been anticipating this for a while, and now she was glad that it had finally come. It would take a few more days to wrap it all up, but the end was in sight. The mine would cease to operate. The Spaniards would go back to La Florida. And she and her family would go back home to New Town where they belonged. *Yes,* she thought, *it's time.*

❧

EVERYONE crowded into the town house at Dahlonega for the big council meeting, and the mood was one of tremendous excitement. The agenda had been announced, and the issue was one in which everyone was intensely interested. The arrival of the Spaniards had signaled a major change in the lives of the people of Dahlonega, and their anticipated departure would be another. The council house was smoke-filled in a short time. Everyone was talking, voicing their opinions on what should be done, speculating on the outcome of the meeting, talking over the time during the Spanish stay just outside their town. When the Raven stood up to begin the meeting, a hush came over the crowd.

The Raven spoke about the initial Spanish request for mining privileges and about the period of negotiations. He reminded the people present of the role played by War Woman in setting things up. He went over the reasons for accepting the agreement in the first place and the benefits they had enjoyed for a while.

Then he talked about the changes that had taken place more recently: how the Spaniards were no longer finding gold, how, therefore, they were no longer making payments to Dahlonega, and how they had become bellicose, sometimes violent. He went over carefully, in other words, all the reasons for wanting them to leave.

He told the people about the opinion of his advisers. He likened his advisers to what the Spaniards called lawyers and explained that their function was to interpret legal ambiguities. He maintained, as had his advisers, that the Spaniards, having ceased payments to Dahlonega, had terminated the agreement between the two parties and, therefore, Dahlonega was no longer obligated to keep the promise it had made.

He urged the people to agree with him to tell the Spaniards that they were no longer welcome in the vicinity of Dahlonega. Then he asked War Woman to speak.

She stood and looked over the crowd. They sat silent, attentive, and respectful. Then she started speaking. She praised the Raven as a great leader and a wise man. She agreed with everything he had said. There had been good reasons for the agreement, and the arrangement had been good for a while for everyone concerned but its usefulness was done. It was time for the agreement to be ended, and it was time for the Spaniards to leave.

When War Woman sat down, the Raven allowed anyone who had anything to say to stand up and speak. Several citizens of Dahlonega took advantage of the opportunity to voice their opinions, but no one spoke in opposition to the views stated by the Raven and War Woman. The proposal was adopted unanimously. The Raven was elated.

THE next morning, Commandante Huelga himself at the head of a troop of twenty Spanish soldiers arrived at the Spanish camp just outside Dahlonega. Capitán Arrredondo rode beside the *commandante*. They found no one in the camp except the *putas*. No soldiers on duty. No miners at work.

Huelga was furious. "What's the meaning of this?" he demanded.

"It's as I told you," Arredondo said. "They've all rebelled against authority. While I was here, they disobeyed my orders. As soon as I left, they deserted."

"We'll find them," Huelga said, "and they'll all hang."

His horse was prancing in circles as the *commandante* looked over the nearly deserted camp. Glancing over a shoulder, he noticed the women. He ordered the men to dismount and, with one holding his own spirited animal, got down to the ground.

"Capitán," he said.

Arredondo hurried to his side.

"Where is your tent?"

Arredondo led the *commandante* to his own tent and provided him with a camp chair. He poured a glass of wine for Huelga. Huelga took a sip.

"Bring those women over here," he said.

Arredondo passed the order to a sergeant who ran over to the women and ordered them to hustle themselves to the *commandante*. The women sauntered over to see him. Huelga pointed out one of the women and called her forward.

"Do you know what's been going on in this camp?" he asked her.

She looked puzzled and raised her shoulders in a kind of half-shrug.

"When did the *soldados* and miners run away?" Huelga asked.

"Run away?" she said.

"Yes," Huelga replied. "Who was leading them, and when did they leave?"

"It was the morning after the slaves killed the soldier and escaped," she said.

"What?" said Arredondo, forgetting his manners and his military decorum in his surprise and interjecting himself into the conversation. Until that moment, he had not thought about the slaves.

"The slaves killed the soldier with the keys," she said. "They unlocked themselves and ran away. In the morning the men found the soldier and Señor Morales led them all after the slaves."

At just that moment Alvarado came out of his tent to see what was going on. Astonished at the sight of Huelga there in the camp, he hurried over to the tent and pushed his way through the women to stand before his *commandante.* He dropped to one knee.

"Commandante," he said. "Thank God you're here."

"How is it," Huelga began, "Alvarado, that you're the only man in this camp?"

"The others all rode out," Alvarado said.

"Why are your miners not at work?"

"They rebelled against my authority and refused to work. I begged Capitán Arredondo to help restore discipline to this camp, but he couldn't control the *soldados,* much less my miners. When real trouble began, he ran away."

"What real trouble?" Huelga asked.

"They were about to have a big fight," said Alvarado, "the soldiers against the miners, and he ran away."

"Did they fight?"

"Well, no."

"Why not?"

Searching for a way to answer the *commandante*'s question, Alvarado hung his head.

The woman out front spoke up. "They got drunk together instead," she said. The *putas* all laughed.

"*Silencio!*" Huelga shouted. "There is nothing funny here. This should not have been a difficult duty here. We had a mine to operate and we had the cooperation of the natives. I sent an officer in charge of troops and a supervisor of the mine. Neither man seems to have been capable of doing his job.

"And where are the miners and the *soldados?* They have gone in pursuit of runaway slaves. Who is leading them? One of the men I left in charge? No. A trader."

"Excellency," said Alvarado, "I can explain—"

"Explain later," ordered Huelga. "For now confine yourself to your tent. You're under arrest."

Huelga gestured toward his sergeant, who in turn pointed to two soldiers. The two hurried forward to stand one on either side of Alvarado. He stood slowly and dejectedly and walked between them toward his tent.

"He has been a problem for some time now," Arredondo said. "I tried talking to him, but—"

"You have also been a problem, Capitán," Huelga said. "You were in command here. You should have been in control. If there were discipline problems with the civilians, you with your *soldados* should have been able to take care of those problems. You failed. If there were discipline problems with the *soldados,* well, what is an officer for? That is exactly your job. If an officer cannot maintain discipline, then he is no good. He is in the wrong profession. You, too, are to consider yourself under arrest, at least until I can sort this whole mess out. Go to your quarters."

Arredondo, crushed, turned and walked away. Now Huelga was left with no one to talk to except the women. He looked them over. Then again he spoke to the one he had singled out earlier.

"Can you tell me how to find the War Woman?" he asked.

41

ARBARO was well nigh exhausted. He had been running almost since having unlocked himself and the others from the chain. They had not eaten, in fact had slowed down only long enough to drink water from a mountain stream. Barbaro kept going partly from fear of capture but mainly from a fierce determination to be free, to be away from the hated Spaniards. He was determined that he would not be a slave again. He would run, or he would fight and die, but he would not be a slave.

The others, the ones following him, only ran because of their fear. They were deathly afraid that they would be captured and all blamed equally for what Barbaro had done. He, after all, was the one who had done the killing. Some of them were even thinking of their defense should they be caught. "We ran with him because we were afraid of him," they would say. Some of them were already thinking that they should give themselves up to their former owners and beg for mercy.

After all, they wondered, where were they going? They were running away from the Spaniards, but whom would they run into while attempting to make their escape to freedom? Indios? And would those Indios be friendly or would they, too, enslave them or even kill them? What kind of freedom were they seeking in this strange land? They were tired and hungry and afraid, and they were beginning to think that they had made a terrible mistake when they had followed the rash and bold Barbaro.

Barbaro was leading the way up the side of a steep hill and wasn't even all that conscious of leading anyone. He was running, and he was not looking back. Even so, the others were not far behind, but they were beginning to fall back quickly. They lacked the determination of Barbaro. They lacked the drive that kept him moving in spite of near-exhaustion.

Barbaro topped the rise and stood up tall. He looked all around. Far below on his trail he saw two Spanish horsemen. His heart pounded in his chest. He knew that he and his followers could not long outdistance men on horseback. He hoped that the others had not noticed their pursuers, for he did not want to listen to their whining fears. He trotted ahead toward the other side of the hill. Looking down below, he was suddenly amazed at the sight of a town built on the edge of a clear running stream.

He wondered who its inhabitants might be, whether they would be friendly or otherwise. He considered the several possibilities. They could capture and kill him and his followers. They could take them and return them to the Spaniards. They could take them and hold them as their own slaves or sell them to the highest bidder. Or they might welcome them and give them protection.

He could lead his followers around the town and on to—where? The horsemen would overtake them soon. He decided that, all things considered, he would approach the townspeople below and take his chances with them. Just as he had reached that decision, the first of the others ran up behind him.

"Barbaro," said the other, but Barbaro stopped him short.

"Look," he said, pointing out the town below.

"Indios?" asked the other, his voice trembling.

"Of course," said Barbaro. "Who else?"

"And the Spaniards are behind us," the other said.

"I know."

"You saw them?"

"I saw them," said Barbaro. "They won't be able to come up here the way we did. Not with their *caballos*. They'll have to find a way around. Look down below on this side of the creek."

The man looked, but he wasn't sure what he was supposed to be seeing. The others came up just then to stand panting there behind Barbaro.

"We're going down there," Barbaro said. "You all wait for me in the brush there by the creek—on this side. I'll wade across and go to the Indios in the town. If they welcome us, I'll call you over."

"What if they don't welcome us?" one asked.

Barbaro looked over his shoulder at his followers and grinned. "If they kill me," he said, "you're on your own."

MORALES ordered his men to break camp, for two of the riders had returned, having found the trail of the escaped slaves. They had followed the trail a short distance to make sure of it, and they had actually seen the slaves climbing up the side of a small mountain.

With everything packed, the men all mounted and ready, Morales and the two scouts led the way. The horses had been ridden hard already, so Morales kept the pace easy. He did not want to wear the animals out or kill them in thoughtless haste.

"They won't escape us," he said. "Don't worry. They're all on foot."

Out on the flat plain, the sun was hot. Perspiration ran down the faces of the Spaniards and soaked their clothing. The *caballos* breathed hard. When they drew near the mountain, the riders who had reported seeing the escapees pointed.

"They were there," said one of them. "They're gone now. They must be on top or going down the other side by now."

Morales signaled a halt. He dismounted and told the others to do the same.

"We'll rest the *caballos* here for a little," he said. Then he studied the tree- and brush-covered mountainside ahead. "We can't follow them up that way on horseback," he said. "We'll have to find another way. A way around."

Sandoval stepped up beside him, and both men squinted, studying the terrain ahead. Sandoval nodded toward his own left.

"Down that way," he said. "It looks like an easier way across the mountain."

"*Sí,*" Morales agreed. "We'll go that way, and once we're on the other side, we'll ride back toward where the slaves climbed over. We'll have them before dark."

❧

THEY had ridden west, then north, to make the crossing. They found a creek there and crossed it, then turned east again. Morales figured they would encounter the escaped slaves somewhere along the creek. All the riders were alert, watching in every direction, looking hard at each bush and tree and rock. Then Morales saw the town. He signaled another halt.

"Rest here," he said. "We don't want to appear threatening to these people. I'll go talk to them."

The other men dismounted and allowed their horses to drink from the stream. Some of the men fell on their bellies and put their heads into the cool water. Morales did not dismount. He rode toward the town. It was walled in the manner of the frontier towns of the Real People and some of their neighboring tribes. Morales wasn't at all sure just where he was, but he thought that he was still in the country of the Real People, and the town had a familiar look about it. He hoped that he was right, for he had become fairly comfortable with the language.

He rode up close to the walls and stopped. He stayed in the saddle for a moment, waiting; then a man stepped out of the entryway and stood with arms crossed on his chest. The manner of his dress told Morales that the man was a Real Person. Morales swung down out of the saddle, dropped the reins to his mount, and stepped forward just a little.

" '*Siyo,* friend," he said.

" '*Siyo,*" said the other. "Who is calling me friend?"

"I'm a Spaniard," Morales said. "My name is Juan Morales. My wife is the War Woman of New Town. Lately we have been living at Dahlonega."

"I know the War Woman," said the other man. "I've heard that she married a white man. You're welcome here. Will you come in and eat with us?"

"I have men with me," said Morales. "They're waiting back there. We're searching for escaped slaves. Black men."

The expression on the other man's face darkened just a little. "What will you do," he asked, "if you find these . . . slaves?"

"One of them killed a Spaniard," Morales said. "Now he must be killed. If they refuse to tell us which is the killer, then all of them will be killed."

"And if they do tell you?"

"Then the murderer will be put to death," Morales said, "and the others will be punished and then sent back to work."

"How do you punish your slaves for running away?"

"They will likely be whipped," Morales said, "but that will not be my decision to make. I'll just take them back. Others will decide what to do with them."

The other man heaved a big sigh. "I don't like it," he said, "that I cannot be of help to the husband of the War Woman of New Town. But I cannot."

"You haven't seen them then?" Morales asked.

The other did not respond.

"Well, we'll just keep searching," Morales said. "We know they're somewhere near."

"They're in my town."

"What?"

Morales was stunned for an instant. The man had said that he couldn't help. Then he had said—

"They're in my town now," he said. "Some black men. They came to us tired and hungry. They were almost naked. They were unarmed, and they said that some white men were chasing them. We told them to come into our town, and we promised them protection. They're my guests, and I cannot let you have them."

Now Morales was silent. Here was a dilemma he had not anticipated. These Real People, though they would accept him as a friend because of his marriage to War Woman, would fight him if they had to in order to protect their guests and keep the promise they had made. The escaped slaves, including the murderer, were under the protection of this town of the Real People.

Morales had lived with the Real People and with his wife, War Woman, long enough to have an understanding of the attitude of these protectors of his prey. And he knew that they would have no particular concern over the killing of a Spanish soldier.

But then Morales, as he had discovered so recently, still had strong patriotic feelings about his homeland. That was the reason he had led this bunch on this chase in the first place. But now what was he to do? He could demand that the Indios turn over the slaves. Then he and his followers would have a real fight on their hands. They would have to fight all the warriors of the town as well as all the escaped slaves. They could not win such a battle. He could report back to the *commandante* in La Florida, and perhaps an army would be sent to attack the town and secure the slaves. By then, though, the slaves might be long gone, and the ensuing slaughter would be all for naught. *What would War Woman say if she were here?* he asked himself.

But it was a foolish question to ask, for he already knew the answer. She would say to him, "Turn around and go home. Forget the whole thing." She would say that if a man had put chains on her, she, too, would kill him the first chance she got and run away. She would say that Spanish law meant nothing in the country of the Real People. And she would look at him and ask him, "Where is your heart? Is it with me, or is it with your *commandante?*"

MORALES rode back to where the others were waiting for him, and they gathered anxiously around to hear what he would have to say. He halted his horse and slowly dismounted. He was tired, and he was beginning to feel old. He recalled that his wife had expressed a desire to go back to New Town. That idea sounded particularly good to him, to return to New Town and a quiet life.

"What did you find out?" one of the miners asked.

"It's a town of the Real People," Morales said, "the Chalakees."

"Did you find the slaves?"

"I saw nothing of them."

"Had the Indios seen them?"

"They said they could not help us," Morales said.

"But they can't be far from us," said another. "Perhaps we can pick up their trail again."

Morales shook his head slowly.

"I don't think so," he said. "The trail is ended. I think we've lost them. Let's go back."

<h1 style="text-align:center">42</h1>

AR WOMAN had invited Commandante Huelga to her house, and the two of them sat in the chairs in front. The rest of the soldiers were denied entry into the town. Huelga sampled the hominy drink that the Real People always offered their guests. He found it strange but interesting. The more he sipped at it, the better it tasted. He would have preferred a glass of good red wine, but this was not a pleasure visit. He had serious business at hand.

"My *capitán*, Arredondo, came riding all the way back to my head-quarters," he said, "to tell me that the soldiers and the miners were ready to do battle with one another. He said that none of them would listen to him. They were all mutineers. If they were ready to fight when he ran away, why are not more of them killed?"

"They did not fight with each other," War Woman explained. "The two groups were facing each other and making threats. They wouldn't listen to the poor young man, and he therefore did the only thing he could think of to do, I suppose. He went to you for help."

"But they didn't fight," Huelga said.

"No," War Woman agreed. "They didn't. They got drunk together instead."

"Then, because they were all drunk," Huelga continued, "the slaves managed to kill a soldier and escape. Is that right?"

"That's probably correct," War Woman agreed.

"And now my soldiers and the miners are trailing the slaves, and they are being commanded by a trader."

"My husband is a good man, Commandante," War Woman said.

"Yes, of course, War Woman. I know that, and I mean no disrespect toward Juan Morales, but he is a trader. He is not a military man. Now I suppose I should take my troops out after them all."

"I would not do that if I were you," War Woman said.

"Oh?"

"I would wait for the return of Juan Morales and the others. See what he has to tell you."

"Well—" Huelga rubbed his chin. He did not really want to ride out into God knew where in pursuit of escaped slaves, recalcitrant miners, and mutinous soldiers. This was a stroke of good luck, for he could stay in the camp outside of Dahlonega and it would seem to have been War Woman's idea, not his own. He was about to speak further, but he saw the Raven of Dahlonega, accompanied by another Indio, walking toward them. The Raven looked solemn. The other man hung his head as if in sorrow or shame.

War Woman saw the same sight. In another moment she recognized the man with the Raven. She sat up straight and stiff and waited until the two men were standing just in front of her.

"War Woman," said the Raven, "this man comes from your own town with news for you. Bad news."

War Woman braced herself to take with dignity whatever it was she was about to hear.

The man from New Town stepped forward. He looked up briefly into War Woman's eyes, then dropped his head again. "I don't like to have to tell you this," he said, "but it has to be told. I was chosen. Your brother killed our war chief. It happened because of our new law that there's to be no strong drink in New Town.

"Your brother and his friends were stealing the trader's drink out on the road where he had left it. Our chiefs, both of them, and the trader went to stop it. Your brother and his friends beat them up, stole all of the drink, and ran away with it. Our war chief was dead."

"And the other two?" War Woman asked.

"They were beaten up, but they have recovered," said the messenger. "Of course, the clan of our former war chief went after your brother. They followed him and the other drinkers for a long ways and found them living in a cave. They beat them all, all except your brother. They told him to go back to New Town with them. He was going to fight them, but then, they said, when he found out that he had killed our war chief, he did not fight them. He went back to New Town with them."

"Then he did not know he had killed . . . our war chief?" War Woman asked.

"No," said the man. "It seems he did not know."

"And how is it that we know," War Woman asked, "that it was my brother who killed the war chief?"

"The other two," the man said, "the trader and our peace chief, both saw him strike the blow and when he came back to town, he did not deny it."

The man fell silent and stared at the ground. War Woman waited a moment. Then she spoke.

"You have more to tell me," she said.

"They brought him back to New Town," the man said. "They were going to kill him, of course. But your mother did not want them to kill her son. I don't know—perhaps she thought it would start a clan war; perhaps it was something else. I don't know.

"But they brought him back to New Town, and he was walking between two of the men who had gone out to get him. They had walked into town and were just at the front of the town house when your mother stepped out from behind a house near there. She stepped out behind them."

The man paused again, as if he did not want to tell the rest of the tale, or as if his voice was choked with emotion. War Woman waited stoically, sitting straight, her jaw set hard.

"Your mother had in her hands a bow and an arrow," the man said. "We all saw her. We stared at her with wide eyes. We could not believe what we were seeing. I myself watched her, and I could scarcely believe it.

"She fitted the arrow to the string, then pulled back the string and aimed. She let the arrow fly, and it drove itself deep into the back of your brother, right between his shoulders.

"He was surprised. He stood a moment with his eyes opened wide. Then he fell forward, and he was dead. That's all."

◦◦◦

WHEN Juan Morales returned to Dahlonega, he found the *commandante* waiting there for a report and found his wife in quiet, dignified mourning over the loss of her brother. Morales explained to Huelga what he had done and why he had done it. He then told the *commandante* that he had failed. He said that he had followed the trail of the escaped slaves as far as he could but had not been able to follow it any more.

"We had to give it up," he said.

Huelga's face was puffed red, but he did not express any anger. If he accused Morales of incompetence, then he would have to go out after the fugitives himself. He would have to show everyone that he could do what the incompetent had failed to do. He therefore decided that he would praise Morales instead. He would praise him for having made a gallant attempt against insurmountable odds.

"So now," said Huelga, "what do we do from here? We've had problems at this mine site from the beginning. I've noticed that the shipments from the mine have dwindled to almost nothing. Are the men not working?"

"It seems," said Morales, "that there is no more gold. We've taken it all out of the mine."

"Does Alvarado agree with that assessment?" the *commandante* asked.

"He disagrees," said Morales.

"Excuse me," said Huelga, "but you, a trader, think there is no more gold, and Alvarez, whose business is mining gold, says that there is more. Who am I to believe?"

Morales shrugged. "I could be wrong," he said.

"Why do you believe that there is no more gold? Why do you doubt Alvarado?"

"Commandante," said Morales, beginning to pace, "I don't like to say anything bad about anyone, especially a countryman."

"Say what you believe," Huelga said. "It's your duty."

"The gold was less and less each day," Morales said. "Then it stopped. Alvarado said we'd find more. We waited. It didn't come. Some of the miners said that it was all gone. They have experience. In the beginning, my wife said we would find gold, and we did. Now she's not at all sure that we'll find more. I don't know. Perhaps it's a feeling and nothing more. As far as Alvarado is concerned, I think that he's talking out of desperation rather than any evidence or experience. He wants to succeed so badly, he refuses to accept reality. That's what I believe."

"I'll consider all this," Huelga said.

WAR WOMAN sat alone thinking about the Little Spaniard. She remembered him as he was in the days before the Spanish drink had gotten its hold on him. He had been young, handsome, bold, and absolutely trustworthy.

Then he had taken to the drink, and it had changed him utterly. It had been some time since she had seen him, but even then he had not looked well. He had been gaunt and his skin sallow. There had been dark circles beneath his eyes, and his eyes appeared to have sunk back in his head. He was skinny, and he was unkempt. And he had become sly and furtive, not to be trusted. Now he was dead by Osa's hand.

War Woman knew why Osa had done the deed. It had not been to prevent clan retaliation. She knew. She knew that her mother had killed her own son because she could not bear the thought of anyone else killing him. If it had to be done, she would do it herself. She had brought him into the world; then she had taken him out of it.

But he had been War Woman's twin, almost a part of her. She felt a terrible loss, almost as if a part of her body had been taken away and she had only just made the startling discovery, as if a leg had been missing for some time, but she had only just now looked down and noticed.

She thought about the Spaniards and their drink. She thought about all the changes the Spaniards were causing among the Real People. She considered the fact that she herself had been instrumental in bringing many of those changes, in establishing the trade, in clearing the way for the miners. She thought about the drink again, and she knew that she was the one who had brought it to her own brother, or had brought him to it. She had introduced him to the thing that had become the cause of his death. And she had done it for gold.

SHE walked toward the Spanish camp. Morales was walking in the other direction, heading toward their home. They met, and Morales turned to walk beside her. She said nothing. She did not even look at him.

"War Woman," he said, "where are you going?"

She did not answer, and she continued walking toward the Spanish camp.

"Are you going to see Huelga?"

She still did not answer, but Morales knew that he was right. She was moving toward the camp, and there was no one else there she would want to see.

"May I go with you?" he asked, and when she did not answer still, he took it that at least she had not said no. He kept walking beside her. Soon they were at Huelga's tent. The *commandante* stood up from his camp chair to greet her.

"Commandante," she said, "the people of Dahlonega wish you to depart. There is no more gold in the mine. The time for you to be here is past. Sleep here tonight, and leave when the Sun begins to light the morning sky."

THEY stood together and watched the Spaniards leave, War Woman, Morales, and the Raven. Many of the other residents of Dahlonega stood around them. No one cheered or yelled or danced with joy, but they were all glad to see the rude Spaniards leaving their land.

The tents were gone, but there was still a mess left by the soldiers and the miners. It would take time for that to vanish. And in the side of the hill the rough tunnel was there, an open sore.

When not even the dust from the Spanish caravan could be seen anymore, War Woman turned and walked back toward Dahlonega. Juan Morales walked alongside her. They walked back into the town, through the streets, and back to the house Morales had built. Consuela and the children were playing beneath the trees. A cooking fire burned on the ground in front of the house.

War Woman stopped beside the fire and looked at her house. She knelt and took hold of the cold end of a burning stick, then lifted it and stood. She walked to the front door of her house and tossed the flaming stick inside. Morales made a movement as if to stop her, but instead he stopped himself. They stood and watched as the flames grew, licking at the walls of the house. At last War Woman turned to face Morales.

"We're going home now," she said.

3

The Darkening Land

1654

43

HE WAS OLD. She felt as if she were as old as the tallest trees in the dense forest that surrounded her home, ancient as the very hills and as the rituals and ceremonies that kept her people alive and continually renewed the world. She knew the old tale of the time in the beginning when the original life-forms had come down from their first home on top of the great Sky Vault. They had found nothing but water, so they had dived under the water until one of them, a water beetle, had come up with some mud. They had spread the mud over the top of the water, and the great buzzard had dried it with his wings. She felt as if she had been there when that all had happened.

She remembered things that had happened so long ago there was no one else alive who could recall them. Others told tales that they had heard from their parents or their grandparents. She had been there at the time of the actual events. She remembered not the tales, but being present when those things happened.

And she had not just been there, she had been involved. She had been a major player in every important event that had taken place among her people over the last—oh so many years. She had met the Spaniards in La Florida and had established trade between them and the Tsalagis back in the old days when she had taken her first husband and had him for such a brief time. All those years ago.

Daksi had been his name. She did not speak it, but she could say it in her mind. Daksi. She could not recall his features anymore, though. She remembered only that he had been young and handsome and bold. She herself must have been very young and beautiful back then. Worlds ago. She remembered also that she'd had a brother, a twin. He, too, had been young and handsome, before he had taken to drink.

There had been another husband, a white man, a Spaniard, and the two of them had made a fortune together. They had owned black slaves and cattle and hogs. They had lived in a big house like white men lived in, but he, too, was gone, long gone. He had lived to be an old man and died a quiet and natural death, but she had lived on and on. He, too, had become a vague memory.

She'd had two children with Juan Morales: Paco and Meli. Both of them were dead. She who had lived such a long life and known so many people was alone in the world. She had outlived everyone. She lived alone in a small house, like the one she had been born in, on the edge of New Town. There were people all around her, but they were all so young and so much a part of this new world that she could not feel like she really knew any of them.

What did they know of her life, of all the things she had done and all the people she had known? What, therefore, could they know of her? How could any of them say that they knew her? If a stranger were to come to New Town and inquire about her, the residents could say, "Yes, there is an old woman here called War Woman. She lives over there in that house." What else could they say? Nothing. They did not know her. Could not.

And so she did not know them. They were children, and they knew nothing but tales of the times that she had known. Sometimes they came to her for advice and for help, for they knew that she had experienced much and had wisdom and powers. They had respect for her—and more than a little fear— but they did not know her.

So she was there among them, yet she was alone. She had been raised her first few weeks of life by an old woman known as the Horn, Uyona, and old Uyona had started her on her life of mysterious power and influence. The old woman had died shortly after that, while she had still been an infant, so she did not really remember Uyona. But she knew what Uyona had done. She knew Uyona.

The Horn had not wanted to die, so she had taken the infant to raise, and it was as if she had put her own life into the infant she had called Whirlwind. *I have become old Uyona,* the War Woman sometimes thought. *I've always been here, and I will never die.*

Sometimes she thought about what the Tsalagis had been like in her youth and what they had become during the course of her long life. They had changed, and she had been the cause of some of the changes. Even that word. Tsalagi. The Real People, Ani-yunwi-ya, had been called Chalakee by the Choctaws, and that word had gone into the trade language, the jargon used by all of the people around. Then the Spaniards had come and the French, and they had picked up the word from the jargon. Now even Real People were using it to refer to themselves. Now a Real Person might say, "I'm Tsalagi," rather than say, "Ani-yunwi-ya."

Ah well, she even caught herself saying it sometimes. *I'm the oldest Tsalagi alive, an ancient Tsalagi woman, as old as the mountains and hills, as old as the very rocks, and older than the oldest trees. Just look at me and you can tell. Just let me tell you the things that I can remember, because I was there when they happened. I was there when they made the world.*

SHE heard some commotion in town. Something was going on. She listened through the walls of her house. There were visitors in town, it seemed. Several visitors. They were not Tsalagis, not Spanish or French. Some other kind of Indios. Some neighboring people. She listened more closely. She caught snatches of the speech, and she did not recognize the language at all.

Ah well, she thought. *It's none of my business. New Town has its chiefs and its council. Let them take care of things. I'm old and tired.* Then she listened some more. Everyone sounded very excited, like something significant, something important, was going on. What did they know? They had never seen anything really important in their lives, not like she had.

She would not bother to go out there. Why should she make them think that anything that might be happening out there would get her excited? They were inexperienced children. She was the War Woman, and she had already seen everything there was to see, much of it several times over. She turned away, but then she turned back, curiosity overcoming her in spite of herself. What was that language they were speaking anyway?

She wrapped a shawl around her shoulders—like the skirt and blouse she wore, it was made of cloth, acquired from Spanish traders—then she reached for her walking stick, and she stepped out of her house. Squinting because of the light of day outside, she located the crowd over near the town house. She could see the backs of the people, gathered around . . . someone. She started to walk, and she set a scowl on her face.

A dog ran across her path, and she swept her stick at it, striking it across the rear end. It yelped, tucked its tail, and ran. She kept walking, and she could hear the voices, Tsalagi voices now.

"These people can tell their tale to us later," said one. "Right now, we should feed them."

"My wife has some stew," said another. "We'll bring it here."

"I'll get *kanohena*."

"*Selu*."

"*Gadu*."

"*Tuya*."

Just about every kind of food was mentioned, and people began running to their homes to get what they had prepared and bring it back to the town house for the guests—whoever they were. She trundled on toward the strangers, and the crowd around them was thinning. As she got closer, she could see Running Man, the war chief of New Town, standing there. He saw her, too, and he walked toward her.

" '*Siyo*," he said. "I'm glad you've come, War Woman. We'll need your advice."

She stopped walking and looked ahead. She could see the strangers now, Indios all right. They were not Tsalagis, Creeks, Choctaws, or Chickasaws. They were not from the southern country, for she knew the people there. She did not recognize these strangers.

They were four men. All of them were barefoot. One wore a matchcoat that slipped over his head. There was a hole for his right arm, but his left arm was inside the coat, and the entire coat reached only to the top of his thighs. He had no leggings. The other three men wore deerskin breechcloths that covered them in front almost to the knees but rode high in back. The hair on their heads was cropped close except for a thin stripe of longer hair that ran from the front at the top of the forehead back to the nape of the neck.

Their ears were adorned with small feathers. One man had facial tattoos that ran horizontally across his eyes and nose. One carried a long bow and had a quiver dangling low on his back. The tail of a mountain lion dangled from the quiver, looking almost as if it were his own tail. Three arrows were in the quiver. The others were unarmed.

"Who are they?" War Woman asked.

"We haven't learned much yet," said Running Man. "One of them speaks the trade language a little. None of them speak our language, and no one here knows theirs. They call themselves Appomattoc, and they are a part of the Powhatan alliance. It seems that they have had a bad fight with white men."

"Spanish?" War Woman asked.

"No," said Running Man.

"French then?"

"I don't think so," said Running Man. "Someone else."

"*Gilisi,*" War Woman muttered, more to herself than to Running Man. She had never seen an Englishman, but she had heard that they were around, not too far away. They were a third bunch of white men, with yet another language. Neither the Spanish nor the French liked the English; so she had heard. If these men had not been Spanish or French, then they must be the Gilisi, the English, she surmised.

"What did you say, War Woman?" Running Man asked.

"Never mind," she said. "Feed these wretched-looking people, and then we'll hear what they have to say."

People started bringing food from all over New Town. They brought deer meat, roasted, dried, stewed, and they brought fish, several kinds. They brought bowls of different varieties of beans and squash and corn, and they brought bread. They laid the food out on long planks, and they invited the strangers to sit and eat. War Woman did not wait for an invitation. She found a place at the plank and sat.

She was old, but she had all her teeth, and they were good. She could bite and gnaw as well as ever, and she liked to eat. She especially liked to eat when someone else had prepared the food. She was an old woman, and she had done her share of cooking and caring for others. Now she was just as glad to be cared for herself. Let them do things for her, if they wanted her to stay around so they could share her wisdom and take advantage of her powers.

She ate venison and fish and beans and squash and bread. She ate some of everything that was there, and then she ate more. She especially liked the deer meat and the bread. She ate several helpings of those. At least the young people could still cook.

She was glad these strangers had come by, for without them the feast would not have been laid out. She glanced furtively at the four Appomattoc men, and she took note of the fact that they ate ravenously, as if they had not eaten for days.

They were tired and hungry, ill dressed, and practically unarmed. They were far from home and had come among a people with whom they could barely converse, a possibly dangerous thing to do. Obviously they were in desperate straits.

She had heard of the Powhatans, a large confederacy of tribes, although she had never dealt with them. The actual Powhatans were the leading tribe of the alliance. Other smaller tribes included were the Chesapeake, Chickahominy, Pamunkey, Potomac, and Appomattoc, represented by these four visitors. Why, she wondered, were these four, coming from such a powerful group, seeking refuge so far from home?

She had never been to the Powhatan country and therefore did not know how many days these four had traveled, but she did know that it was not near. It was north and east of the land of the Tsalagis, near the big water that the white men had come across.

She had heard that these Powhatans were large and powerful and had subjugated a good many other peoples around them. Their lands were vast. She imagined that they were almost as powerful as were the Tsalagis. She tried to imagine how many of these Gilisi it would take to cause serious damage to so powerful a people as the Powhatans, and she could not imagine that there could be so many of them. There were not so many Spaniards or French, and both of those had been around for a much longer period of time. Perhaps these four Appomattoc men were not being completely truthful. Perhaps they were fugitives from their own people. Nothing else made any sense to War Woman, unless the English were far worse than any of the white men she had encountered before.

44

AR WOMAN sat with Running Man and White Crane Feather, the peace chief of New Town. Seven advisers, one from each of the seven Tsalagi clans, sat nearby. The large town house was filled with many of the residents of New Town, all seated in their respective clan sections of the house. Those not lucky enough to find room inside were crowded around the door. All were anxious to hear the tale the Appomattoc men had to tell.

A fire burned in the center of the room. The smoke from that and from the pipes of many of the people present filled the large room in spite of the smoke hole in the center of the roof. No one seemed to be bothered by it, though. The people muttered in low voices to one another, but when Running Man stood up to speak a sudden hush engulfed the smoky air.

Running Man was dressed magnificently, his shoulders draped in his cloak of office: a mantle made of the breast feathers of turkeys. A crown of white crane feathers sat snug on his head. He opened the meeting with the proper formalities and introduced the guests. Then he sat down, giving the floor to the Appomattoc man with the short matchcoat.

That guest stood up to speak. He looked out over the crowd of Tsalagis and hesitated a moment before speaking. Then, using the jargon with some difficulty, he identified himself as He Walks on High, a town chief of the Appomattocs, a member tribe of the once-great Powhatan Confederacy.

"I have lived on this earth for fifty winters," he said, "and the hairs on my head have all turned gray. For most of my life I have enjoyed the association of my people, the Appomattocs, with the great Powhatans. I have enjoyed, too, my own position within that structure. Always, everywhere I have traveled, I have been treated with respect, and when visitors came to my country, they came to me respectfully, sometimes even in fear. I was an important man, an important part of a powerful people.

"In my grandfather's and my father's day, when I was but a small child, no more than three winters old, strangers, these white men who call themselves English and who now call themselves our masters, came to our country in big boats. They came from a land we had never before heard of, from someplace far across the big water. They were strange-looking people, with white skin and hairy faces. They wore strange clothing, and they had animals with them like we had never seen before. They brought with them their women and children.

"They built themselves a town they called Jamestown in honor of their chief across the waters. At first we could not understand their strange speech. Even so we welcomed them as new friends and, when the winter came on us, they were ill prepared for it. They would have starved to death, all of them, were it not for our friendship for them and our kindness toward them. We took pity on them, for we did not like to see anyone starve, especially children. We brought them food and animal skins. We helped them through those cold months.

"Then when the snows at long last melted and the planting time came once again, we gave them seed and showed them what to plant and how to care for it, so that they would have their own crop before the next winter came. We taught them everything they needed to know in order to survive and prosper in this land. We got along well with them. We were friends, or so we thought. One of them even married the daughter of our great chief and took her with him back across the great waters to live there among his people. We have never seen her again.

"But because of our help, they grew stronger, and they became familiar with this land, and soon it seemed they no longer needed our friendship. We should have noticed sooner that they were becoming less friendly toward us. They did not welcome our visits at Jamestown as enthusiastically as they once had. Their faces wore frowns when we went to visit them. They did not offer us food or drink or tobacco as one should a visitor.

"And we had taught them how to smoke and how to grow tobacco. They had been so ignorant when first we met them that they had never seen tobacco before. They did not know what it was or what its use was. They had never smoked, nor had they ever seen anyone smoke. At first the sight of smoke coming out of a man's mouth and nose frightened them. They thought that we were on fire in our bellies when we smoked."

The Tsalagis laughed at the foolish simplicity of these new white men, and He Walks on High paused long enough for the laughter to subside. There would be little enough humor in this talk. Then he continued.

"But they soon learned how to smoke," he said, "and they liked it. They learned how to grow tobacco. We gave them seeds, and we taught them how and when to plant them. Then they took some of it back across the big water, and they sold it there. All the white people back there, it seems, wanted tobacco, and these, our neighbors at Jamestown, began to grow more and more of it. They sold it so much that they wanted more land to grow tobacco on, and then more and more and more.

"They discovered that it was much more convenient for them to just take our tobacco fields away from us than to cut down trees to expand their own fields. They were greedy, but they were also lazy. They took our fields away from us and built new settlements out away from Jamestown, farther into our country, closer to our homes. They pushed us back from them a little at a time, and for a time, we let them.

"Then one day we decided that they had pushed us far enough. We saw that if we did not stop them, soon we would have no land left. We decided that we would not allow them to push any farther. We decided that these English should be taught a lesson in proper behavior and friendship and respect, for we had befriended them and helped them to survive, and now they were paying us back by stealing our lands and pushing us away from them. They should also be taught that the Powhatans were a powerful people and not to be insulted."

Here He Walks on High paused and stood with a long, sad look on his face. He looked as if he might break into tears, but he did not. He continued.

"So we made ready for war," he said, "and we attacked them without warning. We burned up several of their settlements and killed many white men in just one day. More than three hundred, I think. We thought that would be enough. We thought they had learned their lesson. We thought that they had learned that they could not push us away from our own land. But we were wrong, and we soon learned how wrong we had been. I can see now that we should have killed them all."

He Walks on High paused again, and the silence in the town house was thick. Everyone waited anxiously for the rest of the tale. Everyone watched as his breast heaved from exhaustion even at just the telling of the dismal tale. He went on.

"In retaliation, they started attacking our towns, one after the other, and our weapons were no match for their guns and swords. I never saw anyone fight the way the English fight. They burned our towns to the ground, and they destroyed our fields and our grain houses, depriving us of all of our food. They killed everyone they could reach, old men, young men, women, and children. Anyone who managed to escape the slaughter had no place left to live and nothing to eat.

"And they did this in the winter. They did this to one town after another. Many people fled to the west. Some established new towns; some moved in with other people, seeking food and shelter from the cold. People starved and froze to death. Little children, too. We were scattered, and now the great Powhatans are no more. There are some few towns still in the old country, mostly Pamunkey towns, but they have all surrendered themselves totally to the English and will absolutely do the bidding of the English. They no longer have any minds of their own.

"We, who were once proud men, came here as wandering, homeless beggars to tell you our tale, and to ask if we can stay here with you, for we have no other place to go. Our towns are burned. Our families have all been killed. We are alone in this world. We are absolutely no good for anything."

He Walks on High sat down. He had the look of a man who had been totally defeated and demoralized. The smoky air now seemed heavy and oppressive, and it weighed down on all of the people in the big room. His speech was followed by a long and solemn silence in the town house. At last Running Man stood up.

"You're welcome to stay here as our guests," he said. "We'll talk this over among ourselves, and then we'll all talk again in a few more days. For now, you're safe here with us."

The meeting broke up then, and people began to leave for their homes. The four Appomattoc men were given a place to stay. Soon the town house was almost deserted. But War Woman still sat in her place. Running Man waited for her to get up to leave, but it soon became apparent to him that she would not. He walked over to stand before her.

"What are you going to do?" she asked.

"I don't know," said Running Man, with a shrug. "I can't make such a decision on my own. I don't even know if there's anything I should do. I've never met any of these . . . Gilisi, and they're not on our land. I'll have to talk with my advisers, and we have to talk to the women. Then we'll have to—"

"I know all that," she said, cutting him short. "I've lived here for seven lifetimes to your one. You don't have to tell me all of that. What do you think about that man's tale?"

Running Man sat down on a bench facing War Woman. He looked at the ground between them. He sat in silence for a moment, shaking his head slowly.

"I don't know," he said again. "I suppose the story is true."

"I believe it," War Woman said.

"I guess we can give these men a home."

"Yes, we should do that," she said. "Is that all?"

"What else should we do?" Running Man asked. "What else can we do?"

"You've heard of the Powhatans?" War Woman asked.

"Yes," he said. "I have. Of course."

"A powerful people," she said. "Almost as powerful, maybe, as the Tsalagis."

"Yes," he said. "I suppose so. I suppose they were . . . once."

"Then how many of these Gilisi," she asked him, "must there be to destroy so powerful a people?"

"I guess there must be many of them," Running Man said.

"And they keep growing, and they keep taking more land," War Woman said. "Did you notice that man said the Powhatans destroyed several of their settlements?"

"Yes," said Running Man. "Several."

"And all sprung up from just one small, weak town," she said.

Running Man rubbed his chin thoughtfully. "Yes," he muttered. "One town became many."

"How many more settlements will grow from those?" War Woman asked. "How much more land will they want on which to grow their tobacco? When will they reach our country with their long arms?"

War Woman knew of the white man's greed for money. She understood the impulse of the English to grow more and sell more. She had learned from her second husband. She had learned when she herself was busy accumulating wealth in the manner of the white man. She knew that if these men had discovered in tobacco a source of wealth, they would never be satisfied.

"War Woman," said Running Man, "what would you have us do?"

"Who am I, an old woman, to tell you what to do?" she asked.

"You've seen much," said Running Man. "You know many things. Give me the benefit of your years. Tell me what you would have us do."

War Woman tilted her head back and looked toward the ceiling of the town house. Her eyes seemed to glaze over as if she was seeing something there that Running Man could not see, and when she next spoke her voice seemed to come to him from far away.

"I seem to recall," she said, "a time long ago when the tall trees around us were only as high as my knee, a time when the *uk'ten'* could be heard roaring on the other side of the mountain and no one among us had ever seen or even heard of a white man, a time when the world was young and the animals all talked with one another and we could talk to them. I remember that time. I remember it well, for I was there."

Running Man sat in stupefied awe of this mysterious old woman as she said these incredible things. He was also a little frightened. A part of him wondered if she were telling him fanciful tales, but another part knew absolutely that what she said was true.

"One thing I seem to remember," War Woman went on, "a thing I had almost forgotten, the land over that way by the great water, the land that the Powhatans settled on much later, the land that they have just now lost to those English, in the beginning that land belonged to the Real People. It's Tsalagi land. It's our land. I was born on that land once. Who, then, are these ugly and arrogant English to think that they can take it? What gives them the right to just push people aside and drive them from their homes to take more and more land?"

"Do you think that we should—"

"We should go to that land again," War Woman said, "a whole new town of us, two hundred or three hundred of us at least. We should go there where the nearest Powhatan town to the English was and make our own town there, and then we should see what these Gilisi would do. We should see what they would think about that." She raised her walking stick and shook it in the air between herself and Running Man. "That's what I think we should do."

45

HERE WERE discussions and arguments and council meetings but in the end, everyone did what they had all known all along they would do. They did as the old woman advised them to do. They began preparations for the big move to the former country of the Powhatans.

New Town was in a strategic spot along the northern border of the land of the Tsalagis, so it could not simply be abandoned, and therefore the preparations were complicated. Some of the people would have to remain behind, but War Woman had insisted that two or three hundred were needed to establish their town on the site of the abandoned Powhatan town.

Therefore, people were recruited from other Tsalagi towns to either go with them on the long journey or move to New Town to help keep it well populated. War Woman had been among those people who years ago had made the move to establish New Town in the first place, but she had been an infant and had no memory of the process. That made no difference to her.

She had few possessions to carry along and was much too old to be expected to help build houses or a wall. She would simply go along. She could still ride a good horse, even at her age, though she might need to be helped up onto the saddle.

As the preparations moved forward and the word spread, more and more anxious volunteers appeared in New Town. Soon nearly seven hundred Real People were packed and gathered and ready to move to the land that the new white men, the English, or Gilisi, were calling Virginia. He Walks on High and his three Appomattoc companions decided to stay at New Town. They had been assured that they were welcome there, and they were certainly not anxious to revisit the site of their recent miseries.

When the volunteers came from other towns, War Woman stayed in the background, pretending that Running Man was in charge of everything, but everyone knew that it was really War Woman. She was giving directions and making the plans, for if she made a suggestion to Running Man, he followed it as if it had been an order. When anyone asked Running Man what the mission of this migration was, he would answer them in the words of War Woman.

"These English are new to this land," he would say. "They think that they can take all the land they want. So let them attack the Real People if they dare." It was like a battle cry, and all the young men began to repeat it and work themselves up for a good fight.

"Let them attack the Real People if they dare!"

War Woman did not know just how far they were going on this journey or how long they would be in their new homes. At her age, she did not know if she would ever again see New Town. New Town had been her home for almost her entire life. Her mother had brought her to New Town when she was still an infant, and it had been her home ever since, except for the time she had spent at Dahlonega with her second husband. She thought about the way in which she knew every detail of New Town and the surrounding countryside. She knew the houses and streets. She knew each log in the large town house, each pole in the town's stockade fence. The surrounding hills with their rocks and trees were all old familiar acquaintances, and she had spent years' worth of time talking with the waters that ran through the rivers and streams.

She had known several generations of citizens of New Town, and almost all her memories of family were memories also of New Town. She thought about the good years, the early years with her brother and her parents, but they seemed a thousand years in the past, and they had been followed by the time of misery after the Little Spaniard had become a drunk. Even considering all that New Town had meant to her during her long lifetime, she would turn her back on it with ease to go on this long trip. She might see her old home again in this lifetime, and she might not. It did not matter, she told herself, one way or the other, for she had a new and very important task ahead of her.

There were these English who, it seemed, were even more arrogant than were the Spaniards. The Spaniards had come through the land seeking gold and had caused much trouble over the years, but the English seemed to have come for land. If the sad experience of the Powhatans was an example of what to expect from the English, then they had come to stay and to multiply and to expand their holdings. In order to do that, they would have to continue to displace the people who already lived there in the places they wanted.

Alone in her little house in the dark of the night, War Woman had a vision of white men spreading themselves across the land, burning native towns and driving the native people ahead of them. Always moving. Always spreading. Always wanting more and more.

It would be a terrible mistake, she thought, to think that this was just a problem for the Powhatans. Eventually, sooner or later, these greedy whites would reach into the lands of the Real People. The Tsalagis would have to deal with them one day and she wasn't at all sure that she had enough confidence in any of the young people's ability to effectively deal with these foreigners.

So the ungrateful English would have to be taught a severe lesson, one they would not soon forget, and it would have to be done right away, while she, the War Woman, was still around to guide her people. That was her plan of action. She felt as if she were the only one among all of the Real People who could take charge in such times. She was the War Woman.

AT last the day came to begin the journey, and Running Man brought out a strong but gentle gray mare. She was wearing on her back a fine Spanish saddle. He led her to a tree stump and offered her to War Woman. He helped War Woman onto the stump and from there up onto the back of the mare. Once in the saddle, she was at ease. She felt at home. Her personal belongings, packed into a single roll, were tied onto the back of the saddle.

With everyone ready, Running Man led the procession away from New Town, and it was a massive migration. People from all the nearby towns were there at New Town to see them off. There were words of encouragement and there were parting tears, but the general mood was one of great excitement, for everyone knew the mission.

After having ridden a few miles north out of New Town, Running Man sent out scouts to ride ahead and on the flanks of the column. He continued to ride at the head of the column, with War Woman riding beside him. Behind them the line of Tsalagis stretched back farther than any of them could see.

War Woman felt good. Riding along at the head of the column she felt free. It had been a long time since she had made a big trip. She thought about her first major journey when, at sixteen, she had gone south into La Florida. Now, an old woman, she was feeling something of that same youthful spirit of adventure one last time. She did not feel young again, she felt better than young and she liked that feeling.

She also enjoyed the position of importance that had been given to her for this mission. She knew that when people asked Running Man what they should do or what the plans were or what the reasons were they were really asking him to tell them what War Woman had said to him. They knew it, he knew it, and she knew it. Even so, they would go to him and not to her, for that was the proper thing to do. She liked that method, too, because it kept her aloof from the rest of the people.

She enjoyed a special status among her people, one that no one else alive could claim, for she had been known and hailed as a leader and a woman with special powers and gifts for most of her ninety years. Although everyone had tremendous respect for her, many were also afraid of her and most would not dare to approach her on their own. It had been like that, too, for most of her life, and she liked it that way.

At the end of the first day's riding, Running Man helped War Woman down off her horse, and she was sore and stiff from the long ride, but she did not complain. She had expected that. It had been a long time since she had ridden on the back of a *sogwili*. People helped her make her own small camp for the night, and they brought her food. She ate, and she slept well, although again she had dreams or visions.

> She found herself flying over a beautiful green land of rolling hills and forests, much like the land she had known all her life, and then she saw a beautiful river running below. She glided down lower for a better look, and she saw a falls. It looked like a lovely and practical place for a town.
>
> She veered toward the right, toward the bank of the river, and there she saw a blackened blight on the otherwise lush green landscape. Moving in closer, she saw that it was the burned-out site of a town. It matched exactly the description of the site of the Powhatan town that Walks on High had given her.

THE next morning when she woke, she knew that she had visited the site of their next home, the place where the Powhatan town had been burned by the English, the place where the Tsalagis would build a new town with which to taunt the English. She knew she had seen it, but she said nothing about it to anyone else.

They moved on, but the pace of the long column was slow. Hunters were out almost constantly to bring in enough game to feed the seven hundred. Along the way, campsites were carefully selected, having been scouted out ahead. There had to be plenty of space, firewood, water, and grazing for the horses.

On the fourth night out from New Town, War Woman had Running Man gather young men around her, as many as could get near enough to hear, and she told them tales of the bold exploits of past Tsalagi warriors in order to make them anxious to fight. She told of her own fights with Spaniards, including the fight in which her first husband had been killed, the fight that had earned her the title of War Woman.

The young men were anxious to do ferocious battle and the War Woman's tales had exactly the effect she had wanted them to have. Every young man wanted to have the reputation of being a fierce warrior. They wanted to fight the English. They would have fought anyone, any enemy or potential enemy of the Real People. They would have followed Running Man anywhere into battle, would have gone alone anywhere that he or the War Woman might have chosen to send them. They were more than ready. They wanted action.

As the young men who had heard War Woman's tales of war rode their horses back along the long line of encampment to find their own individual camps for the night, they repeated her stories enthusiastically to those who had not been fortunate enough to hear them firsthand.

"She is a great woman," they said. "She's done great deeds."

"In her youth, they say, she could fight as well as any man."

"As old as she is, she could still fight and kill an Englishman."

And in a lower voice, "She could defeat all the English by herself with her powers—if she wanted to."

"Yes. She has great powers."

Running Man knew what War Woman was doing, and he was glad, for when the time came to do battle with the English the young men would all be ready to follow him. War Woman, too, was pleased with the results of her tale telling, but she cautioned herself. *Their mood will have to be maintained,* she thought, *it will not sustain itself. It has to be fed every now and then until the time comes to make use of it.*

She slept and again she dreamed, again of the blackened spot of earth, but now she watched it turn green again, and she watched a town grow up on the spot and cover the scars, and the town was a Tsalagi town, and it was good.

Again she kept the secret of her dream, but she felt good about what she had seen. She was anxious to find the place she had seen and to watch the town grow there and to see for real the things she had seen in her mind. She knew that it would happen, and she knew that it would be good. It was she who had set this whole plan into motion, and she was pleased that the signs she was getting from the spirit world were good signs. Her plans would all work out for the best.

THEY packed up again and started riding. It was getting more difficult each day for the people to climb back onto their horses and ride for another day, more difficult each night to make another camp. These people were used to their permanent homes, their cooking fires and beds. They were not used to wandering day after day and making a new camp each night.

So every fourth night War Woman would tell tales, Running Man would lead a dance, or someone else would be selected to do something to keep the spirits raised, to remind all of the people of their mission, to keep them moving, and to keep them from grumbling, growing too tired, or just giving up and returning home on their own. No one deserted.

The seven hundred kept moving toward Jamestown, toward the abandoned Powhatan town site, toward the English and the land they had dared rename Virginia. Led on by Running Man and urged by the indomitable spirit of the old woman, they plodded ahead. Along the way some babies were born.

Day by day, along the way, Running Man developed a new and warm relationship with War Woman. Like everyone else, he had known of her all his life, had grown up hearing tales about her exploits and about her powers. He had always had great respect and great admiration for her, and a little fear, but as they traveled this long road together he began to love her. He loved her as he loved his own grandmother, but in some ways he loved War Woman even more.

She was like a grandmother, but she was also something more. She was a legend and a power. He began to call her Grandmother, partly out of respect and partly because of the way he felt toward her personally, and he began to take a very special interest in watching out for her safety and comfort. She was, after all, ninety years old, and they were involved in a long and arduous journey.

46

HEY HAD stopped at the edge of a wide river, hesitating to wade in with their horses. Running Man thought that the water appeared to be too deep for a safe crossing. It seemed to have been raining in the mountains. Perhaps they should wait. But the sky gave the appearance of bringing more rain soon and if the water was high, it would likely get higher. If they were going to cross, they should do it soon.

While the debate continued, War Woman nudged her mare, urging her forward. She leaned back as the mare's head and forelegs lowered, dropping down the bank. Soon the water lapped around the old woman's thighs, then her waist. She kept riding. She did not look back to see what the others were doing behind her.

On dry land, the discussion suddenly ceased, and everyone toward the front of the column, everyone who could see and who had been taking part in the argument, watched as War Woman calmly waded the swollen river.

Running Man watched her for a moment and shrugged. He moved forward, riding his horse into the water. Three young men followed. Then others rode on into the river. They would make the crossing, it seemed.

To the west, horizontal lightning split the sky. Soon after, a great clap of thunder shook the ground just as War Woman's gray mare lurched up out of the water on the far side of the river. Riders fought to maintain control of frightened horses. Running Man was unhorsed in the middle of the river, but he caught hold of his horse's mane and held on.

Running Man came out of the water on his hands and knees. He scampered to his feet as quickly as he could and turned to shout back across the river to the ones still over there.

"Cross quickly!" he said.

Other riders then plunged on into the river. Several fell off their horses into the water and floundered, but like Running Man, they caught hold of their horses and held onto them until they reached the other side. War Woman turned her mare and rode back to be near Running Man and to watch what was happening.

There was another flash across the sky, and the dark clouds in the west were coming closer. Another loud clap of thunder sent already-nervous horses prancing and kicking and neighing. Men fought to hold them. War Woman spoke to Running Man.

"We should camp here until the storm has passed," she said. "Tell the others to wait on the other side. The waters will be rising fast now."

As Running Man frantically waved his arms, attempting to attract the attention of the riders on the far side, War Woman felt the first heavy drop of rain splatter on her forehead.

"Wait!" Running Man called. "Don't cross now. Make your camp over there. We'll wait here for you!"

Two young men, ignoring the warnings, plunged into the river. They fought their way halfway across before both of them were swept from their saddles. One of them grabbed a handful of mane. The other reached for a saddle horn, but his hand slipped off. He slapped at the by-now swift-running water, trying to swim or just stay afloat. He went under.

His friend shot him a desperate though brief glance. He was fighting too hard for his own life. The other came up again just as his own horse, also having lost control, was swept into him. The man disappeared again, this time underneath the horse. Horrified people on both sides of the river watched as man and horse rushed quickly beyond their reach and out of sight.

Wailing sounds immediately rose up, probably from relatives of the lost rider. His eyes wide, his mouth agape, Running Man stared after the youth, no longer visible. War Woman turned her horse away from the river and started to ride forward.

"You told them to stay," she grumbled.

RUDE shelters were quickly constructed, and a hasty camp was made on each side of the river. Some mournful voices continued to wail, their sounds not quite drowned out by the rushing waters and the driving rain, which continued throughout the day and the following night. The next morning, though, the rains had gone. The Sun was bright in the eastern sky. The clouds were gone, but everyone and everything the people owned was wet. And some of them were grumbling.

"He Runs Around was a young man," someone said.

"He shouldn't have tried to cross the river."

"It was War Woman who started the crossing," said another. "That crazy old woman."

"You know, it is said that she can control the weather."

"She caused the death of He Runs Around."

"Talk low. She might hear you."

"Why would she cause the death of He Runs Around? She's the one who wants us to go build this new town and teach a lesson to the Gilisi."

"You know that there are some old people who steal the years away from others. You know how they get to be so old."

"She's a witch."

"She can do anything."

"She'll get us all killed."

"We should turn around and go back home. This is a foolish trip we're taking."

"We should kill War Woman first."

ᏋᏫ

THEY waited for the rushing waters to subside before they finished the crossing.

At last all of the people were together again. The horses were all saddled and packed, and War Woman was just preparing to get on her mare. Running Man was moving toward her to help her up. Six men walked up to them. They stared at War Woman with stern faces.

"What do you want?" Running Man asked.

"We came for War Woman," said one.

"We're ready to travel," Running Man said. "Go get your horses."

"We're not going any farther while she lives."

"What do you mean?"

War Woman looked at the men and smiled. "Do you mean to kill me?" she asked.

The men hesitated and looked at the ground. At last the boldest among them spoke. "Yes," he said.

"Why?" she asked.

"You're the real cause of the death of He Runs Around."

"You think so?"

"Yes."

"And you mean to kill me?"

"Yes."

"It's been tried before," said War Woman, "and I'm here. I'm older than all of you put together. I'm as old as that river we just crossed."

"The river that killed our friend?" said one.

War Woman fixed her stare on the bold one, and he felt his skin crawl. He flinched and almost stepped back.

"You said that I killed him," she said. "Was it me or the river?"

"You used the river."

"So how are you going to do it?" she asked. They stood silent. "Which one of you will strike me first?" They all looked at the ground. "Are you afraid of an old woman? An old woman older than your grandmothers? Than all of your grandmothers put together? What kind of men are you? Cowards? And you were planning to fight the English? You? Ha."

"Go to your horses," said Running Man. "We have a long way to go yet. Let's travel."

Reluctantly the six men turned and walked away. Running Man stared after them for a moment, but War Woman turned her back on them.

"Help me up," she said.

The six men rode not far behind War Woman and Running Man. They rode along for a while in embarrassed silence. At last one spoke.

"We should have killed her," he said.

"Then why didn't you?" said another.

"I don't know why, but we should have."

They were silent again for a while. Then another of their number spoke. His voice was low, just loud enough for his near companions to hear.

"We could ride up behind her now and do it," he said.

"How?" asked another.

"With clubs?"

"We could put an arrow into her back."

"Do you believe what they say about her? If we kill her, or even try to kill her, will something bad happen to us because of it?"

"Look what happened to He Runs Around. He didn't try to kill her."

"If we let her live, we might all die."

They talked, but they never arrived at any decision.

⌘

LATER that day Running Man halted the column for a rest and a meal. The people built small cooking fires and began to prepare their meals. The six men sat together again, still looking sullen. Now and then they glanced toward Running Man and War Woman.

"We could do it now," one of them whispered.

"Yes," said another. "We could run up behind her and crack her old skull with our war clubs."

"What?" said another. "One after the other? Taking turns?"

"Well, we could all of us shoot her with our arrows then. That way they can't blame just one of us."

"Yes. We could all shoot at once."

"Shall we do it then?"

"Yes."

The six men stood, looking around themselves furtively to see if anyone was watching. Each found his bow and an arrow. Each nocked his arrow and tested the pull of his bow. They looked at one another, and the boldest of them gave a nod and started to walk. The others all fell in step. Some of the people noticed them and watched to see what they would do.

They walked past campfires where women cooked. The men did not look to the side. They looked straight ahead, toward their goal. They spoke to no one as they passed. No one spoke to them. They were determined to accomplish their mission and avenge their friend. They were determined to protect themselves and others from similar fates in the future. They were resolved. The old woman would die. They were going to kill War Woman.

They walked close enough to her for a bow shot, and they kept walking. They walked close enough so that no one of them could possibly miss. All of their arrows would hit. Any one alone would kill her. They were that close. Her back was turned to them. She was messing around with something in a pot on the fire.

The boldest raised his bow, and then so did the others. Just as they started to pull back their strings, Running Man saw them. He ran to stand between them and War Woman, and he held his hands out toward them.

"Stop," he said.

"Move away from her," said the leader, "or we'll kill you, too."

War Woman looked over her shoulder to see what was happening. She saw Running Man there close to her back, and she saw the six men with their bows and arrows. She recognized the men. Turning to face them, she straightened up, and she had a long wooden spoon in her right hand. She lifted it to her old lips and sipped from it. Smacking her lips, she turned and dropped the spoon back into the pot. Then she put a hand on the shoulder of Running Man and gave a gentle shove.

"Move aside," she said.

"Grandmother," he said, "I won't let them kill you."

"How can you stop them? Move away from me."

He didn't want to move away, but when she spoke to him like that he didn't seem to have any choice. Slowly he stepped to the side, leaving clear shots for the six determined men. Each one of them stood ready to draw back his bowstring, his arrow already aimed at her.

"Will you do it now?" she said.

They stood ready but immobile.

"Will you kill me for . . . that one?"

She stretched out an arm and pointed a bony finger toward the river and off in the direction in which He Runs Around had been swept away, and the six men, in order to see what it was she pointed at, had to turn their heads and look over their shoulders. They looked, and they were astonished, for they saw their friend, whom they believed dead, riding toward them quickly and waving an arm over his head.

"He Runs Around!" one shouted.

"He lives," said another.

They lowered their weapons and ran to meet him. A short distance away from the camp, he reined in his horse and leaped from the saddle. His six friends surrounded him and almost smothered him with their joyful embraces. At last they calmed themselves. They stood in a small silent group away from the rest. One of them nodded his head in the direction of War Woman, and all of them looked toward her.

He Runs Around started walking toward the camp, and the others followed him. He walked to War Woman's fire. His friends stood just behind him, their heads hanging low in shame.

"My friends thought that I had been killed in the river," he said.

"Yes," said War Woman. "I know."

"They told me that they blamed you."

"Yes."

"They were planning to kill you."

"They said so," said War Woman, "but they were afraid. I think they should turn around and go back home. We don't need them here with us."

47

HE RECOGNIZED the town site at once when they came upon it, for she had already seen it clearly. She had flown over it and viewed it from on high, then had swooped down for a closer look. She'd gotten a good look at it, so there was no mistaking it. She knew that it was the place He Walks on High described to her.

"This is where we're going to build our town," War Woman said.

It was a lovely spot there by the river, the rushing falls not far above the town site. War Woman thought that the Powhatan leaders had made a good choice. It was too bad they had let the English drive them away from their homes. Well, the Real People would take the original site and make an even better town, and they would not be driven away.

They would cover up the ugly scar left there on the face of the earth when the English had burned the previous town. And the place cried for a new town to be put up. It was a natural place to build, a natural place to live. Just by the river, with plenty of fresh water for people and animals, open fields for grazing, and woods near enough for easy gathering of firewood and building material, the place would be a natural attraction for both human and other animal life. But it had also attracted white men for those same reasons. War Woman scowled thinking about the white men.

The people were tired from the long journey, but they all felt new exhilaration knowing that they had at last reached their destination and looking at the beauty of the place. They were anxious to get started on their new houses and gardens, their new walled town with its central town house, and some of the young men were equally anxious to find some Englishmen and fight with them. These young men had not yet earned war honors and men's names, and the English offered them a perfect excuse for battle.

War Woman and Running Man calmed these brash young men as best they could without dampening their spirits. There were ceremonies to conduct before starting the town, things that must be done to ensure its safety and success. There was hunting to be done.

In the meantime, the people would camp nearby while they worked. As far as the English were concerned, "they'll find us soon enough," War Woman said. She thought about the cultivated tobacco field she had seen not far away from the town, and she looked carefully around the surrounding landscape. "We should have sentries out," she said to Running Man, and he selected several men for the duty and assigned them strategic posts on all sides around the town site and the temporary camp.

White Heron's Wing, the peace chief of the immigrants, prayed to various spirits in the four directions and sang songs and smoked over the site of the projected town from one end to the other. And each night he led dances in which almost everyone participated.

Hunters were sent on each of those days to bring back meat for the nightly feasts. Everyone was kept busy at something. At the end of the first four days, the women began building their houses. A crew of workmen was assigned the task of building the large town house and another the job of cutting trees to build the wall around the town.

TOM BARRY and Edward Ramsey rode out from their small settlement of farmers located a few miles outside of Jamestown proper. Their tobacco crop was almost ready, and it had to be checked carefully every day. Tobacco had become the mainstay of the Jamestown economy, and a crop failure could mean economic disaster. This day it was their turn to ride out and check the crop.

The Jamestown colonists had not had any trouble from Indians since their big victory over the once-powerful Powhatan Confederacy. In fact, the only Indians left in the area were in a few Pamunkey villages that had surrendered themselves unconditionally into the hands of the colonists, who, because of that bloody episode, had become rather smug and proud of their military prowess. Even so, the bold Englishmen never rode out far from their settlements alone, and when they rode they carried their long rifles. So Barry and Ramsey rode out together to check the tobacco crop.

They stopped their horses at the edge of the cultivated field, dismounted, and slowly walked out among the flourishing plants. Over the last few years, the men had become fond growers of the Indian weed, as they sometimes called it, and Barry lovingly fondled a large leaf with both his hands.

"It won't be long now, Ned," he said.

"Two or three more days, I'd say," Ramsey answered.

" 'Twill be a good crop this year."

"A bounteous crop indeed, and 'twill fetch us a fine penny."

"Yes," said the other. "I daresay."

"I say, Ned," responded Ramsey, a mischievous grin on his face, "do you reckon our good Lord Cromwell has yet learnt to smoke an Indian pipe?"

"I don't know about that, Tom," said Barry, grinning back. "I don't believe that his damned Puritan church allows such pleasant indulgences."

They got a raucous laugh out of the mild joke and then continued on, strolling casually among the plants, making small talk. They had seen what they wanted to see, but they were in no hurry to get back to the settlement. There would be more work to be done there, and they had been glad for their turn to check the tobacco field. They could waste a little time and get a rest.

And besides, talk was freer out away from the others. Back in the settlement one had to watch one's tongue. One never knew what spy of the government might be listening in, ready to run and tell a tale. Ramsey turned his head to look out over the field, and he caught a sudden and surprising glimpse of a few long, thin spires of smoke rising out of the horizon not too far away. The rolling hills blocked their source from view. He looked again, and a frown darkened his face.

"Tom," he said. "Look there."

He pointed and Barry looked.

"What do you make of it?" Ramsey asked.

"Several small fires," said Barry. "Like campfires."

"Who would be camping there?" Ramsey asked.

"They're small fires," Barry said.

"Like Indian fires?" said Ramsey.

"I think we'd best go take a look and see," Barry replied. "We'll have to report the details of this back in the settlement."

They walked quickly back to their horses and mounted up, then rode quickly toward the rising smoke. They had gone perhaps halfway toward the source when they slowed their pace. They looked questioningly at one another, then halted their horses. For a long uneasy moment they sat there in silence. Then Barry spoke.

"What do you think of it?" he asked.

"I think they're at the site of the old Powhatan town," Ramsey answered. "It looks like it from here. But who the devil would be over there?"

"The Devil," Barry said. "The words came from your own mouth, and they were prophetic. The Devil, I'd say, or savages, his minions. Same thing. You said it yourself. Like Indian fires, you said."

"You don't think the damned Powhatans would come back here now, do you?" Ramsey asked. "To this place? After the sound drubbing we gave to them?"

"There's no telling what goes on in the mind of a savage," Barry said. "They might be back. We have to find out, though. We'll have to find a way of getting closer without being seen."

"Let's go back to the settlement and get some more men," Ramsey suggested.

"And tell them what when we get there? That we saw some smoke and we need some help to look at it? Come on, Ned, let's go."

Barry urged his mount forward, and Ramsey, though still hesitant, followed along. They moved slowly down a road that ran between the old Powhatan town and Jamestown, a relic of earlier and friendlier times. Beyond the tobacco field, the road had not been much used since the late war, and it was therefore slowly being overtaken once again by the hardy plants that grew along its edges. Left alone long enough, it would disappear.

"If we continue right down the middle of the road in this manner," Ramsey said, "the savages'll spot us sure, and if they're indeed unfriendly they'll be upon us before we know what's happening."

"You're right," said Barry. "Let's ride into that dark grove of trees ahead and leave our horses hidden there. Then we'll make our careful way up the hill yonder and on over to the falls. From there we can look down on them and see everything that's going on."

They rode a little farther on, then veered off the right side of the road, moving into a nearby thick stand of trees. Dismounting, they tied their horses to saplings and started shoving their way through the thick and darkly shaded underbrush.

Small insects annoyed their faces as they pushed branches and vines out of their way with their arms, getting cuts and scratches for their pains. They roundly cursed the dark American wilderness and the bloody savages with every labored step, eventually coming to the base of the hillside on the other side of the grove. They stood there for a moment breathing deeply, grateful to be out of the thicket.

The hillside before them was steep and rocky and brush-covered, but they felt that they had no choice, and so they assaulted it, and the resulting climb was slow, tedious, and sometimes even painful. At long last, they reached the top, and there, crouched low to hide themselves from the Indians below. They paused briefly to catch their breath and then ran toward the roaring falls.

Down below, where the river was calm again, sure enough, Indians were building a town right where the other town had been. A horse herd grazed and watered along the edge of the James River. A wall was going up around the town. There were men and women and children. Obviously they meant to stay. The two startled Englishmen stared in disbelief. They looked at one another dumbfounded, then looked again at the stir of activity beside the river down below them.

"Well, they're back," said Ramsey.

"How many, do you think?" Barry asked.

"I don't know," said Ramsey. "A great many for just one town. More than were there before. I'd estimate five hundred—or six. Maybe more."

"I'd say a thousand at least," said Barry. "And maybe half of them are warriors. Would you say half?"

"I think so. Yes," said Ramsey. "I'd say half at least."

"Are they the damned Powhatans come back here then?" Barry asked. "Do you think they've come back seeking revenge upon us?"

"There aren't so many Powhatans as that left alive to come back like this," said Ramsey, "and even if there were, I think they'd lack the courage. They wouldn't want to take us on again. Not after what we did to them before. No, I think not. In fact, I'm sure of it. These here have a decidedly different look about them, don't you think? I can't quite pin it down, but it's a different look. They're not the Powhatans, I'm sure of it."

"Yes," Barry agreed. "I think you're right. I don't think I've ever seen these savages before. They've come in from some other part of the country and don't know about us yet."

"Well, by God," said Ramsey, "I'll wager they'll soon find out."

"Yes, they will," said Barry, "and if they won't listen to reason, they'll learn a hard lesson."

"Like the Powhatans."

"Just like the Powhatans," Barry said. "By God, they were the most powerful Indians of them all, and just look what we did to them. These down below must not know what it was that happened here."

"Likely," Ramsey mused, "they came across this place by accident and thought it looked like a good town site. That's all."

"We'll inform them different, and they'll pack up and look farther," said Barry. "Well, do you think we've seen enough?"

"I'd say so," said Ramsey. "Let's get back to our horses and ride back to tell the others."

WAR WOMAN sat smoking a short clay pipe on a newly made bench at the edge of the town site watching the building proceed. Off to one side, she could see Running Man, the war chief, her adopted grandson, in conversation with one of the young men who had been appointed sentry.

She recognized the young man and knew where he had been standing watch. She pretended disinterest in the conversation. In another moment the young man left, presumably to return to his post, and Running Man walked over to where War Woman sat. He squatted down in front of her and looked up at her through a cloud of blue-gray smoke.

"Grandmother," he said, "two white men are up there by where the water falls down the hillside. They're watching us."

War Woman nodded slowly and puffed her pipe, and Running Man still could not see her face through the blue-gray cloud.

"Are they English, do you think?" he asked.

She nodded again. "I knew they'd find us soon enough," she said.

"What do you think we should do? Should we kill them?"

"Just two of them?"

"Yes. Soft Shell Turtle saw them coming from the tobacco fields and watched them all the way. He thinks they saw the smoke from our fires and came here to see what was happening."

"Yes," said War Woman. "Of course they did. Only two of them."

"Yes," he said. Two.

"Let them go," she said. "Let them think that they have not been seen. They'll go home and tell the others that we're here. That's exactly what we want them to do."

48

OFT SHELL TURTLE, the young sentry who had reported seeing the white men to Running Man, was on his way back to his post. His spot was on top of the very hill the two Englishmen had climbed in order to overlook the activities of the Tsalagis. He knew that they were still up near the falls and thought that he could make his own way back to his observation post without being seen by them, but he was wrong.

He was still a good run from the base of the hill when the two white men, about halfway down, spotted him. One pointed and shouted. The other shouted something. Then they began hurrying down the hill. They were coming after him.

One's foot slipped on a rock, and the man flew forward with his feet high in the air. He fell hard on his rear end and slid for a distance. Just as the other came up behind him, he managed to scramble to his feet. The other ran into him, and they both tumbled on down, rolling over each other two or three times. At last they both managed to get up again, and they started running downhill once more, this time a bit more cautiously.

Soft Shell Turtle had turned to his right when first he saw the white men and noticed that they had also seen him. He was running away from them and away from the new town, running along the base of the hill. He had been told not to start anything with the whites, not to fight with them, not yet. His job had only been to watch and report what he saw, nothing more.

Now he had been seen by the English, and they were running after him. He told himself as he ran that he was not afraid to fight two Englishmen, that he was running because he had been told not to fight. He was sure that he could outrun them. He had glanced back over his shoulder a few times and seen how clumsy they were. It irked him just a bit that he was obligated to run from these foolish men.

He looked back again, and the two had finally reached the flatland and were still pursuing him. He knew, though, that they wouldn't be able to catch him. They were too far behind. He considered turning left and running up the hillside, but then he remembered the clump of trees to his right, the trees the white men had ridden into, where they had left their *sogwilis*. He veered to his right and headed for the trees.

"HURRY it up, Ned!" Barry shouted between puffs and pants. "He's getting away from us."

Ramsey, puffing along a few paces behind his companion, didn't answer. His lungs were too busy trying to gulp in some air. He felt as if his chest would burst open soon. He was not used to such exertion, a long, hard day's work perhaps, but not a long run. He wondered how Barry was managing.

Then Barry began to slow down. Ramsey caught up with him and passed him, then took a few more long strides and slowed. Up ahead the Indian had disappeared into the grove of trees. Ramsey leaned forward to rest, his long rifle, clutched in both hands, laid across his knees, and he sucked in air. Barry staggered up beside him. He panted heavily, leaning on his rifle, trying to get enough air in his lungs to speak.

"Ned," he said, "he's gone in there with our horses."

Ramsey straightened himself up and took a deep breath. "What'll we do?" he asked.

Barry stood silently staring at the trees for a moment. "Move in on him," he said, "cautiously. He's not carrying a long bow. Just a club, I think."

"All right," said Ramsey.

The two Englishmen began walking slowly and cautiously toward the dark grove of trees, and as they walked they moved away from one another just a little. Each held his long rifle ready to fire. Their eyes darted nervously about, as if they expected a surprise attack from any direction at any moment. They drew closer to the trees and squinted their eyes as if that might help them see into the dense foliage ahead. They stopped. They looked at each other.

"What now?" Ramsey asked.

Barry took a deep breath and let it out. "We go in," he said.

Another six paces would take them into the woods. Just then a shriek like the sound of a turkey pierced their ears. It was followed by a crashing and a thundering of hooves, and their own two horses came tearing out of the woods, running right toward them. On the back of one was the Indian they had been pursuing.

Both Englishmen yelled, as much out of surprise as fright. They jumped to the sides, and the two horses ran right between them. With the Englishmen behind him, the Indian turned loose the extra horse, and he ran off on his own. Ramsey and Barry each turned quickly, and each got up onto a knee. They fully expected the Indian to turn around and try once again to run them down, but he did not turn. He just kept riding away.

Barry thumbed back the ornate hammer on his flintlock musket and raised the weapon to his shoulder. He took a quick aim and pulled the trigger. There was a clack and a spark and a fizzle, followed by a poof. Up ahead, the Indian yelped and the horse reared, spilling the Indian onto the ground.

"You got him!" Ramsey shouted.

Soft Shell Turtle hit the ground hard, but he rolled as soon as he hit and bounded to his feet, turning to face his antagonists. He had heard the shot, and then he had heard the ball whiz close by his ear. He felt a moment of indecision. He remembered his instructions from Running Man, but the fight had already been started. The Englishman had taken a shot at him and the other Englishman also had a gun.

Soft Shell Turtle knew that the white men's guns could only shoot one time, and that it took them a while to reload. If there had only been one gun, he would have rushed the shooter in an attempt to reach him before he could reload and shoot again. But there were two of the long guns facing him.

It did not seem wise to race toward the second shot, but neither did it seem wise to just stand there and wait for the second Englishman to take aim and shoot at him. The white man's guns had a long reach. Perhaps he should run farther away, at least until the second gun had been fired. He glanced toward the horse he had been riding, but the animal had shied and run away. If he fled, it would have to be on foot.

⌐ᕲ

RAMSEY'S face fell when the Indian stood up. "You missed," he said.

Barry was pouring powder down the muzzle of his rifle. "You shoot him then," he snarled. "He's just standing still out there now."

Ramsey raised his rifle to his shoulder and took careful aim. "I won't miss," he said. Slowly he squeezed the trigger.

SOFT SHELL TURTLE saw the man aim the gun, saw the sparks fly as the hammer fell, and dived to his right, almost as if he had been diving into water. While he was in flight he heard the poof and landed and rolled. Then he came again to his feet. He looked. The man who had first shot his gun was still trying to get it loaded, and he had stopped for a moment to stare at Soft Shell Turtle. Now both guns were empty.

Soft Shell Turtle smiled. He held his arms out to his sides and flapped them like wings. He jumped straight up into the air, bending his knees out to the sides. Then he did it again.

"You're ugly white men," he shouted, "and you're clumsy and stupid!"

But, of course, he shouted at them in his own language, and so the Englishmen had no idea of his meaning. Then he turned, leaned forward, raised the back flap of his breechcloth, and slapped himself on the bare buttocks. Laughing, he ran away.

"Filthy savage," Barry said. "How I wish my shot had been true."

"Or mine," said Ramsey.

"Yours should have been, Ned. He was standing still when you fired your shot."

"He leaped out of the way," Ramsey protested. "I'm as good a shot as you any day. Well, what shall we do now?"

"He's too fleet afoot," said Barry. "We can't chase him down."

"Our horses have run away."

"We'll have to catch them. We'll go after yours first. He's just over there."

"We could split up and go after both at the same time," Ramsey said.

"Do you want to be caught out here alone?" Barry cautioned. "We've fired two shots. The rest of the savages may have heard them."

"You're right," Ramsey said. "We should stick together."

They reloaded their rifles and then started to walk toward the horse that was still in sight. The animal had calmed down and was grazing contentedly. The two Englishmen moved slowly, careful not to spook the already-jittery horse. They separated as they walked, one going around behind the horse, the other still headed toward the animal's mounting side.

They drew within about twenty paces when the horse raised his head, nickered, and trotted off a safe distance. He began again to graze as if nothing were wrong. Ramsey and Barry ran after him a few steps, then stopped.

"Bloody beast," Barry said. "Bloody awful nag."

"Easy," said Ramsey, "easy," and it was difficult to tell whether he was talking to the horse or to the other man. They started moving again, more slowly and more cautiously than before. They got about as close as they had on the previous attempt, and the horse trotted casually away again.

"Blast and damn!" Ramsey shouted. "How are we going to capture that damnable beast?"

Barry looked around. The horse seemed to be working his way toward the rocky hillside.

"We'll keep doing as we've done," Barry said. "If we don't get him sooner, he'll be up against the mountain, and we can catch him there."

They moved again on the horse, and the horse trotted away, closer to the hillside. They moved again. The horse nickered and turned and saw the steep and rough hillside there blocking his path. He started to climb, thought better of it, and turned again. He trotted straight toward Barry.

"Grab him, Tom. Catch hold of him!" Ramsey shouted, and Barry reached out for a handful of mane. The speed and weight of the big horse jerked Barry off his feet, but he held tight, and after dragging him only a short distance the animal stopped and stood as if nothing were wrong or had ever been wrong. Barry gathered up the reins and mounted. Then he looked over his shoulder to find Ramsey.

"Come on, Ned," he said. "Climb on behind."

Ramsey got up behind Barry, and Barry kicked the sides of the horse. They rode in the general direction they thought the other horse had gone. Soon they found themselves at the river's edge, and they had not seen the animal or any sign of him.

"You don't think he swam across, do you?" Ramsey asked.

"I doubt it," said Barry.

"Then where did he go?"

"How should I know," Barry snapped. "It's your bloody horse, isn't it?"

They followed the river a little ways farther west, then stopped.

"We're getting too close to the damned village of savages for my comfort," said Barry, "and still no sign of the damned horse."

"Let's head for home," said Ramsey. "Maybe we'll find him along the way."

Barry shrugged. "It's your horse," he said. He turned the head of his mount and started back east. Still they did not see the runaway.

IT was late when the two Englishmen rode up to their small settlement, an offshoot of Jamestown. Several others came running to meet them. A big, burly man with a full red beard was the first to speak.

"Where the devil have you two been?" he asked. "We've been looking for you to come back for hours." Then as if just noticing, he added, "And on one horse. What's happened?"

A woman pushed her way through the small crowd of settlers.

"Ned," she said, "are you all right?"

Ramsey slipped off the back end of the horse and stepped over to her. He put his arms around her and hugged her tight.

"Yes, darling," he said. "I'm all right, but I've lost our horse."

The man with the red beard spoke up again as Barry stepped painfully down out of the saddle.

"What the hell happened?" he demanded.

Barry looked at Ramsey and then back at the red-bearded man.

"We were attacked by painted savages," Barry said. "They got away with poor Ned's horse, and we barely escaped with our lives."

"Blast," the other responded. "Who the hell were they?"

"They were like no savages I've ever seen before," said Barry, "but there's close to a thousand of the grinning heathens out there, I'd say, and they're hard at labor building up their wretched hovels right there on top of the ruins of the old Powhatan town just below the falls, in the very spot from which we ran the others off. And, it sure looks as if they mean to stay."

49

HASTY meeting was called of all the men of the settlement, and Barry and Ramsey again told their slightly embellished tale. Now and then they gave each other furtive looks, but no one else seemed to notice, for their story was never questioned. The rest just took it as natural that unknown savages would move in on their territory and attack peaceable settlers for no reason. The red-bearded man stood up in front of the gathering.

"You've all heard what these two had to tell us," he said. "Now what do you propose we do about it?"

"We should get our guns and ride out there!" one man shouted.

"Wipe them all out," another added.

There was general agreement voiced by most of the rest all at once, and the red-bearded man let it go on for a while before he held up his hands for quiet.

"I agree," he said. "We should arm ourselves and ride out there and wipe the bold savages off the face of the earth."

There were more murmurs of agreement, and he paused to allow the voices to vent themselves.

"That's what we should do," he said, "but let's think about it a moment. Let's consider what's practical. Our good friends here told us that there were upwards of a thousand of them out there. They're a good day's march away from us, and we're two days' ride from Jamestown. We have eighty fighting men amongst us."

There were more murmurs from the crowd, but they were subdued now. Now that the odds had been specified, it did not sound at all good to them. Apparently no one had considered the logistics until the red-bearded man brought them up.

"Do we attack a thousand with eighty?" he asked. He looked the crowd over, staring at one face after another. As he focused on them, they lowered their eyes. An embarrassed silence settled over the room for a moment, and then a tentative voice spoke up.

"Do they have guns?"

The red-bearded man looked at Ramsey.

"I don't know," Ramsey said. "I didn't see any of them with guns."

"I did," Barry broke in. "Some of them have guns. I don't know how many."

Again there was a moment of silence. A man in the back of the room stood up.

"We should go to Jamestown and raise an army there," he said.

"Perhaps we should do that," said the red-bearded man. "But all the time we're traveling the Indians will be building their strength. They might even attack the settlement while we're running for help."

"Then what do we do?" someone asked. "Just sit here and wait for them to attack us?"

"I have a suggestion," said the man with the red beard. "Barry and Ramsey should ride to Jamestown and tell them what the situation is out here. At the same time, we send to Red Tail's village and tell him to gather up his Pamunkey warriors and send us a man who can talk to these Indians, whoever they may be. We'll ride out to the village and give them a warning to leave in peace. If they fail to heed our warning, we'll set the Pamunkeys on them. Now what do you say to that?"

"Who'll ride out there to meet with a thousand savages and make such a demand?" someone asked.

"I will myself, by God," said the red-bearded man, "with Red Tail and his interpreter. I an't afraid to stand up to them, whoever they may be."

There were murmurs around the room again. Then, "All right, let's do it!" someone shouted. There was little more discussion after that, and everyone agreed to the plan put forth by the red-bearded man.

❧

BARRY and Ramsey rode hard toward Jamestown, and a Pamunkey man the settlers called Indian John was sent to deliver the orders to the village of Red Tail. The rest of the settlers were busy preparing their weapons, getting ready for the worst.

❧

WAR WOMAN had a small fire burning in front of the new house that some of the women had built for her. She leaned over and plucked a hot coal from the fire, holding it between her forefinger and thumb. She dropped it into a small clay pot. Then she bent over to go inside her new house.

She walked over to a corner where she had stashed her few belongings and picked up a leather pouch. Slipping the strap over her shoulder, she took up her walking staff and went back outside, still carrying the coal in the pot. She walked through the town, not bothering to look at the work going on around her, not speaking to anyone. No one bothered speaking to her either. They knew better. When she was like that, they knew, she would just ignore them if they spoke to her.

She trudged on away from the town and down to the river's edge. It wasn't a long walk, but it took her a while to make it. She was old, she moved slowly and, sometimes, a little painfully. It wasn't far from the town, but everyone was busy either working on houses or the town house or the wall or out on sentry duty, so she was alone at the river.

She didn't bother looking back over her shoulder to make sure she was alone. She knew that she was alone. She knew that no one would follow her. They could tell when she wanted to be alone, and they wouldn't dare come near. They would be afraid of her, afraid of what she might be doing, afraid of her power.

At the water's edge, she sat down, exhaling long and loud. She put the clay pot on the ground on her left. She laid the staff down beside herself on the right, and she took the strap off her shoulder. Then she leaned forward, turning her head to one side, and she listened to the water as it ran by her, listened to the voice of the river, the voice of Long Man, and she heard it speak. She listened for a long time.

At last she sat up straight again. Her back and her neck were both stiff from the strain. She ignored the minor pain and picked up her bag. Opening it, she drew out a smaller bag and opened that one. From the small bag she withdrew a crystal, transparent on one end and cloudy on the other. She clutched the cloudy end of the crystal tightly in her bony, wrinkled hand and held it up in front of her face.

She stared long and hard into the crystal, and she saw things in there. Tiny human figures moved around. She paid close attention to their actions. Then she put the crystal back into the small bag and put the small bag back into the larger one. She felt around in the bottom of the larger bag until she found something else in there. She withdrew her clenched fist, held it in front of her eyes, and opened it slowly to reveal two small beads, a black one and a red one. She placed the black bead on top of the crease between the pressed-together forefinger and thumb of her left hand. The red one she placed the same way on her right hand, and she held her hands up in front of her breasts. She bent her head to watch the beads intensely, and she held her hands still.

Suddenly, all of its own, the black bead quivered, moved forward, then rolled back to its original position. The red bead rolled forward then and stayed. She waited a moment. There was no more movement of beads.

Satisfied, she put the beads back into the bag and drew out a small tobacco pouch and a short clay pipe with a river cane stem. She filled the small bowl of the pipe with ancient tobacco from her pouch, replaced the pouch in the bag, and stuck the stem of the pipe between her puckered old lips. Then she picked up the pot, took the coal from inside, and dropped it into the bowl of the pipe. She sucked to get the tobacco burning and sent a cloud of smoke up into the air.

She put the strap of the larger bag back over her shoulder, took up her staff, and used it to help her stand up again. She was stiff. That was what came with being old. She turned to face the east.

She puffed her pipe four times, sending her thoughts with her smoke up into the heavens to the spirits who lived in that direction. She turned to the south and did it again. She faced west and puffed four times, and she faced north to finish off her ritual. The tobacco in the small pipe bowl was consumed, and she knocked it loose, dropping it on the ground at her feet.

She put the pipe back into the bag and, with a groan, bent to pick up the clay pot. She put that in the bag and turned to walk back to the town.

☙❧

"WAR WOMAN," said Running Man, "what should we do? By now the English know that we're here. Will they attack us, do you think?"

"No," she said. "They'll come to talk first. They'll tell us to pack up and move away. They'll tell us that this is their land and that we have no right to be here. They think that, because they broke the back of the Powhatans, they can do anything and that we'll be afraid of them."

"So what should we do?"

"Wait until they come," she replied, "and then tell them to go back to their settlements and mind their own business."

"Then what will happen?"

"Then they'll come to fight," she said, "and we'll be ready. That's all."

"Maybe they won't come to talk first," he said. "Maybe they'll just come to fight."

"Then be ready for them," she told him, "if that's what you think."

RUNNING MAN studied the lay of the land. He looked carefully at the way the town was situated between the river and the plain with the grove of trees, the mountain with the falls back behind. Some men in the trees, he thought, and some more up on the mountain ridge. The wall would be finished soon, and there would be more men there looking out over the wall.

At the river's edge, the bank dropped down to the water. More men could be hidden there. If the English chose to attack, they would ride into a trap with Tsalagis in front of them and on two sides. Then some of the men from each of the two sides could sweep around and close the white men in a circle. He was satisfied that it was a good plan. He just wasn't sure how soon he should deploy his forces.

THE following morning, Indian John returned to the English settlement with Red Tail and another man. The man with red hair met them and spoke with them briefly. Shortly after, the three Pamunkeys, the red-bearded man, and two other white men mounted their horses and set out for the town below the falls.

AT the same time, Barry and Ramsey were starting their return trip from Jamestown. The governor had been abrupt with them. The Indians had been thoroughly subdued all around, he said. There couldn't possibly be any serious threat. Just tell them to get out. If they dared to refuse, then set the damned Pamunkeys on them. That said, he dismissed them.

The two settlers rode out of Jamestown dejected.

"What do we tell them at home?" Ramsey asked.

"What can we tell them?" Barry responded. "Just the truth. Just that the bloody governor wouldn't believe us. 'Take care of it,' he said. The damned fool."

"He'll get us all killed."

"Damn his soul," said Ramsey. "Damn him to eternal hell."

"Maybe the Pamunkeys can drive them out for us," Barry said. "Maybe all's not lost. They might not even know what they've done, and maybe when they've been informed they'll just leave."

"And maybe they won't," Ramsey replied. "There are over a thousand savages in that town, mostly warriors. We need the help of Jamestown, and we have a governor who doesn't care if we're wiped out to a man. Women and children, too. Doesn't he even care a damned little bit about the women and children?"

"He's incompetent," said Barry. "That's all."

"Well," said Ramsey, "let's get back home as fast as we can. The others have got to be told that we can't count on any help from Jamestown. And soon."

The two men whipped up their overworked mounts and raced ahead.

IT was late evening when the small group of settlers and Pamunkeys came within sight of the town beneath the falls. The man with the red beard stopped them. He stared ahead for a moment in silence.

"They're in there all right," he said. "A bunch of them."

"Do we ride on, George?" asked one of the men.

The big red-bearded man, stared hard for a while longer at the town. Then he urged his horse forward. "Yes," he said. "Come along."

UP on the ridge behind the town, young Soft Shell Turtle watched attentively as the riders approached his town.

50

OFT SHELL TURTLE, the young sentry, found Running Man and told him of the approaching group he had seen. There were only six men, he said, all riding *sogwilis.* The war chief thought for a moment. It could be a trick. There could be more men coming along behind them.

He sent Soft Shell Turtle back to his post to keep watching, then went to seek the advice of War Woman. They had a brief consultation and decided to meet the Englishmen outside the walls of the town. Most of the wall was finished on the side facing the Englishmen.

Running Man called for six horses to be saddled. Then he helped War Woman up onto a horse and called four other young men to ride along with them. Once they were all armed and mounted, they rode slowly out of the town and toward the approaching visitors. Running Man had made sure that he and the other men were well armed, and War Woman scoffed at that.

"They didn't come to fight us," she said. "Not just six of them."

A short distance from the wall, they saw the group approaching at a slow pace like their own. They could see then that there were three white men and three Indians.

"Three English," said Running Man, "and three others. Who are they?"

"Pamunkeys," said War Woman, almost spitting the word out. "The whipped ones. Stop. We'll stay here and wait for them."

They halted their mounts and sat waiting for the others to come to them. Running Man and the other Tsalagi men sat tall and straight in their saddles, looking proud and defiant with their rifles laid across their thighs. War Woman leaned slightly forward. A scowl was on her wrinkled old face.

The other group continued to ride forward slowly. War Woman

watched them carefully as they moved closer, narrowing the gap between them. The one in the lead was a burly white man with red hair on his face. There were two more white men. Each looked stout. One had a smooth face and the other had brown hair on his face.

Then there were the three Indians—Pamunkeys almost for sure. Who else would ride with these white men? The Indians didn't seem at all formidable to War Woman. Whipped dogs, she thought. They came closer, close enough to speak, and they halted. The horses stamped and fidgeted nervously. For a moment the two groups sat in their saddles and stared at one another. A horse snorted. Another nickered. At last, the red-bearded man spoke.

"Do any of you speak English?" he asked, looking over the group of Tsalagis.

He waited a brief moment. There was no response, only silent stares, so he turned his head toward one of the Indians in his own group.

"Greet them," he said, "and tell them that we come in peace to have a talk."

The Indian spoke in a language that none of the Real People could understand. They stared at him. He spoke again, still with no effect. At last War Woman grew impatient with his attempts and spoke out loud in the trade jargon.

"Can you talk the trade talk?" she asked.

"Yes," said the interpreter.

"Then why didn't you use it in the first place?" she asked.

"I just thought—"

"What do you want here?" she asked. "You and these white men."

"What is the old hag saying?" George demanded of his interpreter.

"She want to know what we want here," the man answered in halting English.

"Tell her who I am and where we come from," George said.

"My name is Gray Dog," the interpreter said in the jargon. "I'm Pamunkey. This man with the red hair is my captain. He's called George Clinton. He's from a settlement nearby, under the rule of the English colony called Jamestown."

"And you?" War Woman asked.

"I'm Gray Dog, a Pamunkey," he said.

"I heard you say that before," War Woman said. "Why are you riding with these white men?"

"They told me to come with them, so they could talk to you," Gray Dog said.

"Are you the slave of the white men," she asked, "that you do their bidding?"

Gray Dog rankled under the biting, sarcastic questioning of War Woman. Her implications were much too close to the truth, and they hurt what little pride the Pamunkey had left. He was trying to formulate an appropriate response to this old woman when Clinton broke in again.

"What the hell are you talking about?" he demanded.

"Just telling her who we are," said Gray Dog. "Like you said."

"Well then, ask them who the hell they are and what they're doing here!" Clinton demanded. "I mean to know their intentions."

"Captain Clinton asks who you are," Gray Dog said, returning to the jargon.

"We're Chalakees," said Running Man, using the jargon word for the Real People. Gray Dog looked surprised and turned toward Clinton, but before he could say anything, Running Man continued. "I'm called Running Man. I'm the war chief of this town. This is War Woman. Surely you've heard of her."

"No," said Gray Dog. "I have not. What are you doing here? This is a long ways from your homelands."

"Just what you see. We're building a town here," said Running Man.

"We heard," said War Woman, "that some people used to live here and they let someone chase them away."

Gray Dog hung his head for a moment. Then he looked up in the direction of War Woman.

"That was the main town of the Powhatans," he said. "When these Englishmen first came here, in my grandfather's time, they were weak, and we helped them. Then they learned to grow tobacco, and they wanted more and more land for growing. We had a big fight with them, and they whipped us. Many were killed. Men. Women. Children. Some ran away. Those of us who stayed behind surrendered to the English, and now we are subject to their rule. As you suggested before."

"What are you talking about?" Clinton demanded.

Gray Dog turned back toward Clinton and shifted his speech again to English.

"These are Chalakees," he said, "a people from south of here. A powerful people. This one is their chief, and he called the old woman 'War Woman.' "

"War Woman?" said Clinton. "That old hag? What the hell does that mean? War Woman."

"She must have earned it sometime," said Gray Dog.

"Did you ask them what the hell they're doing here?" Clinton said.

"Yes."

"Well," said Clinton. "What did they say? Must I drag the words out of your mouth? I may drag your tongue out for you."

"They say they're building a town."

"We can see that they're building a damned town," said Clinton, growing even less patient. "Why are they building it here?"

"They say," Gray Dog replied, "they heard someone ran off from this town." He shrugged. "They think no one lives here. They build here."

"Ask them their numbers," Clinton said.

"He wants to know how many you are," Gray Dog said, using the jargon again.

"There are enough of us to fill a town," Running Man responded.

"Maybe two towns," said War Woman. "Maybe more."

Running Dog translated into his rough English for Clinton, and Clinton's face reddened. He looked from War Woman to Running Man and then to each of the others. He looked off toward the town, wondering how many Indians were back there behind the wall.

"Well, tell them that they have no business here," he said. "Tell them that this land, all this land, belongs to the Jamestown colony in the name of the Commonwealth of Great Britain. Tell them that we don't want to fight with them, but they can't stay here unless they're willing to get down on their knees and declare themselves loyal subjects of the British Commonwealth. Tell them that we'll give them a week—that's seven days—to pack up and leave. Tell them that. And tell them what it was like to feel the wrath of the English, Gray Dog. I know you remember it well."

Gray Dog sucked in a deep breath and looked back at the Tsalagis there in front of him. He and his people had indeed already felt the wrath of these Englishmen, and he had no doubt the Jamestown army could drive these out, too, for they had devastating weapons, and when they fought they showed no mercy.

However, at the moment, there were just the six of them there, three English and three Pamunkeys, and behind the new walls of the town were almost a thousand more Chalakees, according to the report. He thought that Clinton should be more diplomatic.

"Captain Clinton wants me to tell you," he said in the jargon, "that you can't stay here. This land is now claimed by these English from Jamestown. They even gave the river their own name. They call it James. Clinton wants you to leave this place in seven days' time." He paused a moment before finishing. "Or you can grovel in front of these English like dogs," he said.

"Like you Pamunkeys?" War Woman snarled.

She kicked the sides of her horse and moved forward until she was right alongside Clinton. The red-bearded man watched her carefully, not knowing what to expect, but he held his ground. Even so, what he saw in the old woman's eyes was frightening to him. She looked at him, staring hard.

"Do you think you can frighten Chalakees?" she said, speaking the jargon. "Do you think we're children? Do you think we're weak like the Powhatans? The Pamunkeys? Who do you think you are to come across the big water and claim land here for your own? We came here to this town, and we claim it for our own. Come back in seven days. Come back to see if we're still here. Come back, if you dare, to die."

She turned her mount abruptly, bumping the mare into his horse, causing him to move aside, and she rode back toward the town. Running Man and the other men turned to follow her. The council was over.

Clinton sat stunned for a moment, unable to speak. That part of his face that showed between his hair and his beard turned as red as his whiskers.

"What did she say?" he barked, and when Gray Dog failed to answer quickly enough to suit him, he repeated, "What did she say?"

"She said they claim the land. She said, come back in seven days to die."

"We'll come back all right!" Clinton shouted. "They can be sure of that. We'll come back and wipe out the whole population of these . . . Chalakees. We'll teach them a lesson in manners they'll never forget. Them and their old hag—their witch."

He whipped his horse around and started riding hard back in the direction from which they had come, and the others rode hard after him.

❧

"SEVEN days, Grandmother," said Running Man. "That's when they'll be back."

"And they'll be back in numbers," she remarked. "They'll be back ready to fight. And remember this: These white men fight to kill everyone. That's the only way they know how to fight. They don't quit until everyone on the other side is dead—or until they're whipped."

"I'll remember," Running Man said. "Seven days from now."

He told her his plan of deployment, and she said that it was good. "But don't wait seven days," she added. "He's angry now. I insulted him. He might come back sooner. Be ready anytime."

❦

CLINTON led his small group, riding hard as far as he dared. If he didn't slow down soon, he knew, he would ruin his horses, maybe kill them. Then he would have a long walk back to the settlement. He slowed and walked the horses for a little ways. Then he stopped and dismounted. The others did the same. Clinton paced for a while, his face still red, still fuming, still bristling from the stare and the voice of War Woman. At last he stopped and turned to Gray Dog.

"Tell your chief," he said, "to gather all his Pamunkey warriors. All of them. You three are to go straight from here back to your village. Gather them all up and attack these Chalakees. Kill them all or drive them out. Do it now. But catch that old hag alive, if you can. You hear? Catch her alive."

Gray Dog interpreted in his own language for Red Tail. Then the three Pamunkeys started to mount their horses. Clinton stamped around for a few more moments before he went back to his horse and climbed again into the saddle. The other two white men mounted up.

"Can the Pamunkeys do it?" one asked.

"They'd better," said Clinton, "if they know what's good for them."

"George," said the other, "what the hell do you want the old woman alive for?"

"She's a damned witch," said Clinton. "I mean to burn her at the stake."

51

OE IN THE WATER was young and beautiful and unmarried. She had been pursued before by young men, but she had spurned them all. She had not been interested in any of them. She had eyes only for Running Man, the unmarried war chief of the town, but Running Man had never expressed any interest in her. In fact, he had never even given any evidence of knowing that she existed.

Doe in the Water had made this journey to establish a new town in the old Powhatan country with her family. Her father was not yet too old to fight, and he had readily accepted War Woman's challenge. Her mother's brother, too, was ready and anxious to fight the English. Her mother had accompanied her father, so she, too, had come along.

Doe in the Water had not been looking for a man, but because of the nature of their mission, Running Man had been very much in the front of things. He had been much in evidence, and so she had seen him. She had seen a great deal of him, and the more she saw of him, the more she liked him. But she was getting desperate to find a way to get him to notice her.

She had noticed that Running Man spent much of his time with the old woman known as War Woman, the one whom people both depended on and were afraid of. It was widely said that the old woman had great powers. Doe in the Water didn't know if she believed that or not, but it didn't really matter. The old woman had the attention of Running Man, and that was all she cared about. She would talk to War Woman.

It was evening, already dark, and War Woman was puttering about the fire in front of her house. Doe in the Water walked up close enough to see her and stopped. She watched for a moment, trying to see what the old woman was doing, but she couldn't tell. She might have been preparing food, making some kind of medicine, or doing something else altogether. She was just puttering.

Doe in the Water stepped up closer. War Woman sensed her presence. Without lifting her head, she looked up toward the girl, then continued her puttering. Doe in the Water walked closer, close enough for speaking, and stopped again. War Woman raised her eyebrows to send a stern glance in the young woman's direction.

"War Woman," said Doe in the Water, brave at last, "may I come to your fire to speak with you?"

"What do you want with me?" War Woman asked, her voice gruff.

Doe in the Water walked right up to the fire and looked across it at War Woman.

"Are you trying to frighten me?" she asked. "There's no reason. I only want to talk to you."

War Woman straightened up and looked at Doe in the Water. She was tall and straight and so very young. War Woman thought that she could recall a time long ago when the world was first made and she was that young. She'd had long, strong legs like that back then, too. And she'd had the confidence—or arrogance.

But this girl did not have the reasons for her arrogance that War Woman had possessed when she was young. There was no one with her powers, and she'd had them all her life. This one dared to step up to her fire like that, dared to chastise her for being gruff. This one—she liked this one.

"Sit down," she said.

Doe in the Water looked around and saw a rough bench sitting against the front wall of the house. She stepped over there and sat, her hands on her knees.

"*Wado,*" she said.

War Woman went inside the house and reappeared a moment later with a bowl in her hands. She shoved the bowl toward Doe in the Water.

"Here," she said.

Doe in the Water took the bowl. It contained *kanohena,* and she drank from it. It was very good.

"So," War Woman said, "what's so important that you dare approach the War Woman to talk about it? What can make a young woman want to sit and talk with an old one like me?"

"I want to know you," Doe in the Water replied.

War Woman made a scoffing noise from deep down in her throat. She went back to puttering around the fire.

"No one knows me," she said.

Doe in the Water drank again from the bowl in her hands, looking over its rim as she drank. She lowered it again.

"Running Man knows you," she said.

War Woman turned to look with hard eyes at Doe in the Water.

"He talks to me," she said, "when he needs the advice of an old woman. That's all."

"I need the advice of an old woman," said Doe in the Water.

"There are other old women around."

"I need your advice."

War Woman looked at her again, but this time her look was one of curiosity, not the hard look of before. This one was persistent. War Woman liked that about her. She thought of her own youth again in that time so long ago, and she tried to recall what it had felt like to be a young girl. She dropped something that she'd been holding in her hand and walked over to the bench. She sat down beside Doe in the Water.

"What?" she asked. "How can I help you?"

"Can you make someone love me?"

The question was bold and abrupt. War Woman looked at Doe in the Water for a moment before answering.

"I can," she said. "But I won't do it."

"Why not?"

"Because that's something you should do for yourself. Because if I were to make someone love you, then he wouldn't really love you at all. He'd just be your captive. That's all."

"But this one doesn't even look my way," said Doe in the Water plaintively. "How can I make him look at me? How can I make him talk to me? What can I do to get his attention?"

"Well," War Woman responded, suddenly sympathetic, "why do you care if this one young man looks your way? There are other young men. Many of them. And they're all put together the same way. If this man doesn't look at you, he must be blind, or worse. He's not worth worrying about. Find another one. There must be others who've tried to court you."

"There have been others," said Doe in the Water, getting nervous at the nearness of the old woman, "but I don't like them. And he's not blind. He's very busy, that's all."

"So are we all," War Woman said. "We're building a new town here."

Doe in the Water stood up and paced to the other side of the fire. She stopped and turned to look at the old woman across the flames.

"He's busier than the others," she said. "He's an important man. He's—"

She stopped herself and stared into the flames for a silent moment. She felt suddenly foolish.

"I shouldn't have come here," she said. "I shouldn't have bothered you. I'll go now."

She turned to walk away, but War Woman spoke out quickly, stopping her.

"Who is this important man you're looking at?" she asked.

Doe in the Water stopped. She stood still, her back to War Woman. She thought that she did not want to answer the question. She had said she was leaving.

"Running Man," she said.

WAR WOMAN sought out Running Man early the next morning. She asked him about the sentries, and he told her that they were all in place.

"Are they reliable?" she asked. "Can you be sure of them?"

"They're all good men," he answered.

"Have they had enough sleep? You shouldn't keep them out there too long, you know."

He assured her that the sentries were getting enough sleep. There were plenty of them, and they had reasonable shifts with plenty of time between to get enough sleep.

"Have you put out the men to make the trap ready for the English?" she asked.

"They know where to go," he said. "As soon as a sentry sees anyone coming and warns us, they'll go out and be ready."

"And you," she said. "Are you ready?"

He wondered what was wrong with her. She had never before talked to him like this. She knew everything he was doing. If the plans were not her own, then he had spoken with her about them before setting anything into motion. He always did.

"I'm ready to fight the English," he said.

War Woman looked up over Running Man's shoulder, and she saw Doe in the Water walking toward the river with a water jug.

"Humph," she grunted. "I don't like her."

"What?" Running Man asked. "Who don't you like?"

"That one there with the jug," War Woman said. "Going there. That one. I don't like her."

Running Man turned to look, and he saw Doe in the Water. He recognized her. He had seen her around before. He thought that he had even heard her name once, but he wasn't sure. She was a good-looking young woman and well behaved as far as he knew.

"Why?" he asked. "What's wrong with her?"

"Her legs are too long," War Woman snorted.

Running Man stared long and hard after Doe in the Water, and just then she disappeared over the horizon on her way down to the river. He tried to set her image firmly in his mind. He thought that she looked very lovely. Why would War Woman say that her legs were too long? He wanted to run over to the river and get a better look at her, but he fought off the urge. Instead he turned back to War Woman.

"I think she looks good," he said.

"She has a nasty disposition," War Woman said, and she turned and walked away with no further explanation. Running Man was standing near the wall on the side of the town nearest the river. Men were busy setting poles, and he had been watching the progress. Another day and the wall would be complete. He turned back to watch the work, but every so often he glanced over his shoulder to see if the young woman was returning yet.

At last she reappeared, carrying a jug filled with water. He could tell it was filled by the way she carried it. He tried to watch her without being obvious about it. He was curious about her legs. Were they really too long? He didn't think so. She seemed well proportioned to him. Of course, he was a little far away to get a really good look.

She was walking toward the center of town. If he was to head for the town house to see how things were going there, their paths would intersect. If he hurried, he would cross her path just before she got there. He started walking toward the town house.

He walked with his head down, so she would not see that he was looking at her, but he was looking at her. His eyes were raised as far as he could raise them without lifting his head. It was not the best way to get a good look, but from what he could see she was beautiful. He wondered why he had not noticed before just how beautiful she was and he wondered why War Woman had said those bad things about her.

She stopped and put the jug down, then picked it up with her other hand. He was moving too fast then. He would get there ahead of her and not be able to look at her without turning around. That would be too obvious. He slowed his pace, trying to appear casual, looking around the town. At last he almost walked into her.

" 'Siyo," he said.

She looked at him for an instant, and her eyes were large and dark and lovely. The skin on her face was smooth, and her hair was shiny black. She was like a vision, he thought.

" 'Siyo," she said, and she ducked her head and walked on. He stared after her, thinking that the shape of her body was perfection. What did War Woman mean by saying that her legs were too long? And she had been modest. War Woman had said that she had a nasty disposition. What was wrong with War Woman?

He wondered if maybe the girl was from a family that War Woman had an old grudge against. That might explain her animosity. Such things happened. Or maybe the explanation was even simpler than that. Maybe an old woman simply did not see the same things in a young woman that a young man saw.

Or maybe War Woman's eyes were getting bad in her old age, but if that were the case, this was the first evidence of it that Running Man had noticed. Perhaps the young woman had said something that had displeased War Woman. That would explain the comment about the girl's disposition. But that her legs are too long? That remark didn't make any sense at all to Running Man.

He struggled to recall her name. He knew he had heard it, but he couldn't recall where or when or from whom. He thought that he should know which family she came from, but there were so many here in this new town and they had come from different towns back in the old country.

She turned a corner and he could no longer see her, but he took note of the direction she went. Her house would be somewhere down that way. He would watch for her again. Legs too long? He shook his head in puzzlement.

52

ED TAIL rode at the head of a band of about a hundred Pamunkey warriors. He rode for a cause in which he did not believe, against people he had nothing against, people he did not really want to fight. He was leading these men against disastrous odds in what he could see only as a foolish and dangerous mission. He rode, he was certain, toward his own death, and he would be taking all of these young men with him. He wondered what the next life would hold for him and his followers.

But they had no choice in the matter. He and his people had surrendered themselves to the English monsters unconditionally and had pledged their loyalty to the Crown of England. Then, just recently, the English had said that there was no more Crown. Their loyalty was now to something called a Commonwealth and a Lord Cromwell. Red Tail didn't know what a Commonwealth might be, nor who this Lord Cromwell was. Still, he had given his word.

He had his orders from Clinton, the red-bearded one: "Attack the Chalakees with all your might. Show no mercy. Wipe them out or run them off." And Red Tail had agreed to obey. Well, he would do his best, and he would die in the attempt. He and all of his men. He knew that even as he rode. His main regret was in leaving behind the women and children. He wondered what would become of them. He had told his wife that if he should fail to return, she should lead the rest of the people west and seek refuge with some other people somewhere out there. He hoped that she would do as he had said, and he hoped that they would make it safely.

Of course, he and his men were ready to fight. They were well armed and well mounted. Clinton had seen to that, for Clinton wanted the Chalakees wiped out. All but the old woman. He wanted to take her alive and burn her for a witch. He wanted that very badly, and for all

Red Tail knew, the old woman might really be a witch. She was certainly a powerful old woman. Otherwise she would never have ridden out with the war chief to meet Clinton's group the way she did. Red Tail knew that there were such people. He had known some in his own lifetime. Perhaps this War Woman was a witch.

Red Tail halted his party when they drew within sight of the new Chalakee town. He sat silent in his saddle for a long moment, looking and remembering the good days when there had been a Powhatan town there. He thought about the many times he had visited there and been treated as an honored guest. He remembered the celebrations and the feasts. Then he recalled the time when the Powhatans had decided that the English colonists at Jamestown had pushed them too much and too far. They had decided to push back, but the results had been disastrous.

Now there was this new town, a Chalakee town, right on top of the ruins of the old mother town of the Powhatans, and Red Tail was preparing to attack it because his English lords had told him to do so. It was distasteful to him. He would much rather be killing the English, but he had given his word at that shameful surrender. He had no choice.

He could see the town clearly up ahead, but he was still too far away to begin the attack. He signaled his men to move forward with him, still moving slowly. They rode closer to the walls of the town. He could see some Chalakee heads poking out from behind the wall. They were watching. He knew that. He also knew that as soon as they were within rifle range the Chalakees would begin to shoot at them.

The day had an ominous quietness about it. The only sounds were those made by the Pamunkey horses as they plodded along, their puffing, snorting, and nickering, the clomping of their hooves. Then he heard a sudden commotion behind him, and he looked over his shoulder.

Something was going on back in the rear ranks, and a young man from back there was riding forward, pushing his way through the others to get up close to Red Tail. Puzzled, he halted his men again. The rider from the back pulled up beside him.

"Red Tail," he said, "some of the men back there are running away. I tried to stop them, but they said that they don't want this fight. I told them we made a promise. They said they didn't make it. I told them the English will be angry with us. They said they don't care about the English. They're going home to get their families and then run away to the west."

Red Tail almost smiled. The women and children, the old men even—they would all have a better chance of finding some safe place in the west with some young men along. Even though he would have tried to stop the runaways if he'd had the chance, he was secretly glad to hear the news. He didn't think the men were cowards. Not at all. He just figured that they, like him, saw no sense in this foolish attack.

Now, of course, the odds in the coming battle would be even greater against him than before, but that didn't matter to Red Tail. He had known from the beginning that this would be a suicide mission. The fewer numbers would just result in a shorter battle. It would be over with that much sooner, and as far as Red Tail was concerned, the sooner the better. Furthermore, assuming there was any glory at all to be gained in this otherwise meaningless fight, there would be the more of it for those few of them who stayed to take part.

Red Tail had no stomach for this fight against the Chalakees, but since he had no choice, he had resolved to kill as many of them as he could before he was himself killed. He would go out of this world like a man, like a Pamunkey warrior should go. He looked at the face of the young man who had brought him the news from the rear. He wore a worried look.

"Let them go," he said. "If you or any others want to go with them, go ahead."

"I stand with you," the young man said. "So do the others. All of us who stayed."

"Then the honors will all be greater for us," said Red Tail. "Go back to your place now. Watch for my signal. We'll attack soon."

RUNNING MAN climbed the notched pole that took him up to the narrow platform that ran around the inside of the front wall of the town. He looked out over the edge of the wall and saw the riders coming. It was not an overwhelming number, fifty or sixty, he guessed, and he wondered why so few would dare to attack them. Perhaps they had seriously underestimated the Tsalagi strength.

"Who are they?" asked a man next to him.

"Pamunkeys, I think," said Running Man. "They're the slaves of the English."

He wondered if the Pamunkeys might be coming for some reason other than to make war, to talk maybe. Just then the leader of the Pamunkeys raised a cry, and the whole force began racing toward the walls. One fired a rifle, and the ball struck the wall not far from where Running

Man stood. There were no more questions to be asked. As few as they were, they had started the fight.

Running Man raised his own rifle to his shoulder and took careful aim. He squeezed the trigger. There was a spark and a flash, followed shortly by an explosion that jolted the rifle butt back against Running Man's shoulder. He watched as his ball tore into the chest of the rider in the lead of the attacking force.

RED TAIL fell off the back of his running horse, the first on either side of the battle to fall. His warriors yelled in anger and defiance at the sight but continued the attack. Some of their horses trampled the body of Red Tail in their mad race forward.

AS soon as Running Man had fired the first shot, others began firing from behind the wall. A dozen or more Pamunkey warriors were knocked from their horses' backs. The others, realizing that they were riding into a withering fire, jerked back their reins to turn their confused mounts. As they did, Tsalagis hidden along the riverbank came out in the open and started shooting with rifles and bows. More Pamunkeys fell.

Then Tsalagis came out of the grove of trees on the other side, and the two groups began to sweep around behind the Pamunkeys. The attackers were soon hopelessly surrounded. They were no longer the attackers. They were suddenly trapped and beseiged. Some dismounted and pulled their horses to the ground to use as shields. Some few killed their horses for the same purpose. They got down on the ground behind the horses and shot back at the attacking Tsalagis.

Four especially defiant young Pamunkey men kept in their saddles. One raced toward the rear, one to each side, and the last directly toward the wall of the town, screaming as they rode. Each was soon dropped by a fusillade of rifle shots.

WATCHING from his spot behind the wall, Running Man felt numb. He wished that he could talk to the few remaining Pamunkeys. He longed for an opportunity to give them a chance to surrender. He had

come to teach a lesson to the English. Instead, they had taught him one.
They had taught him that they would not fight if they could find a way
to get someone else to do it for them. They had sacrificed these Pamunkeys, Indian people.

Running Man felt almost sick to his stomach. There was nothing he
could do. He had gleefully laid a trap for the English. Instead, these few
Pamunkeys had ridden into it and it had worked. It worked so well that
there was no way he could stop it. Tsalagis were closing the circle around
the Pamunkeys fast.

Running Man saw a few Tsalagis fall, but not many. Quickly they
were swarming over the Pamunkeys. Then abruptly the fight was over.
It could hardly even be called a fight, Running Man thought. The Tsalagi
numbers had just been too overwhelming. Running Man had a victory
to his credit, but in his own mind it was not a great victory. He would
not boast about this one.

❦

THE victorious Tsalagi warriors came running back into town. They
whooped and bragged. They sang. They danced. Running Man was disgusted. He wanted no part of their celebration. Instead he sought out
War Woman. She was sitting in front of her house alone smoking, seemingly disinterested in what had been happening outside the walls of the
town.

"Do you know what has just happened out there?" he asked her.

"You won a victory," she said.

"Yes," he replied, "but over a handful of pitiful Pamunkey people.
There were not even a hundred of them, and there was not an Englishman
among them. It was a slaughter, Grandmother, not even a battle."

In the background the sounds of the victory celebration filled the air.
War Woman puffed on her pipe.

"Sit down," she said. "Smoke with me."

Running Man sat on the bench beside her, and she handed him the
pipe. He took a puff and handed it back. He was sullen and morose.

"Who were these men you killed?" she asked him. "These men whose
deaths are worrying you so?"

"They were Pamunkeys, of course," he said. He was a little put out
by the question. He knew that he had already told her that, and he was
almost certain that she had known anyway.

"And what were these Pamunkeys?"

"They were people whipped by the English," he said. "Made subject to the English will. They were pathetic slaves."

"And what had they come here for?"

"To attack us," he responded, "because the English made them do it."

"If you had not wiped them out just now," she asked, "what would they have done?"

"They'd have killed us, of course," he said. "That's what the English sent them to do."

War Woman shrugged and handed the pipe back to Running Man.

"Then stop feeling bad about it," she said.

"But I do feel bad. I came here to kill English. I didn't expect this. This land we're living on here should belong to those people we just killed. Not to those white men."

"But it no longer belongs to the Pamunkey people," she said, "or to any of the Powhatans. The English took it from them. We came to teach a lesson to the English. These Pamunkeys had become a part of the English. The English sent them at us, and so your victory was over the English after all."

Running Man puffed the pipe again and thought about War Woman's words.

"You're right, of course," he said.

Even with that admission, he did not feel good. He still sulked.

"Running Man," said War Woman, and she gave him a stern look, "you're the war chief of this town, of all these people here. How will our young men feel if after a fight, which they won, you're pouting? You put them in their places and told them what to do, and they did it. They did exactly as they were told to do and what do they get from you, their leader, for their efforts? A pout?"

He handed her back her pipe. He knew that she was right. He had set these men to battle, and they had won a victory. He owed it to them to make them think that he was proud. It was sad to think about what had become of the Pamunkeys, of all the Powhatans, at the hands of the English, but he could not let that affect him and his people. He stood up.

"Grandmother," he said, "as always, I'm glad that I came to talk with you."

He walked toward the celebration, and he saw some of the men looking in his direction. He puffed himself up with pride. They were good men, and he was their war chief. He would join in their celebration.

Then suddenly there was a young woman just next to him. He hadn't noticed her before. He was almost startled. He paused.

" *'Siyo,*" he said. It was the only word he had ever spoken to her, the woman that War Woman did not like, the one whose legs were too long.

She looked up at him and smiled. "It was a great victory," she said.

He smiled back. "Yes," he said. "A great victory." And he was proud.

53

HE DANCING, singing, and general feasting of the victory celebration lasted well into the night, and much of that time Running Man spent talking with Doe in the Water. The more time he spent with the lovely young woman, the more he puzzled over War Woman's reaction to her. Her disposition was smooth and even, not nasty. Above all, her legs were not too long. *What,* he kept asking himself, *could Grandmother have against her?*

He was beginning to like Doe in the Water very much, but he did not like the thought of going against the wishes of War Woman. His relationship with War Woman had become a very special one, one that meant much to him. He sought out her advice regularly, and he valued her advice. But she could really be grouchy, and if he were to begin to show an interest in a young woman she did not approve of—well, she would certainly let him know about it. She would probably also be terribly rude to the young woman.

He had asked Doe in the Water all the right questions. Their clans were compatible, his and hers, and he could tell that she liked him. He was thinking about asking her if she would like to marry him, but he was worried about War Woman. So, except for the worrying, he spent a very pleasant late evening with her. They danced the appropriate dances together, and in between times they talked.

"Do you like it here at our new town?" she asked him.

He shrugged. "It's a beautiful place," he said. "I like it well enough. We came here for a particular reason."

"Yes," she said. "I know."

"It's far away from other towns of the Real People."

"Yes," she agreed. She glanced up at him for a brief moment. "I'm glad I came, though."

He thought that he understood her meaning, and he smiled at her. "I'm glad, too," he said.

"You won the battle today," she said. It was obvious that she was proud of him, proud to be with him.

"Our young men won," he said. "But I'm sure there will be others. The English won't give up that easy."

❧

WAR WOMAN stayed back away from the crowd, but she watched from the shadows. She saw everything that went on. She watched the young men dance. She listened to the singing and to the bragging over bold deeds in the battle that day. She saw the women bring out their dishes for the feasting, and then she showed herself long enough to get what she wanted to eat. Finally, she watched as Running Man and Doe in the Water got better and better acquainted as the evening wore on. Standing in the shadows, she grinned. Then, having seen enough, she walked back to her house and went inside. She was old, and she needed her sleep.

❧

CALVIN BARTON rode all night long to get back to the settlement. He had been at Red Tail's village when the deserters had returned. He had learned that Red Tail and the rest had been wiped out by the Chalakees, and these were taking the rest of their people and running away. They wouldn't tell him where they were going, and they refused to listen to his warnings when he told them to stay. He had reminded them that they were subjects of the British Commonwealth, but they had told him that they didn't care about that. At last, fearing for his life, he had headed back to the settlement.

He was tired and hungry after his all-night ride, but he was glad to be safely back home. He also felt like he had to report to Clinton as soon as possible that the Pamunkey attack on the Chalakees had been a dismal failure. He would be glad to get the unpleasant business over with, though, for he knew that Clinton would fly into a rage. The man had a terrible temper.

As he rode into the settlement of scattered houses, it was early morning. A few men and women were up and beginning the day. He rode toward the nearest man and nearly fell out of the saddle getting down off his horse. The man ran to grab hold and help keep him on his feet.

"I'm all right," he said. "Fetch Clinton."

As the other ran to get Clinton, Barton staggered to a nearby rain barrel. He leaned over it and reached in with both hands, splashing water into his face. Clinton came running up behind him.

"Barton!" he shouted. "What's the news?"

Barton straightened up and turned to face Clinton. He wiped at his face with a sleeve and shook his head.

"Red Tail's Pamunkeys are all gone," he said. "Before they attacked the Chalakees, half of them deserted and went back home. They packed up everyone and left. The remaining warriors, with Red Tail in the lead, attacked the town and were wiped out—to a man."

"Damn!" Clinton shouted, his red beard bristling. "Damn it to bloody hell." He stomped away from Barton, then turned and stomped back. "Where have the cowardly deserters gone to?"

"I don't know," Barton said. "I asked them where they were going, but they wouldn't tell me. I tried to keep them from running away, but they became so belligerent I was afraid they'd kill me. By then the word had already come back about the massacre, and I left and rode back here. I rode all night to bring you the news."

"Damn it, damn it, damn it!" Clinton roared. "I should have known that the damned Pamunkeys wouldn't be able to do the job right. Go get some food and rest, man. Damn it to hell."

Some others had gathered around by that time, and as Barton walked away, one of them spoke to Clinton.

"What do we do now?" he asked.

"It'll just have to be an army from Jamestown to go out there and whip them," Clinton said. "We'll have to wait for those two to return. They should be able to tell us how fast the governor will act. Blast and damn. They ought to have returned by now."

RAMSEY and Barry returned to the settlement around noon that same day. They listened to Clinton rant and rave about how long they had been gone, and then they delivered their bad news.

"The governor said that we should handle it ourselves," Barry reported.

Clinton surprised them. He did not roar. He looked at Ramsey with wide eyes, with an expression of disbelief, and when he spoke, he spoke softly.

"He refused to send help?" he said. "We should handle it ourselves? Does he not give a damn, then, if we're slaughtered out here, men, women, and children alike? Is that how much our governor cares about our welfare, then?"

Ramsey looked at Barry. Neither had a response for Clinton, nor did anyone else in the room. A heavy silence fell over all. Clinton stood up. He looked around the room.

"Well then, gentlemen," he said, "I suppose we'll have to take care of it ourselves. Have every man look to his weapons. I'll draw up a battle plan. Be prepared. I'll let you know when we'll be going."

☙

ON THE advice of War Woman, Running Man did not wait for the English reaction to the defeat of the Pamunkeys. He gathered up a hundred young men early two mornings after the battle. They were all mounted on good fast Spanish horses. About half of them had Spanish guns, some long rifles, some pistols, and all had bows, arrows, war clubs, and knives.

They had danced wearing wooden warrior masks with rattlesnakes carved on the foreheads to show that they had no fear. They had slept the night before on ashes in the town house, away from women. They were ready to do battle.

They rode away from their town just as the Sun peeped above the eastern horizon, having just crept out from under the edge of the great Sky Vault. They rode toward the nearest offshoot settlement from Jamestown. The English there were the ones who had set the Pamunkeys on them, and Running Man was especially anxious to deal them a stunning blow.

He had made a big speech to the young men the night before. These English, he had said, deserved to be punished. They needed to be taught a lesson. Like the Spaniards and the French, they had come from their own homes across the big water.

"But upon reaching this, our home," he said, "they decided to take it away from us. They seem to think that all land is their land. They whipped the once-great Powhatan Nation, killing many and driving many others away. The few who are left in these parts surrendered themselves wholly into the hands of the English. Then the English, when they want to fight someone, make their subjects fight their battles for them.

"I hate these English because they sent the Pamunkeys to fight us for them and we had to kill the Pamunkeys. We had no choice. They had become a part of the English and were fighting the English fight. The English are cowards and bullies. They're arrogant and greedy. And they think that they can tell us to pack up and move out of here. We'll show them that they can't tell Real People what to do."

The speech had its desired effect, for all the young men who had been chosen to ride against the settlement that morning were anxious for the fight. They shouted and whooped and gobbled the special war cry of the Real People, the imitation of the male turkey in the woods. They were so anxious for the fight that they rode out of town fast, and Running Man let them, even though he knew that they could not ride that hard all the way to the settlement.

He let them ride hard for a little while, and then he slowed them down to a walk. They would walk the horses most of the rest of the way. When they reached the settlement, when they had it in sight, then they could run hard again to make their charge.

DOE IN THE WATER hurried to find War Woman as soon as the young men rode away from the town. She was proud of Running Man, but she was worried, too. He was leading his men against the English, the ones who had defeated the great Powhatans. She had no doubt that the men of the Real People made better fighters than did those of the Powhatans. Still, the English must be able to fight. There must be many of them, and they must have many guns.

"War Woman," she said, spotting the old woman walking along beside the town house. "How are you today?"

"I'm old," War Woman replied.

Doe in the Water hurried to catch up to War Woman, then, alongside her, slowed her pace in order not to rush past her.

"You want to talk about something," said War Woman. It was not a question.

"Yes," Doe in the Water replied. "Running Man knows me now. He talks to me."

"Yes," said the old woman. "I've noticed that. He talks much to you."

"Does he talk about me," Doe in the Water asked, "to you?"

"He has never mentioned your name to me," War Woman said.

Doe in the Water looked disappointed for a brief moment, but she quickly perked up again. "I think he wants to marry me," she said.

"Oh? Has he said so?"

"No," said Doe in the Water, "but I can tell—I think. He likes me. I know he likes me."

"And now that you know him," asked War Woman, "do you like him as much as you thought you would?"

"More," said the other. "I like him more than anyone else I've ever known. I want to marry him." She paused, walking along slowly beside the old woman for a while. "I want to thank you for what you did. I know you told me that you could do nothing for me, but only the next day he saw me and spoke to me. I—"

"I did nothing," War Woman said.

"Well, will he come back?"

"To you?"

"Will he come back safely from this fight today?"

"He'll be back," War Woman said, "and he'll be unhurt and victorious."

"And will he want to marry me?"

"How would I know that? Do I look into his mind?"

"If he does want to marry me," asked Doe in the Water, "who will he ask to speak for him to my mother? Is his mother here among us, or his aunts?"

"He would ask me," said the old woman, "but he has not mentioned your name to me."

54

 LINTON had just finished his noon meal and was preparing to call the men together for a talk to prepare them for battle the next day. He had made his plans. They would gather up early in the morning. Each man would be well mounted and heavily armed. Each man would carry at least a rifle and two pistols, a small ax, and a knife. Those who had them would carry swords. They would mount up with the sunrise and ride out, leaving a small force to guard the settlement.

They would ride straight to the Indian town and attack it without warning. They had used that tactic in the past with success against the Powhatans, and Clinton was certain that it would work with these Chalakees as well. He would tell his men that no one was to be spared, not old men, not women, not children. Wipe them out. If any should survive, they would be totally demoralized.

He downed another flagon of red wine, wiped his mouth and beard on his sleeve, and pushed himself away from the table. Without a word to his wife, he stalked to the door and jerked it open. He was walking to the meeting hall when he heard the alarm.

"Indians!"

He looked to see one of the men running as hard as he could toward a house.

"Indians!" the man cried again.

Clinton swept the horizon with his eyes, and he saw them coming. They were riding right toward the settlement. There were too many of them to be riding in for a talk, and they were riding too hard. It was an attack. A surprise attack. *Damned villains,* he thought.

He turned and ran back inside his house. Grabbing his rifle off the wall, he glanced at his wife. "Indians," he said. "Sound the alarm." He rushed back outside. His wife followed, ready to obey his command, but someone had beaten her to it and was ringing the alarm bell.

Women ran to find their children and then ran for their homes. Men rushed to get their weapons and then to barricade themselves for the coming attack.

The settlement was a line of buildings, mostly small cabins. In the center was a slightly larger house that served as their meetinghouse. The men stacked barrels and rolled wagons, anything they could get, in front of the meetinghouse. They settled behind that makeshift wall for protection and waited for the foe to come within rifle range. But the attacking Indians stopped.

"What the hell are they doing?" someone asked.

They watched as the Indians ran on foot, spreading themselves out in a long thin line, then running toward the line of houses. They were not all moving together in a cluster. They were not all concentrating on the men behind the barricade. Some were racing toward the houses at either end of the settlement.

A man stood up, looking toward his own far right. "My wife and children are down there!" he shouted.

"Get down," Clinton said.

"They're unprotected," the man said. "I've got to go to them."

Just then a shot was fired. The man clutched at his chest, and blood flowed freely down the front of his shirt. He stood weaving, an astonished look on his face. Then he fell forward. And then more shots came, and the Englishmen began returning the fire.

At one end of the settlement, six Real People ran toward the house at the end of the line. As they drew close, the door opened and an Englishwoman stepped out with a rifle in her hands. She aimed and fired, and one of the Real People fell, a ball in his thigh. The woman stepped back inside and slammed the door, but one of the warriors was there to shove it open again before she had time to bar it from inside.

The woman turned to run, and the man cracked her skull from behind with his war club. He heard children scream then, and he looked toward the back of the room. Three small ones were huddled there. She had been running to her children. Two more Real People stepped inside just then, and he looked at them, perplexed. He gestured toward the children.

"What shall we do with them?" he asked.

"Take them with us," said one.

Two of the men gathered up the three small children and left. The third man moved to the fireplace. He saw the poker there beside it, and he picked it up and used it to scrape burning logs out of the fireplace and roll them around the room. By the time he found his companions with the children, the house was burning. They helped their wounded friend up off the ground, and all of them headed back toward the waiting horses.

At the other end of the settlement a similar scene was taking place. Four young men had attacked the house, but they found the door barricaded. They pounded at it with their war clubs and rifle butts, but to no avail. They ran around the house looking for a way in. At last they built a fire under the logs on one side, and then they waited and watched as the flames grew. Soon the door flew open, and a woman came running out screaming. Two of the men grabbed her, and they all started with her back toward the horses.

In the center of the fight, Running Man saw that his plan had worked. He had headed with his mounted men straight for the big house in the middle of the settlement, and the English fighting men had all bunched up there behind their hastily constructed barricade. Then the Real People had dismounted and attacked, not just the center, but the ends as well.

Behind the barricade, some of the Englishmen were panicking. They worried about the unprotected women and children in the houses on down the line. Three men got their heads together, quickly reloaded their rifles, and began running toward the flames at the end of the line to their right. Running Man's warriors cut them down before they had gone half the distance.

Another four ran toward the left. One was hit by an arrow as soon as he emerged from behind the barricade. The other three ran on. A rifle ball in the hip dropped one. One stopped at a house, banged on the door, and called out. The door was opened, and the man was hit in the back by an arrow. The wounded man crawled toward the open door, and a woman from the house helped him in. They shut the door.

The fourth man ducked around the corner of a house and took aim. He fired, and a Chalakee warrior fell dead. The Englishman saw two more rushing toward him. He dropped his rifle and pulled a pistol from his waistband. He raised it and fired too quickly. His shot missed its mark, but the ball sped close by the ear of one of his attackers. Both turned and ran to the side. The Englishman began to reload his weapons.

Behind the center barricade, Clinton was afraid that the settlers were about to be overwhelmed when all of a sudden, as if in answer to some signal he had not heard or seen, the attackers turned and raced back to their horses. They mounted up, gestured and shouted defiantly, and rode away, taking with them one Englishwoman and three small children.

"They're leaving," someone said.

"We've beaten them off," said another.

Clinton stood and surveyed the scene around him. He saw the bodies of at least a dozen Englishmen. The Indians had somehow managed to pick up their own dead and take the bodies away with them. He had no idea how many they had killed.

"You're hurt," someone said.

"What?" said Clinton, as if jerked out of a reverie.

"You're hurt."

He looked down to see his left arm all bloody, a jagged wound just below the shoulder. He didn't know what had hit him. He hadn't felt it.

* * *

THEY had another victory celebration at the new Real People's town that night. They had dealt a severe blow to the English right in their own homes. They had burned houses and killed, and when they felt they had done enough damage and their own losses were too heavy to continue longer they had ridden away with captives.

Running Man was sad for the few young men he had lost. There were also a few wounded, but they would be all right. He was proud of the victory, though. They had fought a good fight, and they had accomplished what they had set out to do. He knew, though, that it was not the last fight.

There were some still hot for blood and some, stinging from their own hurts or losses, who wanted to kill the white woman and the children. They went to the young men who had brought the captives away with them, for the captives belonged to those young men.

"We have a right to kill them," the men hot for blood shouted, "for our young men who died today!"

Running Man did not know what to do. The captives belonged to the young men who brought them in, but the ones who were demanding revenge were right, too. Running Man did not like the idea of killing the helpless captives, but he himself lacked the authority to intervene. He listened as the people argued among themselves there in front of the town house. Then War Woman suddenly appeared before them, and the crowd was suddenly hushed.

"There will be no killing here tonight," she said. "Put them in a house. Guard them. Feed them and treat them well. That's all."

So the woman and the children were put in a house and fed and were left alone, but just outside the house a man stood guard. The matter was settled, and the people began to sing and dance in celebration of their victory. Running Man sought out War Woman for counsel.

"Should I put the sentries out tonight?" he asked. "The English will be seeking revenge."

"But not tonight," she said. "It will probably be a few days before they recover from what you did today. Tomorrow will be plenty of time to put out the sentries. Tonight celebrate and relax. You did well, Grandson."

Running Man beamed with pride. Praise from this old woman was not easy to get. He turned to join the dancing, but War Woman stopped him with a word.

"Grandson," she said. "See if you can find a good-looking woman to spend your time with. Not that skinny, long-legged one. See if you can find one with a better temper."

❧

AT the dance he found her, and he sat beside her. He could feel the eyes of War Woman burning into his back. He knew she was watching him and did not approve, but Doe in the Water was there beside him and she was beautiful and he loved her. There was no one else he wanted to be near. There was no one else with whom he wanted to dance. There was no one else in all of the town, no one he had ever known, whose voice he would rather listen to, to whom he would rather tell the things that were on his mind.

He knew that he wanted to make this woman his wife, but he also knew that he would have to have some woman from his own clan speak for him to the women of Doe in the Water's clan. War Woman had become like his own grandmother, and it was War Woman, he thought, who should speak for him. He had no one else. Of course, there were some older women of his clan in the town, but none of them was close to him. And surely War Woman would refuse. She hated Doe in the Water, it seemed. He did not know what he would do.

"You've had another great victory," Doe in the Water said. "I'm proud that you're sitting with me."

"I'm happy to have you by my side," he responded. "I wish I could always have you by my side."

She ducked her head and sat silent for a moment waiting for him to say more, but he did not. The sounds of the songs and the stomping feet filled the air.

"You could have," she said finally.

"What?"

"What you said."

"I said that I wish I could always have you beside me," Running Man said.

"Yes," she said. "And I said that you could. If you really want that, you could have it. If you want me to be your wife, I want you for a husband. You only need to have someone speak for you, some woman of your clan, to my mother and her sisters. No one would refuse you. Not now."

A worried look took over Running Man's face, and he stared at the ground before him. Doe in the Water looked at him and saw the worry.

"What's the matter?" she asked.

He didn't answer.

"Is something wrong?"

Still he sat silent.

"You don't want to marry me?" she asked.

"Yes," he said, "I do."

"Then why won't you—"

"Doe in the Water," he said, and he looked directly at her face, "what have you done to War Woman?"

"What?" she said. "What do you mean by that? I haven't done anything to her. I like her."

"Then why does she hate you so?"

$$55$$

OE IN THE WATER stalked away from Running Man. She
stomped the ground with each step. He stood as if to try to
stop her, but she did not slow down. He felt as if he must
look the fool, standing there, staring after her, his arm held
out toward her fast-disappearing back. He straightened himself up,
turned back toward the festivities, and tried to look as if everything were
normal with him.

Doe in the Water stomped all the way to the house of War Woman,
but the old woman was not at home. The young woman stomped back
to the dance ground and all around its circumference, but she saw no
sign there of the old woman either. Doe in the Water stalked the town,
walking along every street, and was just about to go outside the walls
and down to the river when she heard a familiar voice come at her from
the shadows beside a house.

"Were you looking for me?" it asked.

Doe in the Water stopped. The unexpected voice frightened her for
just a moment, but she regained her composure quickly enough and
angrily turned to face the old woman.

"Have you been hiding there all this time?" she asked.

"I've been under the ground," War Woman said.

"I don't believe you," the girl replied.

Hidden in the shadows, War Woman smiled. That was what she liked
about this girl. She was bold. She wasn't afraid of anyone or anything.
She reminded War Woman of someone else, someone she had known
long ago when the world was young.

"That's why you couldn't find me," she said. "I just now came out
from under there. I was visiting with the moles. Dirt eaters. They can't
see, you know."

"You were just hiding here behind this house," Doe in the Water said.

"From you?" War Woman responded. "Hiding from you?" She cackled.

"Yes," snapped the girl.

"Why would I hide from you?"

"Because you've said bad things about me," Doe in the Water said. "I thought we were friends, but you've been saying bad things to Running Man. I thought you were helping me, but you were not."

"I told you I couldn't help you," said the old woman. "Ha! I still have dirt in my hair."

"But you didn't say that you'd interfere with bad words."

"You're right," War Woman said. "I did say bad things. You came to me because he wouldn't even look at you. Isn't that so?"

"Yes, but—"

"And that night I told him that your legs were too long. He looked then. Didn't he?"

"Well . . . yes."

"And then I told him that you have a nasty personality, and what did he do?"

"Well, he talked to me, but—"

"I told him to find another young woman, one who's better-looking and has a nicer temper. What did he do then?"

"Well, he—"

"He wants to marry you, doesn't he?"

"Yes," said Doe in the Water. "He does."

"Then why are you stomping the earth so hard? What's wrong with you? Do you have what you wanted?"

"Yes."

"Then tell that foolish man of yours to come and see me," the old woman said, and when Doe in the Water looked for her to respond she could no longer find her. War Woman was gone.

❧

SHE chuckled as she flew through the air. The air was colder up high, and she liked the feeling of the cold air moving against her old skin. It was refreshing and exhilarating. She had to watch out for any passing night birds, though, to avoid an unpleasant collision, and there were the gnats and other small flying night bugs. They could be very annoying, especially when one swept into a whole swarm of them unexpectedly.

She soared around the town in circles, low at first, then higher and higher, and she watched the festivities below her, the people singing and dancing around the fire, smaller cook fires glowing in random spots around the periphery.

She was glad that she could see in the dark. She flew up higher and then started a downward soar that would take her to the settlement where the fight had taken place that day. She hadn't gone along with the fighting men. She was as old as the earth, but she could have made the ride with them. She knew that she could, but they would never have understood. So she had stayed behind. Now she would go look at it in the dark of night, all alone.

She found it with no trouble at all, and she was there in a very short time. Flying was by far the fastest way to travel, faster even than by water in a swift boat. She started to glide and, as she swooped in closer to the settlement, saw where the houses had been burned, and she saw some still-glowing embers from those fires. She saw fresh-dug graves. She recognized them, for she knew how white men buried their dead. Spanish, English, it made no difference.

She swept past the English settlement in an instant, and then she banked and started a long curving turn. As she turned, she reached deep into the pouch she wore hanging by a strap from a shoulder and drew out tobacco—not just any tobacco, but a specially prepared tobacco, a tobacco with a power that only she could impart to it—and, as she floated over the white men's houses once again, she scattered the special tobacco. She smiled as she gained altitude, rising away from the settlement, reaching up into the heavens.

She flew to the East, and there she visited the Red Woman and the Red Man and the Red Sparrow Hawk and the Red Spider and the Red Raven. She flew to the South, where she spent some time with the White Woman and the White Man and the White Sparrow Hawk and the White Raven and the White Spider.

She flew to the West, near to the Darkening Land, and there she saw the Black Woman, Black Man, Black Sparrow Hawk, Raven, and Spider, and then she flew to the North. It was cold in the North, and she did not like it there very much, so she only said hello to the Blue Man and Woman, the Blue Sparrow Hawk, and the Blue Raven and Spider.

She was getting tired, for she was very old, but she had one more visit to make, and she flew hard until she had reached the Sunland, and there she saw the Great Terrestrial Hunter and the Little Men dancing around a fire. She thought about joining their dance, but she was too old and tired for such things, and she still had a long flight ahead of her to get back to her house. The night was almost done, and she would most likely sleep all through the next day as it was. She banked again and started her long dive toward the town below the falls.

☙

"GRANDMOTHER!" Running Man called out. He was standing just outside her door. It was midmorning, and she had not yet made her appearance that day. Usually she was up and about early, almost with the Sun. Her late rising worried him a bit, because she was so old. "Grandmother!" he called again. "Are you in there? I need to talk with you."

"Come back later," she said. "I'm sleeping."

He was relieved to know that she was in there and was all right, but he was impatient to talk to her. He had something very important to discuss, and there was no one else. He found some young men and sent them out as sentries to watch for the English, and then he went back to her house and paced, waiting for her to decide to come out.

☙

IT was midday, but she still slept, and she dreamed about her adventures of the night before. She dreamed of flight, and she dreamed of her youth in the long-ago times. She dreamed of a brother she once had, young and handsome, and she dreamed of another young man, a husband and lover. She dreamed of Spaniards and drunkenness and death, and she dreamed of mountains of gold.

Then she dreamed of the Powhatans, a powerful people, and she saw them swept away by a new kind of white man called English, and she dreamed of her own young men sweeping the English away. Then she saw the English towns in flames, saw the men dying and the women being carried away in tears. She saw big fights, and she saw Running Man, he who was now her grandson, leading the fight, and then she saw him leading the dance, and she saw him with his young wife, and her legs were not too long.

She dreamed of a whirlwind and of crashing thunder and lightning flashing across the sky, and she dreamed of the earth when it was young, and then she dreamed of the Darkening Land.

RUNNING MAN was still pacing, still waiting for War Woman to show herself to the world that day. It was very unlike her to sleep all the day long. He thought several times of calling out to her again, but the recollection of her harsh voice from the first time he called out to her made him wait.

It was midafternoon when she at last came out. She stopped in her doorway and looked at him.

"Have you been out here all day?" she asked.

"Yes," he said. "Well, I—" He felt foolish, but he was relieved to see her at last.

"I'm hungry," she said.

They went to find her something to eat, and he waited with her. He ate with her, but he wasn't hungry. He ate a little to be polite. He thought that she would never finish. She ate slowly, like most old people, but she also ate much. Her appetite was voracious. That, he thought, was unusual for an old woman, but then, everything about this old woman was unusual. At last she was done.

"Grandmother," he said, "may we talk?"

"Do you have your sentries out?" she asked.

"Yes," he said. "I want to talk about—"

"Let's walk out to the river," she said.

She walked slowly, as old people do, and he slowed his own pace to walk alongside her. His patience was wearing out. He bit his lower lip as they walked. He had important things to say, and she kept putting him off. He resolved that he would not be put off longer. When they reached the water's edge, he would talk to her. If she interrupted again with some other suggestion, he would talk anyway. He would not wait longer. At last they came to the water, and she sat down.

"Grandmother," he said, and she held up her hand for silence. She leaned forward and tilted her head as if she was listening to the water or listening to the voice of the river. He knew what she was doing, and he dared not interrupt, in spite of what he had sworn to himself. He wondered what the water was saying to her as it rushed by them on its way to wherever it was going. At last she sat up straight.

"Now," she said, "sit down beside me."

He sat, and he stared out at the rushing water.

"Well?" she said.

"Grandmother?"

"Yes."

"You told me that her legs were too long."

"Whose?" she asked.

"Doe in the Water," he said. "And you said you didn't like her."

"Did I say that?"

"Yes," he said. "You pointed her out to me, and you said you didn't like her because her legs were too long."

"Oh," she said. "That one. Yes. I remember now."

"And later you told me that she had a nasty disposition. Remember?"

"Yes," she said, slowly nodding her head. "I did say that about her. I remember that."

"And then—"

"Wait a minute," she said. "I want to smoke."

She dug into her pouch for pipe and tobacco, and when she had her pipe bowl filled she realized that she had no fire. Running Man had to run back to the town and find a fire. He brought back a stick with a glowing red end, and she lit her pipe. Clouds of gray smoke surrounded her head and clouded her features. She sighed a satisfied sigh.

"Grandmother," said Running Man.

"I'm listening," she responded. "What takes you so long to tell me what's on your mind?"

"I don't know why you hate her so," he said, "but I love Doe in the Water, and I want to marry her. I need you to talk to her mother and the other women of her clan for me. I hope you'll do that for me and I hope that you can learn to like her, because—"

"Is that all?" the old woman asked. "Why didn't you say so in the first place? I'll take care of everything. She's a nice girl. I like her just fine."

<h1 style="text-align:center">56</h1>

 OU'RE THROUGH, George," Calvin Barton said. "There's been a vote, and the command has been handed to me. We lost eighteen men and one woman. Another woman and three children are being held captive right now by that savage horde. No telling what horrors they're suffering as we speak. The men blame you."

"Take the command then and be damned," Clinton said. "You'll find it a thankless job. I can tell you that."

"Don't blame me, George," said Barton. "There was a vote. I'm just reporting the findings to you. That's all."

Barton turned to leave the room. As he was reaching for the door, Clinton spoke again.

"Calvin," he said.

Barton hesitated and turned back to face Clinton once more.

"Calvin, when you've determined your course of action, just tell me what it is you want me to do. I'll do it."

Barton nodded and left the house. The meeting was still in progress. Clinton had not been invited, because of the vote. Barton had left the meeting to give the news to Clinton. That was all. He lacked the authority to invite Clinton back for the rest of the meeting.

He walked back to the meeting hall and found everyone talking at once. As he moved to his new place behind the head table, the voices hushed.

"Have you told him?" someone asked.

"I've told him," Barton said.

"Did he give you any trouble?"

"No trouble at all," said Barton, "and now we must get back to the business of this meeting. Replacing George Clinton as captain of our militia was only the first step. Now we have to proceed to a strong plan of action.''

⟡

THE militia from the settlements marched toward the Tsalagi town. There were 150 mounted men, and behind them walked 200 infantry-men. Each man carried a long rifle, a pistol (some had two), a powder flask, a bag of lead balls, and a knife. Some men carried short axes, and some carried swords. They marched in good, dignified British fashion.

As they drew near the town and Barton was about ready to sound the attack, a hundred or more Tsalagis appeared from behind the wall. They fit arrows to their bows and aimed high. Barton realized what was about to happen. In near-panic, he ordered a retreat. The sky above was suddenly filled with arrows, and the Englishmen ran into one another in an effort to turn and run. Some even ran toward the town.

Then as the arrows dropped, many finding marks in the crowd of Englishmen, men and horses screamed in pain. Those who were not hit and those hit but still able to move raced in full retreat. But from the riverbank another hundred or so Tsalagi archers appeared to send yet another shower of deadly arrows raining down on the heads of the mi-litiamen.

"Follow me!" Barton shouted, turning toward the mountain. He kicked his horse viciously in the sides in a mad race toward imagined safety. Those who were able followed him. There was no immediate pursuit. As the Englishmen rushed toward the mountain in shameful retreat, Tsalagis from the riverbank and from the town ran out to scavenge weapons and shot from the bodies that the others had left behind.

⟡

FROM his place on the walkway behind the wall Running Man watched. So far his plan had worked perfectly. He was satisfied. He felt much better about this fight than he had about the previous one, for this time they were killing English, not Pamunkeys. He was satisfied, but he was not done. He turned and looked toward the falls above the town.

"Batwing," he said to a young man standing nearby on the platform, "go on now with your group. It's time enough."

AT the foot of the mountain, Barton scampered first in one direction, then the other, until he found a place he thought he could climb. Then he turned his horse into the rising ground and lashed at the poor beast, urging it up the side of the mountain. It slipped. It fell and regained its feet. It struggled, panting and blowing, but at last it reached the top of the mountain. The others were following.

Barton rode back and forth along the mountaintop looking for pursuit. He saw none. These Chalakees had tricked him twice, though, and he knew that he could be none too careful at this point. He decided that he would have to make a stand right there. His horse was just about spent, and so must all the others be. He looked around again. Finding a place along the ridge that was naturally lined with boulders, he dismounted and waved the men to him.

"We'll make a stand here," he said. "Fill in the gaps between these boulders with loose rock."

The horses were let loose to run or graze as they chose, while the men busied themselves following Barton's instructions. Soon they had a rock wall along the mountaintop, and they huddled down behind it waiting for an attack from below. They saw no Chalakees except those back at the town. There was no one coming after them.

"What the hell are they doing?" one asked.

"I don't know," Barton snapped back. "Just shut up and wait and see."

"They're not coming after us," said another. "Let's get on our horses and get the hell back home."

"Shut up, I say!" Barton shouted. "The horses would never make it. Not just now. And we don't know what those heathens are planning. They surprised us twice down there. So be still and watch. Be ready for anything."

They lay behind the rock wall in silence then, their rifles ready. Barton thought about the dead and wounded he had left behind. He wondered who they were. There had not been time to look. No time to count either. How many had been lost? How many were left?

He thought about poor Clinton back at the settlement in disgrace and knew that he himself would be next in line. Surely he, too, would be deposed for this dismal failure. Well, he would just have to find a way to turn the tide, to change the drubbing into a victory or at least something more like a draw, a fight that he could claim a victory from. He'd have to kill at least as many of the enemy as they had killed English. *How many?* he wondered again.

"Jones!" he called.

"Yes, Captain Barton," Jones answered, and Barton thought that he detected a tone of sarcasm in the voice. He chose to ignore it.

"Make a count," he said. "How many of us are left here?"

While Jones began the count, Barton concentrated his attention again on the Chalakee town. The men who had been picking over the bodies all seemed to have gone back into the town—or somewhere else. They were no longer in sight. Barton could tell little about what might be going on. He could make out some movement inside the walls, and he could tell that men still stood overlooking the wall. He could see no sign of activity outside the town. Perhaps there would be no pursuit. Maybe the best thing to do would be let the horses rest a bit, then mount up and head home.

"Ninety-seven," Jones said.

"What?" said Barton.

"There's ninety-seven of us up here. Twenty-three are hurt. Five pretty badly."

Barton did a quick calculation in his head. "Seventy-four able-bodied," he said.

"I've heard there's a thousand warriors down there," said Jones.

"I've heard that figure, too," Barton said. "It might be exaggerated a bit."

"If it's only exaggerated a bit," Jones said, "then we're still the hell outnumbered, ain't we?"

Barton didn't bother answering. He watched the town below. Still there was no sign of activity. He stood up boldly to address his militia.

"Men," he said, "we were surprised down there and badly hurt. We have wounded to consider, and we know we're outnumbered. We'll let the horses rest a bit longer, and then we'll head back. This is too big a job for us here. We'll have to go to Jamestown again and impress upon the governor just how damn many savages are out here. It'll take an army from Jamestown to deal with them, and that's for sure."

There was a twang and a whiz and a sickening thud, and Barton stiffened with a jerk. His eyes opened wide and his jaw dropped. Then his body relaxed and fell forward. An arrow protruded from between his shoulder blades. The remaining Englishmen grabbed their weapons and turned, but they found no one to shoot at.

"Where the hell are they?" one asked.

"I don't know."

"I can't see anyone."

"Well, they're out there somewhere."

"They killed Barton."

"It was his own damn fault."

"Look!" one shouted, pointing.

Ahead in the brush a lone Tsalagi warrior stood, revealing himself long enough to aim a long rifle. The Englishmen all quickly swung their own rifles into play, but the Tsalagi fired his before any of them could take aim. The man who had first seen him screamed and clutched at a smashed shoulder. The Tsalagi dropped down and vanished from sight. The Englishmen all fired their rifles at the spot where they had seen him. All of their shots were wasted.

"They're taking our horses!" Jones yelled, and they looked again, and sure enough, the horses were being led away. Few of the Englishmen had managed to reload their rifles. None of them could find clear shots, for the men taking the horses were keeping to the far side of the animals as they led them.

"What'll we do?" asked one Englishman.

"Come on!" another shouted, jumping up and running in the direction of the horses. "We'll stop them. We'll be lost without those mounts."

He didn't run far. An arrow struck him in the chest. The others all dropped flat and huddled into the ground. Their protective rock wall was now behind them.

"We're lost, all right," Jones whispered.

"They'll kill us all," said another.

"I have an idea," said Jones.

"Well, what is it?"

"Let's surrender."

"They might kill us."

"They'll kill us if we don't surrender," Jones said. "That much is certain. If we do surrender, they might kill us. Then again, they might not."

❧

THEY met on the open plain in front of the town beneath the falls, and Running Man accepted the surrender of the Englishmen. He had to speak with them through the Pamunkey, the one they called Indian John, for none of the Tsalagis knew English, and the English, of course, could not speak the language of the Real People.

"Lay your weapons down," Running Man demanded of them, and they did as they were told.

"Your horses will be brought back to you," he said, "and the woman and the children we took. Go on now to Jamestown."

The English settlers then protested that their homes were not in Jamestown but in the settlements that had grown out of Jamestown.

"Go to Jamestown," Running Man repeated. "We're going to watch you go. If you stop at the settlements, we'll kill you."

"We have some people there yet," they said.

"As you go by," said Running Man, "call them out to join you. If they refuse, they'll die."

So the settlers' militia agreed to all of Running Man's terms, and their horses and the woman and the three children were brought out to them. Humiliated, they mounted their horses, leaving all their weapons there on the ground. They turned the horses and rode slowly away. Running Man and some others stood and watched them go.

WHEN the settlers reached their own settlement, the group did not ride too close to the buildings, for they knew that they were being watched and had been warned not to stop there. One man rode in quickly to call out to the ones in the houses.

"Come out!" he cried. "Come out and ride with us to Jamestown!"

A man stepped out of a house. "What for?" he yelled. "What's going on?"

"There's no time to explain!" the rider called. "Get everyone out and all you follow us. The Chalakees are right behind us. They'll kill anyone who stays."

The settlement was quickly abandoned, and as the English men, women, and children rode slowly toward Jamestown, they looked back over their shoulders and saw the rising smoke from the flames that were engulfing their former homes.

57

 ET ME A HORSE," War Woman said. "I want to ride out to the settlements and watch."

Running Man had not planned to go to the settlements. He knew that the men he had sent would take care of things out there. But War Woman wanted to go, so he called for two saddled horses, which were soon brought to him. He helped War Woman up onto the back of one horse, and then he mounted the other. The two of them rode along together in the tracks of the Tsalagi men he had sent to trail the abject settlers to make sure they did as they had agreed to do. About halfway to the nearest of the settlements, they met the men on the road.

"What has happened?" Running Man asked.

"They did just as you told them to do," said one of the men. "They called the other people out of their houses, the ones they had left behind, and all of them started together on the road to Jamestown. Then we burned their houses. All of them."

"Good," said Running Man. "Then everything has been done."

"Yes," said the other. "Everything."

Running Man started his horse moving again, and so did War Woman. The rider who had been speaking to him looked confused.

"Are you going there?" he asked.

"Yes," said Running Man.

"Do you want us to go back there with you?"

"No," Running Man replied. "We'll be all right. There are no English left there, are there?"

"No. Of course not."

"Then everything's all right!" Running Man shouted as he rode on. "Go on home."

The man shrugged, and he and the others continued on their way back to their own town, while Running Man and War Woman rode on alone toward the settlements. The Sun was already low in the western sky, and they still had some distance to go.

The first thing they saw was the red glow from the flames. The sky was darkening by then. They rode on, and the flames danced in the old eyes of War Woman. She kicked her horse into a faster gait and rode ahead of Running Man.

By the time they reached the settlement, the buildings were already almost consumed. The flames that still burned were low. The rest had become glowing embers. The smell of smoke filled the nostrils of War Woman and made them flare. She asked Running Man to get her down off her horse, and he hurried to do that.

"Ah," she groaned as she stood on the ground. She was stiff and sore. She looked around for a place to sit, and she found the stump of a tree nearby. She walked to it and sat down with a long and deep sigh. Running Man stood behind her.

"Have you seen enough?" he asked.

"We'll stay here tonight," she said.

He wondered how long she would just sit there staring at the flames, watching them slowly die down, watching the glowing embers turn to black ash. He was tired from a long day, and so at last he found himself a place on the ground to lie down. For what seemed like a long time to him, he lay awake wondering about the old woman, the one he now called Grandmother.

When Running Man at last fell asleep, War Woman was still sitting there and watching the remains of the English settlement. She watched as the last walls crumbled, and she watched smoke rising from the still-hot black ash. She smelled the smoke and felt it sting her old eyes. She sat still on the stump and watched for most of the night.

WHEN Running Man came out of his sleep, the Sun was already crawling along the underside of the Sky Vault. The darkness was gone. He was a little embarrassed to find that he had slept so late. Looking around and rubbing his eyes, he found War Woman sitting just where she had been the night before. He wondered if she had slept a little and then returned to that place or if she had just been there all through the night.

He was just a little afraid that she would chastise him for his late sleeping, and he was about to speak, to greet her, but without looking at him, she spoke first.

"We sure whipped them," she said. "Those English."

He smiled behind her back.

"Yes, Grandmother," he agreed. "We whipped them pretty good."

"You know," she said, "the Spanish and the French aren't really so bad. I know them, I know how to deal with them, but I don't like these no-good, ugly Englishmen. I don't think it's so good after all to be living so close to them."

Running Man waited for more from the old woman. He didn't know what to say to that. A part of his mind wanted him to tell her that the whole long and tedious move, as well as the war with the English, had been her idea in the first place, wanted him to remind her that seven hundred people had gone to all this trouble just because of her whim. He didn't say anything, though, and in another moment she spoke again.

"This country is not nearly so pretty as the country back there where we came from either," she said. "It's not as good here as it is back there. I don't think we really ever lived here before. I don't like it very much."

Now he knew what she was getting at. She was not just complaining. She wanted to move back to New Town. She had been the one who had decided that they should make this move, and the people had gone along with her. Of course. She always got her way, didn't she? She had convinced them to make the move and to then teach the English a lesson. That was done, and now she wanted to go back home. *Well,* he thought, *if that's what she wants, then we will probably move back home.*

"Grandmother," he said, "I, too, think the land around New Town is better. It's better for us. I don't like this place here very much either."

❧

OF course, they had to have a big council meeting, and all of the people had to be allowed a chance to speak their minds. There were actually a few voices in favor of staying in Virginia. After all, they said, they had made a major move and had gone to a great deal of trouble. They had come a long way, and they had worked hard to build this new town in this strange land. They had also fought hard to keep it, and they had won. "Why?" they asked. "Why give it all up now?"

War Woman had not taken part in the discussion. She did not even attend the meeting. She was aloof to the proceedings. She knew what she wanted, but she did not feel the need to go before the people and plead her case. She had let Running Man and others do that for her. And they had used her own arguments: The English were very unpleasant people, and they lived too close to the town below the falls. The country of this land the English were calling Virginia was not as pretty as was the country at home, and the weather was not as agreeable. But the argument that seemed to have at last won everyone over, or at least shut up the opposition, was that all of the other Real People were too far away. They had left too many friends and relatives too far behind. So, of course, in the end, the people had decided to move back home.

And they did just as they had done before, preparing for a major move, a long journey with a great many people, one that would take many days to accomplish. They prepared food they could carry along with them. They readied weapons, clothing, all the things they'd need for the trip. Finally they packed it all and loaded it onto the backs of horses. Just before they started, they set fire to the town they had worked so hard to build. As they rode away from it, no one looked back.

THE trip back was not like the original trip had been. There was an excitement, but it was a different kind of excitement. It was not the excitement of the young men anticipating war. Everyone was anxious to get back home and see their relatives and the friends they had left behind. They were anxious to get back to the familiar land with the places they had known all their lives. Hunters were anxious to get back to familiar hunting territory. Gardeners were anxious to dig in familiar ground.

The traveling back seemed to go faster than it had gone before, probably because the people knew the way this time. They knew how far they would be traveling, and they knew just about how many days they could expect to be on the trail. They had not known that before. Each night when they camped, they were surprised and pleased to realize just how much ground they had covered that day.

And no one seemed to feel as if they had wasted their time and energy on the frivolous whims of a crazy old woman. On the contrary, everyone seemed anxious to get home and brag to friends and relatives about the things they had accomplished on a worthwhile journey in a just cause. All of the young men who had taken part in the battles would have a new stature in their own home communities. It had been a good trip.

Running Man was especially pleased. As war chief, he had led his people in a major victory against the English settlers, a people they had never even met before, a brutal and warlike people who had smashed the once-powerful Powhatan Confederacy. Running Man would be talked about far and wide for that accomplishment. He would become one of the most famous of the war chiefs of the Real People. He was certain of that.

Just as important, he had gotten himself a wife, for War Woman, just as she had promised to do, had spoken to the women of Doe in the Water's clan, and they had agreed to the proposed match. As soon as the people had returned to New Town, preparations for the wedding would begin. Running Man was anxious for that.

But one thing still puzzled him a great deal. He couldn't figure out yet why War Woman had been so strongly set against Doe in the Water at first and then had so suddenly and completely changed her mind about the young woman.

And War Woman was the most pleased of all. She was as ancient as the trees and the rocks and the water, and even so, still, at her age, she could get whatever she wanted. She had made seven hundred Real People pack up and move a great distance to avenge a wrong done to a people they did not even know. She had brought them to a great victory over those English, then had gotten them to pack up and head for home once more. She felt smug and self-satisfied. She had needed one last adventure in her long life, and she had gotten it. Her powers were still strong. They were not worn out. Not yet.

But she thought much about the Spanish and the French and now those English. She had heard that there were even other kinds of white men. She didn't know their names. She knew that there had been a time, not too long before her own birth, when there had been no white people in the land. None. No one had ever even heard of them. She had herself even known a few years in her life when there had been none in the land of the Real People.

Now the white people had come to stay. She knew that. She could tell that much about them. They would not go away. In fact, more of them would come to this land from the other side of the big water. She thought about looking into her crystal to see what the future would hold for the Real People, but she didn't really want to see it. Not just now. She knew that it would be hard for them. Perhaps she had done something with her life to help prepare them for what they would have to face.

THEY had ridden for several days, and she was tired. She was old. She was ready to stop when the day's travel at last came to an end and the people dismounted, unburdened the pack animals, unsaddled the riding horses, built their fires, and made their camps. Someone prepared a small camp for her, and she sat down heavily. She rested a bit before taking out her pipe and tobacco for a smoke.

Running Man came to see her and told her that someone had prepared a meal for her, but she told him that she was not hungry. That worried him some, for he had always been amazed at her when it came time to eat. She always seemed to eat so much for such an old woman. But this night she said that she was not hungry. She refused the food that was offered to her. She sat and smoked.

"Grandmother," Running Man said, "are you all right?"

"Of course I'm all right," she responded. "What can be wrong with an old woman like me?"

She finished her pipe and put it away.

"I want to lie down now," she said, and Running Man helped her stand up from where she sat. He helped her walk the few steps to where her bed had been prepared on the ground and helped her lie down.

"Are you comfortable, Grandmother?" he asked her.

"Yes," she said. "Just fine."

"Well," he said, straightening himself up. "I hope you sleep well this night."

"Stay with me awhile," she said.

He squatted down beside her. "What is it, Grandmother?" he asked.

"Nothing," she said. "I'm just going away tonight. That's all."

"Going away?" he said.

"I'm going to the other side of the Sky Vault," she said, "to the Darkening Land. I'm kind of anxious to get there. I've never been there before. I don't know what it looks like in that place. I think I'll just fly over there."

"Grandmother," he said, "are you sure? Is there something I can do for you?"

"Just sit here," she said, "and be quiet. I'm going very soon now, and there's something I want to tell you before I go."

She was quiet then for such a long time that Running Man began to worry. He wanted to ask her to hurry and say what it was that she wanted to tell him, but she had told him to be quiet. He sat still and waited patiently, and then finally she spoke again, and her voice was weak and distant.

"Nothing will ever be the same," she said, and those were the last words she ever spoke.

THEN once again, as she had done so many times before, she was soaring high above the world that she had known for oh so many years, and she was looking down on the scene below, the scene from which she had just departed, and the soaring was familiar, comfortable, free and easy, unconstrained by age and infirmity. She realized that there were differences now. For now she could see not only the others down below, the ones she had left behind, but she could see herself as well, or rather, she could see her wrinkled old body lying there. She knew that the ancient, withered form on the ground was not really her at all, for she could tell that she was no longer old. She was not young, but rather ageless, and there was another difference as well, for she knew that, unlike her previous flights, from this final flight there would be no return. She went higher and higher, and the human figures down below became tiny in her sight, like ants, then dots, and then they vanished altogether, and she was looking down through undulating clouds at an earth that had become a ball, and it was then she knew for certain that she was on her way to the house of the daughter of the Sun and, from there, on beyond to the Darkening Land.

Glossary

Ada yuhs desgi, rum, literally: "I'll get drunk with it."

Ani-Gilisi, English, apparently a "Cherokeeization" of the word *English.*

Ani-Gusa, Creek or Muskogee People (Ani: plural prefix, Gusa: Cherokee name for a Creek person). See *Gusa* below.

Ani-'Squani, Spaniards (Ani: plural prefix, 'Squani: Spaniard). See *Asquani* below.

Ani-tsisquah, Bird People (Ani: plural prefix, tsisquah: bird), loose translation: "Bird Clan," one of the seven Cherokee clans. Tsisquah might be spelled *Jisquah* or *Cheesquah.*

Ani-wahya, Wolf People (Ani: plural prefix, wahya: wolf), loose translation: "Wolf Clan," one of the seven Cherokee clans.

Ani-yunwi-ya, the Real People (Ani: plural prefix, yunwi: person, ya: real or original), Cherokee designation for themselves.

Asquani, Spaniard, apparently originally an attempt to render the Spanish word *Español* in Cherokee. Also, here a man's name.

Atsila, Fire, here a man's name. It might be spelled *Ajila* or *Achila.*

Chalakee, the Choctaw and trade jargon word for the Real People, in whose own language it became Tsalagi.

Coyatee, an ancient Cherokee place name, the word can no longer be translated.

Daksi, Terrapin, here a man's name.

GLOSSARY

Dijali-yanah-hida—mules or donkeys, literally: "long-eared."

Eliqua, that's enough.

Gadu—bread.

Gahawista, parched corn. It can be boiled to make a corn mush.

Gano luh' sguh, Whirlwind.

Gatayusti, a game played with a stone disk and a spear. It's usually referred to by the Creek or Muskogee name, "chunkey."

Gayahulo, saddle.

Gusa, Cherokee designation for a Creek or Muskogee person.

Guwisti, Sifter or sieve, and here a woman's name.

Kanohena, drink made from hominy, traditionally served to guests.

Kituwah, an ancient Cherokee town, perhaps the original, or "mother" town. The word can no longer be translated. Cherokees sometimes refer to themselves as Ani-Kituwah or Kituwah People. Also spelled *Keetoowah*.

Olig', contraction for Oliga, below.

Oliga, the redhorse fish, here a man's name.

Selu, corn.

'Siyo, contraction for Osiyo, a greeting, like "hello."

Sogwili, horse, literally: "he's carrying it on his back."

'Squan', contraction of Asquani, see above.

'Squani, as above.

'Squan' Usdi, "the Little Spaniard." See *Asquani* above and *Usdi* below. Here a man's name.

Tohiju, roughly, how are you?

Tsola, tobacco.

Tuya, beans.

Ujonati, rattlesnake.

Uk'ten', contraction of ukitena, "keen-eyed," a mythological monster in Cherokee lore.

Usdi, little.

Uyona, Horn, here the name of an old woman, now deceased.

Wado, thank you.

Woyi, Pigeon, here a man's name.

Yona, bear.

BRANCH

	DATE DUE	
	RECEIVED	
	DEC 4 1997	
By		

BRANCH